The Peony Pavilion

Mudan Ting

The Peony Pavilion

Mudan Ting

Tang Xianzu

Translated by Cyril Birch

Cheng & Tsui Company

Boston

This book was brought to publication with the assistance of a grant from the Andrew W. Mellon Foundation.

First Cheng & Tsui Paperback Edition 1994
Second Printing 1999

Reprinted with corrections by arrangement
with Indiana University Press

Cheng & Tsui Company
25 West Street
Boston, MA 02111-1213 USA

Library of Congress Cataloging in Publication Data
Tang Xianzu   1550-1616.
The peony pavilion–Mudan ting.
(Chinese literature in translation)
Play.
Includes index.
I.Title   II.Title:Mudan ting.   III.Series.
PL2695.M8E5   1980   895.1'24   79-9631
ISBN   0-88727-206-1

Manufactured in Canada

The front cover and the frontispiece are reproduced from a photocopy of one of the woodblock prints used to illustrate an abridged version of the play under its alternate title *Huan hun ji* ("The Return of the Soul") printed in 1618, two years after the dramatist's death, and now rare. The abridgement, by Zang Mouxun, was included in a collection of four of Tang Xianzu's plays under the title *Yuming xinci sizhong* published by the firm of Diaochongguan. (*Photocopy courtesy East Asiatic Library, University of California, Berkeley*)

To Alison

CONTENTS

Introduction

Has the world ever seen a woman's love to rival that of Bridal Du?

Dreaming of a lover she fell sick; once sick she became ever worse; and finally, after painting her own portrait as a legacy to the world, she died. Dead for three years, still she was able to live again when in the dark underworld her quest for the object of her dream was fulfilled. To be as Bridal Du is truly to have known love.

Love is of source unknown, yet it grows ever deeper. The living may die of it, by its power the dead live again. Love is not love at its fullest if one who lives is unwilling to die for it, or if it cannot restore to life one who has so died. And must the love that comes in dream necessarily be unreal? For there is no lack of dream lovers in this world. Only for those whose love must be fulfilled on the pillow and for whom affection deepens only after retirement from office, is it entirely a corporeal matter. . . .

These words are from Tang Xianzu's preface, dated 1598, to his own play. Close in time but halfway across the globe, William Shakespeare had completed *Romeo and Juliet*, his tragedy of star-crossed lovers consumed by the fire of their passion in an inimical world. But for Tang Xianzu love, passion, *qing* was a force he must celebrate. It was part of the new, humane currents of thought, in those late years of the Ming dynasty, to extol the spontaneous affections of the heart, to demonstrate their triumph over the conventions of the coldly rational.

In Tang Xianzu's day the Southern style of drama was at its peak of popularity. This style favored a play, or rather opera, of great length, with a large cast and many scenes, offering a kind of cavalcade effect as shifting groups of players paraded and sang their way through the leisurely days of some protracted celebration. The basic mode was romantic comedy: boy meets girl; obstacles to their match arise from family opposition, fortuitous separation, or the machinations of some boorish rival; obstacles are overcome and all celebrate union and reunion. It was the perfect vehicle for the presentation of a story Tang had read in a collection of storytellers' tales.

The story lacked any kind of distinction beyond the fantastic nature of its theme, of a girl resurrected by the lover for whom she has pined and died. Yet the girl, Bridal Du, becomes through Tang Xianzu's portrayal one of the most adored heroines in all of Chinese literature. Like Yingying in *Romance of the Western Chamber*, she embodies the ultimate mystery of Woman. She is unforgettable as a young girl in the early scenes, cloistered and shy, yearning for love yet hiding her feelings even from the pert maid, Spring Fragrance, her confidante. She flowers through love's experience, first in dream only, then as a shade in the nether realm, more and more openly sensuous, gaining in courage and self-possession, until she can emerge full-fledged at last as wife and helpmeet. Her archetypal quality is strengthened by many allusions to earlier heroines: to ladies in portraits who came to life and stepped forward from the painted silk, or to Qiannü, in the poignant fourteenth-century play, who lay comatose in her chamber while her disembodied spirit valiantly pursued her lover to the capital.

Bridal Du's story, crudely fantastic in the original tale, grows glamorous under Tang Xianzu's lyrical brush. But both fantasy and glamour are undercut by a rich, earthy comedy that establishes *The Peony Pavilion* on a satisfyingly sturdy foundation. With a character such as Scabby Turtle present at Bridal's exhumation, we have no choice but to suspend our disbelief. The mysteries of love can never cloy when they are constantly being shot through, by the cheeky flower lad who propositions Spring Fragrance in scene 9, by Sister Stone's bawdy autobiography in scene 17, or by the extraordinary amatory history narrated by the infernal Judge in scene 23 through the medium of puns on the names of thirty-eight different flowers.

We are asked also, usually by Bridal herself in her arias of reminiscence, to consider the dichotomy between real and unreal in the light of Buddhist-Taoist concepts of the illusory nature of all phenomena. This play, with its vindication of passion, shows much less commitment to the transcendent than do Tang's later plays on Taoist themes, *Handan ji* and *Nanke ji*. But already in *The Peony Pavilion* the dramatist draws on elements of karma and of the noumenal to develop his story of Bridal Du from mere fairy tale into profound philosophical statement.

The rivals for the control of Bridal's destiny are her lover, Liu Mengmei, and her father, Du Bao. Liu Mengmei is a considerable advance on the conventional Chinese stage lover. He is, of course, of good family, handsome, and (most important) a gifted scholar. But his great qualification is the courage born of his devotion to Bridal. At the ghostly advent of the girl he has seen before only in a dream, love conquers fear. We need have no doubt of Liu's belief in ghosts, nor of the author's. We have a real-life account of a parallel situation in a moving passage from the eighteenth-century memoirs of Shen Fu, *Six Chapters from a Floating Life*. After the death of his beloved wife, Yuen, Shen Fu keeps a lone vigil in her chamber in the fearful hope of a visit from her spirit:

> Opening my eyes, I looked into all four corners of the room. I saw the two candles burning brightly on the table; but, even as I looked at them, their flames began shrinking slowly until they were no larger than beans.
>
> I was horror-struck. My hair stood on end and my whole body was seized with an icy shiver. To stop my trembling, I rubbed my hands together and wiped my forehead, staring steadily at the candles all the time. Suddenly, both candle flames commenced to rise until they were more than a foot high and in danger of setting fire to the paper ceiling, and the light had become so bright that the whole room was lit up. Then, just as suddenly, the flames began shrinking and growing dimmer, until they were just as tiny as before.
>
> By this time my heart was pounding and my legs were trembling. I wanted to call Chang to come in and look, but, remembering Yuen's gentle spirit and retiring nature, I changed my mind, afraid that the presence in the room of a living stranger might distress her. Instead, I began calling her name and implored her to appear to me. But nothing happened. I remained alone in the silence and dimness. Finally, the candle flames became bright again, but did not rise high as before. Then I went out and told Chang what I had seen. He thought me very strong and fearless, not knowing that mine was only the strength and bravery of love.[1]

Where Liu Mengmei, instructed to disinter Bridal's body, never flinches, her father, Du Bao, refuses until the very last moment to acknowledge her living reality. Du Bao is a Chinese father, and thus even in a stage comedy commands respect. Substitute for him the sort of gullible old pantaloon who would be the girl's father in Roman comedy or in the plays of Molière, and we would lose the whole point of the play. Du Bao is a decent man, fondly appreciative of his daughter and filled with tender sorrow by the falsely reported death of his wife. The set piece of scene 8 shows his paternal concern for the rustic populace in his charge as Prefect. He is heroic, later, in his determination to defend besieged Huaian, though held down to less than heroic proportions by the rather cheap trick he employs against the rebel Li Quan and his dame. Above all, Du Bao is the blinkered Confucian rationalist. His

---

1. Translation by Shirley M. Black.

daughter, too young to be prey to the unworthy emotion of passion, died three years ago and was buried, and there's an end on't. Her resurrected self can be only some malevolent harpy, Liu Mengmei can be nothing more than a grave robber, nothing will induce this father to acknowledge them—until, in the great climactic moment of the final scene, Bridal swoons away and Du Bao, overcome by spontaneous affection, exclaims "My daughter!"

Like other older males in the play, Du Bao is an instrument of topical satire. Not long before Tang Xianzu was writing his play, peace agreements with raiding Mongols under their leader Altan Khan had included the offer of a fief of land to one of Altan's wives. That kind of truckling to the "barbarians," which was crippling the late-Ming courts, is directly satirized in Du Bao's bribery of Dame Li. In like manner, the Judge's songs of scene 23 satirize official venery, and Miao Shunbin, in scene 41, epitomizes the incompetence of chief examiners (not that the candidates themselves are spared: their essays on the burning topic of national defense contain nothing but sexual innuendo).

Other dramatis personae more closely resemble the staple figures of Ming romantic comedy, but all are clothed with rich invention. Tutor Chen is a bumbling old pedant, picking his teeth through the spring afternoon that sets Bridal's heart aflame, but he develops in the most interesting way to become her eventual champion against her stiff-necked father. Spring Fragrance is the pert abigail in the tradition of Hongniang of *Western Chamber;* it is a pity her role diminishes after the vibrancy of her early scenes. Later scenes offer instead the comic relief of the henpecked traitor Li Quan and his lusty dame, and the uproarious scene 47 introduces another stock type in the person of the ridiculous barbarian.

The structure of the Southern-style opera served both musical and dramatic ends. A variety of scene types was *de rigueur*. In major scenes such as scene 10, "The Interrupted Dream," leading personages engage in important action. The lyrics are at their most poetic here and are set to outstanding tunes selected from the large existing repertoire. Stateliness is the hallmark of lyrics and music in the grand scenes such as the finale, when a large grouping of characters fills the stage and when the locale (in the case of the finale, the Imperial audience chamber) gives scope for splendid costumes and a general air of celebration. Transitional scenes, of short or medium length, are more purely narrative in function. There are comic scenes with plenty of action such as scene 7, "The

Schoolroom"; in modern performance this scene runs to slapstick, with such inventions as Tutor Chen's groping blindly after Spring Fragrance, who has just smeared ink all over his spectacles. Martial scenes such as scene 43, "The Siege of Huaian," bring on halberds and pennants, marching and wheeling, gongs and drums and cymbals. As an operatic technician, Tang Xianzu was criticized for "cracking the throats of the Empire" with his unorthodox rhymes and for such gaucheries as burdening Liu Mengmei in his opening scene with an aria pattern *(Jiu hui chang)* more appropriate to some long, slow, lyrical meditation than to a simple self-introduction. But we, who cannot hope to see or hear an actual performance of *The Peony Pavilion*, can only admire the literary skill with which he varies his pace while never failing to move his plot forward, to enliven it with comic relief, or to explore its significance in thoughtful lyrics.

The prologue in which the playwright announces his intentions and outlines the impending action is in keeping with the conventions of Southern drama. So are the successive introductions of the male lead in scene 2 and the female lead in scene 3. With scene 3 we enter the mainstream of the action, the events in the Du household. But from time to time Tang Xianzu uses a technique that may at first disconcert the reader. With a new scene he will open up a kind of freshet, a spring of future action as yet unrelated to the mainstream. An egregious example of such a freshet is the Judge of scene 23. This is a long scene, and we are two-thirds of the way through it before we discover its connection with the story of Bridal. Meanwhile, of course, we have been entertained with a splendid comic vignette. Miao Shunbin, in scene 21, is another such freshet: it is some time before we realize that the jewels of which he prates at such length are all an elaborate metaphor for the "hidden jewel," the as yet unrecognized scholarly talent of the hero, Liu Mengmei.

The original text of the play is furnished with quite explicit stage directions, to which I have added very little beyond an occasional reminder to the reader that, for example, the "boat" in scene 36 is an imaginary one, indicated by the boatman's pole or oar and by the elaborate miming of the characters as they "board" and are "rowed" away. We have to picture, always, a stage devoid of sets or lighting effects, and one calling therefore for such conventions as the invisibility of two characters to each other, though each is in full view of the audience, until an imaginary door is opened and passed through. Bridal, already on stage, "emerges" from Liu's "study" to

greet him in scene 32, and in scene 50 Liu is on stage with Du Bao
for some time without ever being "admitted" to see him.

Other conventions to which the reader will quickly grow accus-
tomed include self-introductions and the sometimes irritating re-
capitulations of plot. Tang Xianzu is no very serious offender,
though, in the latter regard, especially if we bear in mind the
drifting in and out, over two or three days, of the original audiences
for whom he wrote. Bridal sometimes seems to be given excessive
opportunities to reminisce about her years in the shades—to Liu, to
Sister Stone, to her mother, to Fragrance—but each time brings a
new aria, a new set of images, a further deepening of the tints of
this marvelous portrayal.

Tang Xianzu lived from 1550 to 1616. He passed the metropolitan
examinations (though Liu Mengmei's Prize Candidacy eluded him)
at the age of thirty-three and began his career as a dramatist during
a spell of service in Nanking, when, as a secretary under the Board
of Ceremonies, his duties were less than all-consuming. A loyal but
hortatory memorial to the Emperor resulted in demotion for him.
He never again reached higher rank than district magistrate, and in
his late forties he retired into private life. In addition to essays and
poems he wrote five plays, of which *The Peony Pavilion* is the
masterpiece. In retirement he personally supervised productions of
the play, and it rapidly won wide popularity. Probably a quarter of
the scenes were still in the repertoire in the late nineteenth century.
Though a performance of the entire play was mounted in Peking
during a national drama festival in the mid-1950s, in general only
"The Schoolroom" and "The Interrupted Dream" (scenes 7 and 10)
are performed today. But at least Bridal Du still graces the Chinese
stage, and college students in Taiwan are still willing to spend
sunny Sunday afternoons painstakingly practicing her arias under
the guidance of elderly aficionados.

A Note on Layout

I have based this translation on the editions of the play, with the invaluable annotation by Xu Shuofang and Yang Xiaomei, published in 1958 (Shanghai) and 1963 (Peking).

The three constituents of the play's text, or libretto, are prose dialogue, intoned verses, and arias. I have marked these distinctions by half-indenting verse passages and by fully indenting arias. In the standard scene opening, a single character appears on stage, sings one aria, recites a verse, then descends into prose to introduce himself and state his business. The verse may take the form of a *shi* (poem in regular meter) or a lyric (*ci*) with lines of irregular but prescribed length. I have not given the "tune titles" of the *ci*, since they are recited rather than sung and are therefore not a part of the musical structure. Nor have I marked whether a recited verse is *shi* or *ci*, but this should be apparent from the metrical regularity or otherwise of the translation. All these verses are rhymed in the original, but the translation on the whole uses rhyme only for comic effect.

Roman numerals mark the beginning of new aria patterns and refer to the appended index. Repeats of a pattern are indicated by lettering—for example IIa, IIb, and so on—the first repeat occurring in scene 3. All arias are rhymed in the original, and the rhyme is usually constant for the whole scene (even, for example, in the long scene 23), though there are numerous cases of "intrusive" arias (using a different rhyme) or even of a total switch of rhyme in midscene. As with the intoned verses, I have rhymed the arias only when rhyme seemed necessary to aid the comic effect, as in the arias to the tune *Zi zi shuang* sung by Camel Guo in scene 13 and by Scabby Turtle in scene 35.

The tryst between Liu Mengmei and Bridal in ghostly form (scene 28).

SCENE ONE: *Legend*

PROLOGUE SPEAKER:[1]

    1 By busy world rejected, in my own world of retreat
I pondered a hundred schemes
finding joy in none.
Daylong I polished verses for the bowels' torture
for the telling of "love, in all life hardest to tell."[2]
Dawns warmed and twilights shadowed my White Camellia
    Hall
till "with red candle I welcomed friends"
—and always "the hills and streams raised high my pow-
    ers."
Let me only keep faith with the history of this longing,
of the road that led
through three incarnations[3] to the peony pavilion.
To the Prefect Du Bao
was born a daughter Bridal,
who longed to walk in the spring light.
Roused by dream of young scholar
who broke off branch from willow
she pined and died of love
but left her portrait memorial

---

    1. The player of the role of Chen Zuiliang, the old tutor who first appears in scene 4. Here he speaks in the voice of the author himself. Usually it is the player of a less prominent, "older male" role who is given the prologue.

    2. Quotation, slightly altered to suit the present rhyme scheme, from a poet of the Tang dynasty. Quotations are extremely frequent throughout the play and most are from Tang poets. The annotated editions give the sources; here I simply mark them as quotations.

    3. The history of the girl who died and through the power of love returned to life. "Three incarnations" is an exaggeration born of the belief that it requires three lifetimes for a perfect love to attain consummation. There is probably a reference here to the "rock of three incarnations": during the Tang period a strong friendship grew between Li Yuan and the monk Yuanguan [or Yuanze]. Approaching death, Yuanguan told Li that in twelve years' time they would meet before the Tianzhu Temple in Hangzhou. When the time came Li Yuan found there, by the "rock of three incarnations," a herdboy who was the reincarnation of Yuanguan.

1

in the Apricot Blossom Shrine where her cold grave lay.
Three years passed
and a scholar, named Liu for "willow,"
Mengmei for "dream-of-apricot,"[4]
found at this Gaotang his dream of love.[5]
Then in truth she returned to life and became his bride.
But when the examinations took him to Lin'an
bandits arose at Huaiyang,
besieged Prefect Du
and filled Bridal with fear.
Sent by her to seek news
Liu raised doubts and anger
in the mind of Du Bao, now First Minister.
A romantic tale
but a tale whose execution
almost caused the execution[6]
of Prize Candidate Liu Mengmei,[7]
announced in the nick of time.

> Bridal Du takes colored inks
>   to portray herself after dreaming,
> Tutor Chen uses his tongue
>   to subdue the "pear-blossom spear,"[8]
> The graduate Liu escorts by stealth
>   a girl returned to the living,
> Minister Du strings up and flogs
>   the young Prize Candidate.[9]

---

4. I use "apricot" throughout for *mei*, the flowering tree that is actually a Japanese apricot, though conventionally translated as "plum."

5. According to the *Gaotang fu* by the pre-Han poet Song Yu, Witch's Mount [Wushan] at Gaotang was where Prince Hui of Chu made love in a dream to a beautiful woman who told him, "At dawn I am the morning clouds, at dusk the driving rain."

6. Pun on the phrase *shixing*: "put into practice/ apply punishment." So far as possible such puns will be retained in the translation, at the risk of some prolixity and occasional inventions.

7. *Zhuangyuan*, winner of first place for the entire country in the examination held in the palace for the final proving of scholars.

8. "Pear-blossom spear" is a synecdoche for the rebel Li Quan. It was his (or rather his wife's) favored weapon, a spear with an incendiary device at the tip.

9. The *zaju* drama of the Yuan period concluded with a verse presenting a synopsis of the action in capsule form. This was known as "topic and title proper" (*timu zhengming*). Under the conventions of the Ming *chuanqi* play, this verse was brought forward to the first scene, the prologue, which it concluded.

SCENE TWO: *Declaring Ambition*

LIU MENGMEI:

    1 The house of Liu, preeminent
of old clans East of the River,
ruled by the constellation
Zhang, for Letters, adjoining
Gui, whose meaning is "Ghosts."
But leaves of Liu the Willow
buffeted by the storm
suffered many a fall
before the generation
of this poor wintry scholar.
"In books lie fame and fortune," they say—
then tell me, where are the jade-smooth cheeks,
the rooms of yellow gold?
Ashen from need and hardship
I yet maintain my "overflowing breath."[1]
The successful scholar "rides the giant turtle"
but I have merely scraped frost from its back.
My winter poverty warmed by the fiery south
and blessed to some slight extent by the Creator
I have inherited fragrance of classic books.
Drilling the wall for light,
hair tied to beam in fear of drowsing,[2]
I wrest from nature excellence in letters [3]
and soon the ax of jade to prove its worth
must fell the cassia high in the moon's toad palace.[4]

---

1. The quotation from *Mencius*, which originally seems to have referred to some kind of yoga technique, here indicates scholarly purpose.
2. Classic examples of scholarly application: Kuang Heng, too poor to buy oil, bored a hole through his wall to use the neighbor's light for his reading; Sun Jing, fearful of nodding over his books, tied his hair to a beam.
3. Reference to lines by the Song poet Lu You: "Literary skill is Heaven's creation/ but an able student may gain it."
4. "Breaking off the cassia bough" was a metaphor for success in the literary examinations. The cassia tree in the moon figures in the legend of Wu Kang, banished to the moon and there condemned eternally to fell a cassia which eternally springs up again. Another legend defines the moon as the palace of a celestial toad. Yet another, as the residence of Chang E, who fled there after stealing the elixir of immortality from her husband; forevermore, assisted by a "jade hare," she pounds medicines with mortar and pestle.

I am Liu Mengmei. Liu means "willow," Mengmei "dream-of-apricot," and I am styled Chunqing, "spring lord." I am a descendant of Liu Zongyuan the poet, Prefect of Liuzhou in Tang times, through a branch of the family resident in Lingnan. My father held the title of Doctor-at-Large, my mother as wife of an official of the fifth grade held the title of Lady of the County. *(Sighs)* It was my sorrow to be orphaned at an early age and left with the most meager livelihood. But I rejoice that I am now a grown man, past my twentieth year, talented and of high purpose, and have acquitted myself well in the secondary examinations. Still I have not "met my time" to be placed in office, and so I remain in hunger and cold. My ancestor the Prefect Liu had in his service a certain "Camel" Guo who tended the gardens of the official residence in Liuzhou.[5] This Camelback Guo had a camelback descendant who tends trees here in Guangzhou prefecture, and it is with his help that I manage to live. But this is no place for a man to fulfill himself. "My days are a daze of thoughts of love"—and about two weeks ago I had a dream, out of nowhere. In my dream I entered a garden where a lovely girl stood beneath a flowering apricot. She was of pleasing height, and her manner seemed inviting. In my dream she said, "Master Liu, Master Liu, I am the one you must meet to set foot on your road to love and to high office." This is why I changed my personal name to "Dream-of-Apricot" and took the style "Spring Lord." Truly,

"brief dream, long dream, still a dream;
this year, next year, when is the year?"

     II   Though I changed both name and style in readiness
can the fair sprite I dreamed of
know, without diviner's magic, who I am?
Against the time of our union
I pant to break the cassia in the moon[6]
—and Liu Mengmei, this "Willow Dream-of-Apricot"
has no "mountain pear for sale,"[7]
no vendor's cry, full of false claims.
I fear only the wilting of my precious dream flower

---

5. One of the best-known pieces of the celebrated poet and essayist Liu Zongyuan (773–819) is a brief allegory in which "Camel" Guo, a hunchbacked gardener, lays down rules for the cultivation of trees which are found to be the perfect prescription for wise government.

6. See note 4.

7. Pursuing his sequence of blossoming trees, the author here refers to a Yuan play, *Baihuating*, in which a vendor of mountain pear claims that it will bring happy marriage, the cure of all ills, and so on.

before the jealousy of Chang E, goddess in the moon,
and with this waiting
"the flowering apricot yields sour fruit,
the willow has frowning brows"
—my senses reel.

Possessing no fireflies
I have riddled with holes the neighbor's wall[8]
but the garden wall to the east
—don't say we may not peep over that![9]
Some day spring sun will touch in the dimness
the willow to yellow gold
and the snow's approach burst open
the apricot blossom white as jade.

Ah, then shall I ride in pride before the palace,
accept the tasseled whip of betrothal,
take for my own the star queen of all flowers.
Be all this as it may, I have a friend, Han Zicai, who is a descendant
of Han Yu[10] and who resides at the moment at the Terrace of Prince
Zhao Tuo.[11] For a temple acolyte he is an excellent talker and I must
make a short pilgrimage in his direction.

Envoi:

Willow and apricot flourish
    their splendor at the gate   [Zhang Yaotiao] [12]
in dream I stood before my prince
    but doubt assailed my waking. [Wang Changling]
In my heart a hundred blooms
    not yet their time to open   [Cao Song]
seek first the support
    of an enduring branch.   [Han Wo]

---

8. See note 2. Fireflies in a bag were used for their light by Ju Yin, a third-century scholar too poor to afford oil.

9. Song Yu describes in a poem a girl who for three years has been "peeping over the wall," and the Yuan play *Dongqiangji* ("Story of the Eastern Wall") has a love affair for its theme.

10. Famous poet and scholar (768–824), leader of the "ancient-style" movement of his time and close friend of Liu Zongyuan.

11. Zhao Tuo proclaimed himself Prince of Nanyue on the collapse of the Qin dynasty in 206 B.C. His "Terrace" is above the sea near Guangzhou.

12. From here on each scene ends with a rhyming quatrain made up of separate lines from the classical Tang poets. I give the poets' names in the present case only.

SCENE THREE: *Admonishing the Daughter*

PREFECT DU BAO:

    1 Sichuan scholar of renown
       now Prefect of Nan'an
       I have trodden in turn the covered halls of court
       and the riverbanks of retirement.
       Robe of purple, girdle of gold
       can hardly be said to represent
       no achievement whatsoever.
       Hair frosted now, I dare not look back,
       but long to unpin my cap of office
       and seek, west of the Bridge of Myriad Miles,
       the retreat of my ancestor, the great Du Fu.[1]
       I fear, however, that the favor of my prince
       has not yet extended thus far,
       and so my prefectural carriage
       hesitates uncertain.
    Capping a lifetime of honored office
      here I govern Nan'an
    —and let no one mistake me
      for a Prefect of the common run.
    Always I have drunk
      "only the local water";[2]
    in retirement I shall feast my gaze
      on "the hills before my door."

I am Du Bao, Prefect of Nan'an, styled Zichong and descended from Du Fu of the Tang dynasty. My family residence is in Sichuan, my age past fifty. I reflect that I was twenty when I gained my *jinshi* degree, and now after three years as Prefect here my name is widely synonymous with honesty and benevolent administration. My lady wife, of the Zhen clan, is in direct line of descent from the Empress Zhen of the Wei dynasty. Her family resides at Mount Emei and for generations has been a byword for integrity and virtue. This lady has borne me one daughter only, a girl of good gifts and pleasing

---

1. Du Fu (712–770), generally acknowledged to be China's greatest poet, built a retreat by this bridge at Chengdu in Sichuan. Prefect Du thus neatly caps the claims to distinguished ancestry made in the preceding scene.

2. That is, "I have been content with my official emoluments and accepted no bribes or perquisites of corruption."

person named Bridal. No arrangement has yet been made for her betrothal. It is evident that no virtuous and eligible young lady should fail to be properly educated, and today, having some respite from my official duties, I have summoned my lady wife to discuss this matter. Truly,

> Cai Yong, rich in learning, had one daughter only,
> Deng You, poor in office, lacked sons altogether.[3]

MADAM DU (*enters*):

> 11a Of Sichuan family, in direct line
> from Empress Zhen, Goddess of the River Luo,[4]
> wife of Du Bao, I bear from the court
> the title Lady of Nan'an.

> (*She greets her husband*)

DU:

> In late years to prefecture of note
> though unworthy of such honor

MADAM DU:

> and what have I done that I should deserve
> proud title from the court?

DU:

> In the women's chambers, days of spring
> are hard to fill

MADAM DU:

> daylong in the blossom-patterned shade
> we pattern our sewing.

DU: When it comes to sewing and embroidery our daughter shows exceptional delicacy. But it is evident that a virtuous and eligible young lady has always needed an understanding of letters, so that when the time comes for her to marry a learned husband she will not be deficient in conversation. Is this not also your view?

MADAM DU: I bow to your judgment.

> (*Enter* BRIDAL DU, *followed by maid* SPRING FRAGRANCE *bearing tray with wine vessels*)

BRIDAL DU:

> 11b Voice of oriole falters
> before such radiance of spring.

---

3. Deng You, an honest and therefore poor official of the Jin dynasty, disowned his son to save the life of his nephew in a time of rebellion.

4. The claimed ancestress was consort to the poet Cao Bei, who became Emperor Wen of the Wei dynasty. His brother, Cao Zhi, wrote a poem to the Goddess of the River Luo. The present speaker makes the two figures one.

How can this heart, mere wisp of straw,
give thanks for light by loving parents shed?

(She greets her parents)

Blessings on you, dear Father and Mother.

DU: What is the purpose of this wine your maid brings, child?

BRIDAL *(kneeling)*: The spring sunlight is so delightful today that I am taking the liberty, as you sit at ease here in the rear hall, of offering three cups of wine to you with my respectful wishes for a thousand such springs.

DU *(smiling)*: That's kind of you.

BRIDAL *(offering the wine):*

> IIIa   Blessings on you, my parents,
> for boundless joy to your daughter given.
> May a hundred springs brighten the Prefect's hall
> and this wine be "Heaven's reward" to our family.
> O mother gentle as lily,
> father as cedar strong,
> though the faery peach comes only
> after thirty centuries to fruit
> and even so I your child
> was born of your evening years
> yet with careful guarding
> you bring me now to ripeness.

DU, MADAM DU:

> Then raise the wine jar
> for the "fledgling phoenix" nurtured
> amid the flowers, shaded by tall bamboo.

DU: Fragrance, fill a cup for the young mistress.

> IIIb   Our ancestor Du Fu,
> "wandering, drifting, felt shame before wife and children."

(He weeps)

My state, dear wife, is yet more pitiable than that of the noble Du Fu. He at least had

> a son who could "recite his father's verses"

when all I have is

> a daughter who "models her eyebrows on her mother's."

MADAM DU: Do not be distressed, my lord. If we can only find a good husband for our daughter, won't that be the same thing as a son of our own?

DU *(laughs)*: The same thing?
MADAM DU:

>When the Emperor of Tang showered favors
>on Yang Guifei, "Honored Consort,"
>families wished for a girl
>to be born to them, rather than a son.
>Now, in your middle years,
>why indulge in this complaining?

DU, MADAM DU:

>Then raise the wine jar
>for the "fledgling phoenix" nurtured
>amid the flowers, shaded by tall bamboo.

DU: Child, take the wine things away.

(Exit BRIDAL)

Fragrance, tell me, how does your young mistress spend her time all day long in the "brocade chambers"?
SPRING FRAGRANCE: In the brocade chambers? She does brocade.
DU: And what does she embroider?
FRAGRANCE: Fabrics with a nap.
DU: What sort of nap?
FRAGRANCE: A catnap.
DU: Oh, very good. Madam, you were speaking just now of "patterning your sewing in the blossom-patterned shade," and here I find you permitting your daughter to doze in idleness-what sort of upbringing is this? Call the girl here.
BRIDAL *(reenters)*: What does my father wish?
DU: I was just asking Fragrance about you. What is the meaning of your drowsing in broad daylight? If you have time to spare from your embroidery, there are books on the shelves that are there to be read. Then at some future date when you enter your husband's family, your understanding of learning and of the rites will reflect credit on your own. But this your mother has been neglecting.

>IVa Empty chests are mine as I strive for integrity,
>nor have my studies dishonored the name of scholar.
>You, so long a guest in your parents' house,
>will see the day when you rule a home of your own.
>Your father, by duties distracted, neglects your discipline
>-it is after all your mother should be your model.

MADAM DU:

>IVb You, daughter, before my eyes
>bring joy to my heart through my limbs already weary.
>Delicately nurtured, jewel held in the palm,
>now she comes forth the pearl of all her peers.
>Child, note well the meaning of your father's words

—only a backward "creature of the comb"
"reads characters backwards"!

BRIDAL:

ıvc Favored in the Prefect's mansion
I have indulged myself in idle pastimes
painting one day a "garden scene with swing"
the next embroidering mating ducks for a trousseau.
From now on every idle waking minute
I'll use to the full
at the bookshelves that will line my dressing table!

MADAM DU: Very well, but we must still have a lady tutor to instruct you.

DU: That is not possible.

ıvd The tutor engaged by an official residence must be
a scholar soaked in orthodoxy from the academy.

MADAM DU:

A daughter has no need for all of Confucius,
the *Book of Songs* or the *Documents*
but you must gain some knowledge
of the Duke of Zhou's *Book of Rites.*

DU, MADAM DU:

Shameful waste
for a "Silver Maid" or "Jade One" to ply her spinning
    wheel
when she could be a Lady Collator of Texts
like Xie Daoyun or Ban Ji of ancient times.[5]

DU: It will not be difficult to find a tutor, but he must be treated with respect.

v Lady, as you love your daughter grudge no expense,
let the tutor's "rice and tea" be of quality suited
to the quality of his learning.
Observe how there are volumes of instruction
in my mode of regulation
of state affairs and of my own household.

Envoi:

Why in those bygone years
    was a tutor summoned?

---

5. Xie Daoyun, poetess of the Jin dynasty. Ban Zhao (Ban Ji) of the Later Han period completed the *History of the Han* of her brother Ban Gu.

His the duty of vernal breeze
  to foster youthful flowering.
No son to follow me
  in the evening of my days,
shall my daughter rival the Lady of Wei
  in calligraphic skill?

SCENE FOUR: *Pedant's Lament*

TUTOR CHEN:

    1 Mumbling of texts by lamp and window light
freezes and sours the taste of hopes once bright,
my progress through the halls of examination
thwarted, here I dither in desperation.
'Mid sighs for scholarship run down to waste
only my asthma flourishes apace.
While my coughing waxes
  wine cups tend to wane
an income supplied by village lads
  brings little smoke to my kitchen.
"Is there no one at home
  up there in Heaven
to take pity on the sorrowful
  crane-white locks of a sage?"

I am Chen Zuiliang, styled Bocui, graduate of the prefectural academy at Nan'an. My father and grandfather both were medical practitioners; I myself followed the path of learning from an early age, entered the academy at twelve and was eventually included among the recipients of government support. Fifteen times in forty-five years I sat for examination until I had the misfortune to have my stipend cut off by the Supervisor, merely because I was placed in the lowest grade. On top of that, for two years past I have failed to find any post as tutor and am reduced to short commons and a meager wardrobe. So now, instead of Chen Zuiliang, "Chen So Good," the young fellows delight in calling me Chen Jueliang, "Chen No Food,"[1] and, because of my expertise in medicine, divi-

---

1. Confucius, according to the *Analects*, "went without grain in the state of Chen." This elaborate pun has thus an additional layer of classical allusion.

nation, geomancy, and such, they have changed my style from Bocui, "Lord of Pure Essence," to Bozasui, "Jack of All Professions." Next year I shall complete my sixth decade, but I have no expectation of any improvement. I still keep going an herb shop started by my grandfather. "When a scholar turns to medicine his diet turns to pickles."—But no more of this. Yesterday news came that our Prefect Du was seeking a tutor for his daughter. Applicants came swarming for the post—and why? Reason one: to have something to brag about in their own village. Reason two: to have the chance of a bribe or two for a bit of dirty work. Reason three: to hitch their wagon. Reason four: to get in with the servants on the job of cooking the books. Reason five: to puff themselves elsewhere to advance their prospects. Reason six: to lord it over their inferiors. Reason seven: to deceive their wives. Seven good reasons why they all came tumbling head over heels. Little do they know the perils of service in an official's yamen! Moreover, a girl pupil is always a problem. It won't do to be either too lenient or too strict, and, if one runs into a problem of face now and then, one can neither laugh nor weep. Some old fellow like myself would be best:

> No other cure for heart sore vexed:
> just let me bury my head in a text.

JANITOR *(enters):*

> Show me the teacher who isn't a pauper
> or the janitor who isn't a cunning rogue.

(Greets CHEN)

Congratulations, Professor Chen!

CHEN: Congratulations on what?

JANITOR: Prefect Du is seeking a tutor for his daughter and has turned down a dozen names proposed by the Director of the Prefectural Academy because he wanted a responsible man. I went to the Director's office and recommended you, and here is Prefect Du's letter of invitation.

CHEN: "The human vice is the urge to teach others," as Mencius said.

JANITOR: Don't worry about the "human vice." What about "human rice"? At least you'll be fed.

CHEN: Let's leave it at that, then.

(They begin to walk)

11a   Now to sew my scarf when it's worn to holes,
repair my shoes when they need new soles.

JANITOR:

Now that you're in the tutor's seat
you'll be able to get a new seat for your pants.

CHEN:

If I'm not to sour
the rice that will come my way
I must rinse my mouth
with water from my writing tray
and to guard against the stench from the pickles I've eaten
from now on a toothpick will come in handy.

JANITOR:

11b   If it hadn't been for my efforts
you'd never have found this post.

CHEN:

Let me first see if I can keep it
before I repay your kindness.

CHEN, JANITOR:

Fifth of the fifth month, ninth of the ninth,
when the teacher's fees are paid
then you'll see him leave the yamen
clutching his bulging sleeves.

JANITOR: Now here we are at the Prefect's gate.

Envoi:

JANITOR:

Fickle and fleeting
the honors this world bestows

CHEN:

and who pays any heed
to beard now white as silver?

JANITOR:

In resplendent ease
the Prefect sits above

CHEN, JANITOR:

while endless is the line
of those who seek his favor.

SCENE FIVE: *Engaging the Tutor*

Enter DU BAO with attendants and underlings

DU BAO:

        1a The mountains are at their loveliest
        and court cases dwindle.
        "The birds I saw off at dawn, at dusk I watch return,"
        petals from the vase cover my seal box,
        the curtains hang undisturbed.
    Though I may not aspire to the noble standard
        of ancient Du Shi, "father and mother of his prefecture,"
    yet may I take my ease here in Nan'an
        as once Duke Zhao of Zhou beneath the sweetapple.[1]
    Many are the unsung acts of grace
        my government has accomplished,
    but still I find on "the steps of my hall"
        no "jade tree," no "orchid"—no son at my knee.

I, Du Bao, Prefect of this region, have a family limited to my wife and a single daughter for whom I am seeking a tutor. Yesterday the prefectural academy recommended a salaried scholar for the post, one Chen Zuiliang. This is a sexagenarian who has filled his belly with books, a man most suitable both as instructor for my daughter and as companion for myself. Today I shall suspend official duties so that I may welcome him with wine and due ceremony. Let my runners be prepared!

        (ALL chorus assent. Enter CHEN ZUILIANG in
           scholar's cap and blue robe)

CHEN ZUILIANG *(sings):*

        1b Screw the courage,
        twist the argument:
        gown and cap slip awry as my old age withers
        but still I "overflow"[2] and must be treated
        "with equal pomp as one who shares this hall."

ATTENDANT: Professor Chen is at the gate.

---

    1. "Sweet apple" (*gantang*) is in fact used as a metaphor for a respected official, following the poem by this title in the *Book of Songs*, which is a eulogy of Duke Zhao of Zhou.

    2. See scene 2, note 1.

DU: Invite him in.

ATTENDANT *(announcing CHEN):* The graduate of the prefectural academy of Nan'an.

(Exit ATTENDANT. CHEN kneels, rises,
bows, and kneels again)

CHEN: The graduate Chen Zuiliang prostrates himself. *(He does so)*

"Let learned discourse lighten library"

DU:

"exalted scholar, gem of our assembly"

CHEN:

"be trencher and flagon readied for exchange"

DU:

"and seats for guest and host drawn in due order."
While Professor Chen and I engage in lofty conversation, dismiss my staff and have my household servants wait on us.

(ALL chorus assent and withdraw, making way for serving boys)

I have long been aware, sir, of your learned reputation. May I venture to ask your age and your family history of scholarship?

CHEN: Permit me to declare:

IIa Already I "incline my ear"
to the Way, being close to sixty;
I approach the "historically rare"
—that is, when I shall be seventy.
Beneath the blight of scholar's cap
my temples are ruined with white hairs.

DU: And most recently?

CHEN:

The study of healing marks the Superior Man:
the "sign of the hanging pot" has been passed
down generations of my house.

DU: Oh, so your family have been medical practitioners. What other skills do you possess?

CHEN:

The miscellaneous schools
I can attempt to interpret
and with philosophers generally
I can claim some acquaintance.

DU: Well, all these things will come in useful.

11b Name long known
though now first met,
indeed a great scholar worthy of our nation.

CHEN: I should not presume. . . .

DU:

My daughter has some claim to learning:
I would wish you, as a textual critic
to impart to her a certain gloss.

CHEN: I shall do as you wish, but I fear I may not be cut out to be a tutor for young ladies.

DU:

To this girl-scholar
you shall be another Ban Zhao,
who taught the ladies of the palace.[3]
Today is selected as of good omen
to have her salute you as tutor.

Sound the "cloud board," in the yard there, to summon the young mistress.

(Enter BRIDAL DU, attended by SPRING FRAGRANCE)

BRIDAL DU:

11c Brows limned black with emerald sheen,
pendants swaying at waist,
pictured beauty steps as from broidered screen.
Lotus feet in tripping measure
set long ago as mark of reverence
by the son of the Master, Confucius himself,
scion of scholars' line I now appear.

SPRING FRAGRANCE: Now that your teacher is here, what are we to do?

BRIDAL: We must go. Understand, my bondmaid,
the virtuous young lady
is ever a very mirror of decorum.
You also must gain some little learning
to improve yourself as my maid.

ATTENDANT: The young mistress!

(BRIDAL greets her father)

_____

3. See scene 3, note 5.

DU: Come here, child.
"Jade unsculpted
unfit for use;
person untutored
unaware of the Way."
Make obeisance before your tutor on this auspicious day.

(Drums and pipes sound from within)

BRIDAL *(making obeisance)*: Your student, to her shame "wavering as reed or willow," still dares to seek instruction "ripe as peach or plum."
CHEN: Unworthy to accept the regard of a "jewel held in the palm," still I make bold to "sculpt the jade."
DU: Fragrance, prostrate yourself before Tutor Chen as the young mistress' "reading companion."

(FRAGRANCE prostrates herself)

CHEN: May I enquire what books the young lady has studied?
DU: She has memorized the *Four Books* and the *Four Books for Ladies,* so now she should study something of the classics proper. The *Changes* set forth the cosmic duality of yin and yang in mysteries too profound for her; the *Documents* treat of government and are of no concern to a woman; the *Springs and Autumns* and the *Rites* are "orphan texts," in that each exists in a single version only. The *Book of Songs,* however, devotes its very first lines to the virtue of the consort, [4] and the four-syllable meter makes it an easy text to memorize; moreover, as my ancestor the great Du Fu once wrote, "the *Songs* are our family occupation"-she should study the *Songs.* Of course, all the other works and histories would be very well, did she not have the misfortune to be a girl.

> 11d   Through twoscore years and ten,
> books have been my delight,
> "my shelves hold thirty thousand ivory tallies."

(He sighs)

Like Cai Yong lacking sons, to whom shall I pass
this rich inheritance of learning?
Tutor Chen, let her read what she should read. If she falls short of the standard, beat the maidservant.

---

4. In the view, that is, of the orthodox Confucian commentators, who glossed the opening *Song* (a love lyric) as a eulogy to the consort of the prince.

FRAGRANCE: Ai-yo!

DU:

> For my daughter "capped and grown"
> she will be a lady secretary
> so this little "fragrant apricot blossom"
> of a maid must be carefully watched.

CHEN: I shall take note of this.

DU: Fragrance, help the young mistress to her chamber while I take wine with Tutor Chen.

BRIDAL (*with an obeisance*):

> A tutor may get high at "high table"
> but can a lady be a "gentleman-scholar"?[5]

(She exits with FRAGRANCE)

DU: Now, sir, take a drink with me in the rear garden.

Envoi:

DU:

> Daylong the impartial tutor
> governs his little realm

CHEN:

> a hundred years of coarse husks
> form the sour pedant's diet.

DU:

> Delicate maiden substitutes
> for "scepter-wielding son"

DU, CHEN:

> parting the blossoming branches
> to seek the tutor's seat.

SCENE SIX: *Despairing Hopes*

GRADUATE HAN ZICAI:

> 1a Of line descending from the great era of Tang,
> Chaoyang the seat now of my family residence.

---

5. Bridal is punning here on quotes from the *Analects*.

Before my gaze from the Terrace of Prince Zhao Tuo
sea and sky meet at horizon:
  will the "roc's flight" of my future be as limitless?
Ancient Terrace eluding
  reach of banyan's branches
commands the perilous walls
  of Jiazi Cove below.
Where once the Prince of Yue
  made merry with song and dance
now only the partridge
  wheels on the silent air.

I am Han Zicai, descendant of that celebrated Han Yu who was banished to Chaozhou in the far south for presenting his "Memorial against the Bone of the Buddha." No sooner had he set out than he found the Blue Pass blocked with snow and his horse could make no progress—"A first omen," my ancestor told himself. Suddenly in the midst of his distress there appeared before his eyes, all dressed in tatters, his nephew Han Xiang, who in reality was none other than Han Xiangzi of the Eight Taoist Immortals. My ancestor Han Yu was very upset. Breathing on his brush to thaw out the hairs, he composed a poem in the posting station at the Blue Pass. The last couplet was addressed to Han Xiangzi:

  "I can discern the purpose
    of your journey from afar:
  it is to order my dead bones
    by the noxious southern waters."

Han Xiangzi placed the poem in his sleeve and with a great roar of laughter ascended into the sky. And later on, true it was[1] that my ancestor Han Yu died of the noxious vapors of Chaozhou without a single relative before his eyes. Chancing to notice this from up in the clouds, Han Xiangzi called to mind the poem Han Yu had written. He brought his cloud to land and decently composed his uncle's corpse. When he entered the official residence, there was not a soul about other than his own former wife, all by herself there. Their eyes met, and such mortal fleshly desires as Han Xiangzi still retained began to rise up within him. And that was how a branch of the family came to be resident in the Chaozhou area to continue

---

1. But not in historical fact: Han Yu returned from his banishment in Chaozhou. The lines quoted from Han Yu are authentic, but are deliberately misinterpreted to suit this legend.

the ancestral line. I am a member of that branch in direct line of descent. Troubled times tossed me to Canton, whose Prefect out of compassion for the descendant of a sage of former times secured an Imperial edict appointing me assistant in the Temple of Han Yu. And here I lodge for the time being at the Terrace of Prince Zhao Tuo. Truly,

> though beggarly the student in appearance,

> breath and bone are formed of the Way's pure essence.

But, hello, here is a friend come to visit me. Who can it be?

LIU MENGMEI (*enters*):

> 1b Like Bian Shao, who dozing by daytime
> was mocked for the size of his belly and explained
> it was full of learning—mine too
> bulges with weight of Classics and Histories.
> Yet after daylight dreams
> weary I wake from longing.
> I long to stand where peaks soar above cloud and mist
> and confront the vast plain of the shining sea.

(They exchange greetings)

HAN ZICAI: Liu Mengmei! What wind brings you here?

LIU: I climbed to this terrace by chance in my solitary wanderings.

HAN: The view from the terrace is quite impressive, isn't it?

LIU: But what a climb to get here!

HAN: I have a good deal of pleasure here.

LIU: But as I recall, this was the pleasure of an illiterate.

HAN: Who?

LIU: Why, Prince Zhao Tuo.

> 11a When Qin's First Emperor died, when the "dragon soared,"
> the "deer of Qin" was harried across the land.
> Then Zhao Tuo, Garrison Commander
> of this southern coast, used these unscalable cliffs
> to wall off for himself a corner of the sky,
> and in heroic fashion called himself "orphan,"
> "solitary one"—the formulae of a king.
> Fruitless taking of rivers and hills,
> frenzied building of palace halls.

—but men like you and me, who have studied myriad books to the last word of the last page, have we a single clod of earth in our possession?

Where are the hills and streams
our studies should win for us
as with "half the *Analects*"
Zhao Pu won an empire?[2]

LIU, HAN:

Heaven will ordain
and it is vain to search for precedents
all up and down the length of history
while cold mist shrouds the trees' decay
on weed-grown terrace.

HAN: Your manner and your words give an impression of despondency. My ancestor Han Yu once wrote:

"Care not if those in office be not bright,
care only for the skill with which you write;
care not for an official's unjust earnings,
care only for the mastery of your learning."[3]

I suspect that your accomplishments are still incomplete.

LIU: Let's not speak of it. Even my ancestor Liu Zongyuan and your ancestor Han Yu ran afoul of their time for all their learning and ability. Your ancestor made the mistake of composing his "Memorial against the Bone of the Buddha" and was banished to Chaozhou. Mine was playing chess with the Chief Minister Wang Shuwen one day in the Palace of Morning Light when the noise woke the Emperor, and for that he was banished to the magistracy of Liuzhou, like Chaozhou a coastal district of fogs and noxious vapors.[4] The two men met on the road and engaged in a long conversation by lamplight in their inn. "Zongyuan, Zongyuan," says your ancestor to mine, "your writing and mine are pretty evenly matched. I wrote a 'Life of Wang the Plasterer,' you wrote a 'Biography of a Carpenter'; I wrote a 'Biography of Mao Ying, Mr. Brush,' you wrote a 'Camel Guo the Gardener'; I wrote 'To the Crocodile,' you wrote 'The Snake Catcher.' So much for those. Then I submitted my 'Memorial on the Pacification West of the Huai' to

---

2. Zhao Pu (921–991), a devotee of the *Analects*, told the brother of the founder of the Song dynasty that by the use of one-half of the *Analects* he had won the empire for the founder; now he would rule it for the brother by the use of the other half.

3. Han Yu, in his essay "On the Advancement of Studies," expressed these sentiments in dignified prose; the author puts them into doggerel in accord with the speaker's role of clown.

4. Another invention, based on Wang Shuwen's acknowledged liking for chess. The more pertinent factor behind Liu Zongyuan's banishment was his involvement in Wang's political defeat. The conversation en route to exile is also apocryphal, though the titles attributed to the two great essayists are authentic.

win favor at court, and what should you do but submit in your turn your own essay 'On the Pacification West of the Huai.' With one piece after another you pitted yourself against me. And now, skulking off to banishment in the poisonous south, we meet together in one and the same place. What is this but 'our Time, our Chance, our Destiny'?" But you and I, my friend, can let them go, these happenings of a distant age. If we turn to our own two fates, what have we done to deserve this neglect from the world? My ancestor wrote an essay, "On Seeking Fortune"—why does no fortune come to me, twenty-eight generations later? Your ancestor wrote a definitive "Farewell to Poverty"—then why, in twenty-odd generations down to yourself, has poverty still not taken its leave? As I see it, Time and Chance must bear the blame.

HAN: Very true. You see, Chunqing,

> 11b put all your resources in learning rather than land
> and—who could foretell?—in tranquil times
> it brings back not a cent.

And yet, just the same, back in the days of Prince Zhao Tuo, a learned sophist, Lu Jia, once came to this place as an envoy from the Imperial court, was received by Prince Zhao Tuo with the greatest respect, and then

> turned back his carriage north to the court
> piled high with yellow gold.

In those day the Han Emperor Gaozu detested men of learning, and if he came across a scholar's cap would piss in it. Along came this Lu Jia for audience before the Emperor, all complete with his square scholar's cap and gravely swaying his long scholar's robe. "Another piss pot for me," says the Emperor to himself as he watches Lu Jia's approach. Then as Lu Jia stood before him he snarled, "Sonny, I won the empire from the back of a horse. What do I need of your *Songs* and *Documents*?" Now, this was Lu Jia's cleverness. He made no elaborate reply, just one sentence: "Your Imperial Majesty may well have won the empire on horseback—but can you rule it from there?" The Emperor at this gave a great "Ha!" and said, "Have it your own way then. Let me hear you recite something—anything will do." Cool and collected, our Courtier Lu drew from his sleeve a scroll that comprised the "New Words," in thirteen chapters, previously composed by himself by lamp and window light. These he now delivered in a ringing voice before the throne. By the time the Emperor Gaozu had heard the first chapter, the dragon countenance wore an expression of delight. As chapter followed chapter he praised each one in turn. On the spot he bestowed the title Marquis within the Pass. What an honor for him that day! Not to speak of praise from the Han Emperor himself: every one of the officers civil and military who witnessed the scene cried out, "Ten thousand years of blessing!"

> One word dropped to the ground
> and "Ten thousand years!" deafens the sky.

LIU (*with a sigh*):

> And yet no eye has seen
> one sheet of all my dustheap of despatches.

LIU, HAN:

> Heaven will ordain
> and it is vain to search for precedents
> all up and down the length of history
> while cold mist shrouds the trees' decay
> on weed-grown terrace.

HAN: Let me ask you, Chunqing: how do you manage to live?

LIU: I live off the earnings of my gardener.

HAN: I should say the best plan would be to seek support for your advancement from some powerful patron.

LIU: But you must realize there are few people of real sympathy in these times.

HAN: But haven't you heard, there is an old gentleman, Secretary Miao, Imperial Commissioner for the Examination of Gems, who is a most sympathetic person. His tour of duty ends this autumn, but first he will go to assess gems in the Temple of the Many-jewelled, in the Vale of the Incense Mountains in Guangzhou prefecture. Why don't you go see him at that time?

LIU: I shall do as you say.

Envoi:

> Recalling the sad days
>   of solitary sojourn,
> not mine the destiny to reach
>   the azure clouds of office.
> The Prince of Yue laughed aloud
>   inspecting his high Terrace,
> the heroes of Han's founding
>   had never opened a book.

SCENE SEVEN: *The Schoolroom*

CHEN ZUILIANG:

Droning verses, re-revising
   lines composed last spring,
pondering, my belly filled,
   the taste of the noontime tea;
ants climb up the table leg
   to skirt the ink-slab pool,
bees invade the window
   to raid the blooms in my vase.

Here in the Prefect's residence I, Chen Zuiliang, have "hung my bed curtain" so that I may instruct the daughter of the house, following family tradition, in the *Book of Songs*. The mistress, Madam Du, is treating me with the greatest kindness. Now that breakfast is over I shall immerse myself for a while in the *Songs*.

(He intones)

"*Guanguan* cry the ospreys
on the islet in the river.
So delicate the virtuous maiden,
a fit mate for our Prince."[1]

"Fit," that is to say, "fit"; "mate," that is to say, "seeking." *(He looks about)* How late it gets, and still no sign of my pupil. Horribly spoilt. Let me try three raps on the cloud board. *(He raps the cloud board)* Fragrance, summon the young mistress for her lesson.

*(Enter BRIDAL DU, followed
by SPRING FRAGRANCE bearing books)*

BRIDAL DU:

   1 Lightly adorned for morning,
   to library leisurely strolling,
   unconcerned I face
   table's gleam by window's brightness.

---

1. The first stanza of the first of the *Songs*. Actually a folk love lyric, this, like many more of the *Songs*, was traditionally interpreted in didactic fashion as expressing popular esteem for a benevolent prince or whatnot. I use Legge's translation both to accord with this kind of interpretation and for the sake of its by now somewhat fustian quality.

SPRING FRAGRANCE:

    Words of Worth from the Ancients

    —What a deadly thought

but when I'm through

    I'll be able to teach the parrot to order tea.

(They greet CHEN)

BRIDAL: Our best respects, esteemed sir.

FRAGRANCE: We hope you're not vexed, esteemed sir.

CHEN: As the *Rites* prescribe, "it is proper for a daughter at first cockcrow to wash her hands, to rinse her mouth, to dress her hair, to pin the same, to pay respects to father and mother." Once sun is up then each should attend to her affairs. You are now a pupil and your business is to study: you will need to rise earlier than this.

BRIDAL: We shall not be late again.

FRAGRANCE: We understand. Tonight we won't go to bed so that we can present ourselves for our lesson in the middle of the night.

CHEN: Have you rehearsed the portion of the *Songs* I presented yesterday?

BRIDAL: I have, but await your interpretation.

CHEN: Let me hear you.

BRIDAL *(recites)*:

    Guanguan cry the ospreys

    on the islet in the river.

    So delicate the virtuous maiden,

    a fit mate for our Prince."

CHEN: Now note the interpretation.

    "*Guanguan* cry the ospreys":

the osprey is a bird; "*guanguan*," that is to say, its cry.

FRAGRANCE: What sort of cry is that?

(CHEN imitates the call

of the osprey; FRAGRANCE ad libs an imitation

of CHEN imitating the osprey)

CHEN: This bird being a lover of quiet, it is on an island in the river.

FRAGRANCE: Quite right. Either yesterday or the day before, this year or last year some time, an osprey got trapped in the young mistress' room and she set it free and I said to myself, if I try to catch it again, *I land* in the river.

CHEN: Rubbish. This is a "detached image."

FRAGRANCE: What, a graven image? Who detached it?

CHEN: To "image," that is to say, to introduce thoughts of. It introduces the thought of the "delicate virtuous maiden," who is a nice, quiet girl waiting for the prince to come seeking her.

FRAGRANCE: What's he seeking from her?

CHEN: Now you are being impudent.

BRIDAL: My good tutor, to interpret the text by means of the notes is something I can do for myself. I should like you rather to instruct me in the overall significance of the *Book of Songs*.

CHEN:

> IIa   Of all six Classics
> the *Book of Songs* is the flower
> with "Airs" and "Refinements" most apt for lady's
>   chamber:
> for practical instruction
> Jiangyuan bears her offspring
> "treading in the print of God's big toe";
> warning against jealousy
> shine the virtues of queen and consort.

And then there are the

> "Song of the Cockcrow,"
> the "Lament for the Swallows,"
> "Tears by the Riverbank,"
> "Longings by the Han River"
> to cleanse the face of rouge:
> in every verse an edifying homily
> to "fit a maid for husband and for family."

BRIDAL: It seems to be a very *long* classic!

CHEN: "The *Songs* are three hundred, but their meaning may be expressed in a single phrase":

> no more than this,
> "to set aside evil thoughts,"
> and this I pass to you.

End of lesson. Fragrance, fetch the "four jewels of the scholar's study" for our calligraphy.

FRAGRANCE: Here are paper, ink, brushes, and inkstone.

CHEN: What sort of ink is this supposed to be?

BRIDAL: Oh, she brought the wrong thing. This is "snail black," for painting the brows.

CHEN: And what sort of brushes?

BRIDAL (*laughing*): Mascara brushes.

CHEN: Never did I see such things before! Take them away, take them away. And what sort of paper is this?

BRIDAL: Notepaper woven by the Tang courtesan Xue Tao.

CHEN: Take it away, take it away. Bring such as was woven by the noble inventor of paper, the ancient Cai Lun. And what sort of inkstone? Is it single or double?

BRIDAL: It's not single, it's married.

CHEN: And the "eye" patterns on it—what sort of eyes?

BRIDAL: Weeping eyes.[2]

CHEN: What are they weeping about? —Go change the whole lot.

FRAGRANCE (aside): Ignorant old rustic! (To CHEN) Very well. (She brings a new set) Will these do?

CHEN (examines them): All right.

BRIDAL: I believe I could copy some characters. But Fragrance will need your hand, sir, to guide her brush.

CHEN: Let me see how you write. (As BRIDAL writes, he watches in amazement) Never did I see writing of this quality! What is the model?

BRIDAL: The model is "The Beauty Adorns Her Hair with Blossoms," the style transmitted by the Lady Wei of Jin times.

FRAGRANCE: Let me do some characters in the style of "The Maid Apes Her Mistress."

BRIDAL: Too early for that.

FRAGRANCE: Master, I beg leave to be excused—to leave the room and excuse myself. (She exits)

BRIDAL: Esteemed tutor, may I inquire what age your lady has attained?

CHEN: She has reached exactly sixty.

BRIDAL: If you would let me have the pattern, I should like to embroider a pair of slippers to congratulate her.

CHEN: Thank you. The pattern should be from *Mencius*, "to make sandals without knowledge of the foot."

BRIDAL: Fragrance isn't back yet.

CHEN: Shall I call her?

(He calls thrice)

FRAGRANCE (enters): Clapping like that—I'll give him the clap!

---

2. Inkstones of a highly prized variety made at Duanxi in Guangdong were decorated with patterns of "eyes" carved to follow the natural grain of the stone. If the "eyes" were not "bright eyes," clear-cut, they were known as "weeping eyes," or worse, "dead eyes."

BRIDAL (*annoyed*): What have you been doing, silly creature?

FRAGRANCE (*laughing*): Peeing. But I found a lovely big garden full of pretty flowers and willows,[3] lots of fun.

CHEN: Dear, dear, instead of studying she is off to the garden. Let me fetch a bramble switch.

FRAGRANCE: What do you want a bramble switch for?

> 11b   How can a girl
> take the the examinations and fill an office?

All it's for is to
> read a few characters and scrawl a few crow's-feet.

CHEN: There were students in ancient times who put fireflies in a bag or read by the moon.

FRAGRANCE:

> If you use reflected moonlight
> you'll dazzle the toad up there;
> as for fireflies in a bag
> just think of the poor things burning!

CHEN: Then what about the man who tied his hair to a beam to keep from nodding off, or the scholar who prodded himself awake with an awl in the thigh?

FRAGRANCE: If you were to try
> tying your hair to a beam
> you wouldn't have much left
> and pricking your thighs
> you'd be even scabbier than you are.
> What's so glorious about that?

> (*A flower vendor's cry comes from within*)

Listen, young mistress,
> a flower vendor's cry
> drowns out the drone of studies.

CHEN: Again she distracts the young lady. This time I shall really beat her. (*He moves to do so*)

FRAGRANCE (*dodging*):

> Try and beat me then,
> poor little me —
> tutor to young ladies

---

3. "Flowers and willows": this euphemism for "syphilis" reinforces the "clap" of her previous speech. We are no doubt to assume that Bridal remains innocent of these suggestions of her maid, aimed at Tutor Chen.

scaring this poor malefactor
within an inch of her life!

(She grabs the bramble switch and throws it to the floor)

BRIDAL: You wicked creature, kneel at once for such rudeness to the
tutor. *(FRAGRANCE kneels)* Since this is her first offense, sir,
perhaps it will be enough if I give her a scolding:
    IIC Your hands must not touch the garden swing
    nor your feet tread the garden path.
FRAGRANCE: We'll see about that!
BRIDAL: If you answer back, we shall have to
    scorch with an incense stick
    these lips of yours that blow breezes of malice,
    blind with a sewing needle
    these eyes that blossom into nothing but trouble.
FRAGRANCE: And what use would my eyes be then?
BRIDAL: I insist that you
    hold to the inkstone
    stand fast by the desk
    attend to "it is written in the *Songs*"
    be there when "the Master says"
    and do not let your thoughts wander.
FRAGRANCE: Oh, do let's wander a little!
BRIDAL *(seizes her by the hair)*: Do you want as many
    weals on your back
    as there are hairs on your head?
    I'll have you show respect for the "comptroller of the
    household"
    —the stick Madam Du my mother keeps in her room!
FRAGRANCE: I won't do it again.
BRIDAL: You understand then?
CHEN: That will be enough, we shall let her go this time. Get up.

(FRAGRANCE rises to her feet)

    III Except she lacks ambition for the fame of office,
    instruction of the girl pupil parallels the boy's.
Only when your lessons are completed may you return to the
house. Meanwhile, I shall exchange a few words with your father.
BRIDAL, FRAGRANCE, CHEN: What a waste of
    this new red gauze on the sunlit window.

*(CHEN exits; FRAGRANCE points
scornfully at his retreating back)*

FRAGRANCE: Ignorant old ox, dopey old dog, not an ounce of understanding

BRIDAL *(tugs at her sleeve)*: Stupid creature, "a tutor for a day is a father for a lifetime"; don't you understand he has the right to beat you? But tell me, where is this garden of yours?

*(FRAGRANCE refusing to speak, BRIDAL
gives an embarrassed laugh and asks again)*

FRAGRANCE *(pointing)*: Over there, of course!

BRIDAL: What is there to look at?

FRAGRANCE: Oh, lots to look at, half a dozen pavilions, one or two swings, a meandering stream one can float wine cups down, weathered Taihu rocks on the other bank. It's really beautiful, with all those prize blooms and rare plants.

BRIDAL: How surprising to find such a place. But now we may go back to the house.

Envoi:

BRIDAL:

> Catkins floated on the breeze
> in the Xie family court

FRAGRANCE:

> thwarted is my desire to become
> a butterfly in the western garden.

BRIDAL:

> Ask not what sorrows follow spring
> for they are limitless.

BRIDAL, FRAGRANCE:

> Take for a while this loan
> of green shade for your strolling.

SCENE EIGHT: *Speed the Plough*

*Enter PREFECT DU with PAGE BOY,
underlings, and attendants*

PREFECT DU:

> 1a Where should the five steeds draw my
>   carriage to "advance the spring"
> to learn as green shoots burgeon "what songs
>   are on farm folk's lips"?
> From eave of thatch comes call of dove,
> my crimson carriage draws forth the stag
> as once the white deer, happy omen,
> followed the good Zheng Hong
> and I shall rest "beneath the sweet apple's shade."
> The seasons run their course,
> the second month of spring gives way to the third.
> After enriching rains and fruitful mists
> clear shines the sky for the Prefect to go forth
> to speed the plough as the new season deepens.
> Let farm work thrive,
> ease burden of corvée and lawsuit.

Spring comes early to my prefecture here between the River and the southern Guang provinces. I reflect that I have little way of telling, sequestered as I am in my prefectural court, whether there may not be far-off hamlets falling into ruin while their inhabitants roam as vagabonds. Yesterday, therefore, I instructed this particular county to prepare garlands and wine for my reception as I come to speed the plough. I believe they should be ready for me.

COUNTY OFFICIAL *(enters):*

> No secretary carried out
> the Prefect's orders, but only I
> and my farm-folk helpers.

Your Honor, the garlands and wine are all ready for you to speed the plough.

DU: Let the procession start. And when we approach the village I don't want a lot of hubbub.

*(ALL chorus assent and move in
procession with shouts of "Clear the way!")*

Truly,

> "to quicken summer life move I in procession,
> not to enjoy the pleasant signs of spring."

(Exit)

ELDERS (*enter*):

> 1b Less work to do as white-haired age draws on
> we enjoy the children's jokes and merriment.
> The Prefect on his tour of inspection
> riding in benevolent state
> no doubt will proclaim the virtues of toil in the fields?

We are elders of the village of Qingle of Nan'an prefecture. We are here to congratulate His Honor Prefect Du on his three years in office. His administration has been honest and kindly; he has put a stop to corrupt practices and has refined local customs. Regulations have been proclaimed and associations established in every village; public granaries and village schools are in operation everywhere: truly he has brought the greatest of blessings to us countryfolk. Now he is visiting every district in person to speed the plough, and so we are on our way to the official pavilion to receive him. Here come the sergeants now with garlands and wine.

SERGEANTS (*enter, bearing garlands and wine*):

> 11 No thief slick enough to catch us thiefcatchers,
> today we've vanished from the office without trace,
> bearing wine up a country slope.

(They stumble)

> Nearly dropped it—
> don't rely on us to keep the flowers intact.

ELDERS: Welcome to our village.

SERGEANTS: If these jars should seem to have spilled over and there's not enough wine left, please keep it quiet!

ELDERS: Don't worry. Put them down at the side here while you go off for a bowl in the tavern. (*Exeunt SERGEANTS*) Let the heads of village units straighten the seats. His Honor is approaching.

(They move aside)

DU (*reenters with his retinue*):

> III Pink of almond fully open,
> iris blades unsheathed,
> fields of spring warming to season's life.
> Over thatched hut by bamboo fence juts a tavern flag,
> rain clears, and the smoke spirals from kitchen stoves.

(ELDERS greet him)

ALL:

> Warblers call "a jug, a jug,"

woodchuck grate "sow seed, sow seed,"
for a few days the Prefect's court
stands empty of its drawn ranks of officers.
Advance no vanguard,
make no hubbub
such as might startle dwellers in forest depth.

UNDERLINGS (*report*): Here is the pavilion for the reception of Your Honor.

(*ELDERS greet the PREFECT*)

DU: Tell me, uncles, what district is this and what village?

ELDERS: This is the first district of Nan'an county, the village of Qingle.

DU: Let me enjoy the view. (*He gazes about him*) A pretty spot and well named Qingle, "Pure Joy."

To see the pure lines of hills,
the pure stream waters,
one would fancy oneself
on "the fabled road to Shaoxing."
And all the sky white clouds of spring.

ELDERS:

What is pure is the heart of our governor
and the conduct of his officers
so that the farmer, no cause to take to court
spends his day singing.

DU: Uncles, do you understand the reasons for my spring excursion?

IVa Waving in emerald sheen the young wheatfields,
green plots in patchwork even-scissored
or sketched by painter's brush.
Glossy rain
richly muddies the tracery of paths.
Fertile are the veins of this land South of the River,
but I have fears for men who withhold their effort
while fields run rank with weeds
and for senseless wrangling at law
in interference with your livelihood.

ELDERS: In the past we had official messengers all day long and watches to stand against thieves at night. But when Your Honor came to us,

IVb in a thousand hamlets harvests flourished.
As reverence was shown in ancient days, so now
we elders "carry incense bowls on our heads"

while children "ride on hobbyhorse to hail you."
Like a "two-legged summer sun"
you warm our humble homes.
"By moonlight no dog yaps at chrysanthemums,
when rain is past men go to plough fresh fields."
Truly, welcome you are as rain and dew
to hemp and mulberry.

(The song "Slippery Mud" sounds from offstage)

DU: Let me listen to this country song that comes from the village.
FARMER *(enters):*

va Slippery mud,
sloppery thud,
short rake, long plough, clutch 'em as they slide.
After rainy night sow rice and hemp,
when sky clears fetch out the muck,
then a stink like long-pickled fish
floats on the breeze.

DU: Well sung. "After rainy night sow rice and hemp, when sky clears fetch out the muck, then a stink like long-pickled fish floats on the breeze"—that would be referring to the stench of manure. But, uncles, he doesn't realize that manure is really fragrant. There is a poem to prove it:

Incense burns, cauldrons
    are heaped high to honor the prince,
foods costly as gold or jade
    plied for his delectation.
But when to a starving stomach
    comes a whiff of plain boiled rice
then ambergris itself fails to match
    the fragrance of manure.

Give him flowers for his headband and wine to drink.
FARMER *(smiling as he decks himself with flowers and tastes the wine):*
Hurray for His Honor and hurray for the wine.

Drunk on the governor's nectar,
decked with smiles and necked with blossoms,
what pretty fellows we farmers be.

(Exit)

PAGE BOY: Here comes a lad singing.
HERDBOY *(enters, carrying flute):*

vb   Riding in spring,
plying my whip,
blowing a tune
on my flute,
perched on ox back facing the tail
as crows cross setting sun.

(*Pointing with his flute at the* PAGE BOY)

He's as small as I am,
hair in twin tufts just the same,
but he gets to ride a big horse.

DU: Well sung. What did he sing about the page boy? "He's as small as I am, hair in twin tufts just the same, but he gets to ride a big horse." But, uncles, he doesn't realize that an ox is really a steadier ride. There is a poem to prove it:

Often I would envy
    the lord of myriad households,
certain that high-stepping horse
    was safer than humble ox
but today here from my saddle
    wistfully gauging the sky
I wonder how it compares
    with such ox-back freedom.

Give him wine and flowers to deck himself with.

HERDBOY (*takes flowers and wine*):

Drunk on the governor's nectar,
decked with smiles and necked with blossoms,
what pretty fellows we village lads be.

(*Exit*)

PAGE BOY: Here come two women singing.

TWO WOMEN (*enter, picking mulberry leaves*):

vc   Under the mulberry's shade,
willow basket aslant on back,
but careful where the branches fork
to mind one's own fork doesn't get jabbed!

Why, what's this official gentleman doing here?

Long ago
Luo Fu was picking mulberry leaves
when a high official tried to tempt her,
but she resisted;

and Qiu Hu's wife was picking mulberry
and him long absent, coming back a famous man
tempted her with gold
but she not recognizing him
also resisted.
We have our own man,
put your gold away.

DU: Well sung. But tell them I am no Qiu Hu nor prefect of Qin trying to seduce them—I am their own governor come to speed the plough. I respect their devotion to their task of picking mulberry leaves. There is a poem to prove it:

Peach-bloom complexions blush
with joy of pipes and singing
here in these shaded acres
arched with mulberry,
no fickle, wanton blossoms
of the common sort
but in abundant leaf
close weave of gauzy silk.

Wine and flowers are ready for you.

WOMEN (*turning away to deck themselves and drink*):
Drunk on the governor's nectar,
decked with smiles and necked with blossoms,
how elegant now we mulberry pickers be.

(*Exeunt*)

PAGE BOY: Two more women singing.

(*Enter two more women, carrying baskets for tea picking*)

TEA PICKERS:
vd   At time of "Grain Rains"
picking the new crop
leaf by leaf and bud after bud
of rarest "Filigree Tip."

Why, what is this official gentleman doing here?
A scholar like Tao Gu
to please his new mistress
brewed it with snow
and many the weary student
has longed for it
scented with smoke of bamboo fire
and brewed in earthenware pot.

DU: Well sung. But tell them I am no Tao Gu who found a mistress in the posting station, nor that "hard-up student" of Yangxian who in the old story spat a pretty girl from his mouth to thank his benefactor. I am their own governor come to speed the plough. I am sure it is better for you women to be picking mulberry leaves and tea than to be picking flowers. There is a poem to prove it:

> Since no "tea star"
>> stood in the sky,
> the tea came on earth
>> as "fair nymph of all plants."
> Idle maids delight
>> in the "battle of the flowers,"
> but in the tea-brewing contest
>> may be won a finer prize.

Wine and flowers are ready for you.

TEA PICKERS (*decking themselves and drinking*):

> Drunk on the governor's nectar,
>> decked with smiles and necked with blossoms,
>> how elegant now we tea pickers be.

(Exeunt)

ELDERS (*kneeling*): Your Honor, we elders have tea and rice ready to serve you.

DU: You must not trouble yourselves. Please take the flowers and wine jars that remain to distribute among the villagers as a token of my sincere desire to "speed the plough." Tell the sergeants to mount.

ELDERS (*try to detain* DU, *but in vain. They rise to their feet and call out*): All of you village folk who have received flowers and enjoyed the wine, come now to see His Honor on his way.

VILLAGERS (*reenter, decked with flowers*):

> VI In highest state rides our Prefect on spring excursion,
>> his mount of rarest dapple,
>> while taverns radiant with flowers and wine
>> bear witness to his graciousness.

Come now, all in the village,

>> let us wherever he passes
>> set tablets in his praise.

Envoi:

> Paths from village to village
>> wind along the ridge

green, green, the shoots of spring
across a thousand fields.
Carriage drawn by team of five
must halt when dusk descends
where peach bloom blushes pink
beside the bamboo grove.

SCENE NINE: *Sweeping the Garden*

SPRING FRAGRANCE:
1a Little Spring Fragrance
favored among the servants,
used to pampered ways within the painted chambers
waiting on the young mistress,
I mix her powder, match her rouge,
set her feather adornments, arrange her flowers,
ever waiting beside the boudoir mirror
ready to smoothe the brocaded quilt,
ready to light the fragrant nighttime incense,
urged on by Madam's stick on my puny shoulders.
Bondmaid with petaled cheeks
    just into my teens,
sweet and charming, wide awake
    to the spring's arrival.
A real "passion flower"
    is what we need now
to follow our every step
    with admiring glances.

Day and night you will find me, Fragrance, by the side of my young mistress. She, though she might win fame above all others for her beauty, is more concerned with jealous guarding of the family reputation. Maiden modesty composes her gentle features, and it is her nature to be serious and reverent. The master having engaged a tutor to instruct her, she commenced the study of the *Book of Songs*; but, when she reached the lines "So delicate the virtuous maiden, a fit mate for our Prince," she quietly put the book down and sighed, "Here we may observe the full extent of love to the true sage. As men felt in ancient times, so they feel today, and how should it be other than this?" So then I suggested, "Miss, you are tired from

your studies, why don't you think of some way to amuse yourself?"
She hesitated and thought for a moment. Then she got to her feet.
"And how would you have me amuse myself, Fragrance?" she
asked me. So I said, "Why, miss, nothing special, just to take a
walk in that garden behind the house." "Stupid creature," says the
young mistress, "what would happen if my father found out?" But I
said, "His Honor has been out visiting the country districts for
several days now." Then for ages the young mistress walked up and
down thinking, not saying a word, until at last she began to consult
the calendar. She said tomorrow was a bad day, and the day after
not very good, but the day after that is a propitious day because the
God of Pleasure Trips is on duty for the day. I was to tell the gardener to sweep the paths ready for her visit. I said I would. I'm
scared of Madam's finding out, but there's nothing we can do about
that. So let me go give the gardener his instructions. Hello, there's
Tutor Chen at the other end of the verandah. Truly,
> on every side the glory of the spring
>   and what does this old fool see? —Not a thing.

TUTOR CHEN *(enters):*
> 1b Aging book lover
> now for a while "within the green gauze tent"
> where once the learned Ma Rong gave instruction
> curtain flaps against hook in warmth of sun.
> Ha, there on the verandah
> young girl with hair in double coil
> seeming to speak, but wordless,
> closer now, who can it be?

Oh, it's Fragrance. Tell me,
> where is your gracious lord
> and where his lady?
> And why is my pupil absent from her lessons?

FRAGRANCE: Oh, it's you, Tutor Chen. I'm afraid the young mistress
has not had time for classes these last few days.

CHEN: And why is that?

FRAGRANCE: I'll tell you:
> 1c Spring in its splendor
> cruel to a sensitive nature
> —everything's gone wrong.

CHEN: Why, what has gone wrong?

FRAGRANCE: Ah, you've no idea how angry the governor is going to
be with you.

CHEN: For what reason?

FRAGRANCE: Why, that *Book of Songs* of yours, you've been singing a bit too sweetly, my poor young mistress—

> your classical exegesis
> has torn her heart to pieces.

CHEN: All I did was explicate the "*Guanguan* cry the ospreys."

FRAGRANCE: That was the one. *Guan* means "shut in," doesn't it? My young mistress said, "Even though the ospreys were shut in, they still had the freedom of the island: why should a human being be treated worse than a bird?"

> In books the head must be buried,
> but it lifts itself to gaze on a scene of beauty.

Now she has ordered me to take her in a day or two to stroll in the garden behind the house.

CHEN: What will be the purpose of this stroll?

FRAGRANCE:

> Unsuspected the spring has struck
> and before it hastens past
> she must cast off there in the garden
> spring's disquiet.

CHEN: She should not do this.

> id When woman walks abroad
> lest eyes should light upon her
> at every step she should be screened from view.

Fragrance, by the grace of Heaven I, your tutor, have enjoyed some sixty years of life, yet never have I felt any such thing as "spring-struck," nor have I ever strolled in any garden.

FRAGRANCE: Why not?

CHEN: You should learn how aptly Mencius put the matter. The myriad sayings of the sage are devoted to this alone: to urge men to "retrieve their lost goodness of heart."

> Keep to the normal round,
> lay claim to no "spring-struck" state,
> nor demand any sort of "spring stroll."

And in "seeing out the spring" take care

> lest you see out also the springs of goodness
> in your own heart.

For the time being, then, if the young lady will not be taking her lessons, I shall request a few days' leave. Fragrance,

> go often to the classroom,
> take frequent note of trellised window
> for fear the swallows' droppings
> spatter with filth the lute and the books therein.

I shall leave you now.
> Young lady leaves brocaded chamber
>> to idle among the flowers
> while like the ancient Dong Zhongshu
>> I con my texts behind drawn shades
> with never a glance at the garden.

(Exit)

FRAGRANCE: How lovely, Tutor Chen has gone away. Now, I wonder if the gardener's there? (*She calls*) Gardener!
GARDENER'S LAD (*enters, tipsy*):
> II Just a lad who tends the blooms in the garden,
> flower seller too (on the side)—beg your pardon.
> Runners grab me
> sergeants nab me,
> and ooh, this hot rice wine
> makes a pot of boiled sausage out of my intestines.

(Greets FRAGRANCE)

Hello, Miss Fragrance.
FRAGRANCE: You should have a beating, sneaking out on the street to cadge wine, and no vegetables delivered for days now.
LAD: That's the vegetable gardener's job.
FRAGRANCE: No water piped either.
LAD: That's the water carrier's job.
FRAGRANCE: No flowers delivered either.
LAD: I've brought flowers every morning, a bunch for Madam, a bunch for the young mistress.
FRAGRANCE: What about a third bunch?
LAD: I'm sorry, I deserve a beating.
FRAGRANCE: What's your name?
LAD: Flower Lad.
FRAGRANCE: Well, make up a song for me about your name. If it's a good one I'll let you off your beating.
LAD: All right.
> IIIa Bedding plants have I set out,
>> wave on wave like the sea
> but you're as succulent a shoot as ever I did see.
> Let's do some bedding-out today
>> while the sun shines merrily
> but what if my little blossom withers under me?
FRAGRANCE: Now here's a song for you:

111b Troubles you have brought about,
wave on wave like the sea
—just you dare come looking for something nice from me!

LAD: Ai-yo!

FRAGRANCE: Just you wait
till I go tell His Honor, then perhaps we'll see

(She seizes him by the the hair)

how a bamboo rod or two can whip your apple tree!

LAD *(falling flat):* All right, I give up. To what do we owe the honor of this visit, Miss?

FRAGRANCE: The young mistress will be coming to view the garden in three days' time, so make sure the paths are swept.

LAD: It shall be done.

Envoi:

Time of sweetest fragrance
in eastern suburb now,
happy the home in Yangzhou, ruled
by the Woman Star of Aquarius.
Send not young boys
to the realm of rouge and powder
lest the chattering of orioles
take on a lascivious tone.

SCENE TEN: *The Interrupted Dream*

BRIDAL DU:

1 From dream returning, orioles coil their song
through all the brilliant riot of the new season,
to listener in tiny leaf-locked court.

SPRING FRAGRANCE:

Burnt to ashes the aloes wood
cast aside the broidering thread,
no longer able as in past years
to quiet stirrings of the spring's passions.

BRIDAL:

Like one "eyeing the apricot flower to slake her thirst"

at dawn, cheeks blurred with last night's rouge,
I gaze at Apricot Blossom Pass.

FRAGRANCE:

The coils of your hair
dressed with silken swallows in the mode of spring
tilt aslant as you lean
across the balustrade.

BRIDAL:

Rootless ennui,
"where are the scissors can cut
the comb can untangle this grief?"

FRAGRANCE:

I have told the oriole and the swallow
to leave their urging of the flowers
and with spring as their excuse
to come look at you.

BRIDAL: Fragrance, have you given orders for the paths to be swept?

FRAGRANCE: Yes.

BRIDAL: Now bring my mirror and my gown.

FRAGRANCE (*reenters with these*):

"Cloud coiffure set to perfection
  still she questions the mirror,
robe of gauze soon to be changed
  still she adds sweetening incense."

I've brought your mirror and gown.

BRIDAL:

II The spring a rippling thread
of gossamer gleaming sinuous in the sun
borne idly across the court.
Pausing to straighten
the flower heads of hair ornaments,
perplexed to find that my mirror
stealing its half-glance at my hair
has thrown these "gleaming clouds"
into alarmed disarray.

(*She takes a few steps*)

Walking here in my chamber
how should I dare let others see my form!

FRAGRANCE: How beautifully you are dressed and adorned today!

BRIDAL:

      III See now how vivid shows my madder skirt,
      how brilliant gleam these combs all set with gems
—you see, it has been
        always in my nature to love fine things.
        And yet, this bloom of springtime no eye has seen.
        What if my beauty should amaze the birds
        and out of shame for the comparison
        "cause fish to sink, wild geese to fall to earth,
        petals to close, the moon to hide her face"
        while all the flowers tremble?

FRAGRANCE: Please come now, it's almost breakfast time.

(They begin to walk)

Look how
    while on the lacquered walkway
      traces of gold dust glitter,
    there on the lodge at pool's edge
      mosses make a green mass.
    Timid lest the grass stain
      our newly broidered socks
    we grieve that the flowers must bear
      the tug of tiny gold bells.[1]

BRIDAL: Without visiting this garden, how could I ever have realized this splendor of spring!

      IV See how deepest purple, brightest scarlet
      open their beauty only to dry well crumbling.
      "Bright the morn, lovely the scene,"
        listless and lost the heart
      —where is the garden "gay with joyous cries"?

My mother and father have never spoken of any such exquisite spot as this.

BRIDAL, FRAGRANCE:

      Streaking the dawn, close-curled at dusk,
      rosy clouds frame emerald pavilion;
      fine threads of rain, petals borne on breeze,

---

1. A prince of the Tang court strung tiny gold bells on red thread to hang on the stems of flowers and instructed the gardener to tug the thread when necessary to scare off the birds. Here Fragrance, though aware that this was done out of compassion for the flowers, takes sensibility a stage further by lamenting the burden they must bear.

gilded pleasure boat in waves of mist:
glories of spring but little treasured
by screen-secluded maid.

FRAGRANCE: All the flowers have come into bloom now, but it's still too early for the peony.

BRIDAL:

v   The green hillside
bleeds with the cuckoo's tears of red azalea,[2]
shreds of mist lazy as wine fumes thread the sweetbriar.
However fine the peony,
how can she rank as queen
coming to bloom when spring has said farewell!

FRAGRANCE: See them pairing, orioles and swallows!

BRIDAL, FRAGRANCE:

Idle gaze resting
there where the voice of swallow shears the air
and liquid flows the trill of oriole.

BRIDAL: We must go now.

FRAGRANCE: Really one would never weary of enjoying this garden.

BRIDAL: Say no more!

(They begin to walk back)

VI   Unwearying joy—how should we break its spell
even by visits each in turn
to the Twelve Towers of Fairyland?
Far better now, as first elation passes,
to find back in our chamber
some pastime for idle hours.

(They reach the house)

FRAGRANCE:

"Open the west chamber door,
in the east room make the bed,"
fill the vase with azalea,
light aloes in the incense burner.

Take your rest now, young mistress, while I go report to Madam.

(She exits)

---

2. An involved wordplay here. *Dujuan* means both a flower, the azalea, and a bird, the cuckoo. An old legend related that the Prince of Shu in ancient times was transformed after death into the cuckoo, which ever since has wept tears of blood.

BRIDAL (*sighing*):

> Back from spring stroll
>   to silent room,
> what to do but try on
>   the spring's new adornments?

Ah spring, now that you and I have formed so strong an attachment, what shall I find to fill my days when you are past? Oh this weather, how sleepy it makes one feel. Where has Fragrance got to? (*She looks about her, then lowers her head again, pondering*) Ah Heaven, now I begin to realize how disturbing the spring's splendor can truly be. They were all telling the truth, those poems and ballads I read that spoke of girls of ancient times "in springtime moved to passion, in autumn to regret." Here am I at the "double eight," my sixteenth year, yet no fine "scholar to break the cassia bough" has come my way. My young passions stir to the young spring season, but where shall I find an "entrant of the moon's toad palace"?[3] Long ago the Lady Han found a way to a meeting with Yu You, and the scholar Zhang met with Miss Cui by chance. Their loves are told in *Poem on the Red Leaf* and in *Western Chamber*,[4] how these "fair maids and gifted youths" after clandestine meetings made marital unions "as between Qin and Jin."[5] (*She gives a long sigh*) Though born and bred of a noted line of holders of office, I have reached the age to "pin up my hair" without plan made for my betrothal to a suitable partner. The green springtime of my own life passes unfulfilled, and swift the time speeds by as dawn and dusk interchange. (*She weeps*) O pity one whose beauty is a bright flower, when life endures no longer than leaf on tree!

> VII   From turbulent heart these springtime thoughts of love
> will not be banished
> —O with what suddenness

---

3. See scene 2, note 4.

4. *Poem on the Red Leaf* (*Tihongji*) is the title of a play by Tang Xianzu's friend, Wang Jide. The theme is taken from the Tang story of the Lady Han, who wrote a poem on a red leaf, which she set adrift on the water of the palace drain. The leaf was found by Yu You, who returned a message to her by similar means, and eventually met and married her. *Western Chamber* (*Xixiangji*) is Wang Shifu's famous play on the romance, again of Tang times, of the scholar Zhang and Cui Yingying, whom he met by chance on his visit to the temple in which she was lodging. In fact, our text does not name the *Xixiangji* at this point; rather, the *Cui Hui zhuan*, the story of another Miss Cui, but this seems an unnecessary complication.

5. Two states of the "Springs and Autumns" period, whose ruling families for generations made marriage alliances.

comes this secret discontent!
I was a pretty child, and so
of equal eminence must the family be
truly immortals, no less
to receive me in marriage.
But for what grand alliance
is this springtime of my youth
so cast away?
What eyes may light upon my sleeping form?
My only course this coy delaying
but in secret dreams
by whose side do I lie?
Shadowed against spring's glory I twist and turn.
Lingering
where to reveal my true desires!
Suffering
this wasting,
where but to Heaven shall my lament be made!

I feel rather tired, I shall rest against this low table and drowse for a while.

*(She falls asleep and begins to
dream of LIU MENGMEI, who enters bearing a branch
of willow in his hand)*

LIU MENGMEI:

As song of oriole purls in warmth of sun,
so smiling lips open to greet romance.
Tracing my path by petals borne on stream,
I find the Peach Blossom Source of my desire.[6]

I came along this way with Miss Du—how is it that she is not with me now? *(He looks behind him and sees her)* Ah, Miss Du!

*(She rises, startled from sleep, and
greets him. He continues)*

So this is where you were—I was looking for you everywhere. *(She glances shyly at him, but does not speak)* I just chanced to break off

---

6. Allusion to a story of Liu Chen and Ruan Zhao of Han times, who found faery love by following a "peach-blossom spring" into the Tiantai ("Terrace of Heaven") Mountains. Even more celebrated is the Peach Blossom Spring of an allegory by Tao Qian describing, at the stream's source, a secluded Shangri-la upon which a mortal stumbled.

this branch from a weeping willow in the garden. You are so deeply versed in works of literature, I should like you to compose a poem to honor it.

> *(She starts in surprised delight and opens her lips to speak, but checks herself)*

BRIDAL *(aside):* I have never seen this young man in my life—what is he doing here?
LIU *(smiling at her):* Lady, I am dying of love for you!

> VIII With the flowering of your beauty
> as the river of years rolls past,
> everywhere I have searched for you
> pining secluded in your chamber.

Lady, come with me just over there where we can talk.

> *(She gives him a shy smile, but refuses to move. He tries to draw her by the sleeve)*

BRIDAL *(in a low voice):* Where do you mean?
LIU:

> There, just beyond this railing peony-lined
> against the mound of weathered Taihu rocks.

BRIDAL *(in a low voice):* But, sir, what do you mean to do?
LIU *(also in a low voice):*

> Open the fastening at your neck
> loose the girdle at your waist,
> while you
> screening your eyes with your sleeve,
> white teeth clenched on the fabric as if against pain,
> bear with me patiently a while
> then drift into gentle slumber.

> *(BRIDAL turns away, blushing. LIU advances to take her in his arms, but she resists him)*

LIU, BRIDAL:

> Somewhere at some past time you and I met.
> Now we behold each other in solemn awe

but do not say

> in this lovely place we should meet and speak no word.

> *(LIU exits, carrying off BRIDAL by force. Enter FLOWER SPIRIT in red cloak strewn with petals and ornamental headdress on his piled-up hair)*

FLOWER SPIRIT:
> Commissioner of the Flowers' Blooming,
>> come with new season
> from Heaven of Blossom Guard
>> to fulfill the springtime's labors.
> Drenched in red petal rain
>> the beholder, heartsore,
> anchors his yearnings
>> amid the clouds of blossom.

In my charge as Flower Spirit is this garden in the rear of the prefectural residence at Nan'an. Between Bridal, daughter of Prefect Du, and the young graduate Liu Mengmei, there exists a marriage affinity that must some day be fulfilled, and now Miss Du's heart has been so deeply moved by her spring strolling that she has summoned the graduate Liu into her dream. To cherish in compassion the "jade-like incense ones" is the special concern of a flower spirit, and that is why I am here to watch over her and to ensure that the "play of clouds and rain" will be a joyous experience for her.

> ix   Ah, how the male force surges and leaps
> as in the way of wanton bee he stirs
> the gale of her desire
> while her soul trembles
> at the dewy brink of a sweet, shaded vale.
> A mating of shadows, this,
> consummation within the mind,
> no fruitful Effect
> but an apparition within the Cause.[7]
> Ha, but now my flower palace is sullied by lust.

I must use a falling petal to wake her.

> *(Scatters petals in the entrance to the stage)*

> Loath she may be to loose herself
> from the sweet spellbound dream of spring's delight,
> but petals flutter down
> like crimson snow.

So, graduate Liu, the dream is but half-complete. When it is over, be sure to see Miss Du safely back to her chamber. I leave you now.

---

7. In the Buddhist doctrine of karma, every effect is the result of some prior cause in either the present or a previous incarnation.

(Exit. Enter LIU, leading
BRIDAL by the hand)

LIU: For this brief moment
    x   nature was our comforter,
    grasses for pillow, our bed a bed of flowers.
Are you all right, Miss Du?

(She lowers her head)

    Disarrayed the clouds of her hair,
    red petals caught
    by emerald combs aslant.
O lady, never forget
    how close I clasped you
    and with what tenderness,
    longing only to make
    of our two bodies one single flesh
    but bringing forth
    a glistening of rouge raindrops in the sun.
BRIDAL: Sir, you must go now.
BRIDAL, LIU:
    Somewhere at some past time you and I met.
    Now we behold each other in solemn awe
but do not say
    in this lovely place we should meet and speak no word.
LIU: Lady, you must be tired. Please take a rest. *(He sees her back to the table against which she was drowsing, and gently taps her sleeve)* Lady, I am going. *(Looking back at her)* Have a good rest now, I shall come to see you again.
    Rain threatened the spring garden as she approached
    and when she slept the "clouds and rain"
    broke over Wushan, hill of faery love.

(Exit)

BRIDAL *(wakes with a start and calls in a low voice)*: Young sir, young sir, oh, you have left me. *(She falls asleep again)*
MADAM DU *(enters)*:
    Husband on Prefect's dais,
    daughter in cloistered chamber
    —yet when she broiders patterns on a dress
    above the flowers the birds fly all in pairs.

Child, child, what are you doing asleep in a place like this?

BRIDAL *(wakes and calls again after LIU)*: Oh, oh.

MADAM DU: Why, child, what is the matter?

BRIDAL *(startled, rises to her feet)*: Mother, it's you!

MADAM DU: Child, why aren't you passing your time pleasantly with needlework or a little reading? Why were you lying here sleeping in the middle of the day?

BRIDAL: Just now I took an idle stroll in the garden, but all at once the raucousness of the birds began to distress me and so I came back to my room. Lacking any means to while away the time I must have fallen asleep for a moment. Please excuse my failure to receive you in proper fashion.

MADAM DU: The rear garden is too lonely and deserted, child. You must not go strolling there again.

BRIDAL: I shall take care to do as you bid, Mother.

MADAM DU: Off to the schoolroom with you now for your lesson.

BRIDAL: We are having a break just now, the tutor is not here.

MADAM DU *(sighing)*: There must always be troubles when a girl approaches womanhood, and she must be left to her own ways. Truly,

> moiling and toiling in the children's wake,
> many the pains a mother needs must take.

(Exit)

BRIDAL *(watching her leave and sighing heavily)*: Ah Heaven, Bridal, what unsought fortune has befallen you today! Chancing to visit the garden behind the house, I found a hundred different flowers in bloom everywhere, and the beauty of the scene set my heart in turmoil. When my elation passed and I came back, I fell into a midday slumber here in my incense-laden chamber. Suddenly a most handsome and elegant youth appeared, of age just fit for the "capping ceremony" of the twentieth year. He had broken off a branch from a willow in the garden, and he smiled and said to me, "Lady, you are so deeply versed in works of literature, I should like you to compose a poem in honor of this willow branch." I was on the point of replying when the thought came to me that I had never seen this man in my life before and did not even know his name. How should I so lightly enter into conversation with him? But just as this was in my mind he came close and began to speak fond words to me; then taking me in his arms he carried me to a spot beside the peony pavilion, beyond the railings lined with tree peonies, and there together we found the "joys of cloud and rain." Passion was matched by passion, and indeed a thousand fond caresses, a million tendernesses passed between us. After our bliss was accomplished he led me back to where I had been sleeping, and many times said, "Rest now." Then, just as I was about to see him off, suddenly my mother came into my room and woke me. Now perspiration chills all my body—it was no more than a "dream of Nanke, the human world in an anthill." I hastened to greet my mother with the proper decorum, and was duly given a good talking-to. Though there was nothing I could say in my defense, how can I now free my mind from memories of all that happened in my dream? Walking or sitting still, I find no peace, all I can feel is a sense of loss. Ah mother, you tell me to be off to the schoolroom to my lesson—but what kind of book has lessons to lighten this heavy heart! *(She weeps, screening her face with her sleeve)*

> xi Through scudding of "clouds and rain"
> I had touched the borders of dream
> when the lady my mother
> called me, alas! and broke
> this slumber by window's sunlit gauze.
> Now clammy cold a perspiration breaks,
> now heart numbs, footsteps falter,
> thought fails, hair slants awry,
> and whether to sit or stand
> is more than mind can decide
> —then let me sleep again.

FRAGRANCE *(enters):*

> Against the coming of night
>   rid cheeks of powder's traces,
> against the damp of spring
>   add incense to the burner.

Young mistress, I have aired the bedclothes for you to sleep now.

BRIDAL:

> xii For heart spring-burdened, limbs
> now lax from garden strolling,
> no need of incense-aired
> brocaded covers to entice to slumber.

Ah, Heaven,

> let the dream I dreamed be not yet fled too far.

Envoi:

Idle spring excursion
　　begins from painted hall,
sweet-scented is the shade
　　of apricot and willow.
You ask where Liu and Ruan
　　met with their faery loves?[8]
Look back, and on the east wind
　　heartbreak comes again.

SCENE ELEVEN: *Well-meant Warning*

MADAM DU:

Day by day I decline,
　　older this year than last.
My daughter by study window
　　to sad seclusion holds fast.

For several days I had not visited my daughter in her chamber. When I called on her this noon I found her alone and listless, lying drowsily in her room. On inquiring the reason for her weariness, I discovered that she had just returned from the garden behind the house. She is too young to realize the impropriety, for a girl of tender years, of a pleasure stroll in all her finery in such a deserted place. It was that scamp Fragrance lured her into this. Fragrance!

SPRING FRAGRANCE (*enters*):

Try to take a rest,
　　always some new behest.

Madam, it's so late, isn't it time you retired?

MADAM DU: Where is your young mistress?

FRAGRANCE: After your visit to her chamber, Madam, she fell to talking to herself, and then drowsed off into a spring slumber. I expect she's having a dream.

MADAM DU: You good-for-nothing scamp, it was you who enticed your young mistress into the garden behind the house. What if something untoward had happened to her?

FRAGRANCE: I won't dare do it again.

---

8. See note 6

MADAM DU: Now hear my instructions:

> 1a   For a girl it is proper to sit in her chamber,
> busy fingers embroidering flowers.
> And how goes her work by window's light?
> —As the spring day lengthens
> she adds a row of stitches;
> then, if idle hours prove hard to fill,
> she may suitably turn to books and lute.
> But why, why enter the garden?

FRAGRANCE: It's very pretty in the garden.

MADAM DU: There is something you should learn, slave:

> 1b   That garden is a vast and lonely place,
> kiosks and terraces crumbling in neglect.

Even if a person of mature years such as I should think of going there,

> still I should hesitate.
> What could the child have been up to?
> Her conduct tolerable
> only if the star of fortune rides on high.

FRAGRANCE: And what if it doesn't?

MADAM DU:

> If by mischance
> the unforeseen occurred,
> how should a mother respond?

Your young mistress ate no supper—be sure to prepare her an early breakfast. And tell her,

Envoi:

MADAM DU:

> ghosts and demons lurk
> within the storm-swept groves.

FRAGRANCE:

> Sad solitude, not yet the time
> for the one who will pluck the flower.

MADAM DU:

> Chang E, Goddess of the Moon,
> not easily confined.

FRAGRANCE:

> Crimson lips seem to form
> words of mild reproach.

SCENE TWELVE: *Pursuing the Dream*

SPRING FRAGRANCE:

    1 Wash the sleep from your eyes, prop up your hair
with pins bound in rhino hide.
Rising early to serve milady
sleepily stumble
by the closet
through the boudoir
past the painted screen.
Miss Fragrance, an it please you,
milady's maid alway;
but a tomcat of a tutor
hindered the mice at play
till my mistress, stirred by the *Songs*,
found an auspicious day
and dragging me behind her
to the garden made her way.

Now Madam finds her snoozing,
asks what the matter be,
scolds our dear young lady,
then takes it out on me.
What can I say but "sorry,
no more of such liberty"
—but will Madam let me off
without solemn vow? Not she!

VOICE *(from offstage):* And what sort of a vow did you have to make,
Fragrance?

FRAGRANCE:

"If I trouble my mistress again
may I never find a man of my own."
A crow in charge of a phoenix
—what can I do but moan?
Nightlong my mistress tosses,
greets the dawn with a groan,
mumbling away to herself
while bright the day has grown.

VOICE: Hurry up with the young mistress' breakfast!

FRAGRANCE:

> Word from the kitchen: breakfast's ready.
> Tea for milady—forward—steady!

BRIDAL DU *(enters):*

> 11a Curves of arching hills—
> the paint wears from my brows.
> What made my fragile limbs
> twist and turn all night beneath the coverlet?
> Why so weary? No late moon gazing
> kept me from my rest.
> Is it concern for falling blossoms
> draws my dawn thoughts to the garden?

A hazy dream of petal-scented love
threw my maiden thoughts into a turmoil.
A wakeful night, watching the flickering lamp,
scolding my maid, whom nothing could arouse.
Yesterday, a random spring stroll—who was it I met in my dream?
So close we were, so loving, I was sure this was my life's true love.
Now, when I quietly ponder on what passed, my spirits sink and I
despair. Ah, pity me, pity me! *(She grieves)*

FRAGRANCE *(enters with breakfast tray):*

> "Grains of rice the rare parrot pecked off,"
> tea in a "partridge-speckled bowl."

Please to eat your breakfast.

BRIDAL: What mind have I for that!

> 11b Morning toilet just completed,
> mirror stand not yet folded away,
> all seems flat and flavorless;
> how am I to swallow this?

FRAGRANCE: Madam's orders, you are to eat an early breakfast.

BRIDAL:

> You use my mother as a threat
> against one who truly starves!

Tell me, how are people really supposed to eat?

FRAGRANCE: Three meals a day.

BRIDAL:

> Ha! What strength have I to lift this bowl?
> I can make only a pretense of eating

—take it away and eat it yourself.

FRAGRANCE:

Give me the breakfast leftovers
and keep your paint and rouge.

(*Exit*)

BRIDAL: Fragrance has left me. Ah Heaven, how stately were the pools and pavilions where yesterday my dream took place. How I long for that bygone dream in exchange for this new-found sorrow! Pursuing my thoughts through endless twistings, all night I lay sleepless. Now I can seize my chance to give Fragrance the slip and search the garden alone. (*She grieves*) Ah, for me, truly,

in dreams "no fluttering side by side
of splendid phoenix wings,
between hearts the one minute thread
from root to tip of the magic horn."[1]

(*She begins to walk*)

Here is the garden. Luckily the gate is wide open and the gardener is nowhere to be seen. See how the ground is carpeted with fallen petals!

IIIa   Never till now did spring so stir the heart.
High and low over the plastered walls
no place but springtime longings dance and fly.

(*She stumbles*)

Oh, the hawthorn catching at my skirt—
like my heart, it will not let me leave.
And this little meander of a stream! Can it be that

IIIb   faery lovers trace again
the source of the Peach Blossom Spring?
Here too flying petals fleck the ripples.
The Lord of Heaven need pay the florist nothing,
but for us below, what grief for fallen blossoms
as springtime passes unfulfilled!

FRAGRANCE (*enters*): By going off for breakfast I lost my young mistress. I have sought her everywhere—ah, so here you are.

IVa   So graceful a pose
beneath the trailing apricot branches.

---

1. Quotation from Li Shangyin (?812–858), the first word only changed from "body" to "dream"; translation by A. C. Graham. The "magic horn" is the unicorn's.

But what brings you
so early to the garden all alone?

BRIDAL:

Before the gilded porticoes,
in deep shade spying on nesting swallows—
aimless steps have carried me to these wonders.

FRAGRANCE:

But should your mother chance by,
what a start to find an empty boudoir—
"Where does my daughter wander,
where does my daughter wander?"

BRIDAL (*annoyed*):

ivb If she did find out
I suppose she'd call it "youthful fancy."

FRAGRANCE: A bit too fancy—keep it plain.

BRIDAL:

How they bully me,
turning a simple garden
into a forbidden paradise.

FRAGRANCE:

If I may be so bold—
this was the mistress' orders—
spring should be met with a busy needle,
stronger incense, an active writing brush.

BRIDAL: What else did she tell you?

FRAGRANCE:

In this deserted garden
hobgoblins and trolls abound:
back now to small secluded court,
back now to small secluded court!

BRIDAL: I understand. Be sure to find my mother now, and tell her I shall follow immediately.

FRAGRANCE:

Wild flowers by the step recognize their mistress,
but "the parrot irked by the cage knows how to scold."

(*Exit*)

BRIDAL: Now that my maid is gone I can pursue my dream.
v Rock garden above the pool,
path by tree-peony pavilion.
Buds of peony inset along the balustrade,

strand by strand willows hover,
string by string elm seeds dangle—
offerings of coins to mourn the spring!

Ah, but what a story there is to tell of yesterday, when the young scholar sought a poem on his willow branch, before he forced our union of delight!

VI Of whose house was this youth whose sudden visit
lured secluded maid deep into garden?
And then—though words must falter—
he touched my face;
such loving pains he took
and I, I moved my lips
wishing to speak.

How pleasing I found him, my young scholar,

VII though ours no loving bond from former life,
nor all my life had I ever glimpsed his face.
Can it be in my next life he is fated to appear,
in this life only a dream?
So like to life was this young scholar
who took my life into his arms.[2]

How my longings stir to recall that moment!

VIII Against the weathered rock
he leaned my wilting body,
then as he laid my jade limbs down
"smoke issued from jade in warmth of sun."[3]
By balustrade
past swing
there I spread the folds of my skirt,
a covering for earth
for fear of the eyes of Heaven.
Then it was we knew
perfect mystery
of joy ineffable.

And when my dream had reached the summit of delight, there came flower petals scattering down!

IX Tense in his eagerness
he put his lips to the fragrance of my shoulder
while I with thoughtful ease responded to him.

---

2. The original includes the word "life" (*sheng*) in every line: for the playwright, *sheng* has basic philosophical implications.

3. A magical transformation alluded to in Li Shangyin's poem "The Patterned Lute."

Soon the bright mirror of my mind was clouded
to envision such an event,
such a sweet melting.
Ha! Falling from air, red shadows,
petals torn from heart of flower!
Was I fettered by my own dreaming spirit?

Alas, I seek and seek, but nothing remains. The pavilion of the tree peonies, the peony balustrade, how can they stand so chill and lonely, no sign of human presence? How sad they make me! *(She weeps)*

x   So wild a place, no other hut or kiosk near,
so hard to seek, eyes misty with love.
Under clear white sun and bright blue sky,
how can I grasp what happened in a dream?
For a flash it is there before me,
I linger, circling, doubting,
but here, here he crushed my gold bracelet to the ground!

Should I see him again,

xi   could it be false?
Somehow I can picture him before me.
Slowly, slowly he appears,
then lightly, lightly fades.
But gone not far—
before clouds disperse and rain dries away,
he will return among flowers, beneath willows.
From yesterday to today
before my eyes as in my heart,
the couch of love transforms upon the instant.

Let me linger another moment. *(She looks up)* Why! In a place where no one comes, suddenly I find a great flowering apricot, beautiful with its thick clusters of fruit.

xii   How can its fragrance spread so clear,
its shade like a parasol reach full around?
Thriving in this third month of spring
"when rich rain swells the red to bursting,"
its leaves shine glossy green,
its full round fruit hide bitter heart.
Here shaded from the sun
I may find again a dream of Luofu.[4]

---

4. **Allusion to a Tang story** (traditionally attributed to Liu Zongyuan, whom our

So be it: I am so drawn to this flowering apricot, I should count it a great good fortune to be buried here beside it when I die.

    XIII My heart is strangely drawn
to this apricot's side.
Just as we please ourselves
which flower or herb we most love,
ah, could we only live or die at will,
then who would moan for bitter pain?
Let me commit my fragrant spirit,
though rains be dank and drear,
to keep company with this apricot's roots.

(She sinks wearily to the ground)

FRAGRANCE *(enters):*

    Off by spring pavilion she "hunts for kingfisher feathers."
To freshen the noontime court, her maid adds
    incense to the burner.

So, my young mistress is tired from her stroll and is drowsing under this flowering apricot.

    XIVa How has your garden roaming
brought you to rest against this apricot's side?

BRIDAL:

    I raised my eyes,
its branches filled my vision,
and heartache overcame me.

(She weeps)

BRIDAL, FRAGRANCE:

    What reason for this grief,
what cause for secret tears?

FRAGRANCE: What is troubling you, mistress?

BRIDAL:

    XIVb Spring bade adieu,
we gazed, but found no word to say
and I, I too
would snap a sprig of willow
to question Heaven's will
but now, now I must grieve
that I could make no poem in response.

---

hero claims as his ancestor) of a man who woke from drinking to find himself beneath a flowering apricot which the day before had been a beautiful woman.

FRAGRANCE:
> What does this riddle mean?

BRIDAL, FRAGRANCE:
> What reason for this grief,
> what cause for secret tears?

FRAGRANCE: Let's go now.

BRIDAL (*moving away, then pausing*):
> xivc Slower, before we leave
> let me still linger a while.

(Offstage, a birdcall)

> Listen, the late-spring cuckoo
> "better go back" he calls.
> Must I choose
> if I would come to this garden again
> between short sleep of dream
> and longer sleep of death?

BRIDAL, FRAGRANCE:
> What reason for this grief,
> what cause for secret tears?

FRAGRANCE: Here we are, now come with me to see your mother.

BRIDAL: So, so.
> xv Half in a swoon I am brought to painted walkways
> to inquire after the health of my lady mother.
> Ah, Bridal, Bridal,
> "the blossoming branch mocks her who sleeps alone."

Envoi:

BRIDAL:
> Where to seek him
> who at Wuling found faery love?

FRAGRANCE:
> Affections of a wanderer
> so soon out of mind.

BRIDAL:
> Time after time to come
> when dreams of spring arise,

FRAGRANCE:
> sad thoughts of what might have been
> forever bind the heart.

SCENE THIRTEEN: *In Search of Patronage*

LIU MENGMEI:

    1 Scholar of note, though stuffed with learning,
    still winds of hunger swirl in my belly.
    Dreaming I pace the cinnabar courts,
      then open my eyes to this "shabby hut."
My inkstone dry, the dragon of my talent stranded,
fled the wise hare whose fur should tip my brush.
No deed accomplished, a painted tiger merely,
a restless crow seeking in vain to roost.

I, Liu Mengmei, preeminent in the academies of Guangzhou, have struggled to endure through dog days and winter's chill. At this present time my dwelling is a rustic plot where I rely on my gardener to feed me; and the more I ponder on this, the greater my shame. I recall the advice of my friend Han Zicai, to seek a livelihood elsewhere. Truly, "Confined to four bare walls, one seeks a patron;[1] who's satisfied to be served by an orange grove?"[2] Master gardener, where are you?

CAMEL GUO *(enters):*

    11 Hillocks rising bump on bump,
    back a hump,
    surely an archer drew his bow
    to make me so;
    take ten steps to walk along,
    nine go wrong;
    stumble, tumble, roll and fall
    in a ball.

Here I am, Camel Guo the gardener. Camel Guo my ancestor was brought to Liuzhou by the celebrated Liu Zongyuan back in the Tang dynasty, and it's a good few years now since the wars when I ended up here in Guangzhou with the father of Liu Mengmei, Zongyuan's descendant in the twenty-eighth generation. I've been out selling fruit, and now I must report to my master. *(He greets Liu)* Oh, sir, how hard you work at your studies.

---

1. As the Han poet Sima Xiangru sought the patronage of Yang Deyi.
2. Li Heng in the third century planted a thousand orange trees, which he declared would be a thousand "tree slaves" for his descendants.

LIU: Master gardener, I've a matter to discuss with you. My studies have taken me past the age of twenty and still I have no prospects. I've been thinking how long is the road that stretches before me—how can I stay on vegetating here? I am deeply indebted to you for your services of "firewood and water." In return I now assign to you the ownership of this orchard. Hear me explain:

> IIIa In this transitory lodging of life
> no friend have I found like you.
> The salt and bland I've eaten, sour and sweet,
> all hoed and watered, grafted and grown by you.

And what have I done all day long but
> sit like a drunk, "head propped in hands."
> When did I ever share your burden?
> Who but myself to blame,
> "waiting for a second hare to collide with the tree!"[3]
> I give this garden
> to provide your needs.

GUO:

> IIIb For this old hunchback's family
> growing things has been our way of life.

(He bows)

> My shape will not permit prostration,
> I bow as low as I can get.

But, sir, now that you've given this orchard to me, where will you go?

LIU: Better to be off with staff in hand than sit here gobbling my three meals a day.

GUO: What does "staff in hand" signify?

LIU: They call it "free as the autumn breeze"[4]—it means traveling in search of a patron!

GUO: Dear, dear, rather than
> thread your way across the map
wouldn't it be better to
> tread the rungs of the examination ladder?

LIU: If you're against the autumn breeze, didn't you ever hear of

---

3. Like the proverbial man of Song (coming from the land of Song was synonymous with stupidity). A hare collided with a tree and dropped dead; thereafter the man of Song refused to leave the spot, waiting for a repeat performance.

4. Soliciting funds from friends or strangers was known as "playing the autumn wind."

"Young Liu of Maoling, free as autumn wind"—who went on to
become the Emperor Wu of the Han?

GUO: Don't try to faze me, sir, with your historical precedents.
Whose breeze will you try to catch?

> You hope for a favoring wind
>   to bear you to Prince Teng's Gallery;
> but I fear the thunderbolt
>   that shattered the Duke of Lu's tablet![5]

LIU: I am determined to go in search of a patron, don't try to stop
me.

GUO: Then I'll pack some clothes for you:

> IV   pound and scrub the scholar's tattered robe.

LIU:

> A humble citizen seeks for patronage.

GUO: Then, sir,

> I shall watch for your "return in brocaded gown."

Envoi:

LIU:

> Tossed is this poor body,
>   no haven east or west;

GUO:

> I view with a smile my patrimony,
>   pink bloom on every tree.

LIU:

> Where can I roam to seek
>   the end of my desiring?

GUO:

> Spring breeze in examination halls
>   beats the sponger's "autumn wind"!

---

5. The old gardener Camel Guo is doing a little fazing in his turn. The Tang poet
Wang Bo was aided by a divine wind which carried his boat two hundred miles in a
night to a feast in Prince Teng's Gallery; the tablet bearing the Duke of Lu's calligraphy was shattered by a thunderbolt just before the monks in whose temple
it stood could make copies of the inscription to furnish funds for a poor scholar
of the Song period.

SCENE FOURTEEN: *The Portrait*

BRIDAL DU:

    1 By winding walks I left my dream
and lost him, fading.
Now jade-like charms grow chill in chamber's depth
where soul must languish
since as the mist the petal
or the moon the cloud
a flicker of untold love
once touched my heart.

SPRING FRAGRANCE:

Dreading some glimpse of amorous butterfly
leaf-lost in quest of fragrance,
weary she rises, paints her face,
and listens to the harshness of the shrike.
Spring passes, though crimson sleeves still beckon.

BRIDAL:

No man was there at the peony pavilion,
yet though my dream grows dim
there is one who holds my longings.

FRAGRANCE:

In the curving of her eyebrows
shows her beauty, spring-tormented
—but who should depict these "slopes of distant hills"?

BRIDAL:

In my thin gown I tremble,
wrapped against the morning chill
only by regrets
to see red tears of petals shake from the bough.

BRIDAL, FRAGRANCE:

How to depict the fairy maid of Wushan,
whether by sun or rain
against the cloud and shadow of Gaotang?[1]

FRAGRANCE: My young mistress: ever since you took that stroll in the garden you have been careless of your meals and careless of your rest. Do you think it can be the disturbance of the spring that

---

1. See scene 1, note 4.

is causing you to pine and grow thin? I am too stupid to be offering advice to such as yourself, but I do not think you should visit the garden any more from now on.

BRIDAL: Ah, but how are you to know what lies behind this? You must understand how

    vernal dreams mysteriously
      flower with the third month,
  lightly the chill of dawn
      thins out the blossoms.

(She sings softly)

  II So chill the spring's leave-taking
  daily my thoughts grow idler,
  my will more feeble.
  My toilet made at last, I sit alone,
  listless as the incense smoke I watch,
  no peace of mind
    until the choking weeds that breed distress
  are rooted out, and the shoots of joy can grow.
  Whom to please if I mask my sorrow with smiles?
  —My vision quivers in a blur of tears.

FRAGRANCE: My young mistress,

  III if your fever cannot be cooled,
  then why doesn't it dry the cold tears?
  It's clear that in these spring roamings
  you have had no defense
  from the upsetting chatter of oriole and swallow.
  Just think
  what anxiety you will cause Madam your mother.
  Go on with this grieving
  and folk will be far from perfectly enchanted
  with this perfect beauty of yours.

BRIDAL *(with a gesture of alarm)*: Oh, dear, from what Fragrance tells me I must have become completely haggard. Let me see in the mirror what has really happened. *(She looks in the mirror and sobs)* Alas, when before I could boast of an enticing soft fullness, how could I have grown as thin and frail as this? Before it's too late let me make a portrait of myself to leave to the world, lest the worst should suddenly befall me and no one then ever learn of the beauty of Bridal Du who came from far Sichuan! Fragrance, bring plain silk and colored inks, and attend on me while I sketch.

(FRAGRANCE returns with silk and brushes)

FRAGRANCE:

> Easy to sketch
> > freshness of youth,
> hard to portray
> > the pain at heart.

The silk and the colored inks are ready for your use.

BRIDAL *(weeping):* How can it be that Bridal Du must sketch with her own hand the grace of her sixteen years! Ah, that time should have etched

> IV these peach-bloom cheeks of youth
> so swiftly with lines of care!
> Surely a happy lot is beyond my deserving
> —or why must "fairest face be first to age"?
> Many the beauty has been praised as peerless
> only for time to erase the bright vision—so soon.
> Now to damp down the burning
> of desire in the soul's brief resting place of flesh,
> take brush and paper, ink and inkstone,
> the "four jewels of the study," of quality
> such as is found in chambers of princely consorts
> and render eyebrows to rival the Western Maid's
> which arched above the West Lake's loveliness[2]
> twin crescent moons.

> v With a silk cloth
> lightly wipe the mirror.
> Hair tip lightly brushing, deftly limning;
> ah, mirror semblance,
> you must be my close model
> for cheeks with teasing smile
> and cherry mouth
> and willow leaf of brow
> and now in washes of drifting mist
> the cloud of hair.
> Far tip of eyebrow lost in hair at temples,

---

2. The "Western Maid" is Xi Shi, the most celebrated of all Chinese beauties, who seduced the King of Wu into the ruin of his realm. The West Lake is the famous Hangzhou beauty spot.

already the eyes with light of autumn stream
personify the sitter;
hair ornaments bright with feathers and gems
set off the brows curving as hills of spring.

FRAGRANCE:

vi Best fit to smile,
slender waist poised to breath of spring breeze,
yet sensing too the sorrows the east wind brings.

BRIDAL:

A hint of hill and stream,
a gate, a door
and my own self, captured in likeness,
bearing in hand a "green sprig of apricot"
as I recall my lover.
Here see me lean
in a dawn dream against a rocky mound,
grace of bearing to match the wind-stirred willow;
to lines so fine-drawn
add last for contrast broad green leaves of the plantain.

Fragrance, hold it up so that we may see whether I have caught a likeness.

FRAGRANCE:

vii Easy enough to sketch her aspect
in hues red or dark;
harder to portray the rare individual self
when the image reflects the reality
like flowers seen behind closed lids
or the moon on water.

BRIDAL (pleased with her work): But it will make a charming picture. Ah,

surely my painting promises well
with a sweet appeal more marked than in the model!

FRAGRANCE: All it lacks is a husband by your side. If only

your marriage destiny could be soon fulfilled
and a fine handsome husband found
then we should see a double portrait
—happy couple limned against clouds of bliss!

BRIDAL: Fragrance, I have something to confess to you: that time I was strolling in the garden—I found a man.

FRAGRANCE (startled): Oh, my young mistress, how could you be so fortunate?

BRIDAL: Why, in a dream!
   VIII There he stood smiling,
   and I could recall his living likeness,
   catch with the fine lines of my brush
   the very essence of his soul
   but that I fear to reveal my secret love.
And so this portrait must hang by itself,
   lone crescent of an autumn moon
   rising in space where peak is touched by cloud
   —not this the cloud that frames the honored guest
   in the moon's toad palace![3]

Now take good note of this, Fragrance: The young scholar who appeared in my dream had broken off a branch of willow to present to me. Surely this must be a sign that the husband I shall meet in time to come will have the surname Liu, for "willow"? What would you say to my making up a poem now, to inscribe at the head of this scroll, which would contain hints of my spring yearnings?

FRAGRANCE: That would be a clever plan.

BRIDAL *(inscribing the poem, and reciting it as she does so)*:
  However close the likeness
   viewed from near at hand,
  from farther off one would say
   this was some airborne sprite.
  Union in some year to come
   with the "courtier of the moon"
  will be beneath the branches
   either of willow or apricot.

   (She sets down her brush with a sigh)

Fragrance, many a beautiful maiden in past or present time has married early in her youth a loved and loving husband who has painted her portrait; whilst many another has taken up the brush herself to send her own likeness to a lover. But who should receive this portrait of Bridal Du!
   IX Pleasure yields to pain:
   pleasure in the bright vision
   elegantly demure
   as faery pendants sway;
   pain to predict, as the years deepen

---

3. See scene 2, note 4.

the fading of tint from eye and lip
of this Ajiao, locked up in golden chamber.[4]
Vain labor
when to no lover's eye this lovely image
unrolled will bring a tear,
when there is none to call
the living Zhenzhen from the painted scroll.[5]

(She weeps)

O melancholy fate
that this most imminent presence must stay hid
for latter days to witness.
Fragrance, call softly now for the flower lad, I have an errand for
him.

(FRAGRANCE calls)

GARDENER'S LAD (enters):
Like Qingong I have lived
"among flowers all my days"[6]
yet no Cui Hui I have known
rivals the beauty of this scoll![7]
What is your errand, miss?
BRIDAL: I want you to take this self-portrait of mine to the scroll
maker's to be mounted, and tell him I want it done with care:
x Who shall mount this portrait, so to enhance
the happy capture of the living model?
Let the material be flowered damask
bleached to a gem-like gleam of white
and have the margins slender.
Let there be no blabbing
should anyone inquire the painter's name.
Lining and mount must survive

---

4. Emperor Wu of the Han said that if he were given Ajiao as his consort he would build a chamber of gold for her to dwell in.
5. Zhenzhen, in a Tang story, was a lady on a painted scroll who magically came to life.
6. Qingong was the favored consort of the Han general Liang Ji.
7. Cui Hui (alluded to above, scene 10, note 4), in a Tang story, sent her portrait to her absent lover, with the proclamation that, should the day come when she no longer resembled the figure on the scroll, she would have died for love of him. Here the lad, with an improbable talent for literary allusion, is referring to his girlfriends in the village.

burning of sun and buffeting of breeze,
for "finest things are least enduring"
and the delicacy of red stroke or of black
must not be sullied.

LAD: Young mistress, once the scroll is all complete, where shall I hang it?

BRIDAL:

XI To the gentle boudoir none will come to enjoy its
beauty

FRAGRANCE:

more fit to be enshrined in the faery temple of Wushan

BRIDAL, FRAGRANCE:

or will it take its flight
in transformations between cloud and rain?

Envoi:

FRAGRANCE:

Feather-worked jewelry
at odds with the heart's emotions

BRIDAL:

tears sting the eyes
to turn from the flowers' blooming.

FRAGRANCE:

Show them the bewitching grace
captured in this painting

BRIDAL:

portraits of the Consort Yang
pale in comparison.

SCENE FIFTEEN: *A Spy for the Tartars*

BARBARIAN PRINCE (*enters with suite*):

1 At Heaven's will we have destroyed the Liao
and share the empire with the house of Zhao.[1]
The whipcrack summoning all to courtly ritual
drowns out the wail of nomad flutes.

---

1. The Jurchen, a Tungusic people from Manchuria, overcame the Liao to establish
their Jin dynasty in the north of China in 1115. Zhao was the surname of the Chinese

Toll drums, chime bells
for staffs civil and martial to assemble,
and let the southerners guffaw
at beaky noses,
freckled hides,
and stubby hair.
Far-flung dominions, far-flung dust,
to each new ruler his own new court:
why should we northerners put up with drifting sands
when the south enjoys a land of rich brocade?

I am Dignai, Prince of Hailing and Emperor of the Great Jin Dynasty. I am barbarian by birth and a lecher by nature. Some thirty years ago my great forebear Ogda seized the southern realm and forced the Song lord Gaozong to retire to Hangzhou. But they say he has done up Hangzhou until it now outshines the old capital at Kaifeng, and on the West Lake there people make merry day and night: a poem talks about "cassia buds the autumn through, miles of flowering lotus." So what's to stop me from raising a million men and gobbling it up? But military strategy is a business full of ins and outs, and I need a southerner as a guide. Luckily here's the Huaiyang bandit Li Quan,[2] who's a match for any ten thousand men. He's been willing to submit to me, and I've bestowed on him the title of Prince-errant of Jin. I've set him a time limit of three years to raise men, buy steeds, and create havoc in Huaiyang. This will be my pretext for launching my expedition of conquest. Oh, oh, but I can't wait to be taking my pleasure on the West Lake!

    II Heaven's mandate shared,
Heaven's mandate shared between us,
it's still on me that Heaven smiles,
but my astrologers declare
the south's the nicer place.

ATTENDANTS: How can it be nicer?

PRINCE:

Why, think of the smile on West Maid's lips
as on West Lake with charming grace
she leans on oars bedecked with orchids.[3]

---

ruling house of the Song dynasty, who retreated south across the Yangzi to Hangzhou in 1127.
  2. Li Quan was a historical figure, a rebel against the Southern Song, but a century later than the time of "Dignai."
  3. See scene 14, note 2.

ATTENDANTS: Is this West Lake as big as our South Sea and North Sea here in Peking?
PRINCE: A hundred miles around.[4]

>Blossoms sway above the waves,
>"rare scents blow from behind the clouds."
>Nights that know no dawn
>as singers and musicians clad in brocade
>thread the tipsy crowd.

ATTENDANTS: Lord of Myriad Years, let's borrow it and have a bit of fun!
PRINCE: I already sent an artist on a secret mission to make a painting of the entire scene. There's a Mount Wu above the lake and he's painted me on horseback on the peak. And don't I just look fierce!

>Mount Wu is the top
>and I'm on top of Mount Wu,
>"South of the River" will be an easy prey
>and here we see how easy.

(He dances)

>Just watch me star as
>"The Gorgeous Horseman of the Beauteous West Lake."

ATTENDANTS: Lord of Myriad Years, we may not be able to get to West Lake first stop. Where will you rest your carriage?
PRINCE:

>III Eager to let the horse in the painting sniff West Lake,
>first I must wend my way through the beauties of Loyang.
>Soon I'll pick up what's left of the realm of Zhao!

Envoi:

>Long River narrow as single thread,
>   sky the size of a fan,
>like a line of wild geese flying
>   banners float afar.
>Who will ever drain them,
>   the wine jars of the south?
>Hills and streams delivered up
>   all the way to Yan.

---

4. The figure is actually closer to ten.

SCENE SIXTEEN: *The Invalid*

MADAM DU:

    1 What does this life hold?
    Truly, "hard is the lot of beauty"
    and drear the prospect for parents
    soon to be left childless!

(She weeps)

    Jewel in my palm,
    flesh of my inmost heart,
    silent pearls of tears I shed for you.
Ah Heaven, when others can be
    surrounded by seven sons,
      why must a solitary daughter sicken and pine?
    Delicate as a petal
    she should enjoy Heaven's mercy,
    but storm of wind and rain
    cruelly torments the blossom.
    Properly secluded in curtained chamber,
    who brought the moon to peep,
    the breeze to set the eaves atinkle?
    As my hair thins with age
    my bowels twist in sorrow,
    from gummy eyes the tears come coursing down.
Approaching my midcentury, I have been blessed with one daughter only, Bridal. Why now should a sickness have laid her low for so many months? From the way she looks and moves and speaks it does not seem to be any ailment born of inclement cold or summer heat. But if there is anything behind this, Fragrance must know about it, and I will question her. Fragrance, you scamp, are you there?

SPRING FRAGRANCE: Coming.
    Ailing beauty on my hands
    and no little page to help me out;
    down come the mistress' commands,
    must be some leftovers lying about.
Fragrance, Madam, at your service.

MADAM DU: Your young mistress was in perfectly good health until you came into her service, and now after half a year of your attentions she is seriously ill. It's all very distressing. Tell me, how has she been eating lately?

FRAGRANCE:

> 11a Don't call it eating:
> nothing can rouse her interest,
> no question brings response.
> She babbles prettily to herself,
> laughs and makes no sense,
> then stares with vision glazed.

MADAM DU: We must send for the doctor at once.

FRAGRANCE: It will take

> all the eight schools of acupuncture
> to prod her tender feelings;
> the alchemist's pill nine times refined
> won't separate out this shameful sickness.

MADAM DU: What sickness is it?

FRAGRANCE: I'm sure I don't know, but

> I'd have said her thoughts were pure as autumn sky
> and here she gets spring fever.

MADAM DU: What!

> 11b She is no more than a wisp
> "so thin the scale can hardly register."

And it's you have inveigled her into this.

> Mist-laden blossoms do the damage,
> oriole and swallow carry word,
> clouds and moon conspire together.

Kneel, you scamp! Hand me the rod!

FRAGRANCE *(kneeling):* I truly know nothing about it.

MADAM DU:

> What is it has wasted her graceful form,
> what cause had you to stir her gentle nature?

FRAGRANCE: My young mistress went happily sampling the flowers and willows,[1] how do I know why she should get sick?

MADAM DU *(enraged, beats her):*

> Take that for your show of solicitude!
> Your runaway tongue
> leaks what it tries to cover up!

---

1. See scene 7, note 3; "flowers and willows" equal syphilis.

FRAGRANCE: Careful lest you tire your arm, Madam; let me tell you all that happened. It was that day when she'd been for a stroll in the garden and you chanced upon her after her return. She told me about a young scholar who held a sprig of willow in his hand and asked my young mistress for a poem about it. She said she'd never seen him before in her life and she didn't give him any poem.

MADAM DU: Well then, so she didn't give him any poem. What then?

FRAGRANCE: Then . . . then . . . then the young scholar up and carried her good and proper into the peony pavilion.

MADAM DU: And what was that for?

FRAGRANCE: How should I know? It was all just a dream.

MADAM DU: Just a dream?

FRAGRANCE: Just a dream.

MADAM DU: There's some deviltry here. Summon the master, I'll discuss this with him.

FRAGRANCE (calls): The master's presence is requested.

DU BAO (enters):

> Heavy the weight of my gold girdle of office,
> fragile the jade tray bearing the "jewel in my palm."[2]

Madam, what is the reason for our daughter's sickness?

MADAM DU (weeps): Hear my words, my lord:

> 11c   My heart aches to speak
> of this sickness of cause unknown.
> Long are her slumbers, brief her stirrings,
> reasonless her tears and laughter,
> shadow in place of substance.

It seems our daughter went for a stroll in the garden at the rear of the house. There she dreamed of a man with a willow sprig in his hand who spirited her off. (She sighs) I only fear

> her limbs sullied by willow sprite,
> body possessed by genies of the flowers.

Oh, my husband,

> quickly offer invocations
> lest the moon and wheeling stars afflict her.

DU: More of your folly. Here I have engaged Tutor Chen to teach her restraint and decorum, while you her mother freely permit her to go wandering off. (He laughs) This is all the result of some chill she has caught from the alternation of hot sun and cooling breeze. But if you wish to invoke the stars we need seek no Taoist wizard. It will

---

2. The "jewel in my palm" is Bridal; the "jade tray," her emaciated body.

suffice to have Sister Stone of the Purple Light Convent intone a few scriptures. As the ancients put it, "to slight the doctor for the witch doctor is the best way to avoid a cure." I have already sent for Tutor Chen to come examine her pulse.

MADAM DU: Examine her pulse! If only we had found a marriage partner for her in good time, then no such sickness would have occurred.

DU: What! Among the ancients, "man takes wife at thirty, at twenty woman goes as bride."[3] Such a child as our daughter is, what can she understand?

> 11d   A silly girl,
> what can a babe know of the seven passions?
> She has a fever from going abroad,
> an ague of some kind,
> some convulsion or inflammation of the spleen.

I fear that you, as her mother,

> kept fast our jewel too tightly in your palm
> till now, a too delicate blossom,
> she cannot withstand heartsickness.

DU, MADAM DU (*both weeping*):

> A pair bereft of support

we plead to high Heaven for this girl

> the lifeline of our house.

STEWARD (*enters*):

> Visiting Apricot Ridge
> one sails past Solitude Peak.[4]

Master, a messenger to see you.

DU:

> Official duties must claim my attention.

Madam,

> take loving care of our daughter's health
> for autumn's a fell season to the sick.

(Exit, with STEWARD)

---

3. This is the prescription of the *Book of Rites*.

4. Entrance verses for minor characters are not always full of significance. Here the steward plays on the names of two mountains to prefigure the bereavement of the old couple through the agency of Liu Mengmei ("apricot" being the meaning of the last syllable of his name).

MADAM DU (*to* FRAGRANCE):

"Lacking office, one has freedom;

having sons, all things are supplied."

I fear my husband is too preoccupied with his official visitors to concern himself with his daughter's sickness. It saddens me very much. (*She weeps*) Meanwhile, we shall have Sister Stone invoke the stars and Tutor Chen prescribe medicine. But will either have any effect? Truly,

though mother and daughter are closest of all

on doctor and soothsayer still we call.[5]

SCENE SEVENTEEN: *Sorceress of the Tao*

SISTER STONE:

1 Driven by yin and yang,

people rush pell-mell in pursuit of marriage,

but Heaven denied me

woman's proper parts

and so my sole recourse

was to the Way, to don the shaman's robe.

Now as I crook my fingers

four decades have I seen.

What is this life but a dream?

Song from the void fills purple palace

under cold jade sky,[1]

bamboo and rock rise high as hills,

none here may tranquil lie.

We grieve that human heart

can never be as stone,

but we may open it and look

when the good times chance by.

I am Sister Stone of the Purple Light Convent. "Stone" was not my

---

5. Very untypically, the scene ends with recited rather than sung verse, and lacks an envoi.

1. This verse comprises a "pastiche of Tang lines": each is cited from a different Tang poet, but the whole is consistent in meter and rhyme. The lines are from Li Qunyu, Du Fu, Liu Yuxi, and Han Yu, respectively.

surname in lay life, but I got to be called this because of my rock-hard hymen, on account of which I lost my mate. Come to think of it, if I wanted to return to lay life you'd find my family in the *Hundred Surnames*;[2] as for my religious career, *The Thousand Character Text*[3] has a few lines describing that. Heaven knows, it's not for me to expound

the dusty tomes of ancient lore

it's just that

a quiet life the Master praised

and Yu his thoughts to virtue raised.

Why do I live in these halls

their minarets seem to touch the sky

messing about with

perfection of the Golden Mean?

Well, in religious practice

virtue's reward is happiness;

doctrine of karma means that

vice ever ends in wretchedness.

How can it be that

fortune and fame you're sure to seize?

My ancestors were content to

deep in some dusky forest hide.

With me, it's always been

good deeds a good example set

not to speak of

a tranquil mind no passions fire.

I've got a bumhole

rejoice to see the lilies fair

and a piddlehole

and flowerets clustering everywhere

but right there at the fork, unfortunately

---

2. An ancient compilation which worked the various surnames into a rhymed reader.

3. From here on the old bawd's monologue consists essentially of ludicrously misapplied lines of *The Thousand Character Text*. This medieval tour de force is an essay in rhymed quadrisyllabics that uses a thousand characters without repeating a single one. Because of its universal use as a primer and as a calligraphic model, it was familiar to every literate person. To bring out the piquancy of these gross misquotations, I have borrowed the sonorous English version of the *Text* done by the great Herbert Giles over a century ago. It is hoped that some serendipities emerge from the conjoint ingenuities of the author of the *Text*, the author of the play, and the solemn (and wholly innocent) Victorian translator.

where boisterous streams, cliffs hard to mount
there seems to be some obstruction
    deserts, and Dongting's liquid fount.
So Stone is my name, and while on a stone highway
    causes are heard in every street
what's the use of a stone field
    to drop the millet seedlings in?
How could I marry when
    through valleys deep, through empty halls
    echo, reverberating, calls?
Much better to stay home with Mum and
    in filial duties strain each nerve.
Unfortunately there were all
    your nephews and your nieces too
who kept yapping at me
    you girls, your mother's words obey!
Then Mum says, though the way I was made meant that someone
must
    strive hard substantial good to gain
still as far as looks went
    Mao's beauty wore a pensive air;
everyone else gets a partner
    let peace 'mongst high and lowly reign
so why shouldn't I
    the housewife sing her husband's strain?
So we hired a go-between with a flexible tongue
    let your sincerity be known
and got me promised to a son-in-law with a good big—nose:
    no superficial talents own.
All fixed up in no time at all. So we consulted the calendar
    the sun and moon their courses run
and checked the horoscopes
    the stars shine out when day is done.
He sent over his gifts
    gold from the river Li is brought
and I entered the palanquin
    and jade at far Kun'gang is sought.
To hide my face
    there silken fans of matchless white;
we had runners in front of the procession
    and silver tapers burning bright.

And the groom, what a sight,
>> their Prince they follow close behind
>> their feathers fluttering in the wind
and me the bride got up just as fine
>> adjust your dress with equal care.
We invited all the relatives
>> respect for age should be observed
and there they stood all along the road
>> and brimming goblets crowned with flowers.
So we were wed
>> whilst round about a numerous band
>> of robed officials sit or stand
and there I was with the bridesmaids
>> attending in the inner room.
We drank from the bridal cup
>> sweet music charms the banquet hours
and coins and sweets were distributed to the children
>> in spotless lambs the *Odes* delight.
He carefully inspected my face
>> and learn men's characters to read
and went through my trousseau, every item on the list
>> books, read by stealth at stalls, supply
>> learning for those who cannot buy.
Night comes on and the groom gets itchy. He babbles away
>> the phoenix warbled overhead
and then he gets frisky
>> and snow-white colts in meadows fed.
He lays me where the bedsheets
>> compose our mortal tenements
and there in the lamplight off comes everything
>> and men their earliest garments wore.
Dear Heaven! I took one look at that thing like a rearing donkey's
>> affrighted animals betray
>> by hasty flight their wild dismay
and I can tell you it set me back a bit
>> nor dares to raise the trembling eyes.
The groom sees how nervous I am and says, "Bride, you're no chicken,
>> the added months the year complete.
So I'll take it easy with you while
>> the yin and yang in music meet."

I didn't say a word but I smiled to myself, it's up to you
>   the music's measured cadence beat
try your best, mister bridegroom,
>   to others' faults indulgence show
>   *your* merits should unnoticed go.
A couple more watches pass and there he is on the Terrace of Delight
>   collecting clouds form raindrops bright;
but how come he's down in Witch's Gorge
>   and frozen dew is snowy white?
He can't find his way, wonders what's up, and calls for a lamp.
Down he goes to look
>   two vast saloons lie left and right,
>   the "spacious hall," the "mansion bright"
and there he's gazing
>   o'er many a gorgeous ivory bed.
I lay there without a word, but I had a good grin to myself, aha,
mister bridegroom, this thing I've got here
>   for private as for public wear
but don't start thinking you can have it
>   and eaten with a keener zest.
A few more bouts, and him panting away
>   thus men in every age have shown
>   those virtues that support a throne.
But I was made all wrong; he just couldn't get through
>   dark skies above a yellow earth.
And there he'd been inching away all night
>   make every inch of time your own.
I felt quite ashamed of myself
>   for rooms have walls, and walls have ears
and didn't know whether to hang myself or jump in the river
>   make righteousness your end and aim.
Yet if I were to take a scalpel or needle and thread to myself
>   let nought their precious tissues tear.
Of course, I could just run away and
>   live far from men and worldly strife
but wasn't there some way to bring him where
>   joy reigns supreme, while hands and feet . . . ?
Aha, got it! For want of better he's after the "flower in the rear
court"
>   a stream before, a hill behind

so I just present him with my "dry lotus leaves" and let him
    in autumn reap, in winter store.
Ai-yo! Face to face
    let women guard their chastity;
but once turn your back
    and men the sages' rivals be.
Well, although for a while
    nought could their energies arrest
in the end the loving couple had to think of the
    five virtues and four elements.
Why should he keep an impenetrable bride when
    the *wife's* son is the father's heir;
yet he'd be ridiculed if he married me off to someone else
    while hungry men coarse food enjoy.[4]
So I try to persuade him, "Husband, bear in mind
    a concubine should ply the loom
then you wouldn't need to envy other men
    to see good omens sent by Heaven.
Then I would be reckoned
    'mongst monarchs—each resigned the throne
as long as you
    forget not what you've once acquired."
Later on he really did get a concubine and began to
    take heed of good advice the more,
which left me without a leg to stand on
    e'en foreign nations sought their sway.
I didn't blame him
    the more you draw from Fortune's store;
but it was then I decided to become a nun
    to learn the art of government.
Now I've got this convent, in the past it wasn't much
    throughout pavilions scattered lie
so it was my job to clear up the
    chaos before Creation's birth.
I hung up portraits of the guardian gods
    one sword "Excalibur" was hight
and started "pacing the Dipper"
    one pearl was christened "Queen of Night."

---

4. Giles loses the point of this line, which says "do not because your belly is full reject [the wife of your years of] coarse food."

For my altar offerings and table fare
    'mongst fruits and vegetables come
    first mustard, ginger, damson, plum.
I have transcended the distinctions of the mortal world
    the sea is salt, the river sweet
and escaped the meshes of the nets of men
    fish swim, and birds on wing are fleet.
Now that I've taken the veil, I think of that slavering bridegroom of
years ago
    a dirty person seeks a pool
and that foolish itch I had to be somebody's wife
    burnt fingers clutch at something cool.
Only, it's hard being the abbess of a convent
    the restless eagle wings its flight
and I must
    with clearness ever strive to speak.
When I go to a banquet
    the plainest viands are the best;
but when I come round with my begging bowl, then let
    the old with nicer food be served.
I live all alone here, it's really
    a noiseless and secluded life
and nobody even writes, so there's no need to
    in composition terseness seek.
I'm not getting any younger
    like arrows years fly swiftly by
and, when I look in my mirror, compared to me
    the changing moon is constant found.
I'm certainly no portrait model
    the painter's art preserves their fame
though I might get myself into one of those pious biographies
whose message
    in fixity of purpose lies.
I'm too lazy to go roaming
    two noble cities, east and west;
I'm quite content just to sit here
    their sole desire—a noble bent!
Among the nuns I have bosom friends
    as branches of the self-same tree—
I'm just not interested in those miserable priests
    but Shi was blithe as she was fair.
And if there should be some unsuspected tiger of a man

Bu drew the bow, good marksman he
I'd guard my chastity like a cold water fish
  and Ren 'mongst anglers far from worst.
I've got just one young novice
  love, as though they belonged to you
called Scabby Turtle
  for all men love to crack a joke
  at ignorant and vulgar folk.
VOICE (*from offstage*): There you go, Mistress Superior, making fun
of me, when I'm really a little gem.
SISTER STONE: Young rip,
  by shame or insult sorely tried
I suppose you want a bit of flattery
  and all mankind their worth confessed.
VOICE: There's a runner come to haul you off to Prefect Du, Madam.
SISTER STONE: Whatever for?
VOICE: Says you're a thief.
SISTER STONE: So there's a warrant out for me,
  calligraphy one also finds
calling me some kind of monster;
  let death the brigand's fear be made
but I'm innocent,
  no cares to vex while you explore;
so don't try to raise a storm while
  the sun shines brightly in the sky.[5]
PREFECT'S RUNNER (*enters*):
  From the prefectural hall
  on sainted nun I call.

     (He greets SISTER STONE)

SISTER STONE: What is your errand, brother runner?
RUNNER:
    11a Prefect on dais above
    orders from my lady
    clappers sound in court:
    his honor's daughter,
    what age can she be

---

5. By this point Sister Stone has used up approximately one-half of the entire *Thousand Character Text*.

    to fall so sick
    full half a year?

SISTER STONE: But I'm no healer of women's ailments.

RUNNER:

    You are implored
    to say a mass
    to invoke the aid of the stars.

SISTER STONE:

    11b Occult prescription from the sorceress:
    a little magic charm
    to keep about her person
    and all is cured in an instant.

RUNNER: If that's the way of your charm, please hurry!

(They move off)

SISTER STONE: You child there!

(VOICE, from offstage, responds)

    Take close care
    of sacred halls,
    while my altar is vacant
    look to lamp and incense.

VOICE: Understood.

Envoi:

SISTER STONE:

    Ladies burn their nightly incense
      in the Hall of Purple Light.

RUNNER:

    Weedgrown is the road to the old convent
      on the heights where clouds take root.

SISTER STONE:

    Still wearing the silken amulet
      sacred to the Nine-splendored Lady

RUNNER:

    make no excuse of other concerns
      there in the tranquil heavens.

SCENE EIGHTEEN: *Diagnosis*

BRIDAL DU (*enters, ailing, leaning on the arm of FRAGRANCE*):
    1 Fever deepens,
    so frail yet failing still,
    and still no answer
    to the riddle that torments.
    Returned from dream to watch
    swallows buffeted by breeze
    that tosses rustling blinds
    of bamboo flecked with tears.
    How long since spring departed,
    how long since spring departed
    that beauty should fade so fast?
    Dry paulownia leaves beside the well
    scrape on my heart.
Ah, Fragrance,
    fine-drawn spirit,
    body slender as leaf,
    never made to withstand such train of sickness!

SPRING FRAGRANCE:
    By little and little
    were wrought in you
    such delicacy,
    such height of fancy,
    such depth of passion.

BRIDAL:
    Alas, my joy in sprig of apricot,
    my willow-bearing lover
    fade and dim as spring's traces vanish.

FRAGRANCE:
    Then rest through incense-laden noon,
    cool breezes fan your pillowed head.
    For whose sake are your frowns,
    for whom the wasting,
    whose the pain?

BRIDAL: I have lain sick, Fragrance, ever since that springtime strolling. No itch, no hurt, but I lie confused and stupefied. What is wrong with me?

FRAGRANCE: Young mistress, what's the good of forever thinking about what happened in that dream?

BRIDAL: But how can I stop myself!

> IIa Each spell of senseless longing
> mires me in passion ever deeper.
> What good such thoughts—
> but how can thinking stop?
> And so I pine in secret,
> fearing discovery.
> Faint breath stirs my heart
> only to cough.

Alas,

> what sympathy can there be
> for such a secret burning?
> And how withstand the strength
> of yearnings I conceal?
> I rue,

> I rue the springtime sleep that started all.

FRAGRANCE: Madam your mother believes that, if your marriage can be arranged, this will divert the evil spirits.

BRIDAL:

> What hope from such a plan?
> Does she believe that day
> I fell afoul of some wicked garden genie?

FRAGRANCE:

> IIb Spring goes to its rest: what resting-place for her,
> her spring sleep no true sleeping.
> Lingering breath fails as the days lengthen,
> but like the frail Xi Shi[1]
> drawn brows, hands clutching heart
> only enhance her beauty.

Young mistress,

> the dream is done
> and he was never real;
> sickness endures
> and robs you of your true self.
> Thirst struck this sailing cloud at Witch's Mount.[2]

---

1. Xi Shi (see scene 14, note 2) is the archetype of the fragile, or "ailing," beauty.
2. For Witch's Mount, see scene 1, note 4.

All this for nothing,
no evident cause for such lovesickness,
no sultry summer heat,
nor wine fuddling your senses—
why then do you reel like someone drunk?

TUTOR CHEN *(enters):*

Dry your calligraphy in the sun,
   men think the birds left tracks;
pound your prescriptions in the moon
   with juice from warts of toad.[3]

Prefect Du has instructed me to examine his daughter's pulse. Arriving at the inner court I must let them know of my presence. *(He calls)* Is my disciple Fragrance there?

FRAGRANCE *(greets him):* It's Tutor Chen. The young lady is sleeping.

CHEN: Don't disturb her. I'll just peep in. *(He greets her)* Young lady!

BRIDAL *(pretends to wake with a start):* Who is it?

FRAGRANCE: Tutor Chen is here. *(She helps* BRIDAL *up)*

BRIDAL: Tutor Chen, your pupil has been sick and must apologize for long truancy.

CHEN: Ah, my young disciple, as the ancients put it, "Study is perfected through application, neglected through pleasure seeking." I fear that exposure to sun and wind in the garden at the rear has led to your health being affected, your studies rejected. And I, your tutor, though absent, have been ill at ease whether eating or sleeping. Now I rejoice that the Prefect your father has called me in to examine you. But I had not thought to find you so frail as this. Such being your state, how long before you will be able to return to your studies? The Dragonboat at the earliest!

FRAGRANCE: Yes, and Tutor Chen's the dragon!

CHEN: I am speaking of the Dragonboat Festival, miss, and don't think I'm after *your* sweet dumplings![4] Now, young lady: "observe the breath, listen to the voice, inquire the condition, feel the pulse."[5] Tell me, what is the reason for your sickness?

FRAGRANCE: Why need you ask? It's those *Songs* you were expounding, "So delicate the virtuous maiden,/A fit mate for our Prince"—no wonder she's delicate!

---

3. See scene 2, note 4.
4. Sweet dumplings were eaten to celebrate the Dragonboat Festival on the fifth day of the fifth lunar month.
5. The four modes of observation of traditional medicine.

CHEN: But who's the prince?

FRAGRANCE: How should I know what prince?

CHEN: This being the case, since it's a *Songs* sickness we'll use a *Songs* cure. Right in the first section there's a Sacred Simple for the treatment of feminine disorders.

FRAGRANCE: And do you have it right there in your head?

CHEN: We may prescribe accordingly. The young lady's sickness was caused by a prince, so we'll use the Envoy Prince.[6] According to the *Songs,*

> Having seen her prince
> how should she not recover?

All we have to do is get a prince to cover her, and she'll recover.

BRIDAL (*embarrassed*): Oh, dear!

FRAGRANCE: What else?

CHEN: Ten sour apricots. According to the *Songs,*

> Plop fall the apricots,
> seven are left

and then later

> three are left.[7]

Seven plus three equals ten. This is a special prescription for young men and ladies whose thoughts are a little overripe.

(*BRIDAL sighs*)

FRAGRANCE: Anything else?

CHEN: Three Southern Stars.[8]

FRAGRANCE: Only three?

CHEN: Add a few if you wish. According to the *Songs,*

> Three stars of Scorpio on high.[9]

This is a special prescription for young men and young ladies in their seasonal sickness.

FRAGRANCE: Anything else?

CHEN: It is apparent that the young lady has excess of fire in her belly. I want you to clean up a big chamberpot, and I'll flush the fire out for her with wild celery. This is according to another prescription of the *Songs:*

---

6. Name of an herb used in traditional medicine.

7. From a song of courtship: the girl warns prospective suitors that time is passing.

8. Another herb name.

9. The song celebrates the meeting of lovers. Scorpio is the "heart constellation" in Chinese.

She is off to the bridegroom's chamber,
we feed her horses with celerity.
FRAGRANCE: But, Tutor Chen, you've got the wrong chamber, the wrong celerity, and the wrong horse.
CHEN: That's all right, as long as the breeching goes under the asshole.
BRIDAL: As a physician, Tutor Chen certainly doctors the *Songs!*
FRAGRANCE: Such stately periods—he's more like Mammy Chen the midwife!
BRIDAL: Tutor Chen, your prescriptions are beyond description, I think you should stick to feeling my pulse.

(CHEN *attempts to locate her pulse on the back of her hand*)

FRAGRANCE: Tutor Chen, maybe you should turn her hand over!
CHEN: Ladies should be examined with the back turned, according to Wang Shuhe's *Secrets of the Pulse.* However, either way is handy. (*He feels her pulse*) Eh? What a sorry state her pulse has reached!

   IIIa   So trim a maiden,
   so feeble a pulse.
   Young as she is,
   what has worn her so?

(*He rises*)

Fragrance,
   take good care
   of one who hurt by spring
   now fears the summer,
   for fall is cruellest
   to those who suffer sickness.
Young lady, I go to prepare your medicines.
BRIDAL (*sighs*): Tutor,
   where love attacks the marrow,
   how can needle enter?
   When sickness springs from mist-laden flowers,
   what herbs can have effect?

(*She weeps*)

   Your visit honors me
   but when will you call again
   on this disciple fated
   like Yan Hui to die young?

BRIDAL, FRAGRANCE, CHEN:
>   In sickness fear disturbance.
>   Seek rest,
>   avoid the gossip's chatter.

BRIDAL: Be free to leave, Tutor Chen, I'm afraid I cannot see you off. Tell me, have you cast my horoscope?

CHEN: All will be well if you can pass the Midautumn Festival.
>   Eight characters form the horoscope,[10]
>   three generations the good physician.

(Exit)

FRAGRANCE: Here comes a Taoist nun.

SISTER STONE *(enters):*
>   No sound of Nongyu playing her pipes
>   but here comes Chang E stealing elixir.[11]

I am Sister Stone of the Purple Light Convent, here in response to Madam Du's orders to invoke the stars for her daughter.

FRAGRANCE *(greets her):* What are you here for, Auntie?

SISTER STONE: I am Sister Stone of the Purple Light Convent, under instructions from Madam Du to invoke the stars for her daughter. What sickness does she suffer?

FRAGRANCE: She fell.

SISTER STONE: Fell?

FRAGRANCE: In love.

SISTER STONE: Who's the man?

FRAGRANCE: No man at all—something in the garden.

>   *(SISTER STONE holds up three fingers,*
>   *FRAGRANCE shakes her head; then five fingers,*
>   *FRAGRANCE shakes her head again)*[12]

SISTER STONE: No good either way—you tell me what's wrong with her.

FRAGRANCE: No, you go ahead and ask her.

SISTER STONE *(greeting BRIDAL):* Young lady, respects from an old nun.

BRIDAL *(again pretends to wake with a start):* A nun?

---

10. The eight characters establish (two each) the year, month, day, and hour of birth.

11. Nongyu, in a legend, played the pipes with her faery lover. For Chang E, see scene 2, note 4.

12. Three fingers, in sign language, mean the pulse; five fingers, the whole body.

SISTER STONE: Sister Stone from the Purple Light Convent. Madam your mother has instructed me to pray for you. They tell me you were possessed by an evil spirit in the rear garden, but it's hard to believe.

       IIIb How could one smart as yourself be possessed?
           Yet how so distraught without some demon?

BRIDAL *(as if in a trance):* Oh, my love!

SISTER STONE, FRAGRANCE *(aside):*

    Hear her mumble and mutter
    as if her senses had flown.

SISTER STONE: Fortunately I've brought a little charm along.

(She takes a pin from BRIDAL's *hair and sticks it through a charm, reciting as she does so)*

  Bright golden beams,
  sun rise in east,
  fly evil dreams,
  all ills cease.

"Immediate effect, as commanded."[13] *(She returns pin with charm to* BRIDAL's *hair)*

    Amulet or silver pin
    walking or sleeping never laid aside
    repulses idle thoughts and untoward dreams.

BRIDAL *(coming to her senses):* Alas, I fear the charm is useless. My love is no

    slender sprite inhabiting flower or tree
yet he turned me into a
    poor crazed creature clutching at windborne shadows.

SISTER STONE: Any crazier, and we'll have to strike her with a "thunder in the palm."[14]

BRIDAL:

    Unfair, unfair,
    my thoughts are all of cloud and rain[15]
    and you would strike with "thunder in the palm."

BRIDAL, FRAGRANCE, SISTER STONE:

    In sickness fear disturbance.
    Seek rest,
    avoid the gossip's chatter.

---

13. This is the stock conclusion to any incantation.
14. A Taoist magic formula for controlling storms.
15. Sexual love.

SISTER STONE: One last instruction: you must set up a prayer flag
thirty feet in height.
BRIDAL: What will be the good of that?
        IV Willow and apricot dimly I recall.
Holy sister,
        no bamboo prayer staff will serve the purpose.
Leave me to my thoughts, to seek
        by incantation to renew my dream.

(*She exits, supported by* FRAGRANCE *and* SISTER STONE)

Envoi:

FRAGRANCE:

        Moth-antenna brows oppressed
            by cruelty of her fate.

SISTER STONE:

        In Taoist robes, all ready to pray
            for release from this disaster.

BRIDAL:

        Seek her not now
            where flowers blossom red

BRIDAL, FRAGRANCE, SISTER STONE:

        but let us ask the east wind
            to desist from its promptings.

SCENE NINETEEN: *The Brigandess*

LI QUAN (*enters at the head of his men*):
        I Ranks of ancestors
        rank as goats,
        a mongrel genealogy.
        When swords of war flash
        we bandit heroes can barely
        challenge the éclat of the cat burglar.
    A thousand thundering hoofbeats raise
    the dust of war o'er hill and glen;
    I've learned to speak the Tartar's praise
    and curse my fellow countrymen.
Behold Li Quan of Huaian, bold to resist myriad men. The southern

court offered me no opening, so off I rode to be a bandit. Five hundred men I led from the Huai to the Great River and back again, but no base could I establish. Then my chance came when the Emperor of the Great Jin Dynasty sent from afar to enfeoff me as Prince-errant of the Gold, with instructions to raise havoc in Huaiyang and seize whatever places offered. My problem is that I'm long on valor and short on strategy; but luckily my wife, from the Yang family, has mastered the "pear-blossom spear"[1] and is more than a match for a whole army. What majesty when husband and wife ride out together to battle! A pity she's so jealous—any women we capture have to be placed straight under her command, and every man in the army is terrified of her. Truly,

>   rustic dame is queen of the camp,
>   the snake that swallowed the elephant;
>   bandit chief enfeoffed as prince,
>   a fish promoted to dragon.

DAME LI (*enters, carrying spear*):

>   II   A hundred bouts to stir my amazon zeal,
>   you'll see more blood than rouge.

(She performs spear dance)

>   Petal-scattering whirling spear,
>   one by one the blossoms burst.[2]

(She salutes her husband)

Great chief, a thousand years. I've got my armor on so I won't prostrate myself.

LI: Dame, did you know the Emperor of the Great Jin has enfeoffed me as Prince-errant?

DAME LI: What's this "Prince-errant"?

LI: "Errant" means I have an errand to perform for them.

DAME LI: What sort of errand?

LI: They've given me three years to stir up Huaiyang. Then when we're thoroughly armed and provisioned we make one dash across the Great River and wipe out the house of Zhao and their Song Dynasty. And that's when I become Emperor!

DAME LI: What a wonderful thing! Congratulations! Then on the

---

1. See scene 1, note 7.
2. Presumably at this point she explodes the device attached to the head of the spear.

strength of this commission we must start buying horses and raising troops.

> IIIa Thunder rolls
> as by the camp gate painted drums beat out.
> To the clouded eastern shore
> like birds our spies take wing.

LI, DAME LI:

> Man and wife
> rule the strife,
> all Huaiyang in fear for its life.

DAME LI:

> IIIb Pile grain, recruit men,
> pick out high-stepping steeds piebald and black,
> jade hairpins thrust awry by helmet strings.

LI, DAME LI:

> Man and wife
> rule the strife,
> all Huaiyang in fear for its life.

Envoi:

LI:

> Heroes on every hand contend
>   to overthrow the court.

DAME LI:

> Broken halberds sink in the sand,
>   no rust yet mars their steel.
> On pastures ripe for grazing
>   no herdsmen comes in sight
> but wildfire spreads to horizon
>   across the empty grass.

SCENE TWENTY: *Keening*

SPRING FRAGRANCE:

> I Nightlong the harshness of wind and rain
> and she so frail,
> so wasted in her sorrow.

> The gods no help,
>> herbs no effect.
> A time for frowns,
> a time for smiling:
> alas, for one so young
> neither to smile nor frown!

I have waited on my young mistress while her "spring sickness" has lasted deep into autumn. Tonight, full moon, is the beloved Midautumn Festival, but outside a bleak wind buffets the rain. Still I must bring my young mistress here, to distract her from the gloom of her worsening sickness. Truly,

> rain threatens midautumn moon,
> flame of prayer lamp flickers in the wind.

> *(She exits, and reenters, supporting the dying* BRIDAL*)*

> II The moon-viewing hall is vacant
> as clouds jostle down pathways of the sky.
> The chill in the bone
> presages a passing, life like an autumn dream.
> What has the world to show more puissant than passion?
> —Soul cast adrift, heart aching, all is done.

BRIDAL DU:

> Wasting sound of water clock
>> has worn my pillow through;
> one who lies as drunk or stupid
>> finds it not hard to die.
> A dark thread of fragrance
>> lost in the night of rain,
> my body wholly worn
>> dreading the autumn cold.

I have been so sunk in sickness, Fragrance, tell me what night is this?

FRAGRANCE: It is the middle of the eighth month.

BRIDAL: So, tonight is the Midautumn Festival! Have my father and mother been too distressed by my condition to enjoy viewing the moon?

FRAGRANCE: You must not worry about that.

BRIDAL: I remember when Tutor Chen cast my horoscope, he said the important thing was to get past the Midautumn. But it seems that my sickness is growing more severe, and tonight I feel a little worse. Open the window for me, so that I can see the moon.

(FRAGRANCE opens the window. BRIDAL gazes)

IIIa   Where does the ice-toad moon
swim in this sea of sky?
The jade pestle stands in an autumn blankness
—who now will steal herbs to offer Chang E?[1]
What western wind has "scattered all trace of dreams"?
Once gone, hard to find him again,
surely the tricks of sprites or demons have deceived me.
"Vanishing from the brow
a new pain enters in the heart below."

(She gestures her listlessness)

FRAGRANCE:

IIIb   How callous the spring, to leave in passing
a dismal torment of mists and vapors.
A human life, the high concern of Heaven,
might win a brief respite
yet must dwindle so soon.
Whose to enjoy
this beauty of form so carelessly cast aside?
Let me try to divert her a little: My young mistress, the moon has risen!
The moon clearing the sky
must surely flood the dark dreams from your bed.

BRIDAL *(sighs, as she gazes at the moon):*
Counting the watches
longing for Midautumn
yet the Midautumn
finds me still helpless.
No light of new orphan moon
shall touch my life,
which in the rain
of this sad night must end.
But, however fair you may shine,

IIIc   whose happiness do you bring, Midautumn moon?
Paulownias sheared by west wind
drip tears of rain.
My shrunken limbs, feebler than before;

---

1. See scene 2, note 4.

and at the sky's edge, melancholy geese
hasten their departure.
"Wintry crickets in the grass";
the windows rustle their paper panes.

(She faints, then cries in alarm)

A floating numbness:
hands and feet wilt and will not move.

FRAGRANCE *(in alarm):* The chill in my young mistress' body has numbed her limbs—I must ask Madam to come.

MADAM DU *(enters):*

My husband eminent
in old age hale and strong;
so delicate my daughter,
her short life filled with pain.

How is your sickness progressing, my child?

FRAGRANCE: She is worse, Madam.

MADAM DU: How can this be!

IIId Unforeseen
a dream in the garden,
but how to explain
this continued failure to wake?
Her heavy head droops in deep slumber.

(She weeps)

Oh, why did we not have you long ago
"mount the dragon" of a successful match!
Nightly the lone wild goose
strips the soft feather sheen
from this my "fledgling phoenix."
All becomes void
and time now also for your mother's life to pass.

BRIDAL *(revives):*

IVa Now my spirit stirs
like the air of a mirage
as the breeze sets to tinkling
the pendants below the eaves.

Mother, I make obeisance to express my gratitude. *(Stumbles to her knees in prostration)*

From my first years you have prized me
as your "thousand gold pieces"

but I, unfilial,

cannot serve you to the end of your days.

Mother, this is Heaven's decree. In this life

a flower no sooner red. . . .

Ah, let me only serve anew

these parents, lily and cedar, in the lifetime to come.

BRIDAL, MADAM DU, FRAGRANCE *(making gestures of weeping):*

O cruel west wind,

so sudden, so callous

to scatter green leaf and red petal.

MADAM DU:

ivb   Lacking sons

what pains we took with this child all fragrant charm

to smile her joy about us.

Grown now to womanhood, she was to care

for us, her revered elders, at our end

but now, alas, childless and lost shall we

remain at rim of sky.

My child, very soon

from clash of moon and year

a void of time

shall quench your troubled spirit.

BRIDAL, MADAM DU, FRAGRANCE:

O cruel west wind,

so sudden, so callous

to scatter green leaf and red petal.

BRIDAL: Mother, if the worst befall, what will become of my body?

MADAM DU: We shall take you back to your native place for burial, child.

BRIDAL *(weeping):*

va   My spirit, coffin-borne, will see in dream

the thousand thousand folded ranges

that bar the road to home.

MADAM DU: We shall do it, no matter how far.

BRIDAL: Nevertheless, your daughter has one request to make. I have come to love one tree, an apricot, in the rear court. It is my wish that you bury my body beneath that tree.

MADAM DU: Why do you ask this?

BRIDAL: I can become no

ailing Chang E, immortal

in the moon's cassia grottoes,

yet I should wish
>> my bones to powder white
>> the caverns at the ancient apricot's roots.

MADAM DU (*weeping*): See how her
>> eyes blur with tears
>> as she strains to raise her head
>> and the cold sweat pours
>> a chill to her very heart.

Oh, could I only
>> offer my life for hers now
>> to appease the demon of death!

BRIDAL, MADAM DU, FRAGRANCE:
>> A cruel empyrean that sends
>> the flower-despoiling storm
>> when the moon is at her brightest.

MADAM DU: I must go now to arrange with your father for a great mass to be held. Ah child,
>> in vain the silver toad
>> mixes one herb with another;[2]
>> now paper charms are followed
>> by burning of paper ingots.

(Exit)

BRIDAL: Fragrance, do you think a time can come when I may return to life? (*She sighs*)
>> vb Always you have observed my slightest wish,
>> what I desired you would design.

Fragrance, take good care of my father and mother.

FRAGRANCE: Indeed I shall.

BRIDAL: One thing I have to tell you. That portrait scroll on which I inscribed the poem: I do not care to expose it to the general view. When I am buried, put it in a rosewood box, to be placed beneath the weathered Taihu rock.

FRAGRANCE: What is your purpose in this?

BRIDAL:
>> That portrait and those brush strokes
>> telling my heart's desire
>> may reach some day someone who understands.

FRAGRANCE: Mistress, set your mind at rest. If the worst should be-

---

2. See scene 2, note 4.

fall now, then the lone grave mound will cast a single shadow. But if you will rest now and take good care of yourself, then let me bear a message to your honored father, that he take into the family a young graduate by the name of Mei or Liu, "Apricot" or "Willow," who can be your "companion in life or death." Would not this be an excellent plan?

BRIDAL: I fear it is too late. Ai-yo, ai-yo!

FRAGRANCE:

> How to locate the root of this sickness,
> how find a healer for her heart?

BRIDAL: When I am dead, Fragrance, stand often before my spirit tablet and call to me!

FRAGRANCE:

> Syllable after syllable
> strikes my heart with pain!

BRIDAL, FRAGRANCE:

> A cruel empyrean that sends
> the flower-despoiling storm
> when the moon is at her brightest.

(BRIDAL faints away)

FRAGRANCE: Oh, she is going, she is going! Master, mistress, hurry!

PREFECT DU BAO, MADAM DU *(enter):*

> VI Drum's triple boom,
> ten thousand echoes of sorrow,
> cold rain at window
> unlit by lamp's red glow.

The serving girl brings word that our daughter worsens.

FRAGRANCE *(weeping):* Oh, my young mistress!

DU, MADAM DU *(a joint gesture of weeping):* Ah daughter,

> laying aside your own life
> us also you abandon
> as our road's end approaches:
> you were the one we looked to
> to see us off.

DU, MADAM DU, FRAGRANCE:

> So soon, so soon,
> trackless as stream-borne duckweed,
> shadow of passing sea wave,
> hibiscus flower with gleam of jade
> by the wind cut low.

(BRIDAL revives)

DU: See, her senses quicken! Child, your father is here.
BRIDAL *(recognizing him):* Oh, Father, help me into the inner hall.
DU: Lean on me, child. *(He supports her)*
BRIDAL:

> VII   Head to foot the tree stripped
> "ere ever the dawn wind blows."

Set me a

> tablet upon my youthful grave
> telling I died of longing.

Father, tonight is the Midautumn.
DU: Yes, child, it is the Midautumn.
BRIDAL: And all night long we have withstood the rain! *(She sighs)*
Ah, how can

> the moon, once set, rise again
> or the burnt-out lamp glow red?

(Exeunt)

FRAGRANCE *(reenters, weeping):* Oh, my young mistress,

> "No more than in cloud patterns of the sky
> is there a constancy in the fates of men."

My young mistress is dead of her spring sickness, and the master
and mistress are themselves near death in their grief. Oh, you who
watch, what is there we can do? —But let me now make a keening
for her. . . . No more will you have me, my young mistress

> VIIIa   burn incense cakes in the shape of the "heart"
>   character
> for the sweetening of your linen;

no more will you have me

> when the lamp is trimmed
> wipe away the red tears from the candle;

no more will you have me

> tease with a smile and a proffered flower
> the singing bird;

no more will you have me

> turn the mirror to your face, paint
> with crimson your peach-bloom lips.

I shall remember how you would

> lay down your sewing scissors
> as the night deepened

or in the clear dawn light
take up your sketching brush.
—But that reminds me of the self-portrait she made. When the
master saw it he ordered me to bury it with the corpse for fear that
the sight of it would distress Madam Du. But bearing in mind my
young mistress' dying words, I shall have her, as she did in life,

lean once again by the rocky mound
—although I fear
the garden-strolling youth
may find the colors faded when he comes.
Oh, it's you, Sister Stone!

SISTER STONE *(enters):* You're making a good job of your wailing and
I've come to help you. Now, Fragrance, no more will she make your
viiib   painted lips grow warm
as you follow her on the pipes.

FRAGRANCE: That's true.

SISTER STONE: No more will she need your company as
silk skirts wet with dew
you joust with flowers.[3]

FRAGRANCE: Quite right.

SISTER STONE: Now that your young mistress is gone you will find
things a lot easier.

FRAGRANCE: How is that?

SISTER STONE: She won't be needing you
to chitter-chatter over what to wear
in weather cold or hot;
she won't be making you
stay awake late at night,
get up with the dawn.

FRAGRANCE: Well, I'm used to that.

SISTER STONE: And there are other ways you'll be saved a lot of
trouble. You won't have to
pull a wry mouth when you pick her corns
or
stop your nose when you empty the chamber pot.

(FRAGRANCE spits in disgust)

---

3. The "battle of the flowers" was a game young ladies played at the Dragonboat
Festival, on the fifth day of the fifth lunar month.

There's another thing too: a young mistress in the bloom of youth,
no telling when she might have been at it
　　　　when she might have been at it
and Madam her mother would have
　　　　broken your back there in that garden.
FRAGRANCE: Stop your nonsense! Here's the mistress.
MADAM DU (*enters, weeping*): Oh, my own daughter, day by day
　　　　VIIIc　a hundred times you would pass before me
and never once did I see
　　　　irreverent levity in your eyes.
She had studied by heart
　　　　Ban Zhao's "Four Precepts" from end to end;
no need had she for Mencius' mother's
　　　　"three changes of dwelling" to mend her ways.[4]
We feared to see her
　　　　so slender-soft, so delicate
but who could foresee
　　　　a wasting sickness never to mend.

　　　　　　　　(*She wails*)

From this time forth
　　　　a mother none will call for
　　　　—every inch of my bowels a hundred inches of fire.

　　　　　　　(*She falls in a faint*)

FRAGRANCE (*alarmed*): Master, the mistress is dead of grief! Come at
once, hurry!
DU (*enters, weeping*): Oh, my child! What—my wife is lying here in
a faint! Madam, either it was your fate
　　　　VIIId　to meet with some forsaken day when Aries was
　　　　　　obscured[5]
or I
　　　　who sit as judge must pay
　　　　myself the penalty for past sins.
　　　　Better to be old Shunyu Yi of Han
　　　　with all his daughters—and one

---

4. Ban Zhao, woman historian (see scene 3, note 5), wrote also a set of exhortations to womanly virtue. The mother of the philosopher Mencius moved her dwelling three times to improve his childhood environment.
5. Aries, in Chinese astrology, is the star of childbirth.

who saved his life by her pleading;
or why was there none like that other
ancient doctor of Lu
to save my daughter's life?
Ah, Heaven, Heaven, my years advance, my head is white, yet
though I amass great fortune
to whom shall I pass it down?
I live to see
my little edifice torn down!
Madam, you must be careful of your own health. For even if
your bowels every inch were shattered
into a thousand fragments,
still you could no more
call back your daughter's soul
than that of Wangdi, changed into a cuckoo.[6]

STEWARD *(enters):*

The startled crows fly off
with old mortal woes;
now magpies, harbingers of joy,
bring word of celestial favor.

Your Honor, here is the gazette announcing your promotion.

DU *(reads):* Orders of His Sage Imperial Majesty, transmitted by the Board of Civil Office: "Observing the Jin brigands sneaking south, we hereby appoint Du Bao, Prefect of Nan'an, to be Pacification Commissioner charged with the defense of Huaiyang. He is to proceed to his post forthwith, and neither delay nor error will be countenanced. By Imperial command." *(He sighs)* My lady, in view of these orders from the court to proceed north, it will not be possible to make the westward journey for the burial of our daughter. Steward, send for Tutor Chen.

STEWARD: Tutor Chen, the master wishes to see you.

CHEN *(enters):*

A single ditch claims the venerable Peng
and the child dead ere his teens;
the same hall witnesses mourning
and joyful felicitation.

(He greets DU)

---

6. For Wangdi, Prince of Shu, see scene 10, note 2.

DU: Tutor Chen, my daughter has excused herself from your presence for the last time.

CHEN *(weeping):* True indeed. I grieve that the young lady has passed to the realm of the spirits, leaving myself, Chen Zuiliang, bereft of a place. I rejoice, sir, in your elevation, yet by the same token I lose my job!

(All weep)

DU: Tutor Chen, I have something to discuss with you. I am under Imperial orders and dare not delay my departure. But I recall my daughter's dying wish, that she be buried beneath the apricot tree in the rear garden. Anxious to avoid inconvenience to my successor during his residence here, I have given orders that a part of the garden be set aside and an "Apricot Shrine" built therein, for the keeping of my daughter's spirit tablet. I shall ask Sister Stone here to see to the upkeep of the shrine. Sister, will you be able to undertake this duty?

SISTER STONE *(kneels):* I will see to it that the incense is replaced and the water kept fresh. But for all the comings and goings in the maintenance of the shrine, someone else will be needed in addition.

MADAM DU: Then let us ask Tutor Chen if he will be so kind.

CHEN: I shall be happy to do my utmost in carrying out my lady's orders.

MADAM DU: My lord, there should be some lands assigned to furnish the expenses.

DU: There are some thirty acres of grace-and-favor lands lying fallow, whose yield will supply the costs of the shrine.

CHEN: These grace-and-favor fields will grease and flavor my diet!

SISTER STONE: When you see a Taoist sister, it's your duty to assist her; but I can't see any of this coming to you, Mister "Chen No Food"!

CHEN: A poor scholar gobbles wherever he gabbles. You're only one spinster, but I am a scholar and a gentleman too, so it's mine should be the greater portion.

DU: Let us have no squabbling, the income and expenditures shall be Tutor Chen's responsibility. Sir, during the years of my tenancy here I have highly favored the schools.

CHEN: As we well know. And now that Your Honor has received promotion I shall have your scholars, in accordance with time-honored practice, compose a Record of your Fatherly Benevolence, together with a commemorative inscription. Then upon reaching the capital you will find these most useful to include with the gifts you will be making to your superiors and colleagues.

SISTER STONE: Hey, Chen No Food, is this Record of Fatherly Benevolence some kind of a keepsake of his daughter's to show what a good father he was?

CHEN: It's a eulogy of His Honor's administration—what's it got to do with his daughter?

SISTER STONE: Well, and what might a "commemorative inscription" be?

CHEN: We build a hall of worship and carve a statue of His Honor to receive our homage there, and then over the entrance we write "Hall of the Lord Du."

SISTER STONE: But wouldn't it be better to put the young lady there too at the side, so that we could all pay our respects to her?

DU (*annoyed*): Stop this nonsense! Even if these are time-honored practices, I'll have none of them. Tutor Chen, Sister Stone,

  IX our thoughts, like sunset clouds, rise not
   above the three-foot mound of our daughter's grave
   and this one task my wife and I bequeath you:
We dare not ask that you should hour by hour watch over her,
   but at the Feast of the Tombs, on the day of Cold Food
   let her at least receive a bowl of rice.

Envoi:

DU:

  Her airy essences lost in the dark,
   earth soul returned to the springs below

MADAM DU:

  eighteen long years
   of anxious loving care.

CHEN:

  With every call an echo
   and a breaking of the heart

DU, MADAM DU, CHEN:

  now once again we unreel
   our grief's unbroken thread.

SCENE TWENTY-ONE: *The Interview*

ABBOT:

> 1   A tattered cassock all I own,
> my dwelling the Vale of the Incense Mountains.
> Multitude of living souls,
> Many-jewelled Tathagata,[1]
> multitude of bodhisattvas,[2]
> and what a host of gleaming bald pates!

I am Abbot of the Temple of the Many-jewelled, in the Vale of the Incense Mountains here in Guangzhou prefecture. This temple was built by foreigners as a convenient place to receive officials coming here to purchase jewels. The Imperial Commissioner, His Honor Miao, has just completed his term of office here and plans to make an offering of jewels before the throne of the Tathagata. I must prepare to receive him.

> *(Enter* MIAO SHUNBIN, *accompanied by*
> FOREIGN TRADERS, INTERPRETERS, *and* ATTENDANTS)

MIAO SHUNBIN

> 11   Where southern lands give place to streams and sea,
> a ritual welcome to the cave of pearls.

ALL *(as* ABBOT *receives* MIAO):

> Dragon King of Southern Sea,
> Treasure Boy, and Heavenly Maid,[3]
> hear now the rolling tide of Sanskrit chant.

MIAO:

> "The generalship of Ma Yuan of old
>   subdued waves, flattened sea,
> set up bronze pillars, his monument
>   on perilous road to Shore of Pearls.[4]

---

1. Name of the Buddha in his spiritual form—or forms, for there are innumerable Tathagata.
2. Saintly beings who, though qualified for Buddhahood, have vowed to enter Nirvana only when they can be accompanied by all sentient beings.
3. Buddhist divinities: Treasure Boy was a disciple whose birth was magically accompanied by a flood of jewels.
4. Ma Yuan, Han general of the first century A.D., conquered the Shore of Pearls (modern Hainan Island) and the northern part of modern Vietnam; the great bronze pillars he erected marked the limit of his conquest.

The men of Viet of their own accord
 brought tribute of branching coral;
what need for the Han Commissioner
 to display his unicorn emblem?"
I, Miao Shunbin, hold Imperial appointment as Inspector of Jewels.
My three-year term of office has expired, and custom calls for me to
make offerings before the Many-jewelled Tathagata. Interpreter!

> (*He exchanges greetings with the* INTERPRETER,
> *the* FOREIGN TRADER, *who gabbles*
> *in his own tongue, and the* ABBOT)

Interpreter, instruct this Muslim gentleman to present his jewels.
INTERPRETER: All are set out in readiness.
MIAO (*rises and inspects the jewels*): Rare jewels, indeed! Truly,
heaped like a tumbling mountain torrent, rivaling in brilliance the
sun and moon. Not for nothing does this temple bear the name of
Many-jewelled! Light the incense!

> (*He performs ceremonial obeisances*
> *while bells are struck offstage*)

> IIIa   Three Jewels proclaim the Three Abundances,[5]
> Seven Jewels are marvels incomparable[6]
> glory of the world made manifest
> universe bathed in brilliant light
> abundant store
> assuring boundless merit.

ALL:

> For the majesty of the Buddha
> jewels beyond counting
> to bless his sacred name.

MIAO: You monk there, offer a prayer of thanksgiving for this Muslim trader.
ABBOT:

> IIIb   Countless gems from depth of ocean,

---

5. The Three Jewels are the Buddha, the Dharma (doctrine), and the Sangha
(priesthood). The Three Abundances are probably the blessings of good fortune, long
life, and male offspring, though there is a specifically Buddhist set of three beneficial
practices: frequenting virtuous friends, attending sermons, and examining one's
own impurities.
6. Different sources list different metals and gems, but gold, silver, beryl, carne-
lian, and pearl are usually included.

ships beset by wind and wave,
trader bearing priceless treasure
through perils of his voyage
in a trice
calls on the Bodhisattva Guanyin
for the help that is secure.

ALL:

For the majesty of the Buddha
jewels beyond counting
to bless his sacred name.

LIU MENGMEI *(enters):*

IV Yearning for Chang'an
where sun meets far horizon
but born into the world
in remotest corner of the coast.
Treasure-loving lamas,
bead-counting monks
slippery to the grasp as beryl.

What a joke, this Liu Mengmei, leaving his home to wander destitute and friendless. But now by a lucky chance there comes to this
temple the Imperial Inspector of Jewels. I have requested an interview, and who knows but I may move him to support my
endeavors. *(He greets the attendants)* Be so good as to announce that
Liu Mengmei, graduate of the prefectural academy of Guangzhou,
requests permission to view the treasure.

(ATTENDANTS report as requested)

MIAO: These jewels are Imperial property, not for the common view;
but since the request is from a scholar, let him be admitted for the
moment.

LIU *(greeting him):*

By Southern Sea, a palace built of pearls[7]

MIAO:

let the Jade Gate to the west be closed[8]

LIU:

open the heart to one who understands

---

7. Allusion to the palace built in Guangzhou by the extravagant founder of the
short-lived Latter Han dynasty (tenth century).
8. The Jade Gate, in Gansu province, was an outpost beyond which lay the jade-
bearing regions of Central Asia.

MIAO:

   the Lighter of Chariots shines on a man of worth.[9]

May I inquire the purpose of your visit?

LIU: Your humble visitor is destitute and without recourse. On learning of Your Honor's presence here to inspect the treasure I determined to request a view of the jewels for my own edification.

MIAO *(laughs):* Why should I guard these gems of the Court from you, a pearl of the south? Please feel free to inspect them.

LIU *(examines the jewels under* MIAO's *guidance):* Bright pearls and precious jades I can distinguish at a glance. But here are specimens whose names are unknown to me. I beg Your Honor to enlighten me.

MIAO:

   va   Here is the Pebble of the Milky Way,
   here's Elixir of Gold can boil the ocean dry
   and a blossom plucked from the Iron Tree.[10]
   That sparkle there is the Cat's Eye,
   this glow the Emerald of Araby.
   Ha! Gold Willowbud from Tartar realm
   Thermal Goblet from ancient Qin[11]
   Jade Toad that sucks the moon
   Fire-kindling Pearl
   Ice-preserving Crystal.

LIU: In our southern land of the Guang we have night-shining pearls and coral trees.

MIAO:

   They must yield before Inch-deep Pearl
   and three-foot coral tree may still be smashed.[12]

LIU: Without the privilege of this visit, how should I have seen such sights!

   vb   Rarest treasures of earth
   yielded by foreign lands to our Imperial house.

I beg to know from what great distances these gems have come.

---

9. A legendary pearl of classical times.
10. Rarity was proverbially expressed as "the blooming of the Iron Tree."
11. A legendary vessel which heated or cooled wine at the owner's will.
12. The Inch-deep Pearl was discovered, in an old story, by a Persian merchant, but demanded back from him by the Dragon King during his voyage back to his own country. A rich man of ancient times boasted of his coral tree three feet in height, but his rival smashed it and then presented half a dozen larger ones.

MIAO: Some from ten thousand miles away; the nearest from three or four thousand.

LIU: From so far away did they walk or fly?

MIAO *(laughs):* How could they have walked or flown? Sought at great price by the Court, they were brought here by tribute argosies.

LIU *(sighs):* Your Honor, these gems are mere insensate things, yet lacking feet they came here from ten thousand miles away; while I, Liu Mengmei, cherishing my ambition within a thousand miles of the capital, can find no purchaser, no winged feet to reach my goal!

> A high price offered,
> see how crafty trader
> recklessly drives his treasure-ship.

MIAO: Are you suggesting these jewels are fakes?

LIU: Even granting them to be genuine, they can neither feed the hungry nor clothe the naked,

> useless as empty boat or hanging tile.

MIAO: Then what, in your view, is a genuine treasure?

LIU: In all honesty, sir, I myself am a pearl among men,

> and should I bear my treasure to the Court
> none could assign a price.

MIAO *(laughs):* I'm only afraid the Court has all too many gems of this sort already!

LIU:

> Should I present my jewel before the Dragon King himself,
> I could laugh down his treasures
> and I should be the victor
> in such a contest as the Duke of Qin
> held at Lintong to find the greatest treasure.

MIAO: Then you should indeed be presented to His Sacred Majesty.

LIU: But I am merely a poverty-stricken student who has never yet been able to secure official patronage. How can I aspire to behold His Majesty?

MIAO: You should realize that His Majesty is easier of access than his ministers!

LIU: But I have nothing to meet the expenses of a thousand-mile journey.

MIAO: This presents no problem. As the ancients bestowed gold on men of valor, so shall I assist your journey by drawing on my own perquisites.

LIU: In that case, and since I am encumbered by neither wife nor parents, I shall take my leave and set out at once.

MIAO: You attendants, bring funds for this gentleman and prepare wine for a farewell toast.

ATTENDANT:

> Lichee wine drunk here in the south,
> elm-seed cash[13] drift off to the north.

The wine is ready, and here are the funds.

MIAO: Please accept this for the expenses of your journey.

LIU: My gratitude.

(Miao offers wine to LIU)

MIAO:

> VIa From this Vale of Incense Mountains
> setting forth with wine on your lips
> may you make your way
> in splendor to Chang'an.

LIU:

> What merit can surpass this offering
> of a jewel to the throne,
> retrieval of talents scattered and gone to waste?

MIAO, LIU:

> Ply whip of gold,
> discard commoner's gown
> for return of native son
> glorious in flowered brocade.

LIU: I pray only

> VIb though Heaven is blind
> that the all-seeing eyes of our Lord
> with shrewdness of Persian merchant
> may discern this gem's true worth.

MIAO:

> Truth lies not in glitter of gem
> but in sifting gold from gravel bed.

MIAO, LIU:

> Ply whip of gold,
> discard commoner's gown
> for return of native son
> glorious in flowered brocade.

LIU: I beg your leave to depart.

> VII A noble act
> your gift of gold to a man of valor.

---

13. Coin-shaped seed-pods.

MIAO:

> A cup of wine
> to cheer a struggling scholar on his way,
> now may the wave of your ambition
> float your raft to the stars.

Envoi:

LIU:

> Above the scholar's black silk cap
>   shines the cloudless sky.

MIAO:

> Grace of form, splendor of wit,
>   an aura of dignity.

LIU:

> From the golden palace gate
>   flows every benefit.

MIAO:

> As with that ancient worthy of Jin
>   my gift will speed your journey.

SCENE TWENTY-TWO: *Traveler's Rest*

LIU MENGMEI (*enters with traveling umbrella and cloth-wrapped bundle; he is a sick man*):

>   I   A man on the road
> a bird away from its nest.

> (*Storm noises offstage*)

> Dismal dreams
> as wind and snow scrape the sky.
> One day to next
> my spirit numbed by cold.
> Bearing my traveler's bundle
>   from Vale of Incense Mountains
> at Three Waters I embarked
>   on the first boat that chanced to call.
> To comfort my homesick heart

in depth of winter's cold
half a sprig of apricot
was all Lingnan could offer.
The winds of autumn were blowing when I, Liu Mengmei, took my
leave of Commissioner Miao and said farewell to friends and family. By the time I had left my boat behind and climbed Apricot
Ridge the winter was far advanced. North of the mountains the
winds are harsh beyond all expectation and I suffer from the intense
cold, yet there can be no question of giving up and turning back.
Under the storm-filled sky my gaze is set on Nan'an. A bitter road!
      II   From stark branch
the shrill of a hungry kite.
Ridge already far behind
this lone wandering spirit
prey to sickness.
Hailstones whirl
riddling the rags about my head,
whistling through my shredded umbrella
cold wind pierces my thin gown.
Twisting trail,
longed-for inn nowhere in sight.
And the snow seems to take a delight
mocking white-faced scholar.
Frozen stream, broken bridge
stumbling and staggering across
—ah, here's a willow tree I can cling to
humped like a camel to help me over.

(He crosses the stream by holding on to the willow)

Frail support
one withered branch to clutch for dear life,
slithering, sliding
feet cannot hold.

(He falls)

TUTOR CHEN *(enters):*
      III   Poor but unconcerned
like Yuan An of old, I'll bother none for help
but sit at ease while snow buries my gate.

"When your donkey steps more lively
you know Fifth Bridge is at hand."[1]
In some village somewhere, at turn of year
school must be starting?

(He hears LIU groaning)

But what loud plaint is this?

(He searches about)

What poor devil of a Lü Mengzheng
who lived in a disused kiln?

LIU: Help, help!

CHEN: Here I, Chen Zuiliang, come braving the winter's cold to hunt for a tutor's post, and what should be my luck but to meet up first thing with someone who's tumbled in the stream. Well, let him be.

LIU: Help!

CHEN: A call for help, surely this may be the opportunity for a good deed. I must find out what happened. *(To LIU)* Who are you, and why have you fallen down there?

LIU: I am a scholar.

CHEN: Well, if that's so, let me help you up. *(In doing so he slips in his turn. They clown for a while)* Tell me, where have you come from?

LIU:

> IVa   Single boat light as a leaf
> carried me from Guangzhou,
> City of Five Rams, to Nanshao.
> Liu Mengmei my name
> bearing a gift of jewels.

CHEN: What kind of jewels?

LIU:

> Solitary pilgrim to examination halls,
> my frail clothing could not withstand the cold
> and my body is sick.
> Then, unforeseen, a stream, a broken bridge
> and Liu, the "Willow,"
> almost broke his trunk.

CHEN: To be willing to undergo such hardships you must be confident of high achievement in the examinations.

---

1. Fifth Bridge, outside Chang'an, was a common destination for donkey rides. Chen seems to be using this allusion as a sort of proverbial expression of optimism.

LIU: In all honesty I must tell you I am a "jade pillar to support the heavens, a golden bridge to span the sea."

CHEN *(laughs):* So how does a heaven-supporting pillar crack with the frost, a golden bridge collapse in the middle? But let it be. I happen to know something of medicine. Close by here is a certain Apricot Shrine, where you may rest for a while before you travel on in the new year.

> IVb Young Wei Sheng, beneath a flooded bridge
> clung to a pillar and drowned rather than break his tryst;
> the poet Sima Xiangru wrote on a parapet
> that he would return in glory or not at all;
> this is a presage you will "kick the Dipper."[2]
> Yet I, ignorant clod, may find use as a healer
> while you rest at Apricot Shrine.

LIU: How far is it from here?

CHEN *(pointing):*

> Where snow-laden branches smile a welcome
> embroidered banner waves above wall.

LIU: I shall be happy to follow you.

Envoi:

LIU:

> At thirty still
> a homeless wanderer

CHEN:

> no sooner met
> than bound in closest friendship.

LIU:

> Where offerings are made
> in convent of faery love

LIU, CHEN:

> perhaps the east wind will witness
> the start of a new romance?

---

2. Ursa Major, our Big Dipper, to the Chinese was a dipper held by the demon Kui, who was permanently in the act of kicking it: kicking a dipper, to shake down the grain inside and thus allow it to hold more, was a favorite device of corrupt collectors of the grain tax. However, since Kui (first star of the Dipper) was worshipped as god of letters, what he was kicking was obviously an ink dipper; this is why he "gets ink all over his face" in the Judge's words in scene 23. Sometimes, also, Kui is mixed up with an evil spirit by the name of He Kui. Liu's accident at the bridge, seen in the light of all Chen's literary allusions here, is an omen of his success in the examinations.

SCENE TWENTY-THREE: *Infernal Judgment*

JUDGE *(attended by demons, with* CLERK *bearing writing brush and register):*

  I Commissioned officer of tenth tribunal of Hell
  my seal bestowed by Lord of Heaven.
  Mortals the world over
  upon their burial
  must cross this threshold of mine.

I am Judge Hu of the staff of the Infernal Prince Yama. There used to be ten princes, but then in the mortal world the Song imperial house of Zhao began its strife with the Jin barbarians. Terrible losses resulted, the population was decimated. Observing this reduction in numbers, the Jade Emperor ordered staffing cuts. Nine princes were left for the nine regions of China. The one that was abolished was mine, the tenth. But there was nowhere to dispose of my seal of office, and the Jade Emperor, impressed by my honesty and intelligence, has reinstated me acting pro tem in charge of the tenth tribunal. This very day I have ridden here to take up my duties, no small affair as you can see from my dual escort of sword-bearing demon lictors and yakshas.

CLERK *(offering brush):* The new incumbent will have need of this brush to record indictments and to inscribe his signature. May it please the new incumbent to deliver a eulogy of the brush.

JUDGE *(examining brush):* Demon lictor, this offering of the brush is a significant occasion. The stand for it to rest on,

  II lotus flower of human flesh,
  rising before magisterial bench
  like sacred Isle of Potlaka.[1]

Now offering the brush to me is
  a worthy scribe
  charged with all matters documentary.

CLERK: What of the stem?

JUDGE: The stem is the bone of a hand or foot
  whittled round as bamboo tube.

---

 1. Where the bodhisattva Guanyin, who saves souls, manifested herself. There is a grim contrast between the shape (the sacred lotus flower, a common shape for brush stands) and the material this particular stand is made of.

CLERK: And the brush hairs?

JUDGE: The hairs, from the beards of ox-head demons and the scalps
of yakshas,

> twisted wires of flaming red.

CLERK: Your Honor, whose name appears on the brush as selector of
hairs?

JUDGE:

> This pointy-headed gentleman
> was appointed by the ruler of Zhexu.[2]

CLERK: What name and title does the brush hold?

JUDGE:

> Scholar of Tube City,
> holding office in Yelang.[3]

CLERK: What when Your Honor is inspired?

JUDGE (*laughs and begins to dance*): Then I'll whistle whoo-whee
> knocking Zhong Kui's cap awry[4]
and dance swish-swoosh
> till the Demon Kick-the-Dipper
> gets ink all over his face,[5]
> for who touches ink gets blackened.

CLERK: And when merry?

JUDGE: When I'm merry
> I'll write graffiti on the bridge
> over the River of Blood.[6]

CLERK: And when bored?

JUDGE: When I'm bored
> I'll hand in my brush at the Gate of Hell
> and go home.

CLERK: Was Your Honor's name announced among the examination
successes?

JUDGE: I entered the celestial lists

---

2. An elaborate double allusion to Cao Zhi, a third-century poet who in legend
was granted after death, in the imaginary land of Zhexu, the throne he had been
denied in life, and to an ill-favored courtier of the same period who was known as
"Brush Head."

3. Yelang was a tiny principality in modern Guizhou, whose ancient ruler once
asked an envoy whether China was as big as Yelang. The "Tube City" joke is from
"Biography of Mao Ying, Mr. Brush," by the Tang writer Han Yu (see scene 6).

4. Zhong Kui was a legendary failed examination candidate who after death was
commissioned to chase off evil demons.

5. See scene 22, note 2.

6. This is the bridge the wicked must cross after death.

and my name appeared among the successful
on first and fifteenth of month.

CLERK: Are you skilled as a calligrapher?

JUDGE: I can hold my own
    with Gemini and Cancer
    in accomplishments of studio.

CLERK: Your Honor is a man of lofty talent.

JUDGE: Though I may not match
    the "Demon Genius" Li He
    who from his White Jade Lodge[7]
    scraped the sky with his songs,
still I should not disgrace the company
    of Shi Manqing, Lord of Wind and Moon,
    setting down his evening thoughts
    in Hibiscus City.[8]
Though it is beyond me to record
    every motion of sun and moon
    across the Four Continents
yet I can dispatch
    all the Five Bearers of Pestilence
    to summon storm and thunder.

CLERK: What is your jurisdiction?

JUDGE:
    My jurisdiction
    is in the court of Prince Yama
    under the administration of the Dipper.
    Say I have no official residence:
    then how is it you'll find my image
    in every temple to Lord of Eastern Peak
    or City God?[9]

CLERK: To whom do you pay respect?

JUDGE: From this high seat of office
    I salute in my turn
    revered countenance
    of Great Bodhisattva.

CLERK: And who annoys you?

---

7. Built by the Lord of Heaven for the poet's use after death, according to a legend reported by his near-contemporary, the late Tang poet Li Shangyin.

8. The Song poet Shi Manqing was said to have been appointed Lord of Fairyland (Hibiscus City) upon his death.

9. Here the Judge reminds us that he is none other than the court officer whose statue stood beside the images of the Lord of the Eastern Peak and the City God (in general charge of the sentencing of the dead) in every city temple in China.

JUDGE: Why, when my statue is only three feet tall, a little lacking in majesty, and I have to face those

> tiny demon lictors
> grotesquely posturing
> on the steps below.

CLERK: Your black silk hat looks a bit antiquated.

JUDGE:

> I've been standing here so long,
> writing brush poised over register,
> dust gathers thick on my robe and headpiece.

CLERK: Your brush has dried out.

JUDGE:

> It can be moistened—at a price:
> ten gold ingots,
> ten strings of cash
> or a nice pile of paper
> in appropriate denominations.

CLERK: Here is your register of the dead.

JUDGE:

> Carelessly I
> scan the list of names
> on pages marked with fishtails,[10]
> unremittingly I
> note against each name
> the destined date of death.
> Behold me, inscribing my signature
> like an infernal version of the ancient
> incorruptible historian Dong Hu;
> I follow pattern
> of Spring and Autumn Annals themselves
> to record day, month, and year
> of all who are to pass, perish, expire, or decease;[11]
> and just as Yu the Great
> having subdued the fearsome Spirit of the River Huai
> cast his likeness, and all creatures' also,
> all elves, sprites, gnomes, and trolls
> on nine great tripods, so shall I
> clearly distinguish every one from other.

CLERK: Let me grind the ink for you.

---

10. Chinese books of traditional binding had double pages, on the margins of which the title appeared in parentheses shaped like fishtails.

11. The euphemism varied according to the rank of the subject.

JUDGE:

> Scritch-scratch of midnight ink slab,
> effort rewarded with a shiny black pool.

CLERK: The cock just crowed.

JUDGE:

> Bim-bam on clapper board,[12]
> crowing of golden cock
> cuts short their dreams and calls back errant souls.

CLERK: Let Your Honor call the roll.

JUDGE:

> Each name once checked
> may fly to any one
> of forty-eight thousand fates
> in the Three Realms of Desire,
> of Form, and of the Formless.

Born to mortal care

> they scatter like sparks from a firecracker.
> The tip of this brush
> commits to a hundred and forty-two
> levels of Hell, without remission
> till Iron Tree shall blossom.

CLERK: Your signature for each.

JUDGE: Ah, yes, my signature, so each may be
　　　sliced, burnt, ground, or pounded.

CLERK: There should be a "please" somewhere.

JUDGE: "Please" has been said
　　　by the Four Visitants from Hall of Nothingness:
　　　palsy, dropsy, jaundice, consumption.

CLERK: Hang up the scales, there!

(The LICTORS do so)

JUDGE:

> Strung up by the hair
> men's bodies are light
> to the weight of their sins.
> Like jailers of court of Qin
> we process their cases by the hundredweight.

---

12. A wooden block is struck to summon the souls of the recently deceased.

*(Offstage cries of "Ai-yo!" "Let
us go!" "It hurts!")*

CLERK: They're flogging the dead souls in the Ninth Court next
door.
JUDGE: This is the "music of the flesh,"
    hear demons wail and ghosts cry out
    as they did in the time of Xiao He,
    cruel clerk of Han.
    To laugh at a time like this
    were you the mirthless incorruptible
    Judge Bao himself
    would draw men's hatred.

(Offstage wails)

    To hear such sounds
    who wouldn't weep as Confucius wept
    when his disciple Yan Yuan
    died young and coffinless!
CLERK: Your Honor is afraid!
JUDGE *(annoyed):*
    I take my laws and precepts
    from the Bestiary,[13]
    even the blossoms on my courtyard trees
    are knife-edged.
    See the wind ruffle my hairy beard,
    my eyes flash lightning 'neath lifted brows.
    Nor do I lack for demons and spirits
    to be my secretaries and recorders.
Don't compare me with Judge Gold, Judge Silver, Judge Copper,
Judge Cash in the world of the living:
    I prepare my indictments,
    supervise my coroners
    as though the fearsome White Tiger Spirit himself
    were come to sit in judgment.
From this infernal court of mine issues each sentence of rebirth
whether from womb, from egg, from moisture, or from air.

---

13. That is, "I am perfectly prepared to sentence these dead souls to reincarnation
in any form, animal as well as human."

Bluebottle will report pardons I grant[14]
and merit of my achievements
will secure a triple advance in rank.
In solemn dignity
I rule the fates of men,
in sternest majesty
I clear the path of Heaven.

Call the clerk of the court. Everything in this register has been satis-
factorily disposed of. Are there any other cases that still await
sentencing?

LICTOR *(enters):*

One runner less in the mortal world—
here in the shades a lictor am I.

Your Honor, this hell has been unoccupied for three years on account of the vacancy of Your Honor's position. All we have awaiting
disposal are some minor offenders from the City of the Wrongfully
Dead. There are four males: Zhao the Eldest, Qian Fifteen, Sun Xin,
and Monkey Li; and one female, Bridal Du.

JUDGE: Call the male offenders.

CLERK *(leads in the four male offenders):* The males, Your Honor.

JUDGE *(checks off their names):* Zhao the Eldest: for what offense
were you committed to the City of the Wrongfully Dead?

ZHAO: I was guilty of no offense, Your Honor, it's just that I was
fond of singing.

JUDGE: Stand aside. Call Qian Fifteen.

QIAN: No offense, Your Honor, only I built a little hut for myself and
paneled the walls with fragrant aloes wood.[15]

JUDGE: Stand aside. Call Sun Xin.

SUN: I'm just a young lad, Your Honor, and I liked to spend a bit of
money on the "powdered blossoms" in the local brothel.

JUDGE: Call Monkey Li.

LI: I *was* guilty of an offense, Your Honor, I practiced sodomy.

CLERK: And that's the truth, even here in Hell he's been after this
young Sun.

JUDGE *(annoyed):* Who asked you to butt in? Get up and look after
your charges. *(He writes in the register)* Let the offenders hear the

---

14. When Fu Jian, the unifier of North China in the fourth century, was preparing
a pardon, a bluebottle fly hovered about his brush. It then metamorphosed into a
black-robed lictor, who spread the news of the pardon before it was officially issued.

15. This was presumably an offense against the sumptuary regulations.

verdicts. *(The four male offenders kneel)* Since I am in a temporary acting position, I shall not prescribe punishment. You are pardoned and permitted to be reborn from eggs.

LI: May it please Your Honor, by "eggs" do you mean "balls"? If it's Muslim balls,[16] that means rebirth in the border regions!

JUDGE: Tchah, you still have hopes of human form? Off with you, to the insides of *birds'* eggs.

ZHAO, QIAN, SUN, LI *(weeping):* Oh, oh, this means people will cut our heads off!

JUDGE: Very well, we shall ensure that you are not the sort of creatures humans eat. Since Zhao the Eldest likes to sing, he shall be an oriole.

ZHAO: Good, good, I can be Yingying, Miss Oriole of the play *Western Chamber*.

JUDGE: Qian Fifteen lived in a hut scented with aloes wood: very well, you can have a swallow's nest for your pleasure, go be reborn as a swallow.

QIAN: Then I can be the Imperial Consort Flying Swallow!

JUDGE: Sun Xin spent his money on the powdered blossoms, he can be a butterfly.

LI: Let me be a butterfly, too, so I can go with him.

JUDGE: You are the sodomist, Monkey Li: you can be a bee and have a sting in your backside.

LI: Ai-yo, who can I stick with a thing like that?

JUDGE: Now, you four flying creatures, hear my instructions: you, butterfly,

III   what tailor could match your powdered wings?

And you, bee,

a wicked one you are

with sucking mouth and stinging tail.

You, swallow,

your shadow swoops within the curtains

as you bear fragrant clay to your nest;

and you, oriole,

your piping song beyond gauze window

breaks the spell of dreams.

Now you may all

fly away without restraint,

---

16. "Muslim balls" was an ethnic slur on the Muslims who formed part of the population of northwestern China.

four friends of flower garden;
and even though careless children in the world of the living
      pelt you with pellets,
      strike at you with fans,
still you may become
      subjects of paintings for men of taste to cherish.
So off with you now, and let your wings
      bear the stirring burden of spring.

LI: If I'm to be a bee, I'll come back here and sting Your Honor's head.

JUDGE: Do you want a beating?

LI: Oh, spare this tiny life!

JUDGE: Then that's enough. Off with you all, fly away, quick!

      (He gives a puff, and the four exit,
      each imitating his particular way of flying.
      The JUDGE, as they go, gives another audible
      puff in the direction of the exit)

CLERK *(escorting BRIDAL DU):*
    I'm not a man you'll meet on paths of heaven
    but don't blame me if Hell's a cruel place.
Here is the female prisoner.

JUDGE *(aside):* Not a bad-looking one, either! Suddenly before my eyes
      IV a beauty to throw Heaven and earth into turmoil!
      Hey, you there,
      come a little closer!

      (BRIDAL wails)

    Wailing her woe in this basin of blood
    yet lovely as Guanyin herself!

CLERK *(whispering in his ear):* Why not keep her a while as your concubine, Your Honor?

JUDGE: Tush, there's a celestial law that prescribes beheading for anyone who sequesters a female prisoner for his own enjoyment.
      That little head of yours keeps churning out crazy ideas
      but where to get another head if I lose this one?

      (BRIDAL moans)

    Yet never did I see
    one so young
    look so fetching.

Tell her to step forward.

> v   I can envision you with blooming cheeks
> on terrace of flowers and wine cups
> or decked with ornaments
> joining the song and the dance
> or smiling your favors in faery tryst
> in fabulous Qin or Chu.
> What sickness brought you here?
> Of whose family are you?
> Such freshness does not belong
> by yellow springs of Hell.

BRIDAL DU: If I have any youthful freshness it is because I was born this way, and I have neither married nor drunk wine. But I am here because I once dreamed of a young scholar, beneath the apricot trees in the garden behind the Prefect's residence at Nan'an. He broke off a willow sprig and asked for a poem on the subject. He was affectionate and gentle and we loved each other dearly. On waking from the dream I fell to musing, and composed the lines,

> Union in some year to come
>   with the "courtier of the moon"
> will be beneath the branches
>   either of willow or apricot.

Then, falling into longings, I lost my life.

JUDGE: This is all lies. When in the world did anyone die of a dream?

> vi   How could such slip of girl
> cling so strongly to her dream?
> Who was it claimed to interpret your dream
> or told your fortune in character riddles?
> Hey now, tell me
> where is this young scholar?
> And who else did your dreaming spirit encounter?

BRIDAL: There was no one else. But there were indeed flower petals that fluttered down and startled me into wakefulness.

JUDGE: Call for questioning the Flower Spirit of the garden behind the Prefect's residence at Nan'an.

(CLERK repeats the order)

FLOWER SPIRIT *(enters):*

> Showers of pink petal rain
>   and spring is ended,

one chorus of "The Scented Hills"
and maiden's soul dissolves.[17]
My respects to the Judge. *(He salutes)*
JUDGE: Flower Spirit, this ghost maiden claims to have died of a shock she received when flower petals disturbed her dream in the garden. Is this true?
FLOWER SPIRIT: It is true. She was tenderly entwined in a dream of a young scholar when a chance fall of petals startled her into wakefulness. Passionate longings brought about her death.
JUDGE: My suspicion is that the young scholar was none other than yourself in disguise, leading people's daughters astray.
FLOWER SPIRIT: Now, why should I have led her astray?
JUDGE: You think we here in Hades don't know what goes on?

> VII   Spring left alone would know no cares
> but the Bureau of Flowers
> performs all kinds of mischief.
> In a twinkling one's vital strength is sapped
> by boudoir's sudden voluptuous charm,
> licentious scenes on every hand,
> one's fate adrift on a sea of wine.
> Beauty already close to perfect
> you people make irresistible.
> Come, list for me
> the flowers in your bag of tricks!

FLOWER SPIRIT: I will list them.

(As he speaks the name of each flower,
the JUDGE sings a rhyming line in which through pun
or allusion he brings out some erotic suggestion)

FLOWER SPIRIT:	JUDGE:
Double peach:	Place where trysts are made;
pink-flowering pear:	on fan of ghostly maid;[18]
gold-coin flower:	gifts she won't refuse;
embroidered-ball viburnum:	throw it at her you choose;
peony:	never an angry frown;
brushtip magnolia:	write the message down;

---

17. When the song "The Scented Hills" was sung at the Western Queen Mother's fairy banquet, flower petals came raining down.

18. Allusion to the Yuan play *Xie Jinlian*, in which a young scholar is tricked into believing his courtesan ladylove to be a ghost when a sprig of pink-flowering pear appears folded in her fan.

water chestnut:	set her mirror there;[19]
jade-hairpin lily:	stick it in her hair;
rose:	dew to scent her cheek;
wintersweet apricot:	her forehead to bedeck;[20]
"shear spring":	tailor her gown so neat;
narcissus:	silk stockings for her feet;[21]
lantern flower:	shadows glowing red;
yeast flower:	tipsy she's off to bed;
golden goblet:	for the loving cup;
brocade-sash weigela:	bind her waistband up;
"joyous-union" mimosa:	her drowsy head she droops;[22]
willow:	her waist sways and swoops;
trumpet flower:	he's in strongest form;
pepper flower:	her welcome is warm;
smiling magnolia:	passion on its way;[23]
sunflower:	turns his head more each day;
convolvulus:	twines herself about him;
crape myrtle:	such an itch without him;[24]
"son-bearing" lily:	progeny may she bear;[25]
lilac:	clustering everywhere;
mace:	pregnancy confessed;
milk flower:	gently stroke her breast;
gardenia:	charmingly discreet;
patience:	how long can you wait?
orange blossoms:	sweetest thoughts will bring;
crabapple:	drowsy maid in spring;
baby flower:	dimpled infant's smile;
"two sisters":	jealous all the while;
pink:	outlasts any other;
daphne:	smells too sweet to gather;

---

19. The water chestnut was a common motif for the design of mirror backs.

20. Allusion to a Song princess who set a new style of coiffure when apricot blossoms settled on her forehead during a garden nap.

21. The name for narcissus is "water fairy," and the Judge's response alludes to the rhymeprose on the Goddess of the River Luo by the third-century poet Cao Zhi.

22. The leaflets of the mimosa fold together at night.

23. A fragrant variety of michelia, related to magnolia, is called in Chinese the "smiling flower."

24. The crape myrtle is known as "itching plant" because when the trunk is scratched the branchlets quiver.

25. The day lily, worn at a woman's waist, would help ensure the birth of a son—a belief stemming from its use as a drug to relieve the pains of childbirth.

lotus: so much love within it;
pomegranate: over in a minute.²⁶

JUDGE:
        I leave the rest to your imagination:
        how can the Lord of Heaven himself
        counter such snares?
        Why should they be allowed
        to disturb this innocent maid
        and from peony pavilion
        send azalea soul in panicked flight?²⁷

FLOWER SPIRIT: It was the Lord of Heaven himself who decreed
every last variety of flower. All I do is carry out his commands, it's
absurd to accuse me of deliberately enticing people to mischief.
And considering all the beautiful women there have been, who ever
heard of one dying of a love of flowers?

JUDGE: You say no beauty ever died of a love of flowers? Let me list
some for you:

        VIII· Ladies whose youth was sacrificed to flowers,
        ladies whose tragic fates the flowers decreed:
        like that night-blooming lotus
        who, though they clutched her billowing fairy skirt,
        could not be stopped from soaring to the sky;²⁸
        or like that sprig of crabapple bloom
        whose brocade perfume sachet
        bore magic testimony to her griefs;²⁹
        or yet again, the daphne
        that spelled the death of Parting Mist.³⁰
        You ask which beauties died for love of flowers?
        Flower Spirit, here is guilt that you must share.

---

26. Lotus *(lian)* has a homophone meaning "love"; pomegranate *(liu)* has a
homophone meaning "endure."

27. See scene 10, note 2.

28. Composite allusion to the Han Emperors Lingdi, whose orgies were held beside pools of night-blooming lotus, and Chengdi, whose consort was Flying Swallow
Zhao. Once as Flying Swallow danced a breeze filled her skirts and would have carried her off had not onlookers clutched at them. She "could not be stopped" for long,
though, for she took her own life after Chengdi's death.

29. The crabapple ("drowsy maid in spring" in the list above) was the symbol of
Yang Guifei, consort of the Tang Emperor Xuanzong; when her grave was opened
after her enforced suicide, only a perfume sachet was found within.

30. Parting Mist was a concubine whose jealous husband beat her to death after

FLOWER SPIRIT: I confess my crimes. I shall cause no more blooming from now on.

JUDGE: Flower Spirit, I have just now committed four friends of the flower garden to your charge. As for this female prisoner, since she died of amorous longing, let her be reduced to the ranks of the swallows and orioles.

FLOWER SPIRIT: Your Honor, this woman's offense took place in dream, and is as immaterial as dawn breeze or waning moon. In view of her father's reputation as an upright official, and of the fact that she is his only child, she should be treated with leniency.

JUDGE: Who is her father?

FLOWER SPIRIT: Her father is Du Bao, the former Prefect, recently promoted Governor of Huaiyang.

JUDGE: So, a young lady of quality. Very well then, out of consideration for His Honor Du, I shall seek advice from the Celestial Court before I pass sentence.

BRIDAL: If Your Honor graciously pleases: Is it possible to investigate the source of these distressful feelings of mine?

JUDGE: The matter is all noted in the Register of Heartbreaks.

BRIDAL: Then might I trouble you to determine whether my husband was to have the name of Liu or Mei, Willow or Apricot?

JUDGE: Let me see the Register of Marriages. (*He turns away from the defendant to examine it*) Here it is. Here is a Liu Mengmei, Prize Candidate in the next examinations. Wife, Bridal Du, loved in the shades, later formally wedded in the world of light. Rendezvous, the Red Apricot Convent. Not to be divulged. (*He turns again to face the defendant*) There is a person here with whom you share a marriage affinity. On this account I shall release you now from this City of the Wrongfully Dead, so that you may wander windborne in search of this man.

FLOWER SPIRIT: Bridal Du, prostrate yourself before His Honor.

BRIDAL (*does so*): I prostrate myself in gratitude for your clemency, father and mother of my rebirth. And my own father and mother in Yangzhou—may I see them again?

JUDGE: You may.

> IX   A span remains for her in the land of light,
>   the shades do not claim her yet.

---

discovering a poem from her lover; a line of the poem referred to the amorous promise of the daphne's fragrance.

These mist-laden blooms of spring are a shifty bunch
and passion was bound to ensue
from meeting with willow and apricot.[31]
Now to her view of the lily her mother
the cedar her sire
let Heaven place no impediment,
but let her mount our Home-gazing Terrace[32]
to spy across crystal wastes
ashes of spirit money swirl
above night markets of Yangzhou.

Flower Spirit, take her to the Home-gazing Terrace and let her look her fill.

BRIDAL (*follows him onto the Terrace, where she gazes toward Yangzhou and weeps*): There is Yangzhou, and my mother and father! Oh, let me fly to them!

FLOWER SPIRIT: It is not yet time for you to go there.

JUDGE: Come back and hear my instructions. Attendants, prepare a passport for this wandering soul; and you, Flower Spirit, guard her fleshly body from corruption.

BRIDAL: I thank Your Honor for this clemency.

JUDGE:

x   Against time of desire
when fire shall meet dry tinder
let these green hills be undisturbed[33]
by pelting rain or wind or burning sun.
Your marriage vow to Heaven and earth
will follow flights past moon and stars
as spirit-self comes and goes.
No further permit needed for release,
no mortal womb for rebirth.
Four Friends of the Flowers are yours to command,
oriole and swallow, butterfly and bee
to help you seek, to aid your wooing
till the predicted star, the Coffin Breaker
comes to fulfill your dream.

---

31. That is, with Liu Mengmei, "Willow Dream-of-Apricot."

32. The terrace at the edge of the underworld from which lost souls could view their earthly homes.

33. Allusion to a proverb—"As long as the green hills are there, we can always find firewood"—playing on the "dry tinder" of the previous line.

(Exit)

FLOWER SPIRIT: Come, young lady, let me take you back to the rear garden.

Envoi:

FLOWER SPIRIT:

> Threads of hair escape from cap
> drunkenly awry

BRIDAL:

> prayer flags hang limp all day
> untouched by spirit breeze.

JUDGE:

> Year after year reviewing
> the disputes men engender

JUDGE, BRIDAL, FLOWER SPIRIT:

> we await the judgment of Xiao He,
> great lawgiver of Han.

SCENE TWENTY-FOUR: *The Portrait Recovered*

LIU MENGMEI:

> 1 Never did spring torment man so:
> through all my journeying no other thought.
> Winds have rent rough jacket dark-hued as grapes,
> rains discolored light gown of apricot silk.
> In today's mild sun
> airing my coverlet
> I found the cloud stains of a passionate dream.
> Pearl blossom fills the court with gentle fragrance,
> useless to dwell on the past year's discontents.
> How much spring longing can this "willow" bear
> before his waist grows thinner than Master Shen's?[1]

Sickness has detained me in this Apricot Shrine. By good fortune my new friend Chen Zuiliang is skilled in medicine and has restored me to health. But for some days past I have been suffering an

---

1. The fifth-century poet Shen Yue became legendary for his frailness.

ennui born of springtime longings, and I can find nowhere to turn to assuage my sorrows. Ha, here comes the old abbess.

SISTER STONE *(enters):*

> II   A Taoist sister is just the one
> to see through a young scholar's poses.
> Do you want to know where his fond dreams linger
> as he sighs and stretches a thousand times a day?

I trust you are feeling better, sir?

LIU: My health has been mending recently and now I grow weary of sitting about. This Apricot Shrine is such a sizable place, it must surely have a garden where one might amuse oneself?

SISTER STONE: There is a garden to the rear, and although the pavilions and kiosks are in poor repair there are plenty of flowers to brighten it up. You may while away some hours there, but be careful to avoid grieving.

LIU: What would I find to grieve about?

SISTER STONE *(sighs):* What indeed! No matter, if you go on your own. Follow the west gallery past the painted wall. After a hundred paces you will come to a wicket gate. Enter this and you will find pools and teahouses for a mile around. You may enjoy them as you please and amuse yourself there the whole day through. No need for me to accompany you:

> "All may freely enter
>   this noted demesne
> but few can be aware
>   of the sorrows of its past."

> *(Exit)*

LIU: Now that I know of this garden, let me take a leisurely stroll there. *(He mimes the act of strolling)* Here is the western gallery. *(Strolls further)* How overgrown is this wicket gate, and half of it collapsed. *(He sighs)*[2]

> "Still leaning on this marble balustrade
> my sad gaze shuns the walls on every side.
> Such moons, such breezes, nights of long ago!
> Willows once lush as mist now sere and dry."

> *(He mimes the act of arrival)*

---

2. Liu here recites a pastiche of lines from four different Tang poets.

Ha, what a grand garden!

    III   How silently the splendor has eroded.
    One stretch of painted wall still stands,
    the next slants all awry.

            (He stumbles)

    Slipping on mosses,
    stumbling by broken banks
    to a gate shaped as butterfly wings
    bolted for no good reason.

There must have been many visitors in times gone by, to judge
from the names cut into the bamboo stems.

    Guests came
    and as months and years drew on
    a thousand emerald tablets bore inscriptions.

But already

    wildflowers invade the steps
    and weeds form thickets.

Strange! How would nuns like these of this Apricot Shrine have
built such a magnificent garden? There is something very curious in
this. See where this stream winds its way:

    IV   Is it the true Peach Blossom Spring[3]
    behind bolted gate?
    So fair a spot, in such disarray!
    Amid drifts of mist
    lakeside pavilion leans askew,
    painted boat lies on its side,
    girl's sash dangles from motionless swing.
    No pillaging of armed men
    wrought these ravages
    but surely some grieving owner absent far
    fills this place with sorrowful memories;
    try as you may to forget,
    each turn of path by mound or pool
    captures your thought again.

Here is a fine mound of rocks. *(He looks closely)* Ha, a little box there
among the boulders. If I brace myself against this rockface I can see
what it is. *(Mimes the act of dodging as the rock rolls aside)* Yes, a

---

3. Allusion to Tao Qian's famous allegory; see scene 10, note 6.

rosewood box. *(Opens the box, revealing the portrait scroll within)* So, it is a portrait of the blessed bodhisattva Guanyin. Wonderful! Rather than leave it buried here I shall take it back to my study, there to make formal obeisances before it.

(He retraces his steps, with the box held reverently in his hands)

> v   Rosewood box
> entombed beneath miniature peaks
> as in a handsome shrine to the bodhisattva.
> This boulder below the summit
> is surely an Airborne Peak
> or Rock of Three Incarnations.[4]
> Reverently I shall perfume the scroll with incense,
> kowtow before the portrait
> that in light of sacred flames
> her blessing shine upon me:
> accept my diligent service,
> deign to bestow thy mercy.

(He reenters the hall of the shrine)

Now that I am back in the shrine I shall select a place to install the portrait and an auspicious day to perform my obeisances.

SISTER STONE *(enters)*: Back already, Master Liu?

LIU: Aunt Stone,

> VI   so many woes beset a life of wandering
> sun sinks low behind deserted grove.

If you would have me give up my cares, then you must find me some place, if such there be, where no cares come.

Envoi:

LIU:

> Fond as I am of woods and rills
> close by my hermitage

SISTER STONE:

> already the days of dream and rain
> mourn the passing of spring.

---

4. The Airborne Peak is the site of a celebrated temple by the West Lake at Hangzhou: legend claims the Peak flew there from India. The Three Incarnations are the lifetimes (past, present, and future) through which one's karma works itself out; see also scene 1, note 3.

LIU:

    Where is the path that promises
    return to gilded mansion?

LIU, SISTER STONE:

    The green of the Three Peaks
    half-hidden by blossoming branches.

SCENE TWENTY-FIVE: *Maternal Remembrance*

SPRING FRAGRANCE:

    1a Sight of object recalls owner
    but owner once departed
    object itself grows stale.
    True enough the saying
    "faery fruits long in ripening
    choicest blooms first to fade."

    (She sighs)

    Not my fate to be buried by her side
    awaiting resurrection in the Orchid Palace;[1]
    mine only to clear the incense ashes.

I am Spring Fragrance of the household of His Excellency the Commissioner Du Bao, whom with his lady I have accompanied to Yangzhou. It is now almost three years since my young mistress passed away. Never a day in all this time but the old lady has missed her and wailed her grief. Though His Excellency tries for the time being to console her, how is such sorrow to be assuaged? For let alone the old lady, even I am sad at heart when I recall the kindnesses my young mistress always showed me and the words she spoke as she lay dying. Today would have been my young mistress' birthday, and Madam Du has ordered me to set out incense and lamps that she may pour out a libation in the direction of far-away Nan'an. Now, mistress, all is ready for your use.

---

1. The Orchid Palace was where the ghost of a girl named Cheeks-of-Cloud met a lover who secured the resurrection of her body. Cheeks-of-Cloud had been a hand-maid of the celebrated Tang imperial consort Yang Guifei, and had poisoned herself to accompany her mistress in death.

MADAM DU (*enters*):

> 1b Earth ages, Heaven dims
> and this old body finds no place to settle.
> Reckon it up: no kin before my eyes
> and none to summon back
> my soul on its departure.

Ah Bridal, my daughter,

> here at sky's edge my end draws close,
> pain slices my bowels inch by inch.
> Clouds oppress the ridge,
> trees veil the pass.

FRAGRANCE:

> Helpless against spring longings,
> so young to take leave of life.

MADAM DU:

> A thousand tortures ravage her mother's heart.
> The scent of her still clings
> to sewing case and writing satchel.

FRAGRANCE:

> Incense rises pure in blessing,
> candles gleam from silver stands.

MADAM DU:

> On this her anniversary
> before the embroidered Buddha
> with tears of blood we commit our vows to the wind.

(She weeps)

MADAM DU, FRAGRANCE:

> Though soul be summoned from myriad li, may it come
> to swift rebirth in land of holy calm.

MADAM DU: Fragrance, the loss of my daughter has left these old bones a vain burden and my breast consumed with pain. Tears fill my eyes, grief fills my heart whenever I chance upon a book she left unfinished, a flower embroidery she laid by, traces of her powder and perfume, hairpins or slippers she cast aside. Three years now since she left us, and today her anniversary. This offering of incense to Buddha burns in my heart, these waxen candle tears flow from my eyes. Are all the preparations I ordered now complete?

FRAGRANCE: All is ready, Madam, for you to present your observances before high Heaven.

MADAM DU (*prostrates herself, then recites a pastiche of lines from Tang poets*):

> Wisps of incense swirl,
>> tears start and well forth.
> Again as last year, wine is sprinkled,
>> incense turns to ash.
> Where is the four-foot mound
>> of solitary grave?
> Southward returned may she
>> be born again in Heaven.

I, Zhen, wife of Commissioner Du, reverently present my observances to the Lord Buddha on this my departed daughter's anniversary. May Bridal Du find acceptance into Thy mighty power for swift rebirth in Heaven. (*She rises*) Fragrance, now that I have prayed to the Lord Buddha, it is time to present this tea and rice as an offering to my daughter.

> 11a Where to seek Bridal's grave?
> Hard to gain Heaven's answer.
> My eyes too dim for sight of her in dream
> I hear the very sound of her calling,
> start to my feet,
> turn in wild hope,
> but only the failing lamp
> flickers in gusts of dark wind.

> (*She weeps*)

> Ah my Bridal,
> how could you leave me, white-haired, childless,
> myriad li removed!

FRAGRANCE (*prostrates herself*):

> 11b With fragrant incense
> Fragrance kowtows before the Jade Sylph[2]
> in gratitude for boundless grace bestowed
> wearing as I still do your gift of silken skirt
> your own in former years.

> (*She rises*)

Shortly before she departed, my young mistress instructed me to

---

2. Name of a fairy maiden, which was also bestowed on Yang Guifei; see note 1.

call her name loud and long. Today I call her, young mistress, young
mistress, and again I call

but can my young mistress hear me?

MADAM DU, FRAGRANCE (*weeping*):

So fond her longing,
so deep her grief:
our plaint rises to Heaven
that Heaven should cut off
so cruelly mother from child.

FRAGRANCE (*turns again to the altar*):

O my darling young mistress,
can you return to your old home?
Or where will be the place of your rebirth?

(*She kneels*)

Madam, I would remind you that persons mature in years should
beware the ravages of grief. The young mistress is dead and cannot
return to life, but Madam lives on and must not let this death im-
peril her own health. Take good care as age draws on, that you may
relish wealth and honor in the company of His Excellency.

MADAM DU (*weeps*): Fragrance, are you aware that some years past
His Excellency, lacking a son, contemplated taking a concubine?
Only his joy in our daughter persuaded him to carry on as usual.
Now she is gone and there is none to continue our line. What con-
solation can I offer my lord as we face each other in lonely silence?
Ah Heaven, pity me!

FRAGRANCE: Madam, you are too worthy a lady to be advised by one
of my stupidity. But from what you have said, and since His Excellency has contemplated taking a concubine, would it not be the best
thing to follow his wishes and install such a one in your household
that she may bear a son?

MADAM DU: But Fragrance, can a son born of a concubine match
one's own?

FRAGRANCE: Madam, since you have raised me in your service, I
have become a member of your family though none in fact. If you
will look kindly on the child of a concubine, then surely you may
have a son though none in fact.

MADAM DU: A clever tongue, indeed!

Envoi:

MADAM DU:
　Visit to my daughter
　under waning moon

FRAGRANCE:
　how many now will share
　the white aspen's grief?

MADAM DU:
　Know that this is the sorrow
　hardest to assuage

MADAM DU, FRAGRANCE:
　as by the wintry pond
　tears fleck the orchid leaves.

SCENE TWENTY-SIX: *The Portrait Examined*

LIU MENGMEI:
　Raindrops disperse from plantain leaves,
　breezes cease to ruffle peony tips.
　Still studying the painting's guarded secret,
　look where a gleam of spring light holds the clue.
Lone and listless in my wanderings, I took an idle stroll in the shrine's rear garden. There among rocks by a pool I found a painted scroll, apparently a portrait of the great bodhisattva Guanyin, secreted in a precious casket. Continuous wind and rain for the past few days have prevented my viewing it, but happily today is clear and bright and I may inspect my find.

　　　(He opens the rosewood box
　　　and unrolls the painting)

　I　The blessed bodhisattva
　shows her celestial form
　sharp-etched as shadows in clear autumn light
　beneath Heaven's silver river, the Milky Way.
　Each holy attribute complete
　as in the manifestation at Potlaka[1]
　but vouchsafed now to one from Southern Sea.

---

1. See scene 23, note 1.

(He ponders)

Yet why for such majesty
is there no lotus pedestal?
And why, on closer look
does silken skirt reveal
a pair of tiny wave-tripping feet?[2]

If this is Guanyin, why are her feet so tiny?[3] I must examine this
more closely.

II   For a while longer
let me reflect on the image here portrayed.

I have it!

A little Chang E to hang in someone's study,[4]
so delicate, so gracefully portrayed.

If this is Chang E, I must certainly pay my respects.

Please say, Chang E,
shall I be one to break the cassia bough?

—But if it be Chang E,
why does no faery cloud support her?
And why no flowering cassia grove?

But if it is neither Guanyin nor Chang E, how could it be some
mortal girl?

Bewildered,
seeming to recognize her
I search my heart.

Look again: is this the work of a painter, or from the hand of the
beauty herself?

III   Whence comes this lovely maid
portrayed in colored inks
flowing clear as moonlight from brush's tip?
No flower but would hide in shame
before such a maiden as this.
Impossible to render pose so free
and who would attempt her hair,
pale washes of springtime clouds?

What painter could have achieved this!

Surely this brushwork shows
skill of lovely maid herself.

---

2. "Tripping the waves" is a common kenning for the feet of a beautiful woman,
originating in Cao Zhi's "Goddess of the River Luo" (see scene 23, note 20).
3. Guanyin did not have bound feet.
4. For Chang E, the cassia tree, and their associations with studying for the examinations, see scene 2, note 4.

Wait a minute: here at the top of the scroll is an inscription in small characters. *(He peers closely)* Yes, a quatrain:
> "However close the likeness
>   viewed from near at hand,
> from farther off one would say
>   this was some airborne sprite.
> Union in some year to come
>   with the 'courtier of the moon'
> will be beneath the branches
>   either of willow or apricot."

So, this is a self-portrait by some mortal girl. But what does she mean, "beneath the branches either of willow or apricot"? Most mysterious!

> IV How could she know that Liu Mengmei
> crossing Apricot Ridge, over hill and pass
> would reach this spot?
> And what is this talk of "union in the moon"?
> Promise of joy
> but wait, wait—
> how could my name provide such a riddle
> for Chang E to determine?
> Wondering, pondering,
> can it be true that what will come to pass
> was already perceived in dream?

See how she gazes back at me!

> V Image of slender grace
> trailing her silken robe
> where leaves of spring plantain seem to sway:
> love's longings locked between her brows,
> which curve, gentle as spring hills
> to soft mist of hair.
> We meet each other's eyes—
> how can gaze of either lightly move?
> Ah, flashing rays
> transfixing me again and again!

And she bears a green sprig of apricot in her hand, as if somehow she were holding my own self in her arms!

> VI Apricot branch in hand
> softly intoning her verse,
> luring my stumbling heart to thoughts of love.
> Just as I "sketch a cake to appease my hunger"
> so she "gazes at apricots to slake her thirst."

Ah, my young lady, my young lady,
>   tiny mouth like lotus bud,
>   lips unparted
>   yet the corners, so delicately touched,
>   give promise of a smile
>   and of a passionate heart.
>   Sadly she longs to speak, but breathes not.

The young lady rivals in her skill the painting of Cui Hui, the poetry of Su Hui, the calligraphy of the Lady Wei.[5] Though I have cultivated my own talents, how could I ever hope to match this girl! Brought suddenly face to face with her like this, I shall try a verse in corresponding meter:

>   The excellence of the painting
>   is nature's inspiration,
>   a sprite either of heaven
>   or of earth below;
>   the "moon-palace union"
>   may be near at hand or far
>   but hopes of spring are lodged
>   in willow and apricot.
>   VII Equally skilled is she
>   in painting and poetic craft;
>   perfect match of figure's grace
>   with background hill and stream.

Let me call her as earnestly as I can: Lovely lady! Gracious mistress!

>   Till my throat bleeds I cry for Zhenzhen[6]
>   but does she hear?
>   The proverb says
>   one whose name is spoken will sneeze in response:
>   I wait for her feet to move
>   in slow swaying descent—
>   but her image stays immobile.

So, as I stay on, solitary in this place, I shall spend my days before this portrait, to admire her and present my obeisances, to call her and sing her praises.

>   VIII Happiest of omens, to have found this portrait:
>   surely the "willow" of my name

---

5. For Cui Hui, see scene 14, note 7. Su Hui was the author of a famous poem in palindrome form; the Lady Wei was a celebrated calligrapher of the fourth century.

6. See scene 14, note 5

and the apricot branch in her hand
    must form a closer union yet?
Ah my young lady,
        image without form,
        your gaze destroys me!

Envoi:

Useless to go on resenting
    the portrait's gentle hues;
rather let it hang
    forever by the door.
Rhyme your discontents,
    hide among the willows.
Mounting tipsiness of spring,
    waking ever harder.

SCENE TWENTY-SEVEN: *Spirit Roaming*

SISTER STONE:
    1 Radiance of spring fills hall and terrace,
    pillars carved of jade reflect
    from silver-surfaced pools.
    Smoke of incense rises everywhere,
    cadence of chimes ascends to Heaven
    as we unroll
    sacred scriptures of salvation.

(She recites a pastiche of lines from Tang poets)

"For a handful of years, rouge powder
    layered the yellow clay,
on Witch's Mount the moon
    descends to the Twelve Peaks.[1]
I plucked a single blossom
    of the rose

---

1. See scene 1, note 5. Each line of this pastiche suggests the death of a girl from pining.

as on Bank of Withdrawn Maiden[2]
east wind blew."
This burial shrine of Bridal Du has been in my charge for over three
years now. Today is an auspicious day, which I have selected for a
mass to secure her rebirth in the Realm of Jade. Outside the gate I
have set up a banner to announce this mass, let us see who will
attend.

YOUNG TAOIST NUN (*enters, followed by her* NOVICE):

    II Over ridges of river lands
    a particolored cloud supports the moon
    as like bluebird messengers
    of sainted Queen Mother of the West
    we come and go.

NOVICE: It grows late, let us seek rest at this Apricot Shrine.

NUN:

    Incense in a "magpie-handled" burner
    scents south-pointing branches.

I am Abbess of the Azure Cloud Convent at Shaoyang. My wanderings have brought me to this place where a solemn banner indicates
the imminence of a mass. We are just in time to ascend to the altar
and join in the celebration.

(*She greets* SISTER STONE)

    "Beneath the Canopied Heaven
      willows are veiled in mist"

SISTER STONE:

    "with feathered talisman and crimson pennant
      approach the rocky niche"

NUN:

    "among hills and streams
      I seek a lodging"

SISTER STONE: Very well then,

    "surplice sleeves atrail
      attend our mysteries."[3]

Whence do you come, sister?

NUN: From Shaoyang, and I should be obliged for a night's lodging.

SISTER STONE: Our chief guest-room is occupied by a gentleman

---

2. The Embankment of the Withdrawn Maiden, at Loyang, commemorates an ill-
fated Tang slave girl: she was abducted, and threw herself down a well in protest.
3. This exchange is again a Tang pastiche.

named Liu from Lingnan, who is recuperating from a sickness, but there is a side room at your disposal.

NUN: I am grateful to you. May I ask the purpose of this evening mass?

SISTER STONE (*sighs*): Ah,

> young mistress of the house of Du
>> three full years departed;
> tonight her soul is summoned
>> to ascend the ninefold Heavens.

NUN: So this is your purpose.

> For sacrament of prayer
>> this is a favored time;
> let me with incense and burning lamp
>> assist the holy celebrant.

SISTER STONE: You are welcome to do so.

(Bells and drums sound offstage)

CELEBRANTS: We request our head to offer incense.

SISTER STONE: In honor of the First Consort of the Southern Dipper, charged with mortal matters, and of the Lady of the Eastern Peak, charged with reincarnations.

*(She offers incense and
prostrates herself)*

> IIIa Flames of newly kindled fire,
> incense of highest excellence,
> devotions offered on behalf of Bridal Du.

CELEBRANTS (*prostrating themselves*):

> Clouds of incense wreathe about our banners,
> delicate music soars aloft on breeze.

O holy ones,

> in your immeasurable majesty
> receive this frail fragrant soul
> swiftly into Heaven's height;
> or if her mortal longings still persist
> and she would live again in human form
> let her be born again as maid or man
> and grant that she may find
> a partner for eternal bliss;
> let her not once again
> perish so young.

SISTER STONE: I reflect that the young lady died of her passionate grieving for the flowers, and so today I have picked a sprig of flowering apricot to present before her in a consecrated vase.

(She makes obeisance before the spirit tablet)

> 111b In purified vase
> under cold spring sun
> set one last spray of apricot
> its waxen blooms still red.

Ah young mistress,
> spirit so determined—
> by whose side do you walk
> in fragrant dream?

CELEBRANTS: Tell us, revered teacher, what is represented by the consecrated vase, and what by the sprig of apricot?

SISTER STONE:
> Within the hollow of this vase
> is held the mortal world
> while her poor self
> just like this fading apricot,
> watered but rootless,
> still brings a fragrance to our senses.

CELEBRANTS: Young lady, may you accept this offering and find
> cool balm for your flesh,
> sweet fragrance for your soul;
> if you will return to mortal world
> cannot this sprig of apricot
> serve as your canopy?

(Sound of wind offstage)

SISTER STONE: Most strange! A whirlwind rustles and strikes chill!

(Booming of bell offstage)

CELEBRANTS: The hour of the evening meal, let us eat before we return to bring our ceremonies to a close. Truly,
> before morning mirror we laid aside
>   all inconstancy,
> now bell of evening interrupts
>   our song of "Pacing the Void."

(ALL leave the stage)

BRIDAL DU (*enters, wailing as a ghost, and hiding her face with her sleeve*):

> IV In spirit form, as in a dream,
> from Home-gazing Terrace I come
> where graveyards silent lie in shimmering night.

(*She starts at the offstage barking of a dog*)

So, it is only

> false promise of the shadows—
> a puppy barking at the stars.
> Cool and dim
> springtime shade of flowering pear.

Ah, here is the pavilion of the tree peonies, and here the peony walk, and all neglected and overgrown, for three years have passed since my parents left this place.

(*She weeps*)

> Crumbling wall and weed-grown path
> so deeply wound my spirit.
> Now as I gaze, whence comes
> dull gleam of ghostly lamp?

(*She listens*)

> Ah me, surely the sound of human voices!
> In former days, daughter highborn
> cherished as hoard of gold
> but now the stream flows on
> the blossoms have faded:
> alas for this passionate flower
> of the noble house of Du,
> self-willed beyond recourse
> tonight I count the stars alone.
> In life and death
> passion was all to me
> and how can passion be withstood!

You see before you the spirit form of Bridal Du. My death came of a dream, besotted with passion and longing for love. It happened that the tenth judge of Hell was relieved of his post, and for three years I lodged in the women's cells with none to despatch my case. Then it was my good fortune to meet with a judge who took pity on me and granted my temporary release. This is a night of bright moon and

gentle breezes and I roam at will. But here is the old garden to the
rear of the study—how can it have been turned into an Apricot
Blossom Shrine? How deeply this distresses me!

    v   Despair tortures bowels
of one who seems to wake from drunken dream.
Who will make restoration
of my remaining years?
No sister from the ghostly ranks keeps me company,
alone I straighten gauze robes that trailed on the ground.
I pace my realm
of shadows amid forms
where dew settles on breeze,
cloud obscures Dipper
and moon endures eclipse.
First watch, the flowers shadowed—

    (She starts at the sound of chimes in the wind)

my heart suddenly catches in fear
but it is nought but sound of chimes
in breeze beneath eaves of shrine.
How sweet this scent of incense!

    vi   Smoke of incense clouding
where lanterns glow and shimmer,
I shiver at the sight
of saintly portraits mounted high.
What holy images are these? So, the Lady of the Eastern Peak and
the First Consort of the Southern Dipper. *(She performs a deep kowtow)* The spirit of Bridal Du kowtows before the holy ones. From my
obscurity

    bring me to the light
that in full clarity I may be fated
    to find rebirth in human form!
Let me read these charms: so, this shrine is in the charge of Sister
Stone, and here is a mass for my ascension to Heaven. Ah Sister
Stone, I am deeply in your debt. Ha, and here in this consecrated
vase is a sprig of fading blossom from the apricot by my tomb.
Sweet blossom, like Bridal Du herself you fade before your time,
how sad!

    But all these random drumbeats,
    strikings of bells,

intonings of precious scriptures
break in upon my yellow-millet dream.[4]
Stepping where roots of apricot
grip the fissured earth,
here let me leave some sign.

(She weeps)

Unless I leave some trace of my presence, how can I show my appreciation for the devotions of these pious sisters? Then let me scatter petals of the apricot here on the altar.

(She does so)

To each petal cling
myriad loving thoughts.
I long to know where my father and mother are this night, and where Spring Fragrance. Ha, but from somewhere comes a sound of someone moaning and calling. Let me listen.
LIU'S VOICE *(offstage):* My gracious mistress! Lovely lady!
BRIDAL *(startled):* Who calls, and for whom? Listen again!

(The VOICE calls again,
and she sighs)

VII You the living, I in death,
each fated to wander alone.
One full of longings calls forth
from the one he longs for no reply.
But why do you name no name of her you love?
On my solitary spirit
who would ever call?
Voice of mystery
calling continually
yet pausing ever and again.

(The VOICE calls again)

So, in some guest-room of the shrine
some wandering scholar
rambles in his sleep.

---

4. Allusion to a well-known story of a youth who borrowed the pillow of a Taoist adept and passed through a lifetime of illusion in a dream that took less time than the adept needed to cook the yellow millet for his supper.

VIII From heart I thought devoid of love
longings rise
as he calls and calls again.
I shudder chill, and bitter tears start up.
Ah me, could this be him I saw in dream,
beloved "Apricot" or dearest "Willow"?
For I recall
such a pavilion by flowered pool
was witness to our innocent play
of breeze and moonlight.
And yet what starry union
could be the destiny of a lonely ghost?

I would go at once to find out what I could, but the Dipper turns, Orion wheels, and I may not linger!

IX What is this waving now of temple lamps?

NUNS' VOICES *(offstage):* There are sounds of someone at the shrine!

*(The NOVICE stealthily enters and looks
about. A second whirlwind rises)*

BRIDAL:

I set embroidered banners aflutter
and petals fall in the wind,
sign of ghostly presence of Bridal Du.

NOVICE *(comes face to face with BRIDAL as the latter exits wailing. She starts in terror):* Holy sisters, hurry, hurry!

SISTER STONE, NUN *(enter in alarm):* What's all this fuss?

NOVICE: I was hiding in the lantern shadows to see who it was, when I saw this goddess or fairy maid. She shook her sleeve and the banner fluttered, and then she vanished! I'm frightened!

SISTER STONE: What was her appearance?

NOVICE *(gesturing):* About so tall, so thin, a pretty face, feather hair ornaments and a gold phoenix hairpin, red skirt and green jacket, jade girdle pendants all atinkle, must have been an Immortal come down to visit earth.

SISTER STONE: So, this is the very image of the living Miss Du. It must have been a manifestation of her spirit.

NUN: See, here on the altar, petals of apricot scattered everywhere. It is a miracle! Let us offer one more hymn to her.

ALL CELEBRANTS:

X Breezes disperse the incense smoke,
moonlight floods the walks.

Swift apparition of chill spirit form.
Longings of love so quickly wounded
on a spring night when petals fall.
Speedily may you
ascend to Heaven,
ascend to Heaven:
linger no longer where you have no home.

NUN: Of what sickness did Bridal Du perish, and what was the reason for this manifestation?

SISTER STONE:

XI Calm your fears,
do not ask for reasons,
dismantle we now altar and instruments.
For listen, there along the walk
chill breeze still bears
cold pendants' tinkling sound.

Envoi:

SISTER STONE:

Realizing she dared not
make manifest her presence

NUN:

she would relate her history
but feared the bowels' torture.

NOVICE:

If the spring breeze could be taught
to know of mortal longings

SISTER STONE, NUN, NOVICE:

surely it would recognize
the fairy maid Orchid Fragrance.

SCENE TWENTY-EIGHT: *Union in the Shades*

LIU MENGMEI:

I Where to seek fairy maid
who stood before my eyes?
Wavering shade
as cloud-veiled moonlight.

Aimlessly I pace:
silently I ponder
and already evening sun goes down.
A sunlit cloud descended from the heavens
sculptured grace, flower-like smile:
whose brush portrayed this living presence?
Surely she gazed at me with love unspoken.

Ever since I set eyes on the beauty in the portrait I have longed for
her day and night. As the evening watch draws to a close, I shall
devote myself to repetition of the "pearls and jade" of her verses
and to fresh contemplation of what her eyes seem to say. If only she
could come to me in dream, it would be as the spring breeze to my
spirit. (*He unrolls and contemplates the portrait*) Ah, see how my
lovely lady seems to speak, so clear the light from her expressive
eyes! Truly,

"lone wild duck and sunset cloud
a single flight;
wide sky and clear autumn stream
one color only."[1]

II Borne by evening breeze
a wisp of cloud from Peach Blossom Spring[2]
discloses loveliest of mortals
in flawless purity aglow
against fresh crimson gauze of sunlit window.
This one small painting I hang again,
object of all my yearnings.

Ah lady, lady, I die of longing for you!

III Delicately nurtured, demurely shy,
modestly elegant, daughter of honored house.
Yet with what stirrings did she approach
her mirror patterned with water-chestnut flowers?
What secret thoughts prompted this portrait,
what guesses of one who, finding it, would woo her?

IV As the bright moon her image floods
the sky of my sad longings.

On former nights I could sleep face to face with the moonlight, but
in these past nights

---

1. Lines quoted from the Tang poet Wang Bo.
2. See scene 10, note 6.

so dazzling bright against dark shades
the radiance of her beauty
makes clamorous chaos of my thoughts
and there's no night, no daylight hour
I do not pine.
But that to take her portrait in my hands
could soil its delicate hues
I long to embrace her image as I lie.
Surely there must be a love affinity fated between this lady and
myself? Let me recite her verses once again.

(He does so)

v These words she composed
for one who would understand
predestined "willow" or "apricot."
From crevice in poolside mound
spring longings bore her image
like that of fair Green Calyx, fairy maid[3]
soaring aloft, to light on this painted silk.
What I must do is perform reverences before her.

(He does so, lighting incense)

Agony to stare
at blushing face,
clear line of brow
inscribed already in my heart;
here is your love, not lost at sky's far edge!
Here in this respite from my travels, is there no way I can bring
about a moment's rendezvous with my beloved?
vi Could I but urge
the transformation of this solitary image
until our twin souls stood together
as on painted screen
coarse reed may accompany tree of jade![4]
Ah lady, those tiny ears emerging
like tip of crescent moon through cloud of hair,

---

3. Green Calyx was an immortal who, in a fourth-century legend, explained that after nine hundred years of self-discipline she was able to manifest herself or vanish at will.

4. Old metaphor for ill-assorted companions. The "coarse reed" is Liu himself.

do they hear one word
of all my lovelorn pleading?

VII   How laughable
my poor attempts to joke with her!
Like a clear autumn moon
cloud-soaring over sea and sky
her gaze spans distant hills
to forest shades and misty void.
My offering should be tranquil contemplation,
not ribald mockery!

VIII   Then let my incantations,
my prayers of devotion
move stones to nod their heads,
the sky to rain flower petals.[5]
Does all my piety still lack power
to bring the fairy maiden forth?
She is reluctant to step forward
for cause too light.

> (*Sound of wind rising offstage.* LIU *places
> his hand on the scroll*)

In mounting of damask and ivory
I trust to stay my sylph from flight
in wind's buffeting.
But lest the wind tear her portrait, I should seek out some eminent
painter to make a copy.
                    IX   Idle chatter!
How can I bring to share my couch
one who vies in majesty
with the "Moon and Water" Guanyin herself?[6]
Yet could I find a way
to meet with her in her own person
surely my talk of love
would bring such sweet response
as portrait seems to promise?

---

5. These phenomena, in early Buddhist legends, were the effects of sermons by
abbots of great sanctity.
6. The bodhisattva Guanyin was often portrayed gazing at the reflection of the
moon in water (a symbol of insubstantiality).

I'll trim the lamp and look again more closely.

> *(He holds the lamp closer to the portrait)*

> x   Should such angelic grace
> be encountered in mortal world
> surely it would prove false.

> *(Sound of wind from offstage; his lamp flickers)*

Suddenly a chill gust of wind. I must be careful
   to let no lamp spark light on painted scroll.
Enough now, I shall
   screen my window, sleep
   and search for her in dream.

> *(He lies down to sleep)*

BRIDAL DU *(enters):*
   Long my sleep, but dreamless
    in the shades below;
   ended my life, but unspent
    so many loving thoughts.
   Now beneath the moonlight
    a portrait draws my soul
   where sounds of someone's sighing
    carry on the wind.
I am the ghost of Bridal Du, who died of pining after a garden
dream. Before my death I painted my own portrait and buried it
among the Taihu rocks. I inscribed the portrait with the lines,
   "Union in some year to come
    with the 'courtier of the moon'
   will be beneath the branches
    either of willow or apricot."
After several nights of spirit roaming in the grounds of this shrine, I
was surprised to hear a young scholar call out from the guest room,
"Gracious mistress! Lovely lady!" So plaintive was the cry, it
touched my heart. Secretly I slipped into the room, to find a painted
scroll hung high on the wall. Looking more closely I recognized my
own portrait, and a poem in matching meter had been added. It
bore the signature "Liu Mengmei of Lingnan." "Liu" for "willow,"
"mei" for "apricot"—surely this was predestined! Now with the
consent of my infernal judges I come on this fair night to fulfill the
dream I once dreamed. Ah, bitter suffering!

XIa When scent has left the air
and cold lie powder's traces
and tears start by crimson gauze pane
I fear return
to moonlit haunt of love.
Head swiftly turned in shame,
hair fallen awry,
hands clutch at temples.

So, this is his room.

Lest I mistake the path to Peach Blossom Spring
I linger to ensure
that it is he.

LIU (*recites in his sleep*):

"Union in some year to come
with the 'courtier of the moon'
will be beneath the branches
either of willow or apricot."

Gracious sister!

BRIDAL (*makes a gesture of weeping as she listens*):

XIb Ah, the hurt to hear his cry
a tangled rain of tears
word for word my broken lines of verse.

Can he be still lying awake?

(*She peeps. He cries again*)

From the screened couch
his longings issue in sudden sighs!
Startle him with no clamor
but gently tap the bamboo window frame.

LIU (*wakes with a start*): Ah my mistress!

BRIDAL (*weeps*):

Draw near him now
in form of maiden spirit.

LIU: A sound of tapping on the bamboo frame: is someone there or is it the wind?

BRIDAL: Someone is here.

LIU: Someone at this hour, it must be Sister Stone bringing tea. You are too kind.

BRIDAL: No, not so.

LIU: Then it must be the nun who lodges here in her travels?

BRIDAL: No, not so.

LIU: Curious, curious, not the nun either. Who else could it be? I must open my door and find out. *(He does so)* Ha,

XII of what noble family
is this young maiden
whose beauty startles so?

> *(BRIDAL smiles at him and slips into the
> room. LIU hastens to latch the door again)*

BRIDAL *(folds her hands in her sleeves and composes herself to bow to him)*: Blessing on you, sir scholar.

LIU: May I ask whence you come, young lady, and what cause brings you here at dead of night?

BRIDAL: You must guess, sir.

LIU: Can it be

XIIIa the Weaving Maid of the heavens
surprised by old Zhang Qian
borne by his raft along the Milky Way?
Or her serving maid, Clear-as-Jade,
pursued by Heaven's officers
on her earthly escapade?

BRIDAL: Those you name are celestial sylphs, what would they be doing here on earth?

LIU:

Then you are some mismatched mortal beauty,
"phoenix fated to follow crow"?

> *(BRIDAL shakes her head)*

In some former time and place, did we
"tie our steeds beneath green aspen"?

BRIDAL: We have never met.

LIU: Have you mistaken me for

some hero of romance, Tao Qian
or Sima Xiangru, eloping with Wenjun?[7]

BRIDAL: I have not mistaken you.

LIU: Is it a lantern you are seeking? The *Rites* prescribe

---

7. See scene 10, note 6, for the confusion of two allegories on the subject of a peach-blossom spring. From this confusion the great recluse-poet Tao Qian becomes associated wtih amorous adventure. The bohemian elopement of the Han poet Sima Xiangru with the young widow Zhuo Wenjun is a romantic motif especially common in plays.

"maiden at night walks not without her lamp"
and so you come
red sleeves to share the light by my gauze window.

BRIDAL:

XIIIb I am no goddess
come to shower petals from the air
upon a bodhisattva[8]
nor seek I any lamp to weep
its tears of wax through my studies.
I am no consort Flying Swallow
of flawed repute from former days
nor willing Wenjun
early widowed.
But you, sir, you have strayed
in a butterfly dream among the blossoms.[9]

LIU *(ponders)*: True indeed, I did have a dream.

BRIDAL:

And so with sound of oriole pipes
I search the willow grove;
should you now seek the place of my boudoir
like Song Yu, poet of old,
"try next door or the door beyond."

LIU *(reflects)*: So that's it. In the rear garden, looking west toward
the sunset, I did see a young lady walking there.

BRIDAL: It was myself you saw.

LIU: What family do you have?

BRIDAL:

XIVa 'Mid fragrant grasses
beyond setting sun
I dwell with but my two parents alone.
Sixteen my years,
blameless bloom
leaf-hidden against all breezes
but moved to sighs by spring's leave-taking
and by one glimpse
of the elegance of your bearing.

---

8. Allusion to the *Vimalakirti sutra*: the petals clung to the body of Manjusri's disciple, but not to the saint himself.

9. The classic dream of the Taoist philosopher Zhuang Zi, unsure whether his waking self might not be a butterfly dreaming it was he.

No other errand but to join you,
trim lamp as wind rises,
chat by evening window.

LIU *(aside):* Amazing loveliness in mortal form! Jewel bright as
moonlight, chance midnight meeting: how to respond to her?

(To BRIDAL)

xivb Breathtaking beauty,
loveliest of mortals!
In lamp's glow, sudden bewitching smile!
Still bright the moon—
was this the night fairy raft
rose to River of Heaven?
Out of the dark, beauty adorned you come—
or does a heavenly sylph honor my couch?

(He turns aside again)

But who can tell
child of what family
she presents himself in this fashion?
I must question her further. *(To BRIDAL)* The favor of this visit at
dead of night—can this be a dream?

BRIDAL *(laughs):* This is no dream, it is real—but, sir, I fear you
cannot accept me?

LIU: I fear only that it can't be true. But, lovely lady, if I truly have
your love, then this is joy beyond dreaming—how could I reject
you?

BRIDAL: Then my hopes are fulfilled.

xv From cold secluded vale
a flower you bring to bloom in dark of night.[10]
Unbetrothed am I
as you must surely know,
cherished as daughter of good family.
Tenderness
at peony pavilion,
bashfulness
by rocky path,

---

10. As Wu Zetian, Tang Empress, ordered the flowers to be brought to bloom
when she planned a midwinter tour of her gardens.

rustling of breeze
by study window.
Sharing this lovely night
how precious shall we find
cool breeze and brilliant moon![11]

LIU:

    XVI Soul starts as if in dream
but wakes to find moon
still coolly gleaming.
This sudden splendor—
do we dream now on Witch's Mount?[12]

Now, lady, my gratitude to you for
never fearing
to walk in flower-patterned shade,
never stumbling
crossing the cool green moss,
never trembling
to think your parents deceived,
never doubting
that I am your true love.
See Dipper slant,
petals fold
as flowers sleep in deep of night.
We shall laugh,
sing for joy,
never wind and moon so fair.
Willfully I bend to me
your pliant, fragrant softness,
bringing you distress
but for one passing instant.

BRIDAL: Forgive me, sir, I have one thing only to entreat you.

LIU (*smiles*): Say it, whatever it is, my dearest.

BRIDAL: This body, "a thousand gold pieces," I offer you without hesitation. Do not disdain my love. My life's desire is fulfilled if I may share your pillow night by night.

LIU (*laughs*): You give me your love, my dearest: how could I dismiss you from my heart?

---

11. Wind and moon, commonest metaphor for romance: this is her direct invitation to Liu.
12. See scene 1, note 5.

BRIDAL: One thing more: let me leave before cockcrow, and do not see me off but guard yourself against the chill dawn wind.

LIU: I shall do as you ask. But may I know your honored name?

BRIDAL *(sighs):*

> XVII   Flower has root
> and jade its bed of origin
> but once revealed, the storm may rage too fierce.

LIU: I hope you will come to me each night, my dearest, from now on.

BRIDAL: Sir, it is for you

> the spring breeze opens this first bloom.

Envoi:

LIU:

> Outpour of love, disturbing fragrance
> never met before.

BRIDAL:

> Moon slants from tower, and the gong
> strikes the watch of dawn.
> Clouds of morning pass at night
> to realms none ever saw.

LIU:

> Count the peaks: who knows on which
> the goddess makes her home?

SCENE TWENTY-NINE: *Gossip*

SISTER STONE:

> ia   Taoist priestess, to cowl and cloister born,
> partnerless and childless,
> I tend shrine of Three Pure Ones,
> freshen their drinking bowls, light new incense
> to boom of bell and thud of drum.
> But see this wanton wandering nun:
> what mischief behind that pious front?
>   In worldly matters
>   no such thing as trust;

human friendships
usually harbor doubt.

For three years I have served this Apricot Blossom Shrine established by Prefect Du for his departed daughter. "Clear water reveals the rocks beneath": never the slightest cause for suspicion. But now comes this old dog Tutor Chen and brings along a young scholar, Liu from Lingnan, to convalesce in our guest room. The other day he visited the rear garden and returned in a daze as if some demon had bewitched him. I was already beginning to wonder, and now we have this young nun of Shaoyang, no more than twenty-eight and quite an attractive little thing. She alights here in the course of her wanderings, days go by and she hasn't left yet. Well, during the night there's a sound of chitter-chatter comes from Scholar Liu's room, and I hear a female voice. What's this but our young nun slipping in to see Master Liu behind my back, and he "gratefully accepting his illicit prize"?[1] I'll sound her out when she appears.

NUN *(enters):*

> 1b Taoist priestess, pretty as fairy maid,
> blameless and passionless
> I pace the Dipper in breeze of dawn,
> blow tuneful pipe as clear moon rises.

> *(She sighs)*

> But fairy maids have ever found their mate
> while I remain a lonely supplicant.

> *(She greets SISTER STONE)*

"Only he that rids himself forever of desire
can see the Secret Essences."

SISTER STONE:

"He that has never rid himself of desire
can see only the Outer Pubescences."[2]

Sister nun, it seems your holy wanderings took you last night as far as the room occupied by young Scholar Liu. Was it essence or pubescence you found there?

---

1. A quote, comically misapplied, from Sima Qian's *Records of the Grand Historian.*
2. An even more comical misquotation from the *Daodejing,* the early lines of which apostrophize the mystical qualities of the Way. I have modfied the Waley translation in line with Sister Stone's substitution of *qiao* "hole" for *jiao* "outcomes," the last word of her verse.

NUN: Sister Abbess, what are you saying? Who claims to have seen me?

SISTER STONE: I saw you myself.

     IIa Nun's bright cheeks lightly adorned
    blooming like hibiscus,
    crane-feather cassock
    elegant as river cloud,
    jade headpiece at a rakish tilt,
    smiles sweet as incense smoke,
    what turnout could be more appealing?
    Imagine
    how beneath student's window
    "crystal beams of sinking moon
    twinkled secretly across the bed."[3]

NUN: Which "student" are you speaking of? I'm afraid you are wide of the mark.

     IIb Though young my years and comely my appearance
    mortal yearnings have been washed away
    clear as the moon, ice in a jar of jade.
    What call have you to slight and slander one
    who may certainly claim more propriety
    than an aging beauty like yourself!

SISTER STONE: So now she turns round and slanders me!

NUN:

    Consider
    who brought this student to follow his amours
    in the Temple of Womanly Chastity?[4]

SISTER STONE: Oh! Are you accusing *me* of an affair with this scholar? You are a wandering nun, he is a wandering scholar, if it is acceptable for you to stay in this Apricot Blossom Shrine then why not for him also? But, whereas he used to spend the night in tranquil slumber, the moment you arrive he opens his door in the middle of the night and there is a hum of chitter-chatter. Who was he speaking with if not yourself? I'm going to haul you off and accuse you before the Comptroller of Temples.

(She drags at the NUN's arm)

---

3. A quote from the celebrated love scene in Yuan Zhen's *Story of Yingying*, on which the play *Western Chamber* is based (see scene 10, note 4).

4. Ironically, a convent by this name provides an amorous rendezvous in Gao Lian's play *The Jade Hairpin*.

NUN: Then off we go. It's you who've installed some wandering vagabond in the shrine established by the former prefect. Do you think I'm going to let you go?

(*She drags at* SISTER STONE's *arm.*)

TUTOR CHEN (*enters*):

> IIIa Should you roam these cloud-wrapped terraces
> seeking the dwelling of Master Liu,
> just ask the keeper of Apricot Shrine.

(*He sees the two nuns tugging at each other*)

> What's this? Two nuns competing
> for the favors of some benefactor?
> Each one a "gate of procreation,"
> a Way that can be waded[5]—
> let them "package their jewel" and keep it
> for I'll have nun of it![6]
> One the Elder Sister, one the Younger—
> who's the husband, Master Peng's Jetty?[7]

SISTER STONE: Tutor Chen, you don't understand. I heard Scholar Liu's door open in the middle of the night, and then a murmur of conversation that went on and on. In all good faith I ask this young sister, "Was it you talking to Scholar Liu?" "What do you mean, talking to Scholar Liu?" she says, and I don't mind that, but then she starts babbling about *me* keeping a student in my rooms. Tutor Chen, it's for you to say—who was it lured this young scholar here? I'll have her up before the Comptroller of Temples and get things clear, or my name isn't Stone.

NUN: Then what am I—fickle as water?

CHEN: Silence! You will ruin Master Liu's reputation. Now let there be peace between you.

> IIIb That nuns should have such habits![8]
> True or false, these rumors of "moonlit breezes"?
> All empty prattle, for Master Liu
> is an upright man of learning.

---

5. Chen, Confucian male, ridicules these Taoist women with phrases from their own *Daodejing* to which he gives a salacious twist.

˙ 6. Now he reverts to the Confucian *Analects*, punning on *gu* "sell" (the "jewel" of talent) and *gu* "nun."

7. Master Peng's Jetty lies between the "Sisters" hills in Kiangsi province.

8. This song again puns on homophones from the *Analects* for *gu* "nun."

To Comptroller's court you'll both go
banished from holy orders
for these unholy disorders
that proper scholars will laugh to scorn.

NUN: Well, it certainly doesn't look very nice.

CHEN: You should
straighten your coifs and comb your "flowing clouds"
and look to your tattered cassocks.

SISTER STONE: We will do as you say and desist. Tutor Chen, come eat a vegetarian repast with us.

CHEN: Let us wait until Master Liu can join us.

    IV We linger still in this place of holy peace.

(He weeps)

    A rush of tears to the east wind's prompting!
Sister Abbess, shall we visit the grave of Mistress Du?

SISTER STONE: It's raining.

CHEN *(sighs)*: Alas, locked in spring's chill
rain drips from the azalea blossoms.[9]

(Exit)

SISTER STONE: Tutor Chen has left us. I trust you have come to no harm, Sister.

NUN: Let us try together to find out who it was speaking with Master Liu.

Envoi:

SISTER STONE:
    Free as river mist, we still
        indulge the wiles of the world

NUN:
    for few have reached
        true purity and grace.

SISTER STONE:
    From far Longshan come parrots
        can speak in human tongue

NUN:
    who quarrel long and fierce
        with cage's golden bars.

---

9. The azaleas being red, the rain will have the color of tears of blood.

SCENE THIRTY: *Disrupted Joy*

LIU MENGMEI:
>   I   Water clock has dripped
>   half the watches of night away,
>   moon ascends to zenith,
>   is anything left to burn
>   of the evening's incense?
> Speck of glowing red
>   precious as speck of gold,
> ten slender fingers
>   as tapering shoots of spring:
> to find among mortals
>   a creature so lovely
> turns my heart
>   from other goals.

I, Liu Mengmei, dedicated my life to learning and cherished the worthiest ambitions. Now at Nan'an I have found my love: my northward journey has brought me to the Western Maid herself![1] Her smile "taking captive my heart," she touches me as the evening rain; before the fifth watch is struck, the dawn bears her away. Tonight is a time of our tryst: will she come soon? Truly,

>   let the lotus buds of her feet
>   take but a tiny step
>   and "in the shining candle
>   I will cut a notch" to await her.[2]

But I must be fresh for her arrival, and so I shall take a short nap now.

(He covers his face with his sleeve to sleep)

BRIDAL DU *(enters):*
>   II   On roads of darkness struggling
>   my heart consents not to death
>   for I have found one destined for me
>   who waits in lamplight of lonely room.

---

1. For the Western Maid, see scene 14, note 2.
2. Allusion to two friends of the sixth century who cut notches in the candle to time their composition of poems.

(She opens the door and enters LIU's *chamber)*

See, he sleeps, and yet
no coverlet to ward off chill of spring:
surely he waits for me.
I must wake him. Sir scholar!
LIU *(waking):* Lady, forgive me.

(He rises and bows)

With straightened robe
I hasten in formal greeting.
But have not winds of night and heavy dew
"put all the flowers to sleep"?
BRIDAL: Sir,
my night was long beyond endurance;
sleepless I sat, my thoughts of you alone.
LIU: Lady, how can your footfall be so soundless?
BRIDAL:
By nature leaving no imprint,
no speck of dust
LIU:
object of daytime thoughts
and night's repeated dreams
BRIDAL:
reaching your window
I knew you rested not
LIU:
my heart set all on the coming
of the lady of the moonlight.[3]
Lady, you are later than usual tonight.
BRIDAL:
III Delay so long, so longing-filled,
came from no lack or lightness of my love:
how could my thoughts leave you, my one true joy?
As the night's incense lower burned
taking leave of honored parents
I tidied my needlework by my couch
and followed night breeze, ornaments awry,
too swift my flight for arts of paint and powder.

---

3. These four lines are a pastiche from Tang poets.

LIU: You are too good to me, to show such love. But how can we pass so fine a night without wine?

BRIDAL: Oh, I had quite forgotten: I have a flask of wine, fruit and flowers outside on the verandah. I will get them for you.

(She exits, and returns with wine, fruit, and flowers)

LIU: How kind of you. What fruits are these?

BRIDAL: Green apricots.

LIU: And the flowers?

BRIDAL: "Lovely lady" plantains.

LIU: Then the apricots will be sour as my own unfulfilled ambitions, while the flowers will glow pink as my lady's lovely cheeks. Let us drink a loving cup.

(They drink from the same cup)

BRIDAL:

    IV   Into a cup
    shaped of lotus leaves
    pour the sweet wine.

LIU:

    Nectar you have brewed
    to stir hearts to spring:
    cheeks flush
    as flowerbuds the east wind brings
    to reddest glow in leafy bower.

BRIDAL:

    Then seek to pick
    no rarer fruit nor bloom
    for in this apricot, sir, you must know
    all graces gather
    while this fair plantain flower
    flowers for you.

LIU:

    V   To pursue:
    the flower wilts as lovelorn maid,
    fruit's taste sours tongue
    as thwarted hope of amorous swain,
    yet joy is born as heart of plantain flower
    secretly unfolds
    moistened by apricot fragrance in the night.[4]

---

4. This and some later lines of lovemaking are borrowed from the *West Chamber*

How comes this so?
When dimpled smile appears
on cheeks dizzied by tide of wine
then lip drinks lip in eager draught
and soon
lids droop on loving eyes,
plantain petals stain deeper red,
apricot fragrance fills the mouth.

BRIDAL:

vi Twining,
soaring,
love nest unmatched in mortal world.
In shadowed mystery of night
screened by window's gauze
open and free we loved.
How is it
reaching the hour of bliss
there comes this urge to words?

LIU: Time for sleep now.

BRIDAL: Time for moon gazing:
sit quietly awhile
while Chang E, goddess who knows no jealousy,
makes a third with us.

LIU:

vii No other company
than finely traced flower shadows.
Sleep now, my sweet,
my darling, sleep.
Beauty of spring night perfected
so soon to break against midnight bell.
On former nights, beloved,
our loving made you bashful,
robbed you of speech;
tonight your eyes
need not so tightly close.
Sleep now, while I
cradle your swelling breast,
guarding with this kerchief
firm flesh now moist with sweat

Medley, the long ballad by Dong Jieyuan which was the immediate predecessor of Wang Shifu's famous play.

and slender curve of waist
against the springtime's chill.

YOUNG NUN (*stealing unobserved onstage, followed by* SISTER STONE):
"The Way that can be told of"—
who's going to tell?
"The name that can be named"
gets a bad name![5]

(*Sound of laughter from* LIU *and* BRIDAL
behind the door of his room)

Listen, Sister—can't you hear someone in the young scholar's room? How can that be me?

SISTER STONE (*listening*): Sounds like a girl. Quick, let's knock.

(*They do so*)

LIU: Who's there?

SISTER STONE: The Abbess, bringing tea for you.

LIU: So late at night?

SISTER STONE: You seem to have a guest, sir.

LIU: No, I haven't.

SISTER STONE: A lady guest.

LIU, BRIDAL (*in alarm*): What's to be done?

SISTER STONE (*knocks insistently*): Sir, open at once. The patrolmen are at hand, we must avoid any disturbance.

LIU (*panics*): What to do, what to do!

BRIDAL (*laughs*): No cause for alarm. My family are residents of this neighborhood; if the Abbess insists on making trouble. we can bring an accusation of procuring against her!

        VIII If she wants you to open
she must be more polite!
But how can we fend her off
here by gauze-clad window
till rise of morning star?

Master Liu, you may unbolt the door. I shall
conceal myself here in the shade
cast by this beauty's portrait.

---

5. A corruption of the opening lines of the *Daodejing*, commonly used in plays for the entrance of a comic nun.

SISTER STONE, NUN (*bursting in, giggling, as LIU opens the door. BRIDAL has gone to stand in the shadow, and LIU tries to block their view of her*): Our congratulations!

LIU: On what?

SISTER STONE, NUN (*trying to peer past LIU, still hindered*):

> ixa Deep in the sounding watches,
> close-barred the serried convent gates,
> whence comes this enchantress
> to stir to flame as spark to kindling?

LIU:

> Peer as you will
> what is to be discovered?
> Something I've hidden in my bed,
> in my box, in my sleeve?

> (*He can hold them back no
> longer. As they press past him there is a sound of
> wind from offstage and BRIDAL slips out*)

See, you have set the lamp flickering.

SISTER STONE: Surely something moved, yet there is nothing here but this beauty's portrait—has the spirit of the painting come to life?

> ixb Subject of painted screen
> steps forth to dance and sing
> and to an assignation, sir student, with you.
> Say this is no demon—
> what shade flickered by as that wind blew?

Sir, what painting is this?

LIU:

> A masterpiece of grace,
> sacred image I carry on my travels
> to serve with silent prayers,
> which you have shattered with your bellowing.

SISTER STONE: So this is it. I would never have known. Hearing the murmurs coming from your room overnight, I suspected this young nun our visitor. Now I understand. You must excuse me, sir, while I have a word with her.

LIU: Granted.

NUN (*sarcastically, to SISTER STONE*):

> x Now is settlement to be made
> in Comptroller's court, or privately?

LIU:

> So, you have insulted not only
> a law-abiding scholar
> but someone else as well!
> Sister Stone, you have wrecked
> a night of sweetest slumber.

(Exit SISTER STONE with NUN. LIU laughs)

One charming adventure, two nasty-minded scolds. What a let-down, and how they startled my fair one!

Envoi:

> I would roam candle in hand
> by your side in depth of night
> while the spring breezes bring us
> torment without cease.
> Elder Sister's Mount recedes,
> Younger comes into view[6]
> as borne aloft by dream
> I fly to the Faery Isles.

SCENE THIRTY-ONE: *Defensive Works*

TWO OFFICERS *(one of the army, one of the civil administration):*

> Ia   Sea before us, river at our back,
> still we must guard against new dust
> stirred up by frontier strife.
> Now double walls enfold our Yangzhou as we
> "look down on the river, wine cup in hand."[1]

Officers civil and military of Yangzhou, we offer our respects. His Excellency the Commissioner Du Bao has erected an additional outer wall in the face of depredations by the rebel Li Quan. Today

---

6. See scene 29, note 7.
1. Quote from the rhymeprose, "The Red Cliff," by Su Dongpo, which alludes to campaigns around Yangzhou by the generalissimo Cao Cao in the third-century wars of the Three Kingdoms.

we hold a banquet to celebrate completion of these works, and here comes His Excellency now.

STAFF, ATTENDANTS (*enter, with DU BAO at their head*):
> 1b Files of retainers three thousand strong,
> a fort secure against two million.

> (*They are greeted by the TWO OFFICERS*)

DU BAO:
> Yangzhou, set in splendor to top the world:
> highest tower we ascend to gaze afar.

> (*He looks out*)

ATTENDANTS:
> To guard the northern approaches
>   an elder sage and bold

DU:
> whose cunning lacks, alas,
> "a force worth myriad men."[2]

ATTENDANTS:
> Gold Hill is Heaven's gift
>   to be our "Triple Gate"[3]

DU:
> our bodies as jars of iron
>   shall set a Great Wall here.

The efforts of our soldiers and civilians, led by you gentlemen, civil and military, have swiftly completed double defensive walls about Yangzhou.

ATTENDANTS: This is the fruit of Your Excellency's farsighted strategy. We of lowlier station now humbly present a cup of wine, that like the heroes of old you may "carouse at the corner of the wall."

DU: Excellent. Now let me observe the view from the new tower. (*He does so*) A most majestic wall! Truly,
> moat unparalleled north of River
> first tower of all the Southern Huai.

ATTENDANTS: Let the wine be served.
> 11a Stone layered on stone to cloud-brushing height,

---

2. It was said of a Song general that he had "a hundred thousand men in his bosom," that is, his strategic skill was equivalent in value to a force of that size.
3. These are impregnable island strongholds, the first local, the second to the north in the Yellow River region.

chill waters mirror soaring battlements
guarding our hills and streams
like walls of iron, moats boiling with steam
a thousand miles about the Huai.

ALL:

Lofty watchtowers top the battlements,
below our wine cups banners stream in the wind.
Scent still in our nostrils
of Yangzhou's pride, the garnet rose,[4]
our memory still of tears for the southern land
when "sea turned to mulberry groves."[5]

DU: What are those hills that rise in front there, forty or fifty of them, gleaming white like frost or snow?

ATTENDANTS: That is the salt from the various regions, stored here ready for the merchants to collect.

DU: Where are the merchants?

SALT MERCHANTS (enter):

Produce of seashore,
    piles of whitest jade,
treasure of salt wells
    turns to yellow gold.

Greetings from the merchants to Your Excellency.

DU: Merchants, I presume these stocks of salt will be for you to claim in return for your provisioning of our frontier armies. This salt, like

11b   snowy silver hills that rim the sky:
produce of the seas converted
to summer fodder, autumn grain.
A fair sight, this field of salt
awaiting distribution to the suppliers of our troops.

ALL:

Lofty watchtowers top the battlements,
below our wine cups banners stream in the wind.
Scent still in our nostrils
of Yangzhou's pride, the garnet rose,
our memory still of tears for the southern land
when "sea turned to mulberry groves."

DU: We will drink no more. I rejoice in the abundance of our

---

4. The "garnet rose" (*qionghua*) was a flowering tree, celebrated for its beauty and unique of its kind, which grew in the garden of a Yangzhou temple in Song times.
5. Proverbial expression for the process of historical change.

supplies, for whose protection you, my staff, must take all due measures.

ATTENDANTS:

> III Officers civil and military
> setting the frontier watch,
> setting the frontier watch,
> careful to harm no field or grove,
> to disturb no scholar, merchant, or artisan.

ALL:

> We await onslaught of nomad horde,
> ball and arrow, spear and standard.
> When dust clouds darken border
> startled eyes will behold
> the patterned armor of our stalwart generals.

ATTENDANTS:

> IV Days of good omen
> we sacrifice before City God,
> returning thanks to the spirits
> for safety of our land.
> Set up banners,
> issue arms and armor:
> who will resist our sorties?
> Let archers stand
> by their embrasures.

DU:

> V Lines of defense
> laid in accord with classic strategies,
> officers civil and military
> solemn and sternly ready,
> await frontier beacon
> and gun's first report.

Envoi:

> To Chang'an's royal walls, cloud-wrapped
>   by warmth of rainbow banners
> from stout Box Pass a thousand li
>   distant as a dream.
> But now new cliffs startle the eye
>   rising in endless line
> guarded by men whose spirit
>   challenges the stars.

SCENE THIRTY-TWO: *Spectral Vows*

LIU MENGMEI:

      1a Clouds at dusk over gilded cloister,
      prayer flags flap in gentle breeze;
      as bell's reverberation fades
      already heart grows warm.
      Sweet as orchid or musk
      comes love to musty bookworm.

Too early yet.

      Flower shadows tremble
      patching the moonlight.

(He trims the lamp)

      Shield a scene so lovely
      from too brilliant a flame.

(He laughs)

    "Too soon we reach the end
      of an intriguing book
    but the enchanting mistress
      watched for, never comes."

When my fair one visited the other night we were surprised and disturbed by the nuns. Tonight I plan to use this time of waiting to chat with the Abbess in the lecture hall and allay her suspicions.

(He mimes half-closing the door, and leaves)

      Door ajar awaits my visitor
      but oh, what heart have I
      for the call I now must pay?

(Exit)

BRIDAL DU *(enters):*

      1b Lone spirit, timid lest night breeze
      stir my belt ornaments.

(She starts in alarm)

      A shadow moved—is someone there?
      No, only a cloud
      steals light from the moon.

Here is master Liu's study. But ah, where is he?
　　Lamplight sends shadows flickering
　　through dimness of studio,
　　may its gleam reveal
　　the beauty of this spirit form
　　for lamp's flame is one with flame
　　of my own loving thoughts.

(She sighs)

My rendezvous with Master Liu is hidden only from mortals; it is known to all in the shades. *(She weeps)*
　　However deep the temple hides
　　in bamboo shade
　　how can wind's rustling be kept from men's ears?
　　And how can man and wife withstand the miles
　　of winding road through yellow springs of Hell?
　Wishing to speak, but no sound comes,
　　threatening to frown, but brows remain clear.
　Clinging still to vows beneath blossoming branch
　　yet fearful that this self lives only in dream.
Although my name is entered in the ghostly registers, the mortal body of Bridal Du remains incorrupt. My days in the shades are numbered, I am to return to the world of light. On that day long past it was for Master Liu I died, today it is for Master Liu I return to life. Our destiny as man and wife is clear to my mind. But if I do not speak out tonight, how long can we continue this masquerade between mortal and ghost? Still I fear my story cannot fail to startle Master Liu. Truly,
　　words of a night
　　　between man and shade
　　a hundred years
　　　of connubial, joy.
LIU *(reenters):*
　　　II　Bamboos lean on the breeze
　　across painted balustrades.

(Offstage sound of bird calling; he starts)

　　A startled crow alights again
　　by the kiosk where petals fall.
Ha, the door is wide open now.
　　Jade Maiden from the skies descended,
　　her car a purple cloud.

BRIDAL (*emerges from his study to greet him*): Welcome, Master Liu.
LIU (*bows*): Welcome, my love.
BRIDAL:

> I trimmed the lamp
> awaiting my beloved.

LIU:

> Dear one so constant,
> so true to me.

BRIDAL: While I waited I composed a pastiche of lines from Tang poets.
LIU: Please let me hear it.
BRIDAL:

> "Matchmakers I'd engage
>   yet stand uncertain
> so cold the moon
>   on hills as moonlight pale.
> Whose voice that sings
>   this dirge of spring's passing?
> Specter returned to enchant
>   the amorous Ruan Zhao."[1]

LIU: You have an excellent talent, my dear.
BRIDAL: What visit were you making, sir, so late in the night?
LIU: Last night the nuns disturbed us, so tonight while waiting to welcome your arrival I visited the Abbess to make sure she was safely in her cell. I did not expect you so early.
BRIDAL: I could not wait for moonrise.
LIU:

> III How could poor student earn such bliss,
> hand of celestial being
> more true, more loving than mortal woman.
> Gentle is she, smiles flowering in her eyes
> as I, like one whose bite
> inch by inch encroaches on heart of sugarcane,
> I enter by degrees the realm of sweetness.

But those nuns the other night,

> a senseless storm cut short our spring
> and you, my dearest,
>   your tortuous night visit wasted

---

1. For Ruan Zhao, see scene 10, note 6.

your timid spirit jangled by these alarms—
yet instead of showing anger
you come to retrace the path of our joy.

BRIDAL:

　　ɪᴠ　All unprepared for their rude irruption
my senses scattered in fright.[2]
As moon dimmed behind surging cloud
I hid in shadow of portrait scroll;
then, startled, stumbled
among the rocks by the path.
Wild escapade
for one so delicately nurtured!
Risking too
should rumor breathe as far as my father's house
the torrent of my mother's angry words.

LIU: What distress I have caused you, my dear. How can I be worthy of such love?

BRIDAL: You are distinguished above all men.

LIU: May I ask whether arrangements have been made for your betrothal?

BRIDAL:

　　ᴠ　No red-wrapped pledge in return
for horoscope of bride-to-be
did my parents yet receive.

LIU: What kind of husband do you wish for?

BRIDAL:

　　A young scholar whose devotion
would match my own.

LIU: I am such a one, full of love for you.

BRIDAL:

　　Your youth, your loving heart
captured my slumbering soul,
which can find rest no longer.

LIU: Then be my wife, my dearest.

BRIDAL:

　　Since your home
is in far Lingnan

---

2. In fact, Bridal was much more calm and collected than Liu himself, but here she is obviously laying claim to the timidity required of a decorous young lady.

> who knows but that you intend me
> to serve you as concubine?

LIU: Not as concubine, as wife, for I am yet unmarried.

BRIDAL (*smiles*):

> Is there no other house
> of venerable lineage intertwined
> that yours should accept the graft
> of plant from place unknown?

Please tell me, do your parents still live?

LIU: My late father was an officer of the court, my late mother held the rank of First Lady of the County.

BRIDAL: Then you are the scion of an official house. How is it you remain so long unmarried?

LIU:

> VI   Orphaned I drifted year to year
> finding in beauty's common run
> none to command my devotion.
> Who would ride with me
> as with Xiangru in scented carriage
> or how could I like Xiao Shi
> ascend to Heaven in faery love
> with daughter of ducal house?[3]
> So lightly you dispense your smiling graces—
> I tell you true
> were you less perfect
> in talent and youthful beauty
> still could I never bear to see our union
> short-lived as drying dew.

BRIDAL: Since this is your desire, sir, then let a matchmaker be found for our engagement, so that I need no longer suffer such fears and alarms on your account.

LIU: Tomorrow morning I shall present myself at your residence to pay my respects to your honored parents and ask your hand in marriage.

BRIDAL: If you come to my house, ask to see only myself: it is early yet for you to meet my father and mother.

LIU: So you are truly of distinguished family!

---

3. Liu here alludes to two classic elopements of penniless scholars with rich men's daughters. For Sima Xiangru, see scene 28, note 7; for Xiao Shi, see scene 33, note 4.

(BRIDAL *laughs*)

What is behind this?

    VIIa Purity so abstracted

    of beauty sweet as incense, clear as jade,

    banishes thought of mortal origin.

BRIDAL: If not mortal, must I then be some celestial creature?

LIU:

    But why these lone night journeys

    no handmaid in attendance?

Please let me know your name.

(BRIDAL *sighs*, LIU *turns aside*)

    Fearful of disclosure

    like Flying Garnet of the poet's dream.[4]

If you are so unwilling to reveal your name, I can only believe you
to be some celestial sylph, with whom a poor student like myself
dare hold no further tryst:

    though fairy maid bestow her love on me

    how could I hope to escape

    the wrath of those who rule celestial courts?

BRIDAL:

    VIIb Rank my poor self with heavenly spirits

    and you declare my premature death.

LIU: But if not a creature of Heaven, how can you be mere mortal?

BRIDAL:

    What harm in speaking out

    in the close secrecy of our elopement!

LIU: If not mortal, then you must be some sprite of flowers and
moonlight, some demon of romance.

BRIDAL:

    Then in search of truth

    uproot the flower, but do not wait

    for rise of dawn and moon's decline!

LIU: Come, tell me your story.

BRIDAL (*starts to speak, then hesitates again*):

    My secrecy

---

4. Xu Hun of Tang times dreamed of meeting a fairy maiden in the magical Kun-
lun Mountains. He included her name in a poem, and in a subsequent dream received a scolding from her for such an indiscretion.

threatens this joyful rendezvous
yet words rise to my lips
only to sink again.

LIU: My dear,
this way you will not say,
that way you will not say.
Who'll be the one to learn your secret
if not your student lover?

BRIDAL:
Try to tell—
how to tell?
This is my fear, sir scholar:
"betrothal makes wife,
elopement only concubine."
I will tell my story
when incense smoke has sealed our wedding pact.

LIU: If this is your wish, let us light incense and I will take you as proper wife with formal vows.

LIU, BRIDAL (*after formal prostrations*):
    VIII Spirits of Heaven, spirits of Heaven,
accept the incense of this pact.
Liu Mengmei, Liu Mengmei,
sojourner in Nan'an
met with this maiden's favor
takes her for his wife.
In life one room,
in death one tomb;
should heart prove false to word
then death be the reward
swift as this incense melts away.

(*BRIDAL weeps*)

LIU: Why do you weep?
BRIDAL: I weep without wishing to, so deeply does your devotion move my heart.
    IX Wandering scholar committing
your love to me alone,
surely this is no casual oath
lightly to be rejected.
Still my history sticks in my throat
as though tongue were cut out.

Heed now my Lord of Spring,
hold calm your spirit;
I who so long have hesitated
still fear my words
will send you stumbling to the ground.

LIU: What do you have to tell me?

BRIDAL: Sir, where did you find this portrait here?

LIU: Within a mound of Taihu rocks.

BRIDAL: Am I as pretty?

LIU (*looks at the two together, and starts in surprise*): Why, it is the very image of you!

BRIDAL: Do you understand now? I am the girl in the portrait.

LIU (*offers thanks to the portrait, shaking his folded hands*): I did not burn incense in vain. Please, my dear, explain how this can be.

BRIDAL:

> xa   Master Liu,
> now hear my history.
> The sometime Prefect of Nan'an,
> Du Bao, is my own father.

LIU: But His Excellency Du Bao was transferred from here to the Commissionership at Yangzhou: why should he leave his daughter behind?

BRIDAL: Trim the lamp.

(LIU does so)

> As brighter burns the lamp
> so shall hidden truths be clarified.

LIU: Will you tell me your gracious name, lady, and the years of your age?

BRIDAL:

> Hear now the marriage pledge of Bridal Du
> of years sixteen
> fitted for matrimony.

LIU: So my darling is Bridal Du!

BRIDAL: But sir, not yet your mortal darling.

LIU: Not mortal! What then, a ghost?

BRIDAL: A ghost.

LIU (*in alarm*): Oh, terror, terror!

BRIDAL:

> Stand back, sir,
> listen closely to my story.

And I have asked you not to fear
for already I am at the midpoint
between ghost and living woman.

LIU: My dear, how have you been permitted to keep me company here in the world of light?

BRIDAL:

xb   Relegated to the courts of Hades
I found there pity for my gentle birth,
descendant of Prefect Du of Nan'an.
The Lady Registrar I entreated
for permit to return to life,
the Mistress of Reincarnations granted
fulfillment of my remaining span,
which you, sir, are foreordained to share.
Your solemn vow to take me as wife
fills my cold bones with new warmth.

LIU: Now that you are my wife I shall have no more fears. But how am I to secure your return? How can the moon be scooped from the water's surface, or flowers plucked from the void?

BRIDAL:

xIa   Sun, moon and stars still light me,
I walk my way through ghost in form
for still my spirit endures,
years that remain to me
I am permitted to take up again.

Sir, are you not versed in the canonical texts?

My heart is one
whether mortal my being or no:
who is to tell
illusion from reality?
Though seemingly you must
pluck flowers from the void
you are not called on to retrieve
moon from lake's surface.

LIU: Since you are to return to life from death, may I know the place of your untimely burial?

BRIDAL: It is beneath the flowering apricot tree that stands by the Taihu rocks

xIb   there in my beloved garden
where lonely dreams
beneath the apricot's shade
ripened bittersweet as ripening fruit.

LIU: What if you should run from me to some other goal?
BRIDAL:

> In faithfulness as pure
> as incense in secluded vale
> moonlit at dusk
> I'll stay with you, though road
> lead far as the nine springs of Hades.

LIU: So cold you must have been!
BRIDAL:

> Frozen body and soul
> in coldest chastity.

LIU: What if I should cause your soul to start in terror?
BRIDAL:

> XII Through caverns dug by spreading roots
> leads path to mortal world
> and my cold flesh already
> you have caressed to warmth.
> Fear not to start my spirit
> winging away in terror
> for at sight of you my body and soul
> must reunite imperishable.

LIU: There is so much to tell.
BRIDAL:

> Truly, "one night of wedded union
> one hundred nights of bliss"
> but the tale we tell is of a love
> three incarnations long.

LIU: I'll question you no more. But it will be difficult for me to secure your return single-handed.
BRIDAL: Sister Stone will help you.
LIU: Not knowing how deep you lie, I can't be sure how soon we can get through to you.
BRIDAL:

> XIII Ha, a man shows his worth
> by "going through to the end."
> Though three feet round
> the rocks piled on my coffin,
> take tempered spade and dig your way to me
> where shades' cold breath disperses
> so close to light of day.

(Sound of cockcrow offstage)

xɪv   After my endless sleep of endless nights
now cockcrow takes me from your pillow:
untimely cry, banishing dreams of home
of sleeper beyond the frontier
so far from mortal world.
Waning moon
cannot withstand the cuckoo's call
borne on dim-lit breeze of dawn;
and yet I have told
only one part in three of my story.
xv   Halting words
so slow to leave this clove-scented tongue.
Yet you untied my clove-perfumed girdle,
to you belonged my clove-fragrant chastity.
Be swift to act now,
do not delay,
my love is too deep for many words.

(Sound of wind rising offstage)

Ghostly garments swirl in the wind: I go.

(She hastens offstage)

LIU *(filled with alarm and doubt):* Uncanny! Liu Mengmei, son-in-law
to Prefect Du: surely this was a dream? But let me try to recall: her
name Bridal, her age sixteen years, and buried beneath the flowering apricot in the rear garden. Ah, no, it was flesh and blood I held
in my arms, we loved as mortals love. What perversity makes Miss
Du proclaim herself a ghost?

BRIDAL *(reenters):* You are still here, sir.

LIU: Why are you back so soon?

BRIDAL: I have one last instruction for you. Now that you have
taken me as your wife you must look to this at once and not delay.
For if you hesitate, my story is already revealed and I can come to
you no more. Put all your mind to this and let nothing go wrong.
For if I do not return to the living, then I can only follow you with
hatred from the nine springs of Hades below.

(She kneels to him)

xvɪ   Master Liu, you alone
are the lord of my rebirth.

(He kneels in his turn to raise her to her feet)

Have pity on me
—do not make me hate you from the yellow springs below, while
you
revile me as an importunate ghost!

(She exits with a ghostly wailing, and
pauses to look back at him)

LIU *(softly, to himself)*: So it is a ghost who possesses Liu Mengmei.
She has told me her story so openly, and with such troubled grief.
Whatever the truth, I can do nothing but follow her instructions.
The first thing then is to consult with the old Abbess.

Envoi:

Waking from dream, where now
   the clouds that wrapped my love?
The troubling recollection
   a skirt patterned with golden butterflies.
I'd seek the lonely grave—
   but who will guide me?
Let messengers summon
   the Lord of Purple Light.

SCENE THIRTY-THREE: *Confidential Plans*

SISTER STONE:
   1a Priestess in hibiscus robe,
   hair too short to coif and pin,
   by incense stove and booming bell
   teeth clack in reverence as head bows low.
Light breeze murmurs like palace pipes
but in deserted park
   the Rainbow Skirt hangs cold and still.[1]
Where lotus flowers cluster by poolside path
a scent of incense purifies the night.

---

1. "Rainbow Skirt," here used to symbolize Bridal Du, was the favorite dance of
the Tang beauty Yang Guifei; see scene 23, note 29.

Mortals must age,
plans go awry,
dreams end too soon.
Love too deep
a shallow grave may hold
'neath westering sun.

This Apricot Shrine of mine commemorates Bridal Du. His Honor
the former Prefect originally entrusted it to the charge of Tutor
Chen, but for these past three years he has seldom visited other
than to collect rents and offerings. He did manage to solicit contri-
butions from local gentry and commoners and erect a memorial to
Prefect Du after his departure. But, when I chanced to walk by the
memorial hall yesterday, there wasn't just pig dung lying around
but human dung as well. Chen Zuiliang, Chen Zuiliang, why don't
you get someone to give it a good sweeping? Just compare Miss
Du's shrine and tablet: incense and water changed daily, everything
clean and neat and imposing. Truly,

"don't trust the Confucian
   with his bagful of classical quotes;
real concern is the mark
   of the follower of the Tao."

LIU MENGMEI *(enters)*:

        1b Private words in clandestine tryst
        not for public knowledge:
        long I hesitate
        before voicing them abroad.

(He greets SISTER STONE*)*

Fragrance of falling petals
   fills the hall of gold.

SISTER STONE:

Has sight of special blossom
   disturbed your youthful heart?

LIU:

Fairy maiden still delays
   descent in mortal form.

SISTER STONE:

Thrice has she seen the Eastern Sea
   turn to mulberry groves.[2]

---

2. For this metaphor for time and change, see scene 31, note 5.

LIU: Sister Abbess, not once since my arrival here have I had the good fortune to view the central hall of your shrine. May I see it today?

SISTER STONE: Most appropriate. Please follow me. *(They reach the shrine)* Looking up you see the golden palace of the Jade Emperor.[3] Beneath, at either side, stand the Lady of the Eastern Peak and the Consort of the Southern Dipper.

LIU *(bows as a bell is struck offstage):*

> Emeralds massed in Heaven's height,
>> far terraces of jade,
> banners proclaim the lofty court
>> of the Lord Most High.
> Now that Feng Yi the River Spirit
>> comes to strike his drum
> I understand the flute-playing skill
>> of the noble daughter of Qin.[4]

What a magnificent shrine! But I don't understand the inscription on this tablet: "The Ruler, Miss Du." Which "ruler" was this?

SISTER STONE: The character that looks like "ruler" needs an extra dot on top to make it read "host," that is to say, "tablet lodging the spirit of Miss Du." We are waiting for some person of distinction to inscribe the dot.

LIU: And who is Miss Du?

SISTER STONE:

> 11a   You ask the origin
> of this Apricot Blossom Court.
> It was built in a year now past
> by Commissioner Du Bao
> for interment of his cherished daughter,
> Bridal, dead at sixteen years.
> So swift was his departure
> to post of new eminence
> that inscription on spirit tablet
> remains incomplete.

---

3. The Jade Emperor is the highest Taoist divinity.

4. This is the same "daughter of ducal house" referred to in the previous scene (scene 32, note 3). She eloped and ascended to Heaven with her lover Xiao Shi. A homonym of the surname Xiao means "flute," hence Liu's reference in this line, where she clearly stands for Bridal herself, to her "flute playing." This, in turn, is a euphemism for fellatio: the lady's name was Nongyu, "Fondle Jade." See also scene 18, note 11.

LIU: Who conducts the sacrifices and sweeps her grave?

SISTER STONE:

> A bequest of land
> provides the upkeep of the shrine
> but a "host" is lacking
> for the yearly Cold Food offering.

LIU (*weeps*): Your story reveals Miss Du to be my own beloved wife.

SISTER STONE (*startled*): Is this true, sir?

LIU: It is the most solemn truth.

SISTER STONE: Then you know the days of her birth and death?

LIU:

> 11b   "Till you know about the living
> how are you to know about the dead?"[5]
> Dead in a bygone year
> her birth is now.

SISTER STONE: When did you receive the news of her death?

LIU:

> "In the morning I heard" of her,
> "in the evening died"
> she who could content me so.[6]

SISTER STONE: Since you were man and wife it is for you to offer the incense before her spirit tablet.

LIU:

> "Till you have learnt to serve men
> how can you serve ghosts?"[7]

SISTER STONE: Did you ever meet this lady who was your wife?[8]

LIU:

> This Apricot Blossom Shrine
> was our Terrace of the Prince of Chu[9]
> though you were kept in the dark.

SISTER STONE: Which night was this?

LIU:

> Two nights ago you made yourselves a nuisance.

---

5. *Analects of Confucius*, XI, 11 (Waley translation).

6. *Analects*, IV, 8: "In the morning, hear the Way; in the evening, die content!" (Waley translation).

7. *Analects*, XI, 11 (Waley translation).

8. An arranged marriage could be conducted by proxy, and it was therefore possible for man and wife not to meet until years after their wedding.

9. See scene 1, note 4.

SISTER STONE: Sir scholar, you are possessed by a ghost! I don't believe it!

LIU: If you don't believe me I'll produce an apparition to convince you. Bring me a brush. I shall complete the dot on the character "host," and it will move.

SISTER STONE: How can this be? —But here is a brush.

LIU *(inscribes the dot on the character):*

>My brush turns stone to living thing
>
>as husband furnishes "host."

Look there, look there!

SISTER STONE *(amazed):* Wonderful, wonderful, the host truly moved! Oh, young mistress!

>IIC I'd say the apricot before the tomb
>
>was an uninscribed tablet to her
>
>but it was Liu the Willow, all along,
>
>that stirred up the incense stove![10]

Since this is your wife, sir, you should

>drum the pot
>
>through three-year mourning in graveside hut.[11]

LIU: Rather than that I shall raise her from the grave.

SISTER STONE:

>Such marvelous powers:
>
>you must be Yama, King of the Dead!

LIU: But I need men, workmates, to help.

SISTER STONE:

>You are her man,
>
>she is your mate
>
>and the ghosts are at your command.

LIU: I want you to wield a spade also.

SISTER STONE: The Ming Dynastic Code prescribes execution for any person, instigator or accomplice, who opens a coffin to view the corpse.[12]

>Pity that a Song dynasty scholar like yourself

---

10. The reference here is to the willow-wood dolls magicians used, punning of course on the meaning of the surname Liu.

11. A mixture of Taoist and Confucian prescriptions. The Taoist sage Zhuang Zhou drummed on a pot and sang when his wife died, regarding death as inconsequential. "Three years in graveside hut" was the Confucian rite for parents, not for wife.

12. This kind of anachronism is not unusual in plays. What is unusual is the self-conscious, joking use of the anachronism displayed in the remainder of Sister Stone's aria.

should not have read the laws of Imperial Ming.
Don't take this as some ordinary task
digging a posthole or wall's foundation.

LIU: There's nothing objectionable, it is the young lady's own instructions.

　　　　IId　A plea to you
　　　　from one in the springs below;
　　　　whose orders should surpass
　　　　those of the lady herself?

SISTER STONE: Since it is the young mistress' own command, let me
select an auspicious day. *(She consults her almanac)* As it happens,
tomorrow is the *yi-yu* day of the cycle, appropriate for reopening a
grave.

LIU:

　　　　Happy day
　　　　ruled by jade dog or golden cock
　　　　and not the ox.[13]
　　　　Now to secure the help
　　　　of some noble mover of mountains.

SISTER STONE: My nephew Scabby Turtle can help. But what will
ensue when word of this gets out?

LIU:

　　　　Once she returns to life
　　　　let rumor stop,
　　　　argument cease.
　　　　No plunderer of tombs
　　　　sought here to glut his lust on buried beauty!

One thing more: when the young lady has returned to life she will
need medicines and restoratives.

SISTER STONE: Tutor Chen keeps an herbalist's store. We'll just pre-
tend that this young nun who is visiting us fell afoul of an evil
spirit and needs a tonic from him.

LIU: Please see to this at once.

　　　　"Better to save one human life
　　　　than build a seven-story pagoda":
　　　　this is no children's game!

---

13. In *yin-yang* theory, each day was appropriate or inappropriate for various ac-
tivities depending on the animal by which it was ruled in the zodiacal sequence.

Envoi:

SISTER STONE:

> Moist clouds recall his dream,
>> rain swirls like dust

LIU:

>> west of the city wall
>> I seek the magician Li.

SISTER STONE:

>> Reaching at last the spot
>> where the Withdrawn Maiden died[14]

LIU:

>> I part the withered grasses
>> to gaze on the lonely grave.

SCENE THIRTY-FOUR: *Consultation*

TUTOR CHEN:

> Years of poring o'er the classics
>> taught me a thing or two:
> I traded satchel for bag of herbs
>> heavy as a rock.
> Now my houseboy with respect
>> addresses me as "Squire"
> and when I chance to walk abroad
>> the neighbors call me "Doc."

When I lost my post as tutor my only recourse was to set up as herbalist. Let's see what customer today will bring.

SISTER STONE *(enters):*

>> 1 In Heaven as on earth
>> good sense is hard to find:
>> dreams and false illusions
>> in one whose longings lodge
>> among the springs of Hades!

Tutor Chen, may your enterprise prosper!

CHEN: Welcome, Sister Abbess.

SISTER STONE: A fine display you have here, with the placard

---

14. See scene 27, note 2.

"Learned Doctor" bestowed on you by the former Prefect Du, and your "choicest herbs from every source." What are these two clods of earth for?

CHEN: They come from beneath a widow's bed. Dissolved in a little fresh water they will cure a man possessed by ghost or demon.

SISTER STONE: And what's this strip of cloth for?

CHEN: That's the seat of a he-man's pants. When burnt and the ashes swallowed it will cure a woman sick from ghost or demon.

SISTER STONE: Very well then, how about an exchange, five inches of your pants for three feet of the earth I sleep on?

CHEN: I'm not sure you're that much of a widow.

SISTER STONE: Ha! And how much of a he-man are you?

CHEN: Enough of this. What is the purpose of your visit?

SISTER STONE: I'll tell you. It's that young nun of ours, who

          IIa   young and thoughtless
             joined a procession for the River Spirit
             and returned too late at night.

CHEN: Is she possessed of demons?

SISTER STONE:

             Who knows in what deserted waste
             she fell beneath the spell of what foul fiend?
             In evil month of year accursed
             departed never to return.

CHEN: Shows some want of discretion!

SISTER STONE:

             Truth to tell
             your powers, Prince of Healing,
             surely will withstand
             those of the living Yama, Lord of Hades.

CHEN: Is she living or dead?

SISTER STONE: Dead some days past.

CHEN: A dead person still has a mouth that can take medicine? Very well, we'll burn this trouser patch and administer it with heated wine.

          IIb   Magic potion from lands across the sea
             this trouser patch of a potent male.

SISTER STONE: Medicine of this sort, I've had some already.

CHEN:

             Dame, how can you remember
             what a potent male is like?
             Just cut a square inch and burn it,

mix the ashes in sweet wine,
wedge the teeth apart and pour it down.
No common remedy
but a tonic for the soul
surpassing magic root
of fabled Resurrection Tree of Western Ocean.
SISTER STONE: My thanks to you.

Envoi:

CHEN:

Female companions join the procession
to honor the River God

SISTER STONE:

naught can prevent the sickness
brought on by amorous heart.

CHEN:

Cave hidden deep beneath the cliff
guarded by tight-locked gate

SISTER STONE:

urge the lady healer
forth from her flowered bank.

SCENE THIRTY-FIVE: *Resurrection*

SCABBY TURTLE (*spade on shoulder*):
 1 Balls bigs as gourds, like warts on a hog:
no pants.
Dig the soil and it all comes apart:
no chance.
Live bride not good enough, he's after a ghost:
no sense.
Caught robbing graves, get buried alive:
no thanks!

(He laughs)

Here you see Scabby Turtle, nephew of the Abbess of the Apricot
Blossom Shrine. The Abbess has agreed to Scholar Liu's request to
open up Miss Du's grave. What a laugh—says he and Miss Du are

going to be man and wife again. Well, devil talk or not, I've brought some spirit money along; I'll just stick it here on these Taihu rocks and light a stick of incense.

(*Enter* SISTER STONE, *bearing a jar of wine,*
and followed by LIU MENGMEI)

SISTER STONE:

> II Where lies the maiden formed of jade?
> Where lies the maiden formed of jade?
> By her tomb the west wind
> whistles through tangled weeds.
> To the love song "Bamboo Stems"
> responds "The Maid Revives";
> can the cuckoo's calling reach across
> the Brocade River of her birthplace?[1]
> Sorrow lingers in this pit
> but the dream of three lifetimes goes on.

LIU MENGMEI: Sister Abbess, we have reached the rear garden, and all that greets the eye is a pavilion turning to a heap of rubble, brambles and brushwood all around. I seek her brocade sash and find only flowers of twining creepers that fold at night; I pursue her skirt of gauze where greening tendrils lengthen with the spring. I remember these Taihu rocks as the place I found her portrait, but all seems confused as dream, lost in uncertainty. What is best to be done?

SISTER STONE: Don't distress yourself, sir: here is the place, this mound beneath the apricot.

LIU: O my dear mistress, how pitiful! (*He weeps*)

SCABBY: What are you weeping for? Let's get on with it.

(*He burns the paper spirit money*)

LIU (*prostrates himself*): Now manifest your holy powers, Spirit of the Hills, Presiding Deity of this place.

> IIIa Ashes of money sacred to the spirits
> cling to grassy slope,
> red glows our brazier
> beneath smoke-clad hills.

SCABBY:

> Let's hope our digging doesn't fall

---

1. For the legend of Wangdi, turned into a cuckoo at his death, see scene 10, note 2.

beneath the bane of baleful Jupiter
as down we go
in search of this young lady's heels.

LIU: O Presiding Deity of this place, we are reopening this grave for the sole purpose of restoring Bridal Du to life. Let us find no lifeless corpse, but a living woman,

for you as a spirit should rise above jealousy
as we conquer our fear of offending the spirits;
let her beauty, her smiling ways remain unchanged
as if you, Spirit of Earth, gave up your own daughter.
See, spring buds the apricot—

a time to break the ground.

SISTER STONE, SCABBY (*beginning to dig*):

IIIb   Soil like cement beneath the hoe.
Lady, are you here in your narrow grave?

LIU: Be very careful. (*He peers down*) You've reached the coffin.

SCABBY (*drops his spade in alarm*): The officer? Help, we're dead men!

LIU (*waves his hand impatiently*): Silence!

> (BRIDAL DU *groans offstage,*
> *startling the three of them*)

SISTER STONE, SCABBY: That's a living spirit, it made a noise!

LIU: Careful lest you frighten her.

> (*The three of them kneel by the stage entrance,*
> *miming the act of opening the coffin*)

SISTER STONE: The nails have rusted through and the joins have split open. I'd say the young mistress has been off somewhere playing at "clouds and rain"!

> (BRIDAL *moans offstage,* LIU *goes*
> *to lead her forward*)

LIU: The lady is here as she said. A heavenly fragrance greets me, her beauty is unchanged. Ah, see,

though lid be stained with clay
no ant has entered crack or crevice.
These mottled boards of fragrant wood
carried her lovely form
as a soft couch toward the Yellow Springs
and the earth was unguent to her flower-like body.

> (*He supports* BRIDAL, *who*
> *totally lacks the strength to stand*)

Lean gently on me
as I raise your sleeping face
careful lest harm befall
the funeral stone placed in your mouth.

(*BRIDAL vomits a gobbet of mercury*)

SCABBY: A lump of silver, must be a quarter of a pound, how about this as my reward?
LIU: This is a magic essence the young lady has borne in the manner of dragon or phoenix; it must be treasured as a precious heirloom. You will receive some other reward.

(*BRIDAL opens her eyes and
gives a sigh*)

SISTER STONE: The young lady has opened her eyes.
LIU: Heaven has opened its eyes! Oh, my dear mistress!
BRIDAL DU:
　　　IV Can this be real, or is my soul
　　　falsely roused from evil dream?

(*She shades her eyes*)

Light of sun, moon or stars
hard for mortal eyes to bear,
fearful too the wind's capricious breath.

LIU: She fears the wind's blowing; what shall we do?
SISTER STONE (*taking the weight of BRIDAL from him*): Lay her in this peony pavilion while we administer drugs to restore the soul. You, sir scholar, must cut a piece from this trouser patch.

(*LIU does so*)

SCABBY: Let me provide an extra ingredient or two.[2]
LIU: No need. Warm up a little wine.

(*He mixes the drugs in the wine and
applies it to BRIDAL's lips.*)

　　va Life-giving potion
　　enters the jade-smooth throat.

(*BRIDAL vomits some of the medicine back again*)

---

2. In line with the trouser patch motif, Scabby probably breaks wind at this point.

Ai-yo, it spills across her bosom.
Mistress, take more. Of three mouthfuls
not half has stayed down.

> *(He examines her.)*

Ah, good, good,
spring blooms again in cheek and limb!
BRIDAL *(looking about her):* Who are these people?
Surely a gang of scoundrels
come to disturb my peaceful grave.
LIU: I am Liu Mengmei, "Willow Dream-of-Apricot."
BRIDAL:
My eyes blur, yet I fear
you are not he who stood
beside apricot or willow tree.
LIU: This Taoist sister will bear witness.
SISTER STONE: Don't you know me, young mistress?

> *(BRIDAL gazes at her but does not speak)*

vb Still too soon for you to recall me.
LIU: Do you recall this garden?

> *(BRIDAL still does not speak)*

SISTER STONE: No wonder,
all blurs as in a dream.
BRIDAL: But which is Master Liu?

> *(LIU answers, and BRIDAL shows*
> *sign of recognition)*

Ah, sir, you are truly a man of your word.
I thank you deeply for persistence
like one who, seeking snakes,
moves every blade of grass,
for patience like his who waited
by tree where rabbit died.[3]
Let the jewels be saved from my coffin, and all the rest be thrown
into this pond.

---

3. See scene 13, note 3 for the story of the rabbit or hare. It is a classic illustration
of stupidity rather than patience, and oddly inappropriate for Bridal to use at this
point.

(The three do this with exclamations of distaste)

> The world shall see me fresh remade
> as these waters wash away sepulchral traces.

LIU, SISTER STONE, SCABBY: What a trial for you, lady, to have slept these three long years.

BRIDAL:

> Years that flowed
> "carrying as dust
> the springtime of my youth."

LIU: Lady, you should stay no longer in this place of wind and dew. Let us find a proper place for your rest.

> VI   Desperate effort
> rescued you from living hell,
> now fragrant waters shall bathe your body,
> finest foods restore your strength.

BRIDAL: Where will you take me?

SISTER STONE: To your room in the Apricot Blossom Shrine.

BRIDAL: Where the dust of my sepulcher will be washed away
> by gentle showers in the shrine of love.

Envoi:

LIU:

> Heaven's gift
>   the rouge that tints her cheek

BRIDAL:

> lead me now hence
>   from this terrace of the shades.

SISTER STONE:

> There was a purpose
>   in the entering of this pit

LIU:

> inept as I am, I claim
>   your hand in spirit union.

SCENE THIRTY-SIX: *Elopement*

Enter BRIDAL DU, on the arm of SISTER STONE

BRIDAL DU:

    1 Smile one moment,
    vacant stare the next,
    unbroken threads of yearning thoughts,
    realm of dream ever before me.

SISTER STONE:

    Startled from fragrant slumber
    you left the underworld
    your hearse your carriage
    to the terraces of Heaven.

BRIDAL: Aunt Stone,

    I struggle forward,
    relapse in weakness,
    tender infant you must raise anew.

BRIDAL, SISTER STONE:

    The fear remains
    of arms embracing mist,
    enfolding but a shadow.[1]

BRIDAL:

  Moth-antenna brows afflicted
    by sorrows of three autumn's frosts,
  dreams lingered with setting sun
    across the grassy tomb.
  Petals of wildflowers lighted
    on skirt of silken gauze,
  sleep wore away
    the rouge of cheek and lip.

SISTER STONE:

  As bright clouds hover in windless air
  or cold incense burns again at touch of flame,
  goddess or ghost, not to be known until
  she walks again the hills of faery love.

BRIDAL: Aunt Stone, I lay dead for three years, but love's devotion brought a secret pact to new fulfillment. I owe my rescue to Master Liu and yourself for your faithfulness. Now you restore me hour by hour with wine and health-giving tonics, and over these past days I have felt a gradual revival of vigor.

---

1. Allusion to the old legend of how King Fucha·of Wu opposed his daughter's marriage. She died of love, but later appeared to her lover by the side of her grave. When her mother tried to embrace her, she encountered nothing but mist.

SISTER STONE: Very good. Scholar Liu has approached me already half a dozen times, asking me to set a date for your wedding.

BRIDAL: It is too soon, Aunt. First we must send to Yangzhou to ask my father and mother to appoint a matchmaker.

SISTER STONE: How conventional! But I leave it to you. Let me ask you, are you able to remember your earlier life?

BRIDAL:

II My earlier days
I now recall.
Spring-afflicted I languished, pined,
then, spring-strolling, fell prisoner
in a world of dream beyond enduring.
The portrait of my youthful beauty
I painted myself for him to find.
How earnest he was, how worshipful,
gazing as on some sprite of Heaven,
gazing till glassy-eyed,
calling as on the name of Guanyin,
calling till tongue grew numb.

SISTER STONE: I heard some of this myself. But how did you learn of it in the shades below?

BRIDAL:

Though buried deep in earth
my ears burned to hear him.
So strongly moved by such devotion
from death's cold shade I sought the light
and stepped forth living from the infernal springs.

SISTER STONE: Here comes Scholar Liu now.

LIU MENGMEI *(enters):*

III So fair yet buried in the dust
now gracing anew this world of mists and flowers.
See now the smile that wakes as she sets
her hair with golden pin,
see now the sway of trailing sash
as she steps forward.

(They greet each other)

Bridal—my wife!

(BRIDAL turns aside bashfully)

Dearest mistress, I entered the earth itself to carry you forth, a fairy maid.

BRIDAL: Resurrected, I owe you a debt greater than to my own father and mother.

LIU: Then let us be joined in marriage this very night.

BRIDAL: Dazed and confused, I am still not fully recovered.

SISTER STONE: Just now she spoke of renewed vigor: she is trying to trick you, sir.

BRIDAL: Sir, I must remind you of the words of Mencius, that a young couple must "await the orders of the parent and the arrangements of the go-betweens."

LIU: Although a few days ago I did not "bore a hole to steal a glimpse of you,"[2] still I did bore into the grave to reach you. I see that you have recovered your ability to quote the classics.

BRIDAL: Sir scholar, our condition has changed. The other night I was a wandering spirit; now I am a living woman. A ghost may be deluded by passion; a woman must pay full attention to the rites. Let me explain:

> IV From the shades I have stepped
> into the white light of day.

(She prostrates herself before him)

> Accept this salute, in thanks
> for lifetimes past, present, and future
> but grant, before you take me as wife,
> the services of a go-between.

(She weeps)

> And when the nuptial cup is drunk
> let my honored parents be present.

LIU: Their joy will shake the heavens when I take you, as my wife, to visit your honored father and mother. As for a go-between, Sister Stone will serve.

BRIDAL: But why so impatient, sir?

> Through how many dusks
> have we already waited side by side?

LIU: "What night is this?"[3]

BRIDAL:

> So amorous a student!

LIU: Little demon!

BRIDAL *(laughs):* The demon is in you, sir! It is not I

---

2. An act proscribed in *Mencius*, III, part 2, III, 6.
3. From a song of courtship in the classic *Book of Songs*.

       emerged from ghostly state
       to bewitch with deviltry!
LIU: But why this waiting?
BRIDAL *(bashfully):*
       Returned from death's bourne
       I fear the shock of "clouds and rain."
       You have my living self before you
       yet you must grant my body
       a spell of rest.

                 (She turns aside)

       If only for a moment
       I could calm my loving thoughts!
TUTOR CHEN *(enters):*
       va Empty steps to secluded court,
       flower shadows deep across green moss.

                 (He knocks)

       Anyone there?
       Chen Zuiliang seeks Scholar Liu.
LIU *(startled, like* BRIDAL *and* SISTER STONE *also):* Here's Tutor Chen,
what shall we do?
BRIDAL: Aunt, we must retire at once.

                 (Exeunt)

CHEN:
       Curious
       this sound of women's voices from gauze window
       and someone holding the door shut from inside.

                 (Knocks again)

LIU: Who is it?
CHEN: Chen Zuiliang.
LIU *(opens the door and greets him):*
       Your visit honors me,
       my pardon for delay
       properly to adjust headdress and gown. . . .
CHEN:
       Something peculiar. . . .
LIU:
       What's so "peculiar"?

CHEN:

> vb   Not Heaven's portals these
> yet there in the court the breeze seemed to bring
> angelic voices to my ear?

SISTER STONE *(reenters):* Ah, Tutor Chen!

LIU: Tutor Chen says he heard ladies' voices within. It must have been you.

SISTER STONE: Yes,

> on errand transcendental
> comes a young nun to our lotus land.

CHEN: The same one who was here a few days ago?

SISTER STONE: No, another one.

CHEN: Very good, our Apricot Blossom Shrine is flourishing, surely the beneficent influence of Miss Du from the shades. This was the purpose of my call, to invite Master Liu to share a hamper with me at noon tomorrow by the young lady's tomb. I'll take my leave now.

> Time presses, but
> today we plan tomorrow's meeting
> to drink a cup by the young lady's grave.

LIU:

> An honor, sir,
> since barely a cup of tea does the Abbess offer.
> I shall attend you.

CHEN:

> In your own good time.

(Exit)

LIU: Good, Tutor Chen has gone, please ask Miss Du to come back.

(BRIDAL reenters)

SISTER STONE: What now, what now? Tomorrow Tutor Chen intends to visit the young lady's grave. If all comes to light, number one Miss Du will be labeled a demon, number two Commissioner Du will be accused of failing in her upbringing, number three you, sir, will be ridiculed for allowing yourself to be bewitched, and number four I shall have to take the blame for opening the grave. What's to be done?

BRIDAL: Sister Abbess, what do you suggest?

SISTER STONE: Lady, Scholar Liu will soon be leaving for the examinations in Hangzhou. Your best course is to go along with the wedding he proposes, have the lad find a riverboat for you, set sail

late in the night, and disappear from here. What do you think?
BRIDAL: Let it be so.
SISTER STONE: There is wine ready here. The two of you must make your prostrations before Heaven and earth.

(They do so, and take the winecup in their hands)

LIU:

vIA Three lifetimes, a single union,
for harmony all our days
we share this loving cup,
offer the golden chalice
swifter than spring wine drunk by graveside
to flush the cheek with peach bloom.

BRIDAL (grieving):

Spring longings interred my body
like his who slept three years in drunken dream.[4]

Now one thought distresses me:

what match for your dragon-like, phoenix-like bearing
is this poor body of wood and clay?

LIU: How can you ask this?

vIB Though strange the road to our union
yet what doubts could I have
on this our wedding night?
One blissful night
more precious to this "willow"
than the three locust trees of the ducal court;
my study graced by the nymph Orchid Fragrance,
why fear comparison with the romantic Liu Yung?[5]

BRIDAL (sighs):

Hidden longings possessed my ghostly form
too feeble to resist
the surge of the male force.

Master Liu, I am still a virgin.

LIU: We spent nights of love together: how could your precious body have remained intact?

BRIDAL: That was my ghostly form: only now do I bring you my real self.

---

4. One of the early "tales of marvels" tells how Liu Xuanshi drank "thousand-day wine" and fell so drunk he was presumed dead. After three years in the grave he was roused from his slumber by the wine seller.
5. The fairy maid Orchid Fragrance had the same surname as Bridal; Mengmei has the same surname as Liu Yung, a Sung lyricist celebrated for his many loves.

It was my wandering soul visited my lover,
my body remains virgin as before.

BOATMAN (*enters, and sings two ditties*):[6]
Lively lass courts tavern wight,
home at dawn with never a care:
"Goodwife made me stay the night,
needed my help to dress her hair."

Autumn asters, blooms of spring,
gossips all must have their tea.
Lock your storeroom, don't let 'em in,
or with your stock they'll soon make free.

SCABBY TURTLE (*enters*): Hey boatman, boatman! Passengers for Hangzhou!

BOATMAN: Right here, right here! (*He mimes the act of rowing across*)

SCABBY: There's a boat ready outside the gate, please step aboard sir.

SISTER STONE (*preparing to take her leave*): Master Liu, mistress, please take care on your journey.

LIU: There is no one to look after my wife, won't you come with us, Sister Abbess? I will see that you are rewarded when I receive my official appointment.

SISTER STONE: But I have made no preparations. (*Aside*) Yet when the truth comes out I shall be implicated—flight is the best plan! (*To LIU*) Very well then. If you will give my nephew something and tell him to tidy up after me, I will come with you to serve your lady.

SCABBY: Suits me.

LIU: Then I will give him this jacket.

(*Removes his jacket and gives it to SCABBY*)

SCABBY: Thank you, sir. But who's to take the blame if the truth comes out?

LIU: Just say you know nothing about it.

SCABBY: Very good then, I'll leave you.
Shaven-headed kid masquerades as a Daoist
while the Abbess acts as maid!

(*Exit*)

LIU, BRIDAL, SISTER STONE (*boarding the boat*):

---

6. Based on two "Servants' Poems" by the Tang poet Li Changfu.

VIIa　A solitary sail leaves Nan'an in the darkness
in flight to Hangzhou, lovers' goal.
LIU *(as BRIDAL weeps):* But why these tears?
BRIDAL:

> To leave for earth's far corner,
> to leave for earth's far corner!
> Three years I dwelt here,
> three years this was my grave;
> unable in death to return home
> only now, living, may I rejoin my parents.

BRIDAL, LIU:

> "What night is this?"[7]
> Endless our thoughts,
> boundless our joy.

LIU:

> VIIb　Like Qiannü's wandering soul[8]
> I bear you back to life,
> hibiscus flower fresh-plucked.

> *(BRIDAL sighs)*

But why fresh tears now?
BRIDAL:

> So helpless, so alone,
> so helpless, so alone,
> a perfume sachet lost in deep woods,
> a gold hair ornament crusted in clay:
> where in Heaven or mortal world
> would my heart find its desire?

BRIDAL, LIU:

> "What night is this?"
> Endless our thoughts,
> boundless our joy.

SISTER STONE: The night grows late, tell the boatman to moor, time for you both to sleep now.
LIU: Romantic setting of moonlit deck, bliss of wedding night, how to describe this joy?

---

7. See above, note 3.
8. Qiannü, heroine of a Yuan play from which *The Peony Pavilion* draws much inspiration, wandered in spirit to join her lover, leaving her body apparently at death's door until spirit and lover returned together.

VIII   Moonlit breeze at Blue Bridge,
ancient scene of faery love,
dispels the shadows of Hades' stream.

BRIDAL: My love, never before today did I understand what happiness this mortal life can bring.

Three stars of the "Heart,"
two starry lovers
overcame the seven-starred coffin board.[9]
Tonight I come to you
whole in body, full of love,
yours in every desire.

SISTER STONE:

Out on the river
you swathed yourselves against the cold,
now you may take your ease.

LIU:

How could so small a boat
bear burden of anxious frowns?
Happy slumbers await us
far from the terrors
of Mount Tai's "Ghost-scaring Cliff."

IX   Our mutual debt of love
withholds us from the Birthless Realm.[10]

BRIDAL:

Where now the grave of my long waiting
like her who turned to rock, so long she gazed
for sight of absent husband?

Ah my love,

the sea from whose dark depths
you drew me back to living world
is still no deeper than my love for you.

---

9. An elaborate conceit: Antares and its two companion stars (part of Scorpio) form the "Heart" constellation, projected in a poem in the classical *Book of Songs* as propitious for lovers. The "lovers" are Herdboy and Weaving Maid, Altair and Vega, star-lovers who are permitted an annual meeting (seventh day of the seventh month) across the Milky Way. The "seven-starred" board is the floorboard of the coffin, in which seven holes were drilled.

10. Buddhist concept of a realm beyond birth and death. By her return to life Bridal has of course renounced any such goal.

Envoi:

LIU:
> In secrecy departing
>> beneath the shifting moon

SISTER STONE:
>> fair breezes blow on purpose
>> to escort the nuptial pair

BRIDAL:
>> no onlooker understands
>> the mystery of this barge

SISTER STONE:
>> only the happy bride
>> knows all there is to know.

SCENE THIRTY-SEVEN: *The Alarm*

TUTOR CHEN:
> "Treetop catkins
>> motionless in light airs
> humming verses on a spring stroll,
>> how late the shoots this year.
> In the end, a hundred years
>> nothing but a dream,
> blossoms fair as Western Maid
>> buried by last night's storm."[1]

My gratitude to the former Prefect Du compelled me to undertake the care of his daughter's burial place. Yesterday I arranged with Scholar Liu to pay a visit to the grave, and that is my errand now.

(He walks on)

> Grotto gate unlatched
>> still wrapped in cloud;
> no matchmakers, yet the wild grass
>> multiplies apace.

I'll call for admittance. *(He does so)* Ha, this gate has always been kept tight shut, yet today it stands open. I'll pay my respects to the

---

1. Pastiche of lines from four Tang poets.

bodhisattva. What's this? Cold and neglected, no incense lit, no lamps burning. And where is Miss Du's spirit tablet? I'll see what Sister Stone has to say about this. *(He calls her name three times)* Gone home. I'll call my friend Liu. Friend Liu! Master Liu! Still no answer. *(He searches about)* Tchah, Scholar Liu gone too, as soon as his sickness was cured. No respects on arrival, off again without a word of farewell. Not the way to behave, not the way to behave! I'll have a look in the living quarters. Ai-yo, Sister Stone's moved out as well! Ceremonial chimes, pots and dishes, bed and bedding, all gone without a trace! A mystery! *(He reflects for a moment)* That's it. The other day there was talk of some young nun, and yesterday I heard voices. Liu Mengmei has been up to something here! They must have left in the night. Not the way to behave, not the way to behave! But let him be, I'll go through to the rear garden and pay a visit to the young lady's grave.

(He walks on)

i Moss thickens and ages on secluded path.
Moon-watching kiosks, sheltering pavilions
long shuttered up.
Here long ago we laid our jewel to rest.

(He looks about him)
Oh, but where once the grave mound was piled high now all is level! How is it that
no trace of tomb remains?
Have foxes, rabbits burrowed and brought it down?
These Taihu rocks have shifted to one side, only the apricot tree stands as before. *(He starts in alarm)* Ai-yo, grave robbers have violated the young lady's tomb! *(He weeps and cries aloud)* Ah Heaven, my young mistress!
ii What scoundrel hardened his heart to break this tomb?
What buried treasure prompted this cruel scheme?
Ah young mistress, if only you had been pledged in marriage years ago, then your body could have found its resting place![2]
But no jade mirror given as betrothal pledge
could light the shades for her.
Solitary she lay,
worms threading her skull,

---

2. In the burial ground of her husband's family.

tree roots pushing between her bones,
no warning of this calamity.

I have it! Liu Mengmei is a man of Lingnan where grave robbing is a commonplace.[3] He has moved the coffin to some spot nearby, but cut off one corner as proof and sent it with a demand for ransom money. The villain is convinced that once Commissioner Du learns of this he is certain to come forward with a ransom. The coffin must be buried somewhere near at hand. I'll search for it. (*He discovers the coffin*) Ai-yo, half-hidden among these tufts, surely this is the red-lacquered coffin head, and these the rusty coffin nails! I'll pry it open. . . . Heaven! Where is my young mistress's corpse? (*He looks about*) A board floating on the surface of the pond! That's it, they have thrown my young mistress' body in the stream, the callous brutes! Ah Heaven, why, why,

> III   how could you let her vanish beyond trace
> like that world whose ashes lay
> beneath the Kunming Lake?[4]
> Here was no chain-link skeleton of bodhisattva[5] —
> why then this "moon-and-water" fate?[6]
> Tears washed red petals from her lotus cheeks
> as under black moon of the shades
> she plunged anew into karmic sea.

Now I must see that the pond is drained and her body recovered.

> Sifted and scattered, jade-like bones
> will be hard to reassemble:
> better to have laid her from the first
> in watery grave.
> How vicious, how cold this thievish eye,
> pitiless of youth or beauty
> in deadly lust for gain!

The sage Confucius said, "If a tiger or wild buffalo escapes from its cage or a precious ornament of tortoise shell or jade gets broken in

---

3. No doubt a canard, but Lingnan, in the far south, was regarded as remote from civilized ways; see the references to the "poisonous south" in scene 6.

4. When the Han Emperor Wudi made this lake in his capital at Chang'an in the second century B.C., workmen dug down to a layer of black ashes, which a Buddhist monk interpreted as the residue of the world catastrophe that ended an earlier era (*kalpa*).

5. In Buddhist belief, the bones of a bodhisattva are interconnected like the links of a chain.

6. See scene 28, note 6 for the "moon-and-water" depiction of the bodhisattva Guanyin.

its box, the keeper cannot escape the blame."[7] I shall go first to report this to the prefectural office at Nan'an so that the malefactors may be apprehended; then I must leave this very night for Yangzhou to inform Commissioner Du. That old bawd Sister Stone

IV   well knew the grave held gold and jewels

and Liu Mengmei, grave robber

> worse than he who broke a royal tomb
> for scrolls of ancient days.

Ah my young mistress, how could he

> burst like a housebreaker
> these walls of silver and gold?

Envoi:

> The rifled tomb
>> becomes a road to office,
> no mound remains
>> where grasses riot in spring.
> All innocent, you have been made
>> a partner in these misdeeds;
> only the criminal
>> drinks deep and sleeps till noon.

SCENE THIRTY-EIGHT: *The Scourge of the Huai*

Enter LI QUAN with AIDES

LI QUAN:

> Ia Hero above the common ruck,
> drums clamor, crimson banners wave.
> Three years of ceaseless action,
> broidered battle skirts creased and rent
> thrumming on my swordblade I ride
> carved saddle awry.

First of all thugs am I, Li Quan,

heart bound to barbarous overlords;

---

7. *Analects*, XVI, 1. The final clause is commentary by the Song scholiast Zhu Xi.

a "flip of my toe" fills "nature's moat";[1]
the south must quake before my hordes.
I, Prince-errant of Jin, on the orders of my masters have ravaged the region of Huaiyang for three full years. Now I learn that the Jin have completed their mobilization of troops and supplies for a great southern expedition, which I am to spearhead. I must discuss strategy with my wife, my old lecher. Aides, summon her.

AIDES (*shouting in unison*): Our Prince summons his old fletcher!

OLD CRONE (*enters, bearing a bundle of arrows*): Here I am, and here are the arrows I've just fletched.

LI (*at once amused and angered*): What's this, crackbrain?

CRONE: Your majesty said to summon the old fletcher to discuss strategy.

LI: Rubbish! I called for Dame Li, what's she got to do with arrows?

CRONE: Well, I make 'em, she's your butt!

(*LI chases her offstage*)

DAME LI (*enters*):

> 1b Deep in curtained harem
> deepest strategies
> are hatched by brigandess.

(*She greets LI*)

Long life, great prince!

> Your nightlong ferocity at the frontier
> has thoroughly worn me out—at the front 'ere.

Prince, husband, I was tired out and fast asleep. What do you have to consult me about?

LI: I have learned that the Lord of Jin is moving south, and I am under orders to spearhead his advance by attacking Huaiyang. But I've been reflecting that Yangzhou has Commissioner Du Bao to guard it and isn't likely to be taken in a hurry. What's best to do?

DAME LI: As I see it, if you invest Huaian, Commissioner Du will be bound to advance to the rescue. If I then lead a splinter force against Yangzhou I can cut his communications and we've got him.

LI: Deep, deep! Madam, with a plan like this, I'm scared of you myself!

---

1. This nonsensical line is the result of a muddled quotation. As the Southern Song was falling before the Mongols, a defecting general threatened to flatten the walls of the Song capital with a flip of his toe and to cut the flow of the Yangzi River ("nature's moat") with a crack of his whip.

DAME LI: And when were you anything *but* scared of me yourself?

LI: All right. Before I was made prince I was a henpecked bandit, and now I've been ennobled I'm a henpecked prince.

DAME LI: Exactly! Now hurry along and off with you to attack Huaian.

LI:

        IIa Rally our marching banners,
        onward the vanguard presses,
        ranks of a thousand men
        surge of myriad steeds.
        Tum-tum the drum
        tum-tum the drum
        Huaiyang trembles as we come.

AIDES:

        IIb Tigress of our host
        raging in majesty,
        interlocking battle plans
        dictated from distaff side!
        Laugh and jeer
        laugh and jeer
        Huaiyang quakes as we draw near!

DAME LI: Now hear my orders, Prince-errant of the Great Jin: No matter where your armies pass, not one solitary female is to be taken into your possession. Any contravention of this and I'll have your head in a court-martial.

LI: I wouldn't dare!

                  Envoi:

DAME LI:

        Sandstorm at dusk
          on ancient battlefield

LI:

        while tented warriors imitate
          the fashions of the court.

ALL:

        Now beneath our Marshal's
          flag of brightest red
        bird-shaped ornaments in her hair
          leaning in disarray.

SCENE THIRTY-NINE: *Hangzhou*

LIU MENGMEI:
> 1 Mirror like white shell gleaming
> no longer buried in dust.

BRIDAL DU *(enters)*:
> Toilet new-made,
> I mark my reflection.

LIU:
> Spectacle of Qiantang's tidal bore
> banishes quiet of study.

BRIDAL: Ah husband,
> last night a faery perfume
> stole on us from beyond the clouds
> as the cassia in the moon
> burst into flower.

LIU:
> Yet time hangs heavy on man and wife,
> sojourners in a strange city.

BRIDAL:
> Then let us call for wine
> and drink a cup together.

LIU:
> Raging river tide,
> myriad feet of snow

BRIDAL:
> a sudden thunderclap
> across the Dragon Gate.[1]

LIU: Man and wife together we have reached Hangzhou, the new capital Lin'an. Renting this house has furnished a place for me to study the classics and histories. But the time of the examinations is still far off, and one far from home falls prey to sad thoughts. How can they be relieved?

---

1. A fish that leaped the Dragon Gate (Yumen Gorge on the Yellow River) became a dragon; this was a common metaphor for success in the examinations. Bridal sees a portent of Liu's future success in the spectacle of the famous tidal bore on the Qiantang River at Hangzhou, just as in her second song above she refers both to lovemaking and to examination success by the "moon cassia" allusion.

BRIDAL: I already sent Sister Stone for a jar of wine to ease my lord's melancholy. She has not come back yet.

LIU: That's good of you. My dear, there's something we haven't spoken of. In the beginning you told me merely that you were the daughter of a neighboring family, moved while in the shades to feelings of love, so that with little ado we became man and wife. Throughout our journey I have never asked for further explanation. But was it true that we saw each other by chance in the garden of the shrine? How could it be that your line of verse, "beneath the branches either of willow or apricot," alluded to my name? What magical foreknowledge was this?

BRIDAL *(laughs)*: Good Master Liu, my story of seeing you in the garden was pure invention. But in my former life

> 11a I saw you in my garden dream,
> willow sprig in hand, and on your lips
> a plea for a poem from me.

No sooner had I begun to compose it than you carried me off to the peony pavilion.

LIU *(with a smile)*: Was it nice?

BRIDAL *(smiles back at him)*: Alas, just at the nicest part a shower of falling petals startled me into waking. From that time on my spirits could not settle and I fell grievously sick:

> Loving heart by loving heart betrayed
> true devotion found no true response;
> predestined mates engendered debt of love.
> But force of passion too strong to destroy
> brought life to me
> and a new chapter to the story of Bridal Du.

LIU:

> 11b I listen in amazement;
> yet my own passion
> brought me to believe your living presence.
> I feared our ghostly lovemaking
> would anger the minions of the shades,
> your grave too strong a barrier
> between worlds of light and darkness;
> but loved so truly from the realm below
> it was my lot to guard your body from harm,
> to bring you from the grave
> and lay before you now
> the splendors of this imperial city.

SISTER STONE (*enters with jar of wine*):
    "My route passed by Red Phoenix Palace,
    I bought my wine at Gold Carp Lodge."[2]
Master, mistress, there's something you should know. Buying wine on the riverbank I saw young scholars from all over the country on their way to the examination halls. Sir, take care not to miss the supreme event.

BRIDAL (*flustered, as is* LIU *also*): My lord, you must leave at once.

SISTER STONE: The name of this wine is "Joy to the Prize Candidate."

BRIDAL (*raises her cup*):

    IIIa One night of loving harmony
    disturbed by two words, "rank" and "fame."
    To cheer you, three cups of Imperial brew
    that of four graces—
    flower and willow, man and moon—
    both man and moon may come to full perfection.
    Five watches past, steeds halt at palace gate
    and hubbub fills the six great boulevards.
    Talent like his whose poem
    seven paces were enough to complete[3]
    will take you to the moon's eight-jewelled terrace;
    then drunk with joy of spring
    within the nine-fold palace gates;
    a ten-mile tour of victory
    will be your glorious return.

LIU:

    IIIb Ten years by study window
    until in the "frozen nines" the apricot flower opens.[4]
    Horoscope's eight characters[5] proclaim
    a wife resplendent, matching husband's glory:
    your carriage, crafted from the seven fragrant woods,
    bears you to audience in the Six Palaces

---

2. Lines on "spring strolling" in the capital by the Tang poet Yin Yaofan.

3. The celebrated story of the third-century poet Cao Zhi, who met the challenge of his brother the emperor by completing a poem within the time needed to take seven paces. Note that the present song plays on the sequence of numbers from one to ten, the succeeding song reversing the order.

4. The "frozen nines" are the nine-times-nine days following the winter solstice. Metaphorically, Liu Mengmei after long study is ready to "bloom" in the examinations, just as the apricot flower (*mei*) blooms in the coldest part of the year.

5. Two each for the cyclical names for year, month, day, and hour of birth.

and to bestowal of noble patent
inscribed on five-colored silk.
Blest is the fruit of your heartfelt commitment
to the four womanly virtues
of conduct, speech, appearance, and household thrift
and to the three obediences
in turn to father, husband, son.
Gold characters two fingers wide will bring
the news of my examination honors;
one single parasol of state will shade
triumphant husband on his swift return.

BRIDAL: My lord, I recall the lines I composed for inscription on
my portrait.

IV   My union with the "courtier of the moon"
will surely be achieved now
as in one supreme effort you essay
examination before the steps of gold.

Then with your high place secured we shall travel together to present ourselves before my father and mother,
whose loud huzzahs must ring
for daughter from the shades
now mounted to the height of Heaven's bliss.

Envoi:

BRIDAL:

Truly brilliant
shine my husband's talents

SISTER STONE:

destiny impels
to meet the time of challenge.

LIU:

In the powdered boudoir
count the passing days

LIU, BRIDAL, SISTER STONE:

till from Heaven afar descends
the sound of joyous laughter.

SCENE FORTY: *In Search of the Master*

CAMEL GUO (*enters, with his baggage slung from a carrying pole*):
>   1   Ups and downs of life's long road
>   to be a gardener was my sole concern
>   in Master Liu's house of scholarly line.
>   No trade was ours,
>   our simple wants
>   from orchard trees
>   simply supplied.
>   But lengthening years
>   have aged the trees past bearing:
>   the orchard given up
>   where now to seek my master?
>   At a loss, I worry
>   where to find food and clothing.
>   Under master's eye
>   servant's work's well done;
>   trees will fruit no more
>   when the master's gone.

All my life I, Camel Guo, have supported myself growing fruit for the Liu family. But you'll admit it's a very strange thing: when Master Liu was home I could pick a hundred ripe fruit from every tree, but once he'd left all I got was a hundred maggots. Even if a few good fruit did manage to form somehow, the young lads stole every last one. With no master to protect me everyone cheated me blind. In the end I got fed up and crossed the ridge north in pursuit of my master. I traced him as far as this Apricot Blossom Shrine, where he was recuperating from a sickness. But here I find the gate sealed up by order of Nan'an prefecture. People hereabouts speak of a Taoist sister who got into trouble and ran away, but there's a nephew of hers called Scabby Turtle who lives by the west gate. I'll go seek him out. (*He walks on*)
>   Follow eastern road
>   back to western gate.

(*Exit*)

SCABBY TURTLE (*enters, laughing and wearing* LIU MENGMEI's *jacket*):

11 Scabs all over, ugly from a kid,
  ugly from a kid,
  nabbed for what my auntie did
  what my auntie did.
  Up before his nibs,
  bang wallop thud,
  only saved my skin by
  selling up for good;
  now I run court errands
  round the neighborhood.
"Deeds you wish unknown
best were never done!"

There's no one around just now, so let me tell you what happened
to me, Scabby Turtle, at your service. A fine thing they did, my
auntie Sister Stone and that Liu Mengmei, and a fine escape they
made too. Then along comes that old cuss Tutor Chen and reports
it all to Nan'an prefecture, and I get arrested. They beat me, then
"Where's your auntie gone? How come Miss Du's grave got robbed?" Say I'm not so sharp, I sure was smart then. I just hung my
head and never made a sound. "Beat a horse to make it strong,
squeeze a man to make him talk," shouts the damn judge, "put the
hoop around this scoundrel's head and squeeze it for me!" Ai-yo,
ai-yo, that hurt! Now those torturers, they'd already beaten gold
bells and jade chimes out of me, so now they did me a favor, they
said, "This little devil's brains are oozing out!" "Get a bit on your
finger and show me," shouts the judge. Takes a look, wipes it
under his big nose and says, "It's true, you've squeezed the little
devil's brains out!" Never struck him it was pus from the scabs on
my head! So they loosen the hoop and let me go, but I've to stay
within call as a witness. Well, I got out of there in one piece, so
here I come swaggering along in the jacket Master Liu gave me.

(He chants)

Sway and swagger, swagger and sway
  no one around, I'll swagger all day.

GUO *(reenters, and greets* SCABBY *with a bow):* My respects, young
sir.

SCABBY *(makes a great show of not returning his bow, but laughs and
chants instead):*

My back's sore and none too steady,
  can't make a bow;

your old hump is bowed already,
bow wow wow!

GUO: Young ruffian, your tongue's so sharp it will cut you. I'd like to know what you've got on your back anyway!

SCABBY: I'll have your tongue out, you old villain: I've humped nothing from you!

GUO (*goes up to inspect* SCABBY's *jacket*): Never mind anything else, how did this jacket get on to your back when it belongs to Master Liu of Lingnan?

SCABBY: Ha! And why shouldn't a court officer like myself have a decent jacket to wear? If it's some Liu family from Lingnan you're talking about, how could I have stolen their things from here, the other side of Apricot Blossom Ridge?

GUO: The name's woven into this belt. If you won't own up I'll call the runners.

SCABBY (*falls flat as he dodges* GUO's *grab at him*): All right, all right, I'll hand it over.

GUO: Enough of this fooling, it's the owner I'm looking for.

SCABBY: Who's that?

GUO: Where did Scholar Liu go?

SCABBY: Don't know.

(*They repeat this exchange twice more*)

GUO: If you won't tell me I'll call the runners.

SCABBY: Wait, wait, we can't talk here in the middle of the street. Come to the armory.

(*They proceed there*)

GUO: Here's a nice out-of-the-way place.

SCABBY: Now then: there *was* a Scholar Liu, but I don't know if he's the one you're after. If you can describe him, I'll tell you; if you can't, you can call the runners or take me before the judge for all I care, I'm not going to say a word.

GUO: What a young ruffian! All right, I'll describe him:

> IIIa Scion of the family of Liu,
> fair-skinned, of handsome mien
> and elegant deportment.

SCABBY: So far so good. What age?

GUO:

> Evident from his looks
> that he has not passed thirty.

SCABBY: Very good. And what have you to do with him?

GUO:

> Father and son, I've tended
> the growing of their food,
> seen Master Liu grow up
> from earliest infancy.

SCABBY: So you were the Liu family's majordomo! When did you leave him? Do you know the trouble he's got into?

GUO:

> In spring we parted,
> now I've traced him to this place
> but of his troubles I know nothing.

SCABBY: Well, everything the old boy says makes sense. Grandpa, if you want to know about his troubles, phew! (*He draws* GUO *to him and whispers in his ear, but* GUO *can't hear*) Tchah, heck with it, there's no one around. Listen, grandpa:

> IIIb   He reached this shrine a sick man.

He met up with a Tutor Chen, whose pupil was the daughter of Prefect Du. This old Chen lured him into

> recuperating here at the shrine
> and strolling in the grounds.

GUO: And what happened then?

SCABBY: He strolled as far as young Miss Du's grave, where he found a portrait of her. He moped and pined from dawn to dusk, and that's how the trouble came about.

GUO: How was that?

SCABBY: Our young scholar

> taking false for true
> opened the grave, robbed the tomb.

GUO (*in alarm*): Oh dear, what then?

SCABBY: You can't imagine: Tutor Chen reported to the authorities, who had the shrine surrounded. Scholar Liu was arrested and flogged along with my auntie, Sister Stone. Stripped and strung up, fingers squeezed, no fear they wouldn't confess. They signed a statement and were sent before the Provincial Judge of Jiangxi. "What's the punishment for this crime?" says he to his staff, and they look it up in the code and report that, for taking a body from a grave, the sentence is to be pulled.

GUO: What do you mean, "pulled"?

SCABBY (*pretends to strangle* GUO): Like this.

GUO (*in alarm, and weeping*): Oh, my poor master, now your old humpbacked servant is left without recourse!

SCABBY *(laughs):*
> No need to be upset.
After that they were pardoned, and even Miss Du came back to life!

GUO: How could such a thing happen!

SCABBY:
> A life-preserving ghost
> became a young scholar's wife,
> my death-deserving aunt
> went with them as their maid!

GUO: Where have they gone?

SCABBY:
> I saw them off
> on the journey to Lin'an
> and received this old jacket for my pains.

GUO: You scared me to death, but there's good news after all!
> IV   This journey to Lin'an will mean
> his name in gold on examination list.

SCABBY: That's it.

GUO:
> Then to the Imperial city
> I shall bestir my bones.

SCABBY: Keep a lookout on your journey, old fellow, for right at this moment
> descriptions are posted everywhere
> to catch the guilty party!

Envoi:

GUO:
> I marked each hidden pool
> in quest of faery spring

SCABBY:
> from the prefectural city
> southward lay the ford.

GUO:
> Where people gather
> I dare not tell this tale

SCABBY:
> but think of him far off
> prime hero of romance.

SCENE FORTY-ONE: *Delayed Examination*

MIAO SHUNBIN (*enters with* ATTENDANTS):
      1 Beacons flare for tumult
      through the nine border regions
      forcing delay of the examinations:
      now the youth who would "leap the Dragon Gate"[1]
      must face no spring stream, but autumnal flood!
      The cassia in the moon piles high its blossoms
      but who will pluck them from beyond the clouds?
MIAO, ATTENDANTS:
      Close guarded in examination hall
      scholars await our scrutiny and report.
MIAO (*recites a pastiche of lines from Tang poets*):
      The Artificer of the Celestial Will
         awaits the emerging hero
      whose skill will hook and secure
         the giant turtle of success.
      His place will be made known
         when the glory of spring is announced
      and sheen of phoenix plumage
         is seen upon his writings.
Miao Shunbin, at your service. On the strength of the skill I displayed in assessing the tribute jewels brought by Muslim traders to the Vale of Incense Mountains, His Imperial Majesty charged me with the supervision of the metropolitan examinations. For the final palace examination, in view of the turbulent state of the Jin armies on our frontier, the question concerns appeasement, attack, or defense as the most appropriate policy. My assistant examiners have made a selection of the superior answers, and I am under Imperial orders to determine the final ranking. But grading gems is easy compared with grading papers. Why so? Because I have cat's eyes, no different in quality from jasper, beryl, or crystal; therefore, they flash sparks when they light upon a true gem. Now, examination essays are something my eyes have had noth-

---

1. Metaphors for examination success included leaping the Dragon Gate (and thereby changing from mere fish into dragon), plucking the cassia blossom from the moon, and riding the giant turtle.

ing to do with. However, it is the Imperial command and there's
no help for it. Attendants, open the boxes and fetch me the various papers. (*They do so, and he makes a show of looking them over*)
Not very many! Let's see what the three in the top section are like.
The first essay, in answer to the question of appeasement, attack,
or defense as the most appropriate policy: "Your servant understands that the nation's appeasement of bandits may be compared
with a village council's settlement of a squabble." Ha, if the village
elders can't settle a squabble, there's no great matter, but, if the
nation can't settle *its* affairs, what then? Not very bright of my
examiners to propose this man for Prize Candidate. Let's look at
number two, in favor of defense: "Your servant understands that
the Son of Heaven's defense of his realm may be compared with a
maiden's defense of her virginity." That comparison's a bit too
tight! Now number three, in favor of attack: "Your servant understands that the southern court's attacking the north may be compared with an upstanding yang penetrating a yin." Now there's a
novel idea; yet *The Book of Changes* speaks of the interpenetration
of yin and yang. There was a case of appeasement once before,
when the traitor Qin Hui betrayed the nation. We'll put the one
who favors attack in first place, the one who favors defense in second, and the appeaser third. The remaining papers may then be
ranked in order.

> II Every kind of error:
> what a bunch of blockheads
> grinding their ink for nothing,
> not one brush "bursts into flower."[2]
> The Dragon Gate still offers
> while these poor fish would turn each ripple
> into a ten-foot wave.

But what am I to do?

> Here the examinations
> furnish a strong tide,
> but what if no mighty fish enters the stream?

(*He places the papers back in their boxes and seals them*)

LIU MENGMEI (*enters*):

> III Battling the dusty road,

---

2. As once, in his dream, did the brush of the great poet Li Bo.

> battling the dusty road
>
> men of talent cluster like spokes to the hub.

GATEKEEPER: A fine time to arrive, sir scholar, the examinations just ended.

LIU: Ha, the examinations are over! Have the papers been submitted?

GATEKEEPER: Do you think they were waiting for you before submitting them?

> Heroes flocked to the mark,
>
> time now to lock the halls,
>
> submit the papers.

LIU: I'll guarantee there isn't a Prize Candidate among them.

GATEKEEPER: Not many, just three.

LIU:

> Ten thousand nags strive for first place:
>
> which lags behind? The divine Hualiu!

Go at once and announce that a make-up Prize Candidate seeks admission.

GATEKEEPER: These are the examination halls of the palace. You should have applied for make-up admission to the county or prefectural halls.

LIU: Do you really refuse to announce me, brother? *(He weeps)* Ah Heaven, and it was His Excellency Miao himself who provisioned my journey to "present my jewel"!

> Like old Bian He, punished
>
> by loss of both his feet
>
> when the true gem he offered was judged a mere stone,
>
> I stand ashamed, tears streaming.

MIAO *(overhearing them):* Gatekeeper, where does this man think he is? Bring him to me.

(GATEKEEPER drags LIU in)

LIU: Applicant for make-up, I beg Your Excellency to admit me for examination.

MIAO: Ai-yo, the Imperial topic has been set and answered, the halls of the Hanlin College have been locked; who would dare admit anyone at this late stage?

LIU: Humble student as I am, I have brought my family a thousand leagues from South of the Ridge. You leave me no recourse but to dash my head against these steps of gold and put an end to my life.

(He makes to do this, but the GATEKEEPER stops him)

MIAO *(aside):* This young scholar is surely Master Liu, truly a neglected jewel from the Southern Sea. *(He turns to LIU)* Come forward, master scholar. Do you have paper for your answer?

LIU: I have paper here.

MIAO: In that case I shall admit you for examination, to be judged with equal clemency.

LIU *(kneels):* Only once in a thousand years could one hope to meet such favor.

MIAO *(reads out the topic):* His Imperial Majesty puts the question: Now that the troops of Jin menace the frontiers, which is the most appropriate of the three possible policies of attack, defense, or appeasement?

LIU *(kowtows):* I understand the Imperial desire. *(He rises)*

GATEKEEPER: Be seated here at this side.

(LIU takes his seat and writes his answer)

MIAO *(reexamines the three previous papers):* The first advocates attack, the second defense, the third appeasement. I cannot think that appeasement will meet with His Majesty's approval.

(LIU submits his answer)

MIAO *(looking it over):* Ha, "a thousand words completed while shadows move an inch"! My compliments to you! But I shall need more time to read it. Just tell me now, of the three possibilities, attack, defense, appeasement, which do you advocate?

LIU: I do not favor any particular one. Attack may be appropriate at one time; at another, defense may be appropriate; and appeasement may follow later. Just as a wise physician selects his different drugs, use attack for the outer symptoms, defense for the inner, and appeasement to harmonize relations between the two.

MIAO: A farsighted solution! But how would you apply it to the current situation?

LIU: At this time

> IVA the Imperial carriage lingers
> in splendor manifest to all
> by West Lake, where the autumn-seeding cassia
> and lotus scent three miles about
> are overlaid by sad thoughts of the frontier.

He must be stopped,

that creature who would rein in his mount
on the fair hills of Wu.
When shall we move
to recover northern lands
with such ease as a man spits on his hand?
If our policy be of appeasement only,
then southern lands are shamed by that petty court;
for attack and defense alike
let His Majesty's throne be established
closer to sacred heartlands of the north.

MIAO: Your words are full of wisdom, sir scholar.
       IVb Our sacred lord surveys his realm
intent with a single sweep of his net
to gather in this lost pearl
these jade-like tears of your concern.
A thousand and more candidates submitted papers,
yet not one sees the demands of our time,
comprehends the celestial will
or is fit for charge of office.
The triple strategy you speak of
has power to banish His Majesty's cares
while your written treatise fathoms
all secrets of Heaven and earth.

LIU: I am a student, sir, from South of the Ridge.

MIAO (*lowering his voice*): I am aware of that:
skilled angler, you have hooked the magic coral
and proved your right to ride the great turtle's head!
Sir scholar, you must await the Imperial decree before the palace
gate.

LIU (*assents, then speaks aside as he exits*): This Chief Examiner is
actually His Excellency Miao. But while the issue is still in doubt I
cannot presume to make myself known to him.
    May his eyes see clear
      as in the brightest mirror
  while the red-robed visitor
    silently nods assent.[3]

---

3. A legend narrates that when the great Ouyang Xiu was Chief Examiner a
mysterious visitor dressed in red stood beside him and nodded agreement as he
ranked the highest papers.

(Exit)

MIAO: The papers are all ranked in order. You attendants, wait on me now as I submit them to His Majesty.

(He proceeds towards the throneroom)

Writing brushes are stilled
　　in the Hanlin College,
the clepsydra drips on
　　amid the watchtower's drums.

(Urgent drumrolls sound from offstage)

Hai, what drums are these?
GATEKEEPER: They are the drums that stand before the offices of the Privy Council, beaten to announce troubles on the frontier.

(Sounds of horses neighing from offstage)

MIAO: Urgent reports from the frontier. Alas, alas, what is to be done?
AGED PRIVY COUNCILLOR *(enters)*:
　　"Through the walled passage from Sepal Hall
　　　　the royal splendor coursed;
　　to the little park Hibiscus Blossom
　　　　the griefs of the frontier came."[4]
MIAO *(when they have greeted each other)*: Are you here, venerable sir, to report on troubles at the frontier?
COUNCILLOR: That is correct. And you, sir, are you here to submit the examination results?
MIAO: Exactly.
COUNCILLOR: These matters must be presented in the order of their urgency. Excuse me.

(He kowtows and addresses the throne, offstage)

Your servant of the Privy Council, charged with supervision of men-at-arms through the Empire, reverently begs to report to his Imperial Master.
VOICE *(from offstage)*: What is the substance of your report?

---

4. Lines from Du Fu's sequence of poems, "Autumn Meditation." Translation by A. C. Graham.

COUNCILLOR:

> va Word comes,
> word comes of raiding by those men of Jin.

VOICE: Who is the vanguard?

COUNCILLOR:

> The fighting led,
> the fighting led by that Li Quan.

VOICE: How far have they reached?

COUNCILLOR:

> They press on the environs of Huaiyang.

VOICE: Whom may we send against them?

COUNCILLOR: The present Pacification Commissioner for Huaiyang is Du Bao,

> who lest the frontier regions be cut off
> should advance with meteor speed to their aid.

MIAO (*kowtows, and addresses the throne, offstage*): Your servant Miao Shunbin, charged with supervision of the examinations, reverently begs to report to his Imperial Master.

> vb The papers,
> the papers of the palace candidates have been read
> and are presented,
> and are presented for Imperial ranking.
> Let the astrologers
> select an auspicious day
> as all await the ceremonial proclamation.
> Your officers are assembled before the palace
> and preparations well in hand
> for celebration in the Garnet Grove.

VOICE: Let the officials who have made report attend by the palace gate.

(MIAO and COUNCILLOR both rise)

MIAO: Have you heard any reason, venerable sir, for these frontier disturbances?

COUNCILLOR: I have, but didn't dare include it in my report. The Lord of Jin's sole motive in this expedition is to seize for his own enjoyment our beautiful West Lake.

MIAO: That crazy Tartar, the West Lake is for the pleasure of us all. Hangzhou itself will be useless with the West Lake in his hands!

VOICE (*in proclamation*): Hear the Imperial edict: In our government of the Empire there are matters urgent and matters less so, concerns now civil and now military. Since present danger threatens Huaiyang, Commissioner Du Bao is ordered to advance against the enemy. No delay will be countenanced. As to ceremonial proclamation of the examination results, this must await the setting aside of shield and spear, when we shall turn from martial to civil arts. This to be made known to all our servants. Kowtow!

(MIAO and COUNCILLOR kowtow,
call out "Ten thousand years!" and rise)

Envoi:

COUNCILLOR:

> Marshland, hill and stream
>   enter our battle plans.

MIAO:

> Resplendent in trailing robes
>   daylong the officials gather.

COUNCILLOR:

> The man of gifts must set his eyes
>   beyond the distant clouds

MIAO:

>   yet warriors take precedence
>   when frontier guard is set.

SCENE FORTY-TWO: *Troop Transfer*

COMMISSIONER DU BAO *(enters at head of his staff)*:
>   1   West winds toss the trees
>   along the Yangzi's banks;
>   to the north where flows the Huai
>   "sorrowful my gaze."
>   Defenses perforce are set
>   here in Jiangnan, the southern land,
>   but beyond the northern frontier
>   dragging at all our thoughts
>   what fair prospects are closed to us?
> Pounding of washing blocks announces another fall,
> the river flows on, its waters are lost to view.
> The frontier's grassy waves encroach on Central Realm

whence flies a single messenger wild goose
past watchtowers on the Huai.
The Empire's sorrows
line my temples;
shall I commit them to the eastward flow
and like the poet Du Mu of my ancient line
find peace in a "drunken Yangzhou dream"?

It is three years since I, Du Bao, took up my duties in Yangzhou as
Pacification Commissioner for Huaiyang. Aside from the depra-
dations of Li Quan's men we have enjoyed a general tranquility.
But I was deeply disturbed yesterday to learn of an impending
raid by the border troops. My wife, meanwhile, understanding
nothing of these things, grieves for her own part over our departed daughter.

(Enter MADAM DU, attended by SPRING FRAGRANCE)

MADAM DU:

    ii My husband holds the tally of command
and "like a swallow caught in the curtain"
I attend him in this place of peril.

(She sighs)

Beyond the screen the tree-lined Qinhuai River
and the far peaks of Gold Hill and Scorched Hill,
glimpse of a landscape bringing
only regret to sorrowing brows.

Blessings on you, my husband.

DU: My lady.

MADAM DU:

How many years since Nan'an fell behind us?
Spring and autumn alternate, dawn yields to dusk.

DU:

In vain we long for the Brocade River of our home
and Yangzhou's delights are nowhere to be found.

MADAM DU:

Stroking your sword, judging past and present,
how can you bear the idleness of this waiting?

(She weeps)

DU, MADAM DU:

No son to ease our sorrows,
tears veil the cloud-capped ridge and wooded stream.

MADAM DU: My lord, when I speak of our departed daughter you can find nothing to say. How can you understand the grief that fills my heart, not only for her whom we lost but also that we are left deprived of all progeny? It is my wish now, while we are in Yangzhou, to seek out a secondary wife who can provide you with a successor. Does such a plan have my lord's approval?

DU: It would not be fitting to take a girl from a family under my jurisdiction.

MADAM DU: Then would a girl from Nanjing, across the river, be suitable?

DU: I have no mind for such matters at this moment of urgency in His Imperial Majesty's service.

MADAM DU: Oh, Bridal, Bridal, the bitter grief! *(She weeps)*

FIRST MESSENGER *(enters):*

> Glory of Imperial command
> > far-reaching as sun or moon,
> bloodlust of eager warriors
> > rages down Yangzi and Huai.

Instructions from the court for His Excellency!

DU *(having knelt to receive the Imperial messenger, he now rises and reads out the edict):* "Instructions from the Privy Council concerning the raiding of the Huai region by border troops. Edict of His Sacred Majesty: Du Bao, Pacification Commissioner for Huaiyang, to proceed at once across the Huai. No delay will be countenanced. This is Our will." Ha, a desperate crisis at arms to bring forth so stern an edict! My lady, we must transfer our headquarters to Huaian, to leave at once.

POST STATION COMMANDER *(enters):*

> A feathered missive for the Adjutant,[1]
> an ivory tally for the posting stage.

Your Excellency, boats are ready and await your disposal.

> *(Drums and pipes sound offstage.* DU *and his staff, with* MADAM DU, *mime boarding the imaginary boats)*

VOICE *(from offstage):* The officers of your command are assembled to see Your Excellency safely on your journey.

DU: They may rise and return to their posts. *(He turns to* MADAM DU*):* My lady, autumn once more on the river:

---

1. It was army practice to insert a feather in a message to indicate urgency.

III   Signs from Heaven of autumn's approach,
signs from Heaven of autumn's approach:
breath of the "metal" wind,[2]
mist enfolds trees by painted bridge
beneath the city's watchtowers.
Warmth of summer retreats,
gently begins the chill
as a thin drizzle clings to trailing robe.
Now forward our painted bark between faery banks
to meet the rising tide, the wind's stern breath,
and spume of flying spray.
Specks in the sky, white gulls
swoop across our course;
when the wind drops at sunset
our sail's reflection quivers by the rushes' green.
Muffled by thick clouds, sounds of pipe and drum
and somewhere the songs of water-chestnut gatherers
rouse in the mind a longing for rustic peace.

But now, who is this rider who spurs down the bank to us?

SECOND MESSENGER (*enters in haste, waving his riding crop to indicate galloping horse*):

IVa   From saddle I call:
back your oars, halt for the feathered missive.

DU: What is your business?

SECOND MESSENGER:

The prefecture of Huaian
close-menaced by Li Quan's arrogant zeal.

DU: Are there troops to mount guard?

SECOND MESSENGER:

Too few to withstand him;
therefore it lies with the Commissioner
to advance with meteor swiftness:
linger no more on this river route
but speed by land.

DU:

Calm your fears.

My lady,
I ride in haste via the posting stations;

---

2. In five-element theory, the autumn wind belongs to the element of metal, which kills.

do you reverse your course and sail back,
reverse your course and sail back.

MADAM DU: But see, another rider comes to report!

THIRD MESSENGER:

ivb Myriad mounted tribesmen
threaten to cut the mighty Huai
and camp on Lake Tai's shore.

Your Excellency must make haste,
delay no more.

Your servant returns at once
in fear that beleaguered city
soon or late must fall to barbarian horde.

MADAM DU (*weeps*):

What now my lord?
To serve at arms, your temples rimed with age,
while beacons blaze alarm down every highway!

DU:

A desperate pass
if your return to Yangzhou is cut off.
You and I, where shall we meet again,
where shall we meet again?

Lady, I must leave you now. Yangzhou is surely threatened: you
must make directly for Hangzhou.

v To fly apart, as age's shadows close!
To fly apart, as age's shadows close!
Now like Du Fu, sent out on service,
I'll weep for wife deserted in sky's far corner!

MADAM DU (*weeps*):

Alone, no daughter by my side,
now I must send my husband to the wars!

DU, MADAM DU:

Husband and wife of rank and title
no more than wanderers solitary and childless,
each looking to message or to dream
to know if other still lives!

MADAM DU:

vi Old and useless, I hesitate here still.

DU:

But I must do my duty
as Commissioner for this region.

MADAM DU: Then, my lord, my
"old pedant, head stuffed with battle plans,"

please take good care of yourself. *(DU exits)* Ah Heaven, the fires of battle will soon be burning all about Yangzhou. Come then, Fragrance, we shall make straight for Hangzhou.

Envoi:

Desolated is Yangzhou's beauty
    along the Sui Emperor's Dike
the lands of Chu and Han
    turned into battlefields.
Ignorant of war
    the ladies of the inner chambers
turn to each other for counsel
    as evening sun goes down.

SCENE FORTY-THREE: *The Siege of Huaian*

DU BAO, OFFICERS, MEN *(enter in battle array):*
    I In clamor of west wind
    din of slaughter raised by demon hordes
    where clouds of autumn spume
    roil the yellow waters of the Huai.
    Deployed in "wild-goose" columns,
    our "dragon" array prepared,
    we slash through Heyang to the beleaguered city.
DU: I am weary of marching. Tell me, my officers, how far have we come?
OFFICERS: We are close to Huaian.
DU *(peers forward):* Ah Heaven,
    the half of our hills and streams still left to us
    now resound to barbarian flute.
OFFICERS:
    Stench of blood rises
    over the autumn weeds of our old camp.
DU:
    Moans of gibbon and crane fill the air,[1]
    battle robes soaked not with sweat but tears.

---

1. Allusion to a legend of an ancient prince whose officers were turned into gibbons and cranes on a southern expedition.

OFFICERS: Your Excellency,
          with no tears left to plead for Heaven's succor
          let us advance!

DU: Men of my command! My sons! The city of Huaian lies before us in desperate plight. We will set death at a venture and storm the city walls, while at the same time we petition the court for reinforcements. My orders to the army: Courage, advance!

OFFICERS (*tears streaming*): Your orders acknowledged, sir!
          11a Steady in saddle, orders understood,
          advance the banners on every hand;
          let them wave in light of day
          till dust obscure sun's brightness.

DU, OFFICERS, MEN:
          Fierce the pride of Tartar armies,
          long the road for southern troops:
          close invested, in haze of blood
          hazarded city awaits its fate!

DU: Marauders block the road before us: to the attack!

(Exit, with his army)

LI QUAN, DAME LI, MEN (*enter, armed and with wild yells*):
          11b Our leader like General Li of old
          brings down his wild goose shot through the heart,
          handles his steed like a mounted panther.[2]
          Pointed stirrups prick,
          flags and pennants wave.

          Fierce the pride of Tartar armies,
          long the road for southern troops:
          close invested, in haze of blood
          hazarded city awaits its fate!

LI (*laughs*): Prince-errant of the Great Jin, myriad bold warriors at my command, I have laid a siege seven lines deep to the city of Huaian: close enough, I think! (*Drums and shouts from offstage*) Ha, troops ahead, must be the approach of Commissioner Du; I'll lead a detachment of a thousand against him. (*He retires to rear of stage*)

DU, OFFICERS, MEN (*reenter*):
          Fierce the pride of Tartar armies,
          long the road for southern troops:

---

2. A "panther" was a horseman who could catch up with a running steed, grab its tail, and vault into the saddle.

close invested, in haze of blood
hazarded city awaits its fate!

*(LI and his followers come forward and exchange
insults with DU, and LI and DU engage
in a round of single combat. Then LI breaks
off and deploys his men into line to block DU's advance)*

DU: Forward, my men, through their line and slash our way into the city!

LI: Ho, Du's men have fought their way into the city. Well, let them. They'll surrender soon enough when they've come to the end of their provisions.

LI, DAME LI, MEN:

Fierce the pride of Tartar armies,
long the road for southern troops:
close invested, in haze of blood
hazarded city awaits its fate!

(Exeunt)

TWO CIVIL OFFICIALS *(enter):*

III Daylong the swirling clouds of battle
silk caps of office set aside.

FIRST MILITARY OFFICER *(enters):*

With spear and sword I guard the bridge.

SECOND MILITARY OFFICER *(enters):*

Horn and drum like dragons roaring.

(The MILITARY OFFICERS and CIVIL OFFICIALS exchange greetings)

FIRST CIVIL OFFICIAL:

Towers beside the Huai
survey the distant sea.

SECOND CIVIL OFFICIAL:

Tumult of conflict
rises endlessly.

SECOND MILITARY OFFICER:

Drum and cannon
terrify me:
give me wings, to Heaven I'll flee!

FIRST MILITARY OFFICER:

Sword from sheath,

arrow from quiver,
backs to the wall now battle we!

OFFICERS, OFFICIALS:

Saps are our nightmare,
scaling ladders our misery:
when shall we
our bold Commissioner see?

FIRST CIVIL OFFICIAL: We civil officials hold posts as Counselor and Adjutant to the prefectural forces of Huaian. Under close siege by these northern bandits we have long anticipated the arrival of His Excellency Du Bao, the Pacification Commissioner, but there is still no sign of him. May I enquire what strategies our defending generals have prepared?

SECOND MILITARY OFFICER: In my considered opinion: surrender!

SECOND CIVIL OFFICIAL: How can you say this?

SECOND MILITARY OFFICER: Well then, if not surrender, best thing is escape.

FIRST CIVIL OFFICIAL: One man might escape, but not ten.

SECOND MILITARY OFFICER: If that's the case, what am I to do with my little woman?

FIRST MILITARY OFFICER: Lock her in a closet.

SECOND MILITARY OFFICER: What do I do with the key?

FIRST MILITARY OFFICER: Give it to me. If Li Quan doesn't come, I'll take care of your doxy and present you with a son—by proxy.

SECOND MILITARY OFFICER: Suppose Li Quan does come?

FIRST MILITARY OFFICER: Then I'll present your wife and son to him. How's that for foxy?

SECOND MILITARY OFFICER: Some friend *you* are! What moxie!

(Drums and shouting from offstage)

MESSENGER *(enters):* Leave to report! Troops from the south have broken through the siege lines. Commissioner Du is here!

OFFICERS, OFFICIALS: Open the city gates at once to welcome him.

Blood spills each day through Heaven and earth
but who in the court seeks the tasseled badge
of authority to attack?

(Exeunt)

DU *(enters at the head of his OFFICERS and MEN):*

IVa   Din of killing fills the air, a mournful wail,
a mournful wail;

city besieged on every hand, close and tight,
close and tight.
Whistling wind
tears at signal pennants:
open the gates,
let down the drawbridge!

MILITARY OFFICERS, CIVIL OFFICIALS (reenter, with ATTENDANTS):
Officers civil and military
wait in welcome.

(They kneel)

Your Excellency, all officers civil and military are here to receive
you.

DU: You may rise; I will confer with you atop the watchtower.

(They murmur assent, rise, and exit)

ivb   Desert dust stains my robe,
my battle robe;
stench of blood reeks from my sword,
my jeweled sword.

(Drumrolls sound from offstage)

Drums of Huaian,
Yangzhou flutes;
unfurl our banners,
mount the watchtower.

DU, OFFICERS, MEN:
Assemble now
the staffs entire.

(They proceed to the watchtower)

OFFICER OF PROTOCOL (enters): We await Your Excellency's pleasure.
DU:
v   Thousand-league advance of dragon columns:
how may we now, like Liu Kun of ancient Tsin,
by whistling from a moonlit tower
fill these barbarians with thoughts of home,
make them lose heart and retire?

OFFICER OF PROTOCOL: Let all staffs civil and military take their
places.

MILITARY OFFICERS, CIVIL OFFICIALS (enter, with ATTENDANTS, and *kneel to* DU): Our beleaguered city, fragile as piled eggs, faced the fate of massacre; Your Excellency, easy as juggling balls, came to our relief. Accept now from each officer here assembled the ritual kowtow of gratitude.

DU: Spearpoints rose from every quarter to beset you gentlemen with troubles: my fault of dilatoriness was grave. A low bow will be sufficient. (ALL *murmur assent, rise, and bow*) This bandit seems to possess a certain degree of martial skill. There is some ruse behind his permitting me to enter the city.

MILITARY OFFICERS, CIVIL OFFICIALS: It will be no more than saps beneath the walls or "cloud ladders" to scale them. We shall be on our guard against these things.

DU: What I fear is the tactic of the locked city.

SECOND MILITARY OFFICER: Beg to inquire: what is this "tactic of the locked city"? Do they lock up the inside or the outside? If it's the outside, then they lock the Prince-errant out. But if it's the inside, then they lock *me* in!

DU: We'll leave that aside. How many troops in the city?

FIRST MILITARY OFFICER: Thirteen thousand.

DU: Provisions for how long?

FIRST MILITARY OFFICER: Six months.

DU: Then with the administrations civil and military of one heart we may confidently await relief.

(*Sound of drums and shouting from offstage*)

MESSENGER (*enters*): Beg to report: Li Quan's men are close about the city.

DU (*with a drawn-out sigh*): This bandit shows little sense.

    VIA Troops and supplies both plentiful,
      we can withstand his siege
    as long as army and people labor in accord.

MILITARY OFFICERS, CIVIL OFFICIALS, ATTENDANTS:
    Walls patrolled through dusk and dawn
    duties severe for troops and city folk.

(*Yells from offstage.* ALL *weep*)

    Let rebel hordes scream and yell,
    our army guards its silence.

(DU *prostrates himself in prayer to Heaven.* ALL *raise
him to his feet, then join him in renewed prostrations*)

DU:

    Tears bedew beleaguered city

    as silent prayers ascend to Heaven.

MILITARY OFFICERS, CIVIL OFFICIALS, ATTENDANTS:

    vib Defense of frontier is the mission

    laid on our heroic chief,

    whose nonchalant whistling lulls the foe

    from tower hundred feet high.

DU:

    Yangzhou and Huai not to be undervalued

    and so myself gird sword at waist.

MILITARY OFFICERS, CIVIL OFFICIALS, ATTENDANTS:

    Let rebel hordes scream and yell,

    our army guards its silence.

DU: From this day forth let civil officers supervise the defense of
the walls while the officers of the army lead sorties, adjusting tactics to the demands of the situation.

SECOND MILITARY OFFICER: But I'm scared the main armies of the
Tartars are coming!

DU: Armies of the Tartars!

    vii They'll come or not as tide of battle flows

    but we'll not strike the royal standard of Zhao.

And if they do come,

    our answer is to fight for very life!

Envoi:

FIRST MILITARY OFFICER:

    Day after day the swirling

    of dust from raiders' hooves

SECOND MILITARY OFFICER:

    three thousand, armed in rhino hide,

    jostle the crimson chariot wheels.

DU:

    In his bosom, a plan all his own

    to secure the frontier's peace—

ALL:

    to no other man shall belong

    the credit for this deed!

SCENE FORTY-FOUR: *Concern for the Besieged*

BRIDAL DU:

    i Noisy magpies greeted my rising
    presage of dream's fulfillment;
    with happy smile I set my gold hair ornaments.
    Fragrant smoke mingled with autumn haze,
    hopes of gilded placard of success
    burned bright as incense glow.
From ghostly state achieving living form
in poverty aspiring to high office:
what progress toward the goal before us,
exalted husband, honored wife?

As I attended my husband Scholar Liu in his studies for the examinations, there came an Imperial summons to men of worth to present themselves for selection. Now I linger here awaiting the announcement of his success. Truly,

    though close at hand, the Imperial court
      seems a thousand miles away:
    shall my husband be the one man
      to outdistance all the rest?

LIU MENGMEI (*enters*):

    ii A lucky chance in the hall of letters
    but clash of arms heralds misfortune.
    Teased by hopes
    of the gilded placard of my success
    my elegant bride, emerged from earthy cave
    to soar with me up to the ninth heaven,
    has waited, soul adrift
    where evening veils the river.[1]

(They greet each other)

BRIDAL: Back at last, Master Liu. But I had looked for you in lofty carriage, "clad in brocade in broad daylight" for all to see. How is it you come now alone and on foot?

LIU: I'll explain what has happened.

---

1. This is probably an allusion to the story of Qiannü; see scene 36, note 8.

III Latecomer to examination halls
I found them closed, locked up,
aspiring heroes all departed.

BRIDAL: Oh, no, you arrived too late!

LIU:

By happy chance I met an old acquaintance.

BRIDAL: Were you admitted as a make-up candidate?

LIU:

When nought but moonlight filled his boat
the examiner retrieved a rejected pearl.

BRIDAL (*rejoicing*): Wonderful! Has the list been issued?

LIU:

At the very moment
of report submitted to Dragon throne
of publication of phoenix lists—
an untoward event.

BRIDAL: What kind of untoward event?

LIU: You must understand that the armies of the Great Jin Empire
are on the march and are ravaging Huaiyang.

Frenzied urgency at Willow Camp
delays banquet in Almond Park.[2]
Your decorated patent of nobility
cannot be issued yet.

BRIDAL: I shall not mind the waiting. But tell me, is it not this
Huaiyang that is under my father's governance?

LIU: It is.

BRIDAL (*weeps*): Ah Heaven, what will happen to my father and
mother! (*She sobs in distress*)

LIU:

Ah, see her keen distress,
the agony of mind,
the bowels' torture!
Does grief burn fiercer now
than when you sojourned in the shades?

BRIDAL: Let us not speak of that. There is one thing I would ask,
but dare not.

---

2. Willow Camp means army encampment, in allusion to a Han general who
made his headquarters at a place called Willows; the Almond Park was where successful examination candidates feasted in the Tang capital Chang'an. The Garnet
Grove, referred to in scene 41, was outside the Song capital Kaifeng.

LIU: Please ask it.

BRIDAL: It must still be some time before the list of successful candidates is published. I should like to request that you seek news of my parents in Huaiyang, but I do not know if you would be willing?

LIU: I am at your command in this, and yet I am reluctant to leave your side.

BRIDAL: You needn't worry about me, I shall be able to manage here.

LIU: Then I shall leave at once.

BRIDAL:

> IVa "Beneath that white cloud lies my parents' dwell-
>   ing"
> and I, lone shade once buried by apricot's root,
> sad and forsaken was my fragrant spirit,
> which now melts at touch of "willow"!
> Across the miles to Yangzhou
> still my soul would fly
> for few are they who return to mortal world
> and my father and mother will start in amazement
> to learn that I am living,
> to find out of thin air
> a "phoenix son-in-law" before their gate
> as though for Weaving Maid and Herdboy
> a bridge of magpies formed across the void![3]

LIU:

> IVb I start to leave, then stop again,
> my thoughts in two places at once.
> My true wish is to stay by my darling's side.

BRIDAL: I have Sister Stone to keep me company.

LIU:

> Small use, a female companion through the long cold
>   night
> should old longings of wandering soul
> return to impatient heart.

BRIDAL: I shall wander no more.

LIU:

> My talents have won me highest place

---

3. See scene 36, note 9. Magpies (birds of good omen) form a bridge across which the star-lovers can meet.

yet when the lists are published
I fear it may lie beyond my power to be present.
BRIDAL *(sobs):* Oh, father, mother!
LIU:

Out of concern for your parents
you will bear this separation
while I, "half a son" to them, need not demur
to claim such elevated kinship.

But, my dear, when I present my respects before your parents,
their first question is sure to concern your return to the living.
BRIDAL *(sighs):*

va   A tale that must sound
like work of demon monsters—
I fear my father will balk in disbelief.

(She reflects for a moment)

I have it: take my portrait with you.
At sight of portrait painted by my own hand
he will be sure to ask your story.

LIU: But what story can I tell him?
BRIDAL:

Tell him how officers of celestial court
by chance discovered
the due fruition of a predestined match
and hastened to open my grave.

LIU: Should I tell him how before that time you visited me in my
study?
BRIDAL *(turns aside bashfully):*

Don't tease,
don't tell a tale would bring me ridicule
though you may give a hint of it
to that crafty maid of mine.

LIU:

vb   My whole desire, to present myself to your parents
in carriage with team of four,
you by my side, like Qiannü returning in splendor;[4]
who could anticipate such a visit
to bride's parents beset by war's alarms

---

4. See scene 36, note 8.

while scholar-groom still wears
the tatters of his days of poverty!

BRIDAL: No harm in a plain bridegroom. But I fear the loneliness
and hardships of the road before you.

LIU:

In autumn dusk
script forms of wild geese against the setting sun
distracted soul night-moored on Qinhuai River.

BRIDAL: My husband, this time of our separation will be a cold and
lonely time for us. But when you return to be proclaimed Prize
Candidate. . .

LIU:

The list once published,
ah, then the joy of "The Grand Visit"
surpassing "Imperial Son-in-Law Appears at Court"![5]

SISTER STONE *(enters):*

Umbrella good for sun and rain
"spring portrait" till autumn turns to spring again.

Here are your traveling things and an umbrella for you.

(LIU and BRIDAL bow to each other in formal leave-taking)

BRIDAL:

vi My scholar-lover now
will formally enter the family of Du.

LIU:

And great will be the joy
when return to life is known.

BRIDAL: Master Liu, come back to me as soon as all is settled. Do
not be distracted by
pleasures of Yangzhou—flute song on moonlit bridge.

Envoi:

LIU:

Make formal visit in due time
to parents of the bride

BRIDAL:

though empty be the purse
of gift for honored in-laws.

---

5. "The Grand Visit" (by bridegroom to parents-in-law) and "Imperial Son-in-
Law" are operatic tune titles.

LIU:

> My steed now turns its hooves
> into the Yangzhou road

BRIDAL:

> sore the grief of separation
> in one place as in other.

SCENE FORTY-FIVE: *A Spy for the Rebels*

REBEL SENTRIES *(enter, and patrol up and down the stage)*:
> I Our Great Prince started as common thug,
> common thug,
> his Dame a camp wench, cracked old jug,
> cracked old jug.
> Chieftains now of mountain band
> no scruples stay their itching hand.
> Gong and drum,
> gong and drum,
> up hill, down dale
> the sentries come.

Brothers, our Prince is besieging Huaian, and he's looking for someone to take a message in to Commissioner Du. Nobody on the highways, not even a shadow, so now we scour the byways.
> Gong and drum
> gong and drum
> up hill, down dale
> the sentries come.

(Exeunt)

TUTOR CHEN *(enters, bearing umbrella and traveler's bundle)*:
> II Tranquil post in Nan'an
> respectable living now lost.
> It isn't hard to make your fortune:
> just teach school for a thousand years.

Tutor Chen, at your service, on my way to Yangzhou to report to Commissioner Du concerning his daughter. But what am I to do now that he's besieged in Huaian and I'm left with nowhere to turn? Too dangerous to travel the highway, I'll take to the byways instead.

Peripatetic as the ancient sages
in search of a living I dodge and twist
fearful of "drowning in mud or stumbling into fire"
by falling into rebel hands.
Frosts thin the trees' cold shadows,
gibbons wail, tigers scream
and I sigh lackaday!

SENTRIES (*reenter*):

"Knows the hills are full of tigers
so what does he do but head straight for them."

—Where are you off to, you old sod? (*They seize* CHEN)

CHEN: Mercy, Sir Chief!

SENTRIES: Not us, the Chief's someone else.

CHEN: Ah Heaven, what now! Now truly,

"crow and magpie fly together:
will good or ill befall?"

(*Exeunt*)

LI QUAN, DAME LI (*enter with attendants*):

    III Bandits bold brought forth by time of chaos,
who dare call us coward?
"Southern scum" where the north is concerned,
"northern curs" to the south,
for us the Lord of Heaven reserves a special doom.

LI: We've been besieging Huaian a long time now, Mother, but it refuses to fall. What we need is someone to send into the city to negotiate for us, and incidentally find out what Commissioner Du's dispositions are. But there doesn't seem to be anyone we could send.

DAME LI: We need to find someone old Du knows and trusts, and then devise a trick to suit the situation.

CHEN (*reenters as captive, bound, propelled by* SENTRIES):

    IV Lost in byways that twisted like sheep's intestines
now, ah Heaven,
how shall I escape this butcher's yard?

(CHEN *is presented to* LI)

SENTRIES: Beg to report, here's a captured southerner.

LI: An old greybeard. Where from, and what trade?

CHEN: May it please you,

    V the scholar Chen Zuiliang,

native of Nan'an
visiting friends in Huaiyang.

LI: What friends?

CHEN: Commissioner Du,
in whose residence of yore
I sat behind tutor's screen.

DAME LI: So you were a tutor in his residence. How many pupils?

CHEM: By his lady, Madam Zhen, he had only a single daughter,
girl-scholar whom death took early.

DAME LI: Who else?

CHEN:

A goddaughter, Spring Fragrance,
companion to Her Ladyship.

DAME LI (*aside, with a triumphant laugh*): I never knew the details of
old Du's family life. Now that I *do* know, a scheme comes to mind.
(*To her ATTENDANTS*) Take this silly old pedant away and hold him
outside the camp gate.

(*ATTENDANTS shout assent and exit escorting CHEN*)

Prince, I have a scheme. We will pick out a couple of severed heads
belonging to those women we executed yesterday, and claim that
they were the Du womenfolk, killed by our men on their way back
to Yangzhou. The heads will be the evidence. We'll let this old
pedant go, and he can take the message to old Du. This should
cool off old Du a bit, and he won't be as determined to defend the
city.

LI: Brilliant, brilliant! (*Stands up, and speaks in a low voice*) Call my
Adjutant. (*ADJUTANT enters*) I'm going to invite that old pedant in
for a chat. While we are in the middle of it, I want you to present a
couple of heads belonging to those women we killed yesterday.
Announce that they are Commissioner Du's wife, Madam Zhen,
and her maid Spring Fragrance, and don't make any mistake. (*AD-
JUTANT assents, and exits*) Now, you men, let's have that bachelor of
arts back in here.

CHEN (*reenters under escort*): Mercy, great Prince!

LI: No mercy for a spy like you.

DAME LI: Let me beg you, Prince, to untie him, so that we may
benefit from his discourse on the art of war.

LI: Very well, we'll do what Mother says and untie him.

(*ATTENDANTS release CHEN's bonds*)

CHEN *(kowtows):* Humblest thanks, great Prince, Madam, for your magnanimity in sparing my life.

LI: Get up, and let's hear some of your art of war.

CHEN: Duke Ling of Wei asked Confucius about the marshaling of troops. Confucius refused to respond, but said, "I have never yet seen anyone whose desire to build up his moral power was as strong as sexual desire."[1]

LI: Why did he say that?

CHEN: Because at that moment Duke Ling had his Duchess Nanzi sitting beside him, that's why the Master was reluctant to speak.

LI: I don't know about this Duchess; "nanzi" sounds like it was a man he had there, but Mother here is a real woman.[2]

MESSENGER *(enters to offstage roll of drums):* Beg to report! Troops guarding the Yangzhou road have killed the womenfolk of Commissioner Du; they've brought their heads in and want a reward.

LI *(examines the heads):* I suspect a false report.

MESSENGER: True as you're standing there! Du's lady, Madam Zhen, and a maidservant by the name of Spring Fragrance.

CHEN *(glances at the heads, and cries out in terror):* Ah Heaven, it really is the old lady and Spring Fragrance!

LI: Tush, what's the old fool sniveling about! Now to break through into Huaian and kill old Du himself.

CHEN: Spare his life, great Prince!

LI: I'll spare him only on condition that he yield up the city.

CHEN: Then let this poor scholar go there to bear witness to your tiger-like royal majesty, and I'll return at once to report.

DAME LI: Off with you now, old pedant, the Prince will spare your neck this time.

(Drums and yells offstage. The gate is opened)

CHEN *(shaking in terror):*
    VI Display of might
    to stamp on my mind this Prince-errant of Jin!

LI, DAME LI: Go tell Commissioner Du
    his martial pomp is all for nought;
    let him yield without delay

---

1. Chen at this point jumbles together quotations from the *Analects of Confucius,* XV, 1; IX, 17; and VI, 26. Li's bewilderment is fully understandable.

2. There is often a suggestion of sodomy in the pun between *nan* "south" (the name of the Duchess) and *nan* "male."

for 'tis no lie
that we intend to swallow stream and hill.

(Exeunt)

CHEN *(sees them off with repeated bows, then addresses the empty stage)*: Plain thieves and robbers. And they have killed Lady Du and Spring Fragrance: I must report this within the city.

Envoi:

The sea gods' eastward progress
    raises a cruel wind;
as light fades from desert floor
    sand swirls like ashes.
Like Shan of old
    he will take in his former dependents
come to wipe off the dust that now
    must settle on his head.

SCENE FORTY-SIX: *The Rebels Countered*

DU BAO *(enters, sword-girt and in full armor, at the head of his troops)*:
1 Awaiting relief we array our troops
in "wind" and "cloud" formations;
here at the border
a month creeps by like a year.

(Drumrolls and shouting offstage. He sighs)

Cannon thunder like tigers roaring,
swords flutter, a snowstorm of wild-goose wings.
But ah, Li Quan,
    you have me to deal with before you take this land.

(He recites a pastiche of lines from Tang poets)

What easy, bantering hero
  will come to break this siege?
Myriad miles of nomad realm,
  no single bird in flight.

Our task today here in the south,
　　the gateway to the sea:
fortunes of the wars
　　have rimed these locks of mine.

Armed risings have beset Huaiyang throughout my tenure here,
and now this city of Huaian is isolated and under close siege. Our
only course is carefully to husband arms and provisions while we
keep up a constant din of gongs and drums. We cannot hope to
escape with our lives, but commit ourselves to the will of Heaven
and resolve to defend to the last man. Skulking now in this watchtower I think back to the fall of the northern capital, and grieve as
my gaze seeks out the lost homeland:

　　　II　What purpose has Heaven in this
　　when no light of sun moon or stars suffices
　　to distinguish Chinese from Tartar
　　but rank stench of sheep and goat
　　blows throughout mortal world
　　and central lands are turned
　　to a desert of yellow sand?

(His anger rises)

　　Hair beneath helmet bristles with rage,
　　hair beneath helmet bristles with rage!
　　Whose were the machinations
　　that brought our hills and streams to this?

(He sighs)

The central lands are lost.
　　Pass and ford close beset,
　　every hope denied
　　yet Yangzhou shall still be guarded
　　and the Huai River freed!

By the looks of it, Li Quan with his myriad-bandit horde should
find this place easy enough to take. There must be some reason for
his hesitation.
　　I have a plan to raise this siege
　　but lack an envoy.

MESSENGER *(enters to offstage drumrolls):*
　　"Battlefield closed to the very wild geese,
　　here's a man come straight from Hell."

What a laugh—the whole city sealed off like someone had

dropped an iron bucket over it, and here comes Sir Scholar wandering along in search of patronage. Got to report this. Your Excellency, there's an old friend of yours come acalling.

DU: Surely a spy?

MESSENGER: Says his name is Scholar Chen, from Nan'an prefecture west of the river.

DU: What magic wings carried this pigheaded old pedant in here? Summon him at once.

TUTOR CHEN *(enters):*

    III Banners enhance beauty of scene,

    drums and gunpowder crackle away

    though the Lantern Festival's still far off![1]

Where is His Excellency Du Bao?

DU *(steps out of the watchtower to welcome him with a smile):*

    What old friend do I hear

    come a thousand miles to visit?

              (He sighs)

To see you in this place, revered sir,

    fills my eyes with tears of alarm.

CHEN: I note that Your Excellency's hair has turned completely white.

CHEN, DU:

    White-headed both

    after a three-year separation

    ruefully each regards other.

     (They exchange salutations, then recite a
       pastiche of lines from Tang poets)

CHEN:

    White-headed, donkey-borne

    I trail my coarse cloth sack

DU:

    reminded of South Slope's past joys

    by old friend's timely visit.

CHEN:

    Our former haunts in Nanjing

    a thousand miles behind

---

1. The Lantern Festival, first full moon of the new year, was celebrated with a deafening noise of firecrackers.

DU:

in far Taiyuan
we needs must find our home.

CHEN: My best respects to Your Excellency. But I grieve to report the death of your lady wife, at the hands of rebel troops on the Yangzhou road.

DU (expresses astonishment): How did you learn of this?

CHEN: While I was in the rebels' camp I was shown her ladyship's head. I examined it with my own eyes. Spring Fragrance also perished with her.

DU (weeps): Ah Heaven, the pain is more than I can bear!

IV　Companion of my rank and honors
my wife, Madam Zhen, of virtuous name unblemished,
lady of first grade by Imperial decree,
worthy helpmeet loyal and chaste!
I recall your living image,
recall your living image,
dignity of headdress and robes of court
and bitter flow my tears.

(He collapses, weeping, and is raised
to his feet again by OFFICERS)

CHEN: Ah my lady, my lady, how could you meet such an end! Weep for her, you generals and officers all!

ALL (weeping): Ah her ladyship!

DU (impatiently dashing the tears from his eyes): No, there is no call for this! My lady held high honors from the court, it was only fitting that she should die with curses against the rebels on her lips. What right have I to let her loss weaken my will, turn my soldier's heart to ashes?

One who holds general rank
forswears all private sorrows;
come anguish as it may
he can have no regrets.

Tell me, Tutor Chen, is there any other word from this "Prince-errant of Jin?"

CHEN: This is hard for me to say, but he plans to kill Your Excellency.

DU: Ha,

what is his purpose in seeking my death?
I seek *his* for the nation's sake.

CHEN: If a poor scholar may express his views: neither of you needs be killed. (*He draws* DU *aside and whispers in his ear*) What the Prince-errant really wants is this city of Huaian.

DU: Lower, lower, but tell me: in that rebel camp of theirs is there one chief, or two?

CHEN: Li Quan and his wife sit side by side.

DU (*laughs*): If that's the way it is, I can guarantee to raise this siege. —But, Tutor Chen, tell me why you were on your way to see me in the first place.

CHEN: I had almost forgotten until you asked. I came straight here to report the plundering of your daughter's tomb.

DU (*startled*): Ah Heaven, what quarrel could thieves have with dry bones beneath a grave mound? This was surely for the sake of any valuables they could find. Who were the culprits?

CHEN: After Your Excellency's departure, Sister Stone took in a wandering fellow from South of the Ridge, named Liu Mengmei. Sight of the tomb aroused his greed, and when night came he broke into it, then absconded. The young lady's remains were cast into the pond nearby. It was this I came to report, "careless of the length of the journey."

DU (*sighs*): My daughter's tomb rifled, my wife the victim of disaster. True enough the saying,

> "Hard to protect this body
>   till it lies three feet deep;
> harder still to protect the corpse
>   through its eternal sleep."

Well, we must let this be; but I thank you for your kindness and the trouble you have taken.

CHEN: I have known nothing but poverty and hardship since I said farewell to Your Excellency.

DU (*sighs*): Harassed by military matters, I am in no position to reward you. But there is an important service I should like to entrust to you.

CHEN: I shall be happy to undertake it.

DU: Some time ago I composed a brief missive to request Li Quan to withdraw his men. In the absence of any other envoy I must trouble you, sir, to deliver it. You men, bring forward my missive and the accompanying gifts. If you, Tutor Chen, can succeed in your persuasion of Li Quan, your deed will be reported to the court and your further career secured.

ATTENDANTS (*bringing forward* DU's *letter and packages*):

"The scholar employs his three-inch tongue,
the general a single sheet of paper."
Here are the missive and the gifts.

CHEN: I accept them with all deference. Yet it is a frightening task
to deliver such a message.

DU: Be at ease.

    v   Though close the siege as iron bucket
a single envoy may pass through
and the general's scrap of paper
will pacify the foe.

Tutor Chen,

make your best effort to convince these brigands
for treacherous though they be
still they must act as interest dictates.

CHEN: I fear this role of "persuader" is not one for which a scholar
is best fitted.

DU: Yet since they opened their lines to let you through, their intentions are obvious.

A scholar like yourself is my ideal messenger.

CHEN:

Your Excellency's missive, like a new Great Wall,
clothes this poor pedant in awesome might.

(Offstage drums and fifes)

DU:

    vi   Flutes shrill, tongues wag in the watchtower,
and when the task is accomplished
your name submitted to the court
will win its mite of favor
as bearer of this missive
vital to the protection of Huaiyang.

Envoi:

DU:

From sallies across the river
how many will return?

CHEN:

Prefect's carriage faces flood
to await the counselor's coming.

DU:

Sir, this visit from afar
has caused you many hardships.

CHEN:

> Still let the waves of your magnanimity
> wash this poor stranded fish!

SCENE FORTY-SEVEN: *Raising the Siege*

INTERPRETER:

> 1 All under Heaven
> split between contending houses, north and south,
> and in between the two
> a nettle bed of bandits
> openly aid the Tartars against their fellow Chinese.
> As their interpreter
> I specialize in starting quarrels.
> "When strange events befall
> there's reason for them all."

Interpreter in the camp of the Prince-errant of Jin, at your service. What a laugh: here's our chief busily besieging Huaian, aiding the Jin in their campaign against the Song, when what do you know, comes an envoy from the north on a secret mission to the southern forces! It's a true saying,

> "Learn the way they bleat and cheep
> still at heart they're dogs and sheep."

(Exit)

LI QUAN *(enters at head of his men)*:

> II Serrated pennants like tigers' fangs
> reach to the river,
> roosts for our hunters' falcons
> challenge the sky.
> With roll of drum and flags aflutter
> chariots and mail-clad steeds advance
> to surround the city, laid out like brocade
> with cloud upon cloud of dust.
> Ha, Commissioner Du,
> even wings won't help you now.

Prince-errant of Jin, at your service. I have had this city of Huaian under assault for many days, and still it doesn't fall. Though tiger-like my stance as I crouch for the kill, still in my heart I calcu-

late more like a fox. Worry number one, that massive reinforcements will be sent from the southern court; worry number two, a
reprimand from the northerners for failing in this mission. Caught
in this dilemma, I have summoned my dame for a conference.

DAME LI *(enters):*

> True daughter of Chiyou,[1]
>> scourge of hosts, captor of generals,
> leopardess-wife,
>> I manipulate demon and sprite.

Have you heard, Prince, of this envoy sent by the house of Jin to
confer with the southern court? He has just arrived outside the
gates of our camp.

LI: What a thing to happen!

TARTAR GENERAL *(enters on horseback, sword in hand):*

>> III　Post 'orse carry dis emboy from de nort'
>> wid tiger-'ead warrant all fancy an' shinink.

GROOM *(enters on the double, chasing wildly after him):* You're slipping, you're slipping!

TARTAR:

>> Who dat dar sojer
>> scare my 'orse?
>> How come
>> big camp 'ere, nobody 'ome?

GROOM *(bellows):* Prince! Prince-errant! The envoy from the north
is here! *(He runs off)*

LI, DAME LI *(they panic):* Fetch the interpreter at once!

INTERPRETER *(enters, and kneels before TARTAR):* The Prince-errant is
too sick to come out. May Your Highness deign to enter.

TARTAR:

>> Why 'e not
>> say so before—kerboolah!

> *(He dismounts and takes the seat of honor)*

Durr-durrrr!

LI *(to INTERPRETER):* What does he say?

INTERPRETER: He's angry.

> *(LI and DAME LI raise their folded hands in salute,*
> *but the TARTAR turns his head in annoyance and ignores them)*

---

1. Brass-headed, iron-browed chieftain who rebelled against the legendary Yellow Emperor.

TARTAR *(points to LI):* Chelly wondoo dalah!
LI: What's he say?
INTERPRETER: I daren't tell you—he says to kill you.
LI: What for?
TARTAR *(inspects DAME LI, and smiles):* Hooling-hooling! Wow!
DAME LI: What's he say?
INTERPRETER: He says he likes Madam's looks.
TARTAR: Kalao-kalao.
INTERPRETER: Riding has given him a thirst.
TARTAR *(gestures impatiently):* Oo, damn, damn.
INTERPRETER: He wants some koumiss.
TARTAR: Yar wooch!
INTERPRETER: And some roast mutton.
LI: Mutton and koumiss, quick!

(ATTENDANT enters with koumiss, which TARTAR gulps down,
and mutton, which he slices and gobbles)

TARTAR *(gives a satisfied laugh and wipes his greasy hands on his tunic*
front): Eeloo woolad.
INTERPRETER: He's happy now. He accepts your offering.
TARTAR *(sways drunkenly in his seat):* Sotobah, sotobah.
INTERPRETER: He says he's a bit drunk.
TARTAR *(gazes fixedly at DAME LI):* Da-oolah, da-oolah!
DAME LI *(giggles):* What's he say?
INTERPRETER: He wants you to sing for him, ma'am.
DAME LI: Certainly. Ha,

> IVA   how can I stop myself giggling
> as like some bodhisattva, ignorant of his tongue
> I sit here watching this foreign clown!
> Who does he think he is, this booby?
> "Come over here," without a by-your-leave,
> just a "yow-erch-boom-goo-lah."

Here, interpreter, I'll pour a cup of wine, you give it him.
INTERPRETER *(presents the wine):* Aah-err gally.
DAME LI: What was that?
INTERPRETER: I told him it was you offering the wine, ma'am.
DAME LI: That's right.
TARTAR *(sways drunkenly, gapes at DAME LI):* Botty-botty!
INTERPRETER: Now he wants you to dance for him.
DAME LI: Certainly, just let me get my pear-blossom spear.

(She performs her spear dance)

ivb Cold in the gale pear blossoms scatter,
fetchingly the slim waist sways,
whirl and spin, twirl and spin,
floral arch aburst in bloom
till this pop-eyed Tartar's
half beside himself!

TARTAR (*turns aside, flaps his arms, and collapses in laughter*): Hoo-ling! Hoo-ling! Wow! (*INTERPRETER helps him to his feet, he waves his arms around, and falls flat on the floor again*): Ally-bally!

INTERPRETER: He's applauding, and wants you to sing some more.

TARTAR (*smiles, nods, and beckons to DAME LI*): Hasa-hasa.

INTERPRETER: He wants to ask you something.

DAME LI (*smiles*): To ask me what?

TARTAR (*catches DAME LI by the sleeve and lowers his voice*): Hasa-hasa 'airy kalah, 'airy kalah.

DAME LI (*smiles*): What's he saying?

INTERPRETER (*shakes his head*): He wants to borrow something that belongs to you.

DAME LI (*smiles*): What is it he wants?

INTERPRETER: I'd rather not say.

TARTAR (*collapses in laughter again*): Gooloo-gooloo!

LI (*aside, to INTERPRETER*): What's this he wants from Mother? Him and his gooloo-gooloo!

INTERPRETER: He's after something he shouldn't ask for. He can ask, but I don't think Madam will let him have it. Even if Madam will, I don't think you will, and even if you will, I don't think I will.

LI: What *is* this thing that nobody's willing to let him have?

INTERPRETER: Why, he just said it—hasa-hasa hairy kalah—it's something of Madam's that's got hair on it.

LI (*enraged*): This makes me mad! What a nerve, from a stinkpot barbarian like this! Give me that spear!

(*He seizes the pear-blossom spear and runs at
the TARTAR with murderous intent. INTERPRETER helps TARTAR to
his feet, they dodge, and TARTAR, still
yelling "Gooloo-gooloo," picks up wine
jar and parries spear with it*)

LI:

v Block my spear, would you, you sweaty lecher?
Stinking nomad, think an iron wall protects you
all in the name of the mighty house of Jin?

(He grapples the TARTAR *to the floor)*

I'll stamp those red whiskers right down your throat,
wring that foul-smelling filthy neck!

(DAME LI pulls LI off the TARTAR)

TARTAR *(back on his feet)*: Yeelah-yeelah hallay! *(Points at* LI*)* Leelo jeeding moolash, leelo jeeding moolash! *(He exits, flapping his arms wildly)*

LI: I'm burning up! What was all that yeelah-ha about?

INTERPRETER: Calling for his groom.

LI: And what was that pointing at me and leelo jeeding moolash?

INTERPRETER: He's going to report it to his chief and have him send someone to kill you.

(LI trembles in distress)

DAME LI: Well, my old Prince, you shouldn't have done it.

LI: But, but, but—he was after that hairy kalah of yours!

DAME LI: Well, and supposing he'd got it? You're only jealous!

LI *(after a pause)*: I just blew up, that's all. But when this gets reported to the Jin court, this Prince-errantship of mine might wobble a bit.

DAME LI: He'll have to report on his mission to the southern court, he won't necessarily tell them about this.

LI: So what do you propose, Mother?

DAME LI: I'll have to think something out.

MESSENGER *(enters to offstage drums)*: Beg to report! That bachelor of arts we let go a couple of days ago just came galloping back alone from Huaian. Says he has an urgent message for the Prince.

DAME LI: Very timely, bring him in.

TUTOR CHEN *(enters)*:

> VI Necessity's the mother of invention
> and a scholar under orders from the general
> has to think of something smart!

(Loud yells offstage. CHEN *staggers in terror)*

Iron cannon roar
sweeping me off my feet.

Oh dear, oh dear,
> arms of war, shield and spear close-locked
> and me here in their midst!

MESSENGER: Enter, sir scholar!

CHEN *(presents himself)*: The scholar Chen Zuiliang, narrowly spared a thousand deaths, prostrates himself hundredfold before His Highness the Prince, Her Highness the Princess.

LI: Is Commissioner Du ready to hand over the city?

CHEN: The city would be a poor sort of gift. I bear the Commissioner's offer, made with all due respect, of a princedom for Your Highness.

LI: I'm a prince already, have been for years!

CHEN: This is what is meant by "rank piled on rank and title heaped on title." Commissioner Du submits this letter for your perusal.

LI (*reads aloud*): "Du Bao, family friend of generations past, kowtows before the standard of the Prince-errant Li." (*To* CHEN) What friendship has my family ever had with Commissioner Du?

CHEN: Court officers named Li and Du were constant companions during the Han dynasty, and the great Tang poets Li Bai and Du Fu were the closest friends. This is why Commissioner Du presumes to describe himself as a family friend.

LI: That's very nice of him. What does the letter say? (*Continues to read aloud*)

> VIIa They say you serve a foreign lord:
> with one who, tiger-like, wolf-like,
> harbors dreams of conquest
> friendship is hard to maintain;
> do but declare anew
> allegiance to the sacred house of Zhao,
> then treasure and titles will be yours
> and honor's duties all fulfilled.
> Fief and demesne will be secured to you:
> leave ways of darkness, turn to the light
> and swift will be your rise.
> Respond as did Zhao Tuo to Lu Jia's urgings,
> submit as did the descendants of Zhuang Qiao:[2]
> look favorably, we beseech you, on this plea.

(*He laughs*)

This document urges my submission to the Song court, advice I do

---

2. Lu Jia was sent by the founder of the Han dynasty to secure the submission of Prince Zhao Tuo (see scene 2, note 11): Zhuang Qiao of the royal house of Chu carved out an independent kingdom for himself which his descendants eventually yielded to the Han throne.

not welcome. But here's a separate message addressed to Her Highness. *(Laughs again)* Commissioner Du seems to be as scared of you as I am, Mother!

DAME LI: Read it out for me.

LI *(reads the second letter):* "Du Bao, family friend of generations past, bows with folded sleeves before the tent of Madam Yang." Hey, hey, here's Commissioner Du claiming to be an old friend of yours, too.

CHEN: If he's a friend of your family, Prince, then also of your Princess, for she is part of your family, too.

LI: I suppose so. But it's only women, not men, who bow with folded sleeves.

CHEN: If the Princess folded her sleeves to receive him, Commissioner Du would have to bow the same way in return!

DAME LI: Well said. Now read it all for me.

LI *(reads the letter):* "Du Bao, family friend of generations past, bows with folded sleeves before the tent of Madam Yang. It has come to our attention that the Jin Tartars have ennobled your honored spouse as Prince-errant, but have bestowed no title on Madam herself. This is improper and an insult. Your servant has already submitted to the court of our great Song dynasty a proposal that your ladyship be ennobled as Princess Pursuant of the Gold. On bent knee we await your pleasure in this. Witness our hand." —Well there's a fine thing, first he applies for court favors for Mother!

DAME LI: Tell me, Scholar Chen, if I'm made Princess Pursuant of the Gold, does that mean I'm supposed to go and chase the Golden Jin?

CHEN: Your title once bestowed, you can chase any gold you want, just show up at court and they'll give you all you can carry. That's the meaning of Princess Pursuant of the Gold.

DAME LI: I begin to see the beauty of your court of Song.

CHEN: Not to speak of yourself, madam, even the Duchess of Wei used to praise the beauty of the Prince of Song.[3]

DAME LI: I'll believe you. Now if I'm to have a gold headpiece I want plenty of gold in it. I usually wear a helmet, and lately I've

---

3. Tutor Chen jumbles some more quotations from the *Analects,* still with the Duchess Nanzi in mind (see scene 45, notes 1 and 2); "the beauty of Prince Chao of Song" is referred to—though not by the Duchess of Wei—in *Analects,* VI, 14.

dispensed with other adornments, so I'd like your southern court to make me a new helmet in the latest style.

CHEN: I shall see to it, madam.

LI: You're so busy pursuing all this gold, what about me, Prince-errant, what kind of errand is this for me?

CHEN: You'll have a title too, Prince Pursuant of the Gold.

LI: I accept.

CHEN (*kowtows*): I fear only a change of heart on Your Highnesses' part.

DAME LI: My mind is made up. Let's have a deed of submission written out, and we'll have Scholar Chen deliver it to the southern court.

LI:

> viib Submit we to the court of Song
> for house of Jin engenders only disasters.

DAME LI: Scholar Chen,

> undertake this task
> and you may ask for all the gold you wish.

CHEN: Great Prince,

> let sound of chimes from Poyang Lake
> drown out all wild ambitions

and, madam,

> as you turn back from sea of darkness
> may the stars favor you.

LI, DAME LI, CHEN:

> Let fighting cease,
> obey the loyal summons
> that these names may be struck from rebel list.

LI: Scholar Chen, you'll stay for supper, we will draft the deed of submission and see you off this very night.

> (*He raises his folded hands in a gesture of farewell,
> and* CHEN *makes obeisance in ceremonial leave-taking*)

> viii No match myself for the bandit-hero Li Kui,
> still this mighty wife of mine
> is a genuine Honored Lady Yang.[4]

---

4. Li Quan modestly disclaims comparison of his own prowess with that of Li Kui, the "Black Whirlwind," a swashbuckling leader of the *Shuihuzhuan* bandits; but he proudly equates his wife (nee Yang) with the "Honored Lady Yang," Yang Lingpo. This lady, better known in Peking Opera as She Taijun, was the wife of the Song general Yang Ye (or Yang Jiye); herself a mighty warrior, she was matriarch of the Yang family of generals whose saga is celebrated in novels and plays.

CHEN:

> This instrument of submission I carry
> will set the royal house of Zhao
> beside themselves with joy.

(Exit)

LI: Well, Mother, we've given up our "golden" days with the Golden Jin, but we've picked up a handy couple of princedoms. Most people can't manage one princedom, and here we are with two, isn't that a grand thing?

DAME LI: Don't get excited, there may be a third honor coming.

LI: What third honor?

DAME LI: The honor of a sword blade—right across the back of our necks!

LI: What do you mean?

DAME LI: A beheading.

LI: But we've submitted to them—what's all this about beheading?

DAME LI: When you and I were rebels, all our strength came from the support of the Tartars. Now we've changed sides, the southern court can take us any time they want.

LI *(enraged)*: Haha! My valor is a match for myriad men! What fear have I of any "southern court"?

DAME LI: You're another Xiang Yu, won't stop till you reach Crow River![5]

LI: Nothing of the kind! Anyway, if I'm Xiang Yu, you're the Beautiful Lady Yu, and I'm damned if I let His Majesty of the house of Zhao get his hands on you!

DAME LI: Enough of this, you're no Xiang Yu and I'm no Beautiful Lady Yu either. Let's try a scene from another play.

LI: Which?

DAME LI: Fan Li sails off with the Western Maid.[6]

LI: That was on Lake Tai. How do we get there? Let's take to the sea instead and live as pirates.

DAME LI *(to the waiting TROOPS)*: Men, we have declared our alle-

---

5. Xiang Yu, rival of the founder of the Han dynasty, met a heroic death at the Crow River after taking leave of his consort Yu and thereby furnishing the later Chinese stage with one of its favorite scenes of eternal farewell.

6. Closing scene of *Huanshaji*, the most famous play of the previous generation. For the Western Maid, see scene 14, note 2.

giance to the southern court. Dismantle the siege lines about Huaian and await our pleasure at the coast.

TROOPS: The siege is raised. *(Drums offstage)* Your ships wait in readiness, time for Your Highnesses to march.

> *(LI and DAME LI lead them aboard the imaginary*
> *boats and proceed in procession across the stage)*

LI:

> IXa Where Yangzi and Huai debouch,
> where Yangzi and Huai debouch,
> surge waves of open sea.
> Blow wind from east,
> blow wind from east
> to fill our sails of brocade.
> We'll take the Isles of Faery for our lair,
> raise our standard on giant sea turtle's back!

DAME LI:

> IXb Submit to the Way of Heaven,
> submit to the Way of Heaven
> and life gets a little easier.
> Strike your rebel flag,
> strike your rebel flag,
> to fight any further would be no light matter.
> The Jin are "Golden"—mere metal—
> but our mettle came close to melting
> in face of the Song, whose element is fire!
> Fold we now our peaceful hands
> and like sportive dragons roam the seas.

TROOPS: Prince, madam, we have reached the open sea.

LI: We will land and camp here, and set sail at daybreak.

Envoi:

LI:

> While spear still challenges shield
>   each is his own prince

DAME LI:

> clear-cut the rival spheres
>   of dragons male and female.

LI:

> Bear we now our standard
>   downstream to open sea

TROOPS:

> no longer to bend our bows
> 'gainst armies of the court.

SCENE FORTY-EIGHT: *Mother and Daughter Reunited*

BRIDAL DU:

> 1 My body wilted, wasted
> by demons of love longing,
> now freed from the grave's mouldering,
> clad all anew in fragrant flesh
> I wait alone in village inn,
> wife of penniless scholar.

SISTER STONE *(enters)*:

> But he's away
> making his fortune, mingling with the great.

BRIDAL:

> Woven bamboo blind
> hangs cold on autumn window

SISTER STONE:

> ashes of incense gather
> on pillow and pendant bright.

BRIDAL:

> Rivers bar the way
> to him who commands my dreams

SISTER STONE:

> till once again you meet
> beneath the flowering peaches

BRIDAL:

> for here's no misty wraith
> but his true love come again.

BRIDAL, SISTER STONE:

> Moon risen, breezes stopped,
> shadows press close to form.

BRIDAL: Aunt Stone, it was so great a happiness for me to be received back into life and to marry Master Liu. I was so sure of his immediate success and of our joyful return to make obeisances before my father and mother. Who could have foretold that insurrection south of the Huai would compel the court to postpone the examination announcements; and now my parents are trapped by siege and I have had to entreat Master Liu to seek news of them. Now here I lie abandoned in an inn by the Qiantang River: how melancholy a sight, moonlight on rolling waters!

SISTER STONE: But how does this compare, lady, with the yellow springs of Hades?

BRIDAL: Why, no comparison:

> IIa   moonlight on rolling waters,
> lonely village inn;
> still, when I think of years in the cold grave
> rather this glimpse of stars through tattered blinds
> than blackness underground.

Ah then, aunt,

> what could I learn of parents' well-being
> or how serve husband with rice and kindling?
> In anxious torment
> between death and life
> one man in all my dreams.

SISTER STONE: Few indeed have known such adventures!

> IIb   And I kept you company in simple shrine
> through the long waiting for your destined mate.

BRIDAL: That night, aunt, when you came calling at Master Liu's door, did you know that it was I hiding there?

SISTER STONE:

> I'll never know how painted scroll
> could furnish such concealment—
> you would have hoodwinked
> the very spirits that way!

BRIDAL: It's twilight already, see now

> shadowed moonlight, pale-shining stars
> and glowworms green as demon fire.

Time to light the lamp.

SISTER STONE: We're out of oil,

> but here in the dark
> a few glimmers suffice for you
> to doff your robe of gauze.

BRIDAL: The nights are so long, and sleep comes slow. Go borrow a jar of oil from the landlord.

SISTER STONE: Sit here for a while in the garden, then, and I'll go.

> "When all is dark as covered jar
> lotus-bud feet will not get far!"

(She exits, leaving BRIDAL *to gaze at the moon and
sigh. Enter* MADAM DU, *as on a journey,
attended by* SPRING FRAGRANCE)

MADAM DU:

    III Armed uproar north of the river,
south of the river we wander to and fro,
no perfumed carriage to bear us
but traveling sandals that soon must fall apart.
My husband commands the armies:
I gaze beyond the horizon, but how to know
whether he lives or has perished?
Amid the jostling throng
my sole companion little Spring Fragrance:
chignon awry,
haste forbids arrangement in Yangzhou style;
yet somehow we have reached Hangzhou our goal.
Dark shadows fall on wooded hills:
where to find shelter, strangers as we are?

SPRING FRAGRANCE: Thank goodness, Hangzhou at last!

MADAM DU: Truly a chance in a thousand that we have escaped with our lives as far as Hangzhou. But there is no one here we can turn to after all the perils of our long and lonely road.

FRAGRANCE: This gate before us seems to be ajar, let's try it without further ceremony.

MADAM DU *(steps through the gate):* Oh, how empty and silent everywhere! Is anyone here?

BRIDAL: Who is it?

FRAGRANCE: A woman's voice. I'll ask her to open the inner gate.

BRIDAL *(startled):*

    IVa As by sculptured balustrade I lean
whence come these gentle tones
seeking admittance?

MADAM DU:

Benighted on our journey
two ladies seek a moment's shelter.

BRIDAL:

No man, indeed, from the voice.
I'll open the gate to what the moonlight shows.

(They greet each other)

A lady visitor. Please come inside and sit for a while.

MADAM DU:

> I come in hope
> of succor, human or divine.

BRIDAL:

> Excuse this rough reception,
> excuse this rough reception.

(Each, for the first time, examines the other's face)

MADAM DU *(in surprise):* Lady,

> ɪvb in this tumbledown place
> why do you sit alone,
> your lamp unlighted?

BRIDAL:

> Here in the paleness of this empty court
> I watch and wait for the fullness of the moon.[1]

MADAM DU *(aside to FRAGRANCE):* Fragrance, who does this lady remind you of?

FRAGRANCE *(startled):* I daren't say it—the image of my young mistress!

MADAM DU: Go quickly and look if there is anyone else here. If there is no one, I fear this must be a ghost.

(FRAGRANCE exits)

BRIDAL *(aside):* This lady is the image of my mother, and that maid is surely Spring Fragrance! *(To MADAM DU)* Where have you come from, madam?

MADAM DU *(sighs):*

> From Huaian, where my husband
> as Pacification Commissioner
> is beset by armed uprising.
> I escaped with my life to reach this place of haven.

BRIDAL *(aside):* It is my mother! But how can I make myself known to her?

FRAGRANCE *(hastens back and whispers aside to MADAM DU):* Empty house, no trace of anyone else. It's a ghost, it's a ghost!

(MADAM DU trembles in fear)

---

1. The full rounding of the moon is a metaphor for human reunion.

BRIDAL: This is indeed my mother and her story confirms it! *(She throws herself forward, in tears):* Mother! Mother!

MADAM DU *(moves away from her):* Is this you, my child? Forgive me, I have neglected you, and now you are here as a revenant to accuse me. Fragrance, take spirit money from our baggage and scatter it at once.

(FRAGRANCE does so)

BRIDAL: I am your daughter, and no ghost!

MADAM DU: If you are no ghost, I will call your name thrice and you must answer thrice, each time louder than before.

(She calls thrice and BRIDAL answers thrice, but each time weaker than before)

Yes, a ghost!

BRIDAL: Mother, let me tell my story.

MADAM DU:

But first move back
for from your ghostly presence
an icy whirlwind blows.

BRIDAL:

No "ghostly presence" this!

MADAM DU *(recoils in terror as BRIDAL clutches at her hand):* Child, your hand is cold!

FRAGRANCE *(kowtows):* Young mistress, please don't come and pinch me!

MADAM DU: Child, we would have had a great mass said for your soul, but your father was set against it.

BRIDAL *(weeps):* Mother, however much you may fear me, nothing will make me leave you again!

SISTER STONE *(reenters with lamp):*

IVC Gate firmly barred,
what voices these in deserted court?

(She lowers her lamp to light the path)

And how did yellow spirit money
light here on the green moss?

FRAGRANCE: Madam, isn't this Sister Stone?

MADAM DU: It is indeed.

SISTER STONE *(in surprise):* Ha, where can her ladyship and Spring Fragrance have come from, and everyone so confused and bewildered?

See them hover, hesitate,
her ladyship
    recoiling in fear that the lacquerware lamp is unlit[2]
and the young mistress
    in dim shades longing for light to let her draw near.

BRIDAL: Come quickly, aunt, to help my mother overcome her fear of me.

FRAGRANCE: Don't say Aunt Stone is a ghost, too?

SISTER STONE (*takes MADAM DU by the arm and shines her lamp on BRIDAL):*
    An end to fearful doubts!
    Let lamplight aid the moon to show her features:
    surely this is the face of her we lost?

MADAM DU, FRAGRANCE:
    The face of her we lost!

MADAM DU (*embraces BRIDAL and weeps*): My child, ghost or not I couldn't bear to give you up again!
    ıvd   Three years of heartbreak:
    what brings the cruel sea
    to give back now its shining pearl?

BRIDAL:
    For my father's sake and yours
    the court of Hades in pity
    granted my soul's return.

FRAGRANCE: But how did you manage to escape from the grave, miss?

BRIDAL:
    A story hard to tell.

MADAM DU: But how did it come about?

BRIDAL:
    My sad fate moved the Lady of the Eastern Peak,[3]
    who gave a young scholar, in his dream,
    instructions to open my tomb.

MADAM DU: What young scholar was this?

BRIDAL: His name is Liu Mengmei, from South of the Ridge.

FRAGRANCE: What a wonderful thing, there really is a *liu*, "willow," and a *mei*, "apricot"!

---

2. Allusion to the tale of a man named Shen Bin, who desired to be buried at the foot of a tree in his garden. The day he died, an old tomb, which contained an unlit lacquerware lamp and a tablet with Shen Bin's own name on it, was discovered there.
3. Bridal kowtowed before the image of this goddess in scene 27.

MADAM DU: How did he come to bring you here?

BRIDAL:

    It was for the examinations we came here.

MADAM DU: A worthy young bachelor of arts, then! Please invite him in at once to pay his respects.

BRIDAL: At my request

    he left to seek news of my father and yourself

    in embattled Huaiyang

    and this is why I lie

    alone in rustic court,

    alone in rustic court.

MADAM DU *(aside, to FRAGRANCE)*: Can this be possible?

FRAGRANCE: It must be, for how could there be a ghost as lively as this?

MADAM DU *(turns back to BRIDAL, in tears)*: My child!

    va I had believed your pure spirit, risen to Heaven,

    high-placed on lotus throne in western paradise;

    what thought had I of such reunion

    after three years cut off in ghostly caverns?

    I wept till limbs were numbed, bowels tormented,

    heart withered, moistened by nought but tears,

    dreams wracked with grief, and mind distracted.

    One moment you were here on earth;

    the next, your world and mine were not the same.

    Fears grew that offerings of rice to your spirit

    were all cut off

    and sheep and oxen grazed over your grave.

ALL:

    What night is this?

    What night is this?

    Or do we meet now only in dream?

BRIDAL *(weeps)*:

    vb In shallow earth you laid your child

    where bones grew cold and sleep came slow;

    the cold food you offered at the Feast of the Dead

    there South of the River

    was more than I could eat.

    Never dreaming of such a day as this

    now I find that past time

    impossible to relate.

    Unfathomable riddle:

    when, when will Heaven make all things clear?

Ghost no more, accept me now as mortal:
had not my former life been cut off
how could I now take up the threads again?

ALL:

What night is this?
What night is this?
Or do we meet now only in dream?

MADAM DU: Aunt Stone, I am grateful to you for watching over my daughter.

SISTER STONE:

vc But don't ask me to blurt out
the story of what happened
for I go all of a cold sweat just to think of it.
In all good faith I performed
the sacrifices every seventh day,
made offerings middle of the seventh month, All Souls—
how did I know she'd found herself a lover?

(She sings in lowered voice, aside to MADAM DU):

There was I, out demon chasing—
how was I to know this shadow play
was none but herself, returned to human form?

ALL:

Miraculous destiny,
miraculous destiny,
the wheel of karma come full circle.

FRAGRANCE:

vd I've heard of maids like Qiannü[4]
who sent her spirit roaming
but here's the marvel of body and soul
rejoined after three long years.
There I pitied her, encoffined
and never known a husband
and here she's dwelling, mistress of this court!

Truly, my young mistress,
lovelorn spirit so determined
now fulfilled in wifely devotion!
Never a day Spring Fragrance

---

4. See scene 36, note 8.

didn't set a meal for your departed spirit,
never a festival her ladyship
didn't offer sacrifices with her tears,
and all the time
you'd quit the halls of Hades
and joined him on that boat!

ALL:

Miraculous destiny,
miraculous destiny,
wheel of karma come full circle.

MADAM DU:

VI So full my heart:
my daughter restored to life
stands here before the lamp.
Yet your poor father
beset in that nest of rebels can receive no word.
BRIDAL: Do not distress yourself, Mother, for my husband will be
faithful to my plea:
in caves of earth or reaches of the sky
he will complete his search.

Envoi:

The spirit is seen in fancy
that's hidden from the eye;
phoenix wings bear aloft the searcher
for peaches of paradise.
Claim not that warmth of flesh
belongs to mortals only
when the first light of dawn
strikes cold gleams from the mirror.

SCENE FORTY-NINE: *Moored before Huaian*

LIU MENGMEI (*carrying traveling bundle and umbrella*):
1 No easy road to take
in time of strife and disintegration.
To the solitary wanderer

falling leaves announce autumn's coming.
My gentle wife longed for news of her father
and so in Yangzhou I sought him
only to learn of his plight, besieged in Huaian
where now I hasten to his aid.

                    (*He recites a Tang pastiche*)
    How to devise some means
        to visit honored kinfolk
    though far above me in station as
        broad highway from muddy trail?
    Alas, for this simple scholar
        helpless before life's hardships,
    no other occupation
        than the struggle with poverty.

Penniless scholar in this world of men, I, Liu Mengmei, became the
beloved of Bridal Du, who dwelt in the shades, made her my wife,
and journeyed to the metropolitan examinations with her at my
side. By good fortune my paper was accepted in the palace examination, but alarms from the frontier delayed announcement of the
results. Soon my young bride, learning that rebel action threatened
her father's armies in Huaiyang, begged me to undertake this journey to ascertain his welfare. She placed in my hands her own self-
portrait, with the aid of which I shall announce the joyous news of
her return to the mortal world. Yet poverty denied me other means
to finance my journey, and I am dependent on the objects my bride
brought with her out of the tomb. Some of these things are be-
jeweled trifles, not easy to sell or pawn at a moment's notice; some
are vessels of precious metal sadly tarnished by burial. Moreover, I
am a scholar by training and quite ignorant of the marks of the
merchant's scale. I have made but little cash on my journey, and
what little I have made has gone to supply my daily needs. Reaching Yangzhou I learned that my father-in-law had led his armies on
to the defense of Huaian. Rebel troops blocked the road, I could
advance no further. But now, as luck will have it, they seem to be
growing lax and dispersing, so I am making my way ahead as best I
can.

        ii   I'd hoped to follow old Du Mu,[1]

---

1. The Tang poet Du Mu in a celebrated line spoke of waking from a "ten-year
Yangzhou dream," which had brought him nothing but a name for heartlessness in
the pleasure quarters.

drink deep in Yangzhou, dream away
three lifetimes in the houses of flowers and moon—
how could I guess His Excellency had left
to ascend the mighty Huai!
No chance to mount on crane's back
like some immortal sylph
to soar the winds of Heaven,
myriad gold pieces stacked about my waist:
my fate now, to seek food and shelter
from fisherman and woodcutter
where dying lotus, wilting willow
touch Lake Tai with autumn.
Ah, how the breath of autumn speaks
of failure yet to establish name or rank
and of my weeping bride's abandoned plight!
Do not look back
for equal melancholy reigns
south as north of the river.

As I travel my road, now to my joy I see the walls of Huaian rising
to meet the sky, and beneath the walls the clear waters of the great
Huai River. Over the watchtowers stream military banners sixteen
feet long. Drums roll and bugles blow, they must be closing the city
gates. I'll seek out an inn for the night.

INNKEEPER (enters):
    Water my wine as much as I may,
    not much money passes this way.
Is it a night's shelter you are seeking, sir scholar?

(LIU enters the inn)

Will you take the special delicacies with your wine, or just the ordinary?

LIU: I do not drink wine.

INNKEEPER: You'll want a meal, though?

LIU: I'll eat first, pay later.

INNKEEPER: No, pay first, eat later.

LIU: Here are some scraps of silver.

INNKEEPER: I should say they *are* scraps. I'll just weigh them. (He
does so, and calls out in astonishment) Your silver's run away! (He
hunts about on the floor)

LIU: What are you making all this fuss about?

INNKEEPER: Sir, your silver's disappeared down a crack in the floor.

You can see some specks still.

LIU: Very well, here's some more.

INNKEEPER *(takes the silver, but loses it again; all is then repeated a third time)*: Why, sir, it must be quicksilver you've brought with you!

LIU: How could it be quicksilver? *(Aside)* But that's right, it was the quicksilver placed in Miss Du's mouth when she died.[2] "When the clay in its jaws turns to pearl, a dragon will ascend to Heaven; when the quicksilver in its mouth turns to elixir, a ghost may return to earth." This is as things should be, it is a matter of chemical change upon contact with the open air. When the young lady died, the quicksilver died also; now she has returned to life, and so has the quicksilver along with her. But magical substances of this kind, I fear, are beyond the understanding of the common run of men. *(He turns back to INNKEEPER)* Enough of this, landlord, you have frittered away all my fine silver till there isn't a mite left. This book here is one I am constantly reading, it's worth a jug of wine.

INNKEEPER: Book looks pretty worn.

LIU: I'll add a brush to go with it.

INNKEEPER: Brush looks pretty fuzzy.

LIU: With all the customers passing this way, you must have heard of Du Fu's line about "scholarship that wears out ten thousand books"?

INNKEEPER: Can't say I have.

LIU: Or of Li Bai's "dream of a brush that sprouted a thousand blossoms"?

INNKEEPER: Can't say I have.

LIU *(laughs)*:

> IIIa   A droll conceit
> of ten thousand tattered tomes
> and a thousand blooms from a brush head.

My mistake—these are not things one buys wine with.

INNKEEPER *(laughs also)*: But "fairies have given their pendants of jade, ministers of state their gold and sables."

LIU: Ha, but where did they come from, these sables, this gold, these pendants of jade?

> When one fitted to serve the nation
> offers himself to his prince

---

2. See scene 35.

then clad in sables, decked with jades,
he shines forth, learned beyond price.
Don't you realize:

high-born ladies will seek to bring him
their dowry of a thousand gold pieces;
leading ministers of the court
will bow in deference before him.

INNKEEPER: Why, what do they want with him?

LIU:

The brush of a man of true learning
can restore peace to the empire.

You won't take my book, you won't take my brush—how about this umbrella?

INNKEEPER: It's going to rain.

LIU: Then I won't go out tomorrow.

INNKEEPER: Then you'll die here—of starvation.

LIU *(laughs):* Have you heard of Commissioner Du Bao?

INNKEEPER: Who hasn't? There's a feast tomorrow to celebrate his raising the siege.

LIU: Well, I'm his son-in-law, on my way to visit him.

INNKEEPER *(startled):* It's a good thing your lordship told me, there's an invitation for you that His Excellency issued days ago.

LIU: Where is this invitation?

INNKEEPER: I'll take your lordship to see it. *(He ceremoniously leads LIU away)* Let me carry your baggage and umbrella for you, sir.

(They proceed a few steps)

LIU: Where is the invitation?

INNKEEPER: What's this, then?

LIU: But this is a proclamation to the citizenry.

INNKEEPER: That's it! Take a look:

iiib "Interdiction of vagabond cheats and impostors"!

—It seems His Excellency Du is a native of Sichuan province:

"In this place we find ourselves
three thousand miles from our Sichuan home:
no son nor nephew have we summoned to our side
nor yet has our family counted a son-in-law."

—This next bit is about your lordship:

"Should any impostor put forward false claims
the constabulary is authorized to arrest him."

—And this is about your humble servant:

"Any provider of succor or shelter
to be equally implicated in the crime.
This to be proclaimed
throughout our jurisdiction."
"Witness our seal, fifth month, thirty-second year of the Jianyan reign of the great Song Dynasty."[3]—And you can see Commissioner Du's seal at the end, it says "Office of the Imperially appointed Commander-in-Chief and Pacification Commissioner for the Huaiyang Region," all bright shiny red. Now, your lordship, if you'll just wait here a minute, I'll be off and report you and I'll be back in no time.

"Sweep snow from your own gate, that's enough,
don't worry 'bout frost on your neighbor's roof!"

(Exit)

LIU *(weeps):* Ah wife, wife, if only you knew of my helpless misery now I have reached this place! *(He looks about)* Ha, there ahead is a building with an inscription in great gilt characters, perhaps I can find shelter. *(He reads the inscription)* "Shrine of the Fuller Woman." What does this mean? *(He reads further)* Yes, a tablet on the wall:

"The great Han Xin remembered a bowl of rice
and left a story for a thousand ages."
—That's it, the fuller woman was the benefactress of Han Xin, who was Earl of Huaiyin.[4] To think that Han Xin was a pseudo Prince of Qi[5] and still could be fed, yet here am I, a genuine bachelor of arts, and even a cup of unheated wine is beyond me! I should offer a thousand obeisances to this fuller woman.

(He prostrates himself)

IV	Angling for his keep in the wide lands of Chu
the starving princeling met his fuller woman.
She recognized a greatness there
to which Xiang Yu, his commander, was blind
despite his double-pupiled eyes!
The Grand Historian praised her,

---

3. A.D. 1158.
4. Han Xin, principal lieutenant of the founder of the Han dynasty, was saved from starvation in his youth by a fuller woman, whom he rewarded in his years of greatness.
5. After his conquests in Shandong (the ancient land of Qi), Han Xin asked only to be enfeoffed as "pseudo" Prince of Qi.

the city of Huaian commemorates her,
and so a bowl of rice was worth
a thousand pieces of gold.
History shows us so many women of vision!
　　Duke Wen of Jin begged for food and was scorned
　　but the wife of Xi Fuji honored him;
　　Wu Zixu of Chu begged for food and was scorned
　　but a girl washing silk was loyal to him.[6]
　　Before their pointed phoenix shoes
　　I knock my head on the ground
　　three thousand times.
The first watch has begun, I'll take my rest under this covered walkway, and be up early in time for the opening of the city gates. There is no water for my ablutions . . . *(he looks out)* but good, it's raining!

Envoi:

　　No one to talk with
　　　　about the days of old
　　but thinking how the fuller woman
　　　　recognized a prince.
　　Before the commander's tent I bow
　　　　in tattered scholar's gown—
　　do not cause these thin lapels
　　　　to be soaked through with tears!

SCENE FIFTY: *Uproar at the Banquet*

DU BAO *(enters with ATTENDANTS):*
　　1　Endless Huai with roar of thousand steeds,
　　wild geese file across autumn sky,
　　waves curl up to lowering clouds.

---

6. One of the classic models of self-sacrifice, a "girl washing silk" recognized the noble Wu Zixu when he was a fugitive, but jumped into the river and drowned herself so that he need not fear betrayal.

> Here as I gaze from lodge's height
> homesick eyes fill with tears.

DU, ATTENDANTS:

> Turn of circumstance
> brought us our song of triumph.
> Now still we linger here.

DU:

> The road to earldom a thousand tortuous leagues
> and many the pair of sandals I've worn through!
> Now horn and drum on ramparts
> announce the autumn dusk
> and age draws on.
> Beacons last night announced a state of peace
> but dreams of home brought waking tears
> to one detained by duty
> lingering irresolute.

I, Du Bao, serving as Pacification Commissioner was faced with armed insurrection. Besieging forces cut off any hope of relief, but by skillful use of messages I brought about the raising of the siege. Now the rebel Li Quan has left and the forces of Jin have not advanced to replace him. Meanwhile there is work of rehabilitation to be done, and this is what I now occupy myself with. All of you, my staff, await my orders outside the gate there!

> (ATTENDANTS *exit, except for one who takes up his*
> *station as* GATEKEEPER. DU *sighs*)

Rejoice as I may in the salvation of the city, still the pain of the loss of my wife cuts deeper. (He weeps) Ah, my lady wife! Yesterday I submitted a separate memorial to request funeral honors for her and leave for myself to return to my home in the west. How will His Majesty receive this? Truly, "wealth and honors vanish like dew from the grass, family reunion is rare as flowers on brocade."[1] (He sets himself to examining documents)

LIU MENGMEI (enters in tattered gown and cap, and carrying BRIDAL DU's self-portrait):

> 11 Pain of penury, pain of the wanderer,
> season of stricken leaves and wild geese flying.

---

1. "Flowers on brocade" are usually a metaphor for the superfluous, but here suggest something hard to meet with.

(He straightens his garments)

> Straighten my cap to shine
> resplendent as a bridegroom
> for how can I be sure
> of family recognition?

GATEKEEPER *(calls out):* What traveler is this?

LIU: His son-in-law come to pay respects to His Excellency Du Bao.

GATEKEEPER: Is this the truth?

LIU: The word of a scholar.

(GATEKEEPER steps inside to seek instructions)

DU: Our proclamation has stated the position clearly. What does he look like?

GATEKEEPER: Nothing special, but he's carrying a scroll.

DU *(smiles):* A painter—tell him I'm tied up with military concerns.

GATEKEEPER *(returns to post):* His Excellency is tied up with military concerns. You may be at ease.

LIU: At ease—but "ease makes for no success."

GATEKEEPER: Then off with you, for "success can take no ease."

LIU: Is His Excellency out visiting?

GATEKEEPER: There's a peace banquet today for all officers civil and military, the guest register has already been filled.

LIU: What do you mean by a "peace banquet," brother?

GATEKEEPER: It's an annual event at every frontier post, only this year is special because the rebels have been repulsed. The tables will be set with jeweled trees, silver dishes, bolts of silk, ingots, and all sorts; if you're His Excellency's son-in-law you can take some home with you.

LIU: So that's how it is. I'm only afraid that when I'm received I'll be asked for a verse for the banquet, a victory song or a eulogy of the "clearing of the Huai River," not so easy at a moment's notice. I'll just borrow this gatehouse of yours for a while to think something out, for "best prepared is best served."

GATEKEEPER: You'd better be off, sir scholar, here come the officers.

CIVIL OFFICIAL *(enters as LIU exits):*

> III   Fortress walls along the Huai
> shrouded in autumn now
> as we rejoice in armor laid aside.
> Time now for all to join
> in songs of praise for peace.

MILITARY OFFICER *(enters)*:
> Officers civil and military
> generals and ministers alike
> gather to feast our Lord.

After you.

CIVIL OFFICIAL: At our banquet today for officers both civil and military let fruits of field and stream be served in abundance, and let there be no lack of song and dance.

CIVIL OFFICIAL, MILITARY OFFICER *(they salute DU)*: Spirits of earth and air support His Sacred Majesty, the might of our lord is manifest to every corner. With one slim document the rebels were dispersed; time now for feasting in honor of peace and in accord with martial rites. All is in readiness; deign to grace our festive board!

DU: Though my poor services contributed little to the achievement of our armies, it is not for me to set aside an annual rite when all of you gentlemen are here in attendance. I dare claim no song of triumph, but let us use this occasion for our ease and relaxation.

(Drums and pipes sound offstage. ATTENDANT enters, bearing wine)

ATTENDANT: "A three-inch tongue worth more than Huang Shi's *Tactics,* and Five-peels Wine beats Snowbrew from Qinghe." Here's the wine.

DU *(pours the wine)*:
> IVa   North of the Yangzi, south of the Huai,
> Heaven and earth free and clear,
> the soldier's dipper measures our tranquil nights.[2]

CIVIL OFFICIAL, MILITARY OFFICER *(offering wine)*:
> From the Great Wall itself
> what can resist the force of our commander?
> Joy that the clash of arms is stilled,
> our battle pennants motionless,
> for a scrap of paper turned the rebels back.
> We could not bear to gaze on the sacred land
> under the wail of Tartar flutes
> but here's the hub of defense
> for a thousand frontier leagues!

---

2. A sort of soldier's canteen was beaten to mark night watches in the army, but the nights are ruled also, of course, by the Big Dipper constellation.

ALL:

> Where autumn winds sweep frontier grass
> we wait attendance
> at our peace banquet;
> wine like the flowing Huai,
> chivalrous hearts as one,
> wishing our prince long life!

DU:

> rvb Good fortune attend His Majesty!
> The combined skills of my officers
> held firm this sector of our defenses.

CIVIL OFFICIAL, MILITARY OFFICER:

> Clear and strong came your commands
> spontaneous as the great Zhang Liang,
> who laid out strategy for the founder of Han
> with chopsticks at banquet table

DU: With my letters to Li Quan and his wife, I devised a scheme
> as Chen Ping repulsed the Huns with a tale of glamour
> or Liu Kun with his piping in the moonlight—[3]
> one word broke through the besiegers' chains.
> Other than this, what hope of reinforcements?
> With Heaven's aid alone we gather today.

ALL:

> Where autumn winds sweep frontier grass
> we wait attendance
> at our peace banquet;
> wine like the flowing Huai,
> chivalrous hearts as one,
> wishing our prince long life!

MESSENGER (enters to the sound of drumrolls offstage): "Adorned with gold and sables, installed in highest office; outside the Commissioner's brocaded tent, where was our wall of defense to be found?" Your Excellency's memorial has been submitted and I bear the Imperial command, that rather than retire into private life you are to

---

3. With a stratagem of *cherchez la femme* comparable to Du Bao's own, Chen Ping rescued the founder of the Han dynasty from the besieging Huns. He convinced the wife of the Hun chieftain that a beautiful woman was about to be presented to her husband, and she, rather than face such competition, persuaded him to give up the siege and withdraw. In scene 43 Du Bao alluded to Liu Kun, whose piping made the barbarians homesick.

proceed to court to assume the duties of Minister of State. Madam
Du is posthumously created Virtuous Lady of the first rank.
CIVIL OFFICIAL, MILITARY OFFICER: Minister of State means Chief
Minister: we of Your Excellency's staff reverently offer our joy that
your military success is rewarded by ministerial rank!

(They offer wine)

> IVC   One crowned with sable headdress, cicada-winged,
> may months and years preserve
> felicitations now as he joins with dragons and tigers
> gathered at court like spokes at a hub.

At this your departure, sir, we look to lay aside

> our weapons washed in the River of Heaven,
> the world at peace beneath your mighty hand.
> Season of cassia's blooming
> will waft onward your steed with fragrance divine
> flutes and drums sound daylong
> until to the capital you bring the news
> of high autumn here in the south.
> But will you then remember, as washing blocks sound,[4]
> the days of your old adventures?

ALL:

> Where autumn winds sweep frontier grass
> we wait attendance
> at our peace banquet;
> wine like the flowing Huai,
> chivalrous hearts as one,
> wishing our prince long life!

DU: Each of you gentlemen is at the height of his talents and vigor
and destined for noble rank. It is no great achievement for such a
one as myself to be returning white-haired to the court.

> IVd   Each day consulting mirror or gazing from balcony
> tears moisten my gown for the changes time brings,
> for the state of our rivers and hills
> and the ravages of the years.
> Wildly eying my "sword of Wu"
> I hack at the railing;
> then, as the sun sets, turn my head—

---

4. Thudding of clothes on washing blocks, as people make ready their winter
clothing, is a common seasonal metaphor.

but ah, the river flowing east bears off
dreams of return to the south.

(He salutes them with folded hands)

With whom, henceforth, will you banter
as did his staff with General Yü of old?

ALL:

Where autumn winds sweep frontier grass
we wait attendance
at our peace banquet;
wine like the flowing Huai,
chivalrous hearts as one,
wishing our prince long life!

LIU (reenters): Poem completed, ready in my belly; name card yet to
submit! (To GATEKEEPER) Announce me again, brother.

GATEKEEPER: His Excellency is in the midst of a peace banquet.

LIU: Here I have a poem to celebrate the banquet all thought out and
ready, and the banquet is still in progress.

GATEKEEPER: Who asked you for such a thing?

LIU: Brother, I am His Excellency's son-in-law, willy-nilly I must
pay my respects.

GATEKEEPER (turns back to DU): Your Excellency, here's your son-in-
law, Willy Nilly, come to pay his respects.

DU: Beat him!

LIU (as GATEKEEPER angrily shoves him offstage): While father-in-law
still sits at meat, 'tis meet for me to attend his pleasure. (He exits)

SINGING GIRLS (enter):

"Warriors locked in deadly combat
yet swirls the dance by general's tent."

The entertainers salute Your Excellency.

va Fife and drum greet our commander
as clouds of battle lift.
We would plead with His Majesty to detain
our defender of Huaiyang
but sable headdress awaits him,
jade belt to adorn his waist,
and golden seal his wrist;
in whirling autumn wind,
gold stirrups clattering,
he'll smile and wave on the road to the palace
strewn with sand in his honor!

ALL:

Rivers and hills he took in his hand
to present to His Lord our Prince;
now city of jade prepares pipe and song
to greet his triumphal progress.

LIU *(reenters):*

"To see for a hundred leagues
still one more tower to climb."

The feast must be over by now and the singing ended, and I'm famished. No help for it, I shall force my way in.

GATEKEEPER *(seizes him):* What are you, a hungry ghost, that you've no shame?

LIU *(furious):* You low menial who attends His Excellency's horse, how dare you insult one who like myself has "mounted the dragon" to become his son-in-law? Now see if I don't beat you! *(He does so)*

DU *(calls):* Who dares make such a disturbance before the camp?

GATEKEEPER: It's that son-in-law who turned up this morning, says his name is Willy Nilly, tattered gown, tattered cap, tattered baggage roll, tattered parasol, and a tattered portrait scroll in his hand, says he's starving and is trying to force his way in. Anyone who tries to dissuade him gets beaten, he's beaten nine and a half in turn, all that's left is half of me here!

DU *(furious in his turn):* Disgusting! After the interdiction I issued, what fraudulent scoundrel is this to come making up such a tale?

CIVIL OFFICIAL, MILITARY OFFICER: If this young man has truly "mounted the dragon," it's up to us to "flatter the phoenix"—to establish ourselves in his favor!

DU: So you would fall for his scheme! Have the adjutant arrest this rogue, and see that express couriers escort him as far as the Hangzhou jail!

(ADJUTANT shouts assent, seizes LIU and trusses him up)

LIU: Injustice! Oh, my wife, my wife!

For love of Fondle Jade I aspired
to join the noble house of Qin[5]
but now must copy Zhong Yi in scholar's hat,
prisoner from the land of Chu.[6]

---

5. For Fondle Jade, Nongyu, see scene 32, note 3, and scene 33, note 4.
6. Zhong Yi, musician of Chu in classical times, so impressed his Jin captors with the nobility of his character that he was freed and sent home.

(Exits)

DU: You gentlemen cannot know how sharp have been the pangs of separation from my family in these times of trouble. And now comes this nobody with his raging and yelling to stir up my sorrows anew.

CIVIL OFFICIAL, MILITARY OFFICER: The name of your late wife, by the grace of His Majesty, is inscribed on the roll of the paragons of virtue. Do not fear that you will lack worthy descendants. Let the singing girls pour wine!

 vb Your southern duties successfully completed
 and the alarms all ended,
 accept this goblet in the name of peace.
 Good fortune and long life await you
 and offspring manifold
 by a new wife to be.

DU: I'm drunk.

(SINGING GIRLS move to his side to support him. He weeps)

 See how their sleeves "stain with a hero's tears"!
 Not for "autumn's grief alone"
 do I grow haggard!

ALL:

 Rivers and hills he took in his hand
 to present to His Lord our Prince;
 now city of jade prepares pipe and song
 to greet his triumphal progress.

DU: Gentlemen, I leave you. I am anxious to present myself at court, and shall begin my journey as soon as possible.

(Drums and music offstage)

 vi Tomorrow a parting cup of wine . . .

CIVIL OFFICIAL, MILITARY OFFICER:

 before His Majesty requests your portrait . . .

DU *(smiles):*

 yet by the time it hangs in Unicorn Hall
 my head will be snow-white!

Envoi:

DU:

 Westward a thousand leagues of sand
  the rebels pacified

CIVIL OFFICIAL:
>flanked by double banners
>eastward he returns.

MILITARY OFFICER:
>Across the frontier in setting sun
>wild geese all are flown

ALL:
>thoughts linger on waters of Huai
>placid as a mirror.

SCENE FIFTY-ONE: *The Lists Proclaimed*

TWO GENERALS OF THE IMPERIAL GUARD (*enter, bearing the Imperial regalia of orb and mallet*):
>Phoenix dance and dragons soar
>>about the Imperial capital;
>behold, in lofty palace halls,
>>the plumes of His Majesty's Guard.
>The Gate of Heaven waits to announce
>>the candidates' success
>when fresh from river lands is heard
>>the song of martial triumph.

To our places. His Majesty is to hold court, and here we wait in attendance.

AGED PRIVY COUNCILLOR (*enters*):
>1 Under our care, from ordered court
>to provisioning of farthest frontier,
>our rivers and hills stand firm.

MIAO SHUNBIN (*enters*):
>Thriving of letters in Hanlin Academy
>declares the return of peace.

Greetings, and congratulations on the surrender of Li Quan, the credit for which must go entirely, sir, to your dispositions.

COUNCILLOR: It is to report on this to His Majesty that I am here. You, sir, were engaged some time ago in selecting a Prize Candidate. Now comes the sacred edict to lay aside martial matters and promote the arts of peace. It is time for the announcement to be made.

MIAO: It is to seek His Majesty's approval of my selection that I am here. But here's an old scholar comes wandering up. Curious, curious!

TUTOR CHEN (enters, dressed in tattered gown and cap, and bearing a memorial in his hand):

> Confucius my master lamented
> he could not see the Duke of Zhou;
> but here's the Son of Heaven
> gets to see Tutor Chen now!

—And that's no small matter, I can tell you! (He greets MIAO and the COUNCILLOR) The scholar Chen Zuiliang, at your service.

MIAO (startled): Not another belated candidate requesting examination?

CHEN: Not at all, I'm here to be presented to His Majesty by the favor of His Excellency the Privy Councillor here.

COUNCILLOR: This is the old scholar who was sent by Commissioner Du Bao to secure Li Quan's surrender. The memorial he's carrying is the document of submission, that's why I'm presenting him in audience.

VOICE (from offstage, as drums and singing are heard): Let the officers submitting memorials approach the Imperial presence!

COUNCILLOR (moves forward and kneels, motioning to CHEN to kneel behind him; both kowtow): Your Majesty's Privy Councillor charged with the defense of the Empire humbly begs permission to submit: Felicitations to our Lord, whose sacred virtue accords with the might of Heaven! The rebels of the Huai region have surrendered and the troops of Jin remain motionless. Now your servant Du Bao, Pacification Commissioner for Huaiyang, reverently submits his memorial by the hand of the scholar Chen Zuiliang of Nan'an prefecture. This man bears Li Quan's letter of submission for Your Majesty's inspection. Your servant's joy in this is beyond estimation!

VOICE: Let the scholar Chen Zuiliang report in detail how Du Bao secured the surrender of Li Quan!

COUNCILLOR: Long life to Your Majesty!

(They rise)

CHEN: Your Majesty's servant the scholar Chen Zuiliang presents the act of submission and humbly begs permission to report:

> IIa Where Huai and Yangzi seaward flow,
> network of hills and streams a thousand leagues,

sound was the stratagem of your Commissioner
assuring the rebels of Imperial clemency.
Ha, how swiftly did the bandit Li submit!
His document of surrender sealed and delivered,
news of it reached the ears of the master of Jin
yet no move southward dare he make.
To Loyang, to enjoy the blossoms
is as far as he dare advance
and now as we hunt these Tartars
we may retake Kaifeng with ease.

VOICE: Let the memorialist await the sacred command by the Southern Gate.

CHEN: Long life to Your Majesty! *(He rises)*

MIAO *(kneels):* Your Majesty's servant Miao Shunbin, having examined under court instructions the papers of the candidates, now humbly begs permission to submit:

  11b The Advanced Scholars offered their essays
  in examination within the palace
  and still await publication of the lists.
  Now all unrest is stilled and hearts rejoice
  as Heaven smiles once more on the arts of letters.
  Ha, every paper read,
  now cry we forth the names of the successful
  that he who waits to soar dragon-like over all
  need quash no longer his cloud-borne dream.
  Fragrant the cassia blooms in the moon's toad palace[1]
  and chrysanthemums, whose beauty will be sung
  as wine is poured at Imperial banquet,
  already open yellow.

VOICE: Await the sacred command by the Southern Gate!

MIAO: Long life to Your Majesty! *(He rises and moves aside)* Time for the lists to be published, these starving scholars have waited long enough!

COUNCILLOR *(laughs):* Smuggling in a bandit's letter as a crib, it didn't take this Scholar Chen long to get through his examination!

VOICE: On your knees to hear the reading of the Imperial edict: "We are gratified to learn of the pacification of the rebel Li Quan and the repulse of the troops of Jin. These are the meritorious achievements

---

1. See scene 2, note 4.

of Du Bao, whose return to the capital we have already commanded. For his assiduity and skill in negotiation, Chen Zuiliang is appointed Grand Chamberlain within the Palace, hat and girdle of office to be issued. Of the Advanced Scholars in palace examination, Liu Mengmei is decreed Prize Candidate. Let him be escorted with orb and regalia to the banquet in his honor in the Almond Grove." —Give thanks for the Imperial bounty!

ALL (*rising*): Long life to His Majesty!

ATTENDANTS (*enter, bearing hat and girdle of office for* CHEN): "From school gate to palace gate he strides, blue gown laid by for hallowed purple."

CHEN (*dons his new finery*): My deepest respects to you, gentlemen.

MIAO, COUNCILLOR: Congratulations. Tomorrow we will impose on you, as new Chamberlain, to announce the names of successful candidates.

CHEN: Where does this Liu Mengmei come from, the new Prize Candidate in His Majesty's proclamation just now?

MIAO: He is from Lingnan, and his history is a most unusual one.

COUNCILLOR: In what way unusual?

MIAO: It was when I had already finished reading through the examination essays and was arranging them in order of merit for submission. Just at that very moment there appeared this young man outside the Southern Gate, wailing piteously and begging to be admitted as a make-up candidate. It appeared he had been delayed by the obligation of transporting his family to the capital. I included his essay as an appendix to my submission, never dreaming that it would win for him the rank of Prize Candidate!

COUNCILLOR: What a remarkable story!

CHEN (*aside, to himself*): From the sound of it, it's that unspeakable Liu Mengmei—but when did he ever have any "family"? Ha, that's it, he's taken up with that Sister Stone! (*To the others*) I must tell you, gentlemen, this Liu Mengmei is an old acquaintance of mine.

MIAO, COUNCILLOR: All the more matter for congratulations to you!

Envoi:

MIAO:

>Gilded names on the candidates' lists
>radiant in morning light

COUNCILLOR:

>my memorial on frontier strife delayed
>my departure from the palace.

CHEN:

    Speak not of cares of office
      nor of old age hastening on

ALL:

    when there in Cinnabar Court he stands
    in solitary dignity.

SCENE FIFTY-TWO: *The Search for the Candidate*

CAMEL GUO (*enters, laden with baggage and traveling umbrella*):
    I Nine myriad leagues of sky,
    three thousand different roads,
    journey of a month or so
    stretches to half a year.
    Tattered and lousy the rags on my back
    and this burden squashing head down level with navel
    scritch-scratch I crawl
    like a turtle trying to climb to the sky.
Thanks be to Heaven, old Camel Guo has reached Hangzhou at last.
What splendors to be seen here in the capital—but where is Scholar
Liu to be found? I'll go look for him on the main streets—ha, but
here's a squad of stinking troops comes clattering up, I'll get out of
their way. Truly, "unless some fisherman guide us, how shall we
get to see the great billows?" (*He exits*)
TWO COLONELS OF THE GUARD (*enter, preceded by gongs and pennants*):
    II Placards cover the palace gates
    but where is Prize Candidate Liu Mengmei?
    No call for him to act like the rebel Huang Chao
    who failed, chalked up a poem in disgust
    and then went jouncing off.
    Door to door we seek him, for audience on the instant.
    Much longer, and he'll miss
    banquet to honor him in Almond Park.
FIRST COLONEL (*laughs*): What a joke, what a joke, a strange to-do at
our great court of Song. Would you believe it, makes Prize Candidate and doesn't even care! Can you credit it, makes Prize Candidate and stirs up all this fuss! Can you imagine it, makes Prize
Candidate and off he trots! Who'd have thought it, makes Prize

Candidate and disappears! Of all the weirdos in this world there's none to match a man from South of the Ridge. Look at this placard, "Prize Candidate by Imperial edict, Liu Mengmei of Lingnan, twenty-six years of age, medium height, fair complexion." Set out all clear and unmistakable, yet he's nowhere to found in all the Empire! What's he done—gone home? Died? Fallen asleep? Whatever it is, he's going to miss his place at the banquet in the Garnet Grove.

SECOND COLONEL: Brother, how can we sift through all this sea of humanity? Why don't we stick a scholar's cap on one of our lot, and send him off to the feast. Then if the real person shows up later we can reimburse him for the meal he missed.

FIRST COLONEL: Wouldn't work. You could send a substitute to a feast of old comrades of the Guard, but not to a scholars' banquet in the Garnet Grove. He'd have to compose a special poem in the Almond Park.

SECOND COLONEL: Who could tell, brother—how many Prize Candidates' poems have *you* seen? But we'd better go on yelling if you say so. (*They bawl, three times*) Prize Candidate Liu Mengmei, where are you?

FIRST COLONEL: Twelve gates of the capital, east and west, and all along the main streets not a soul answers, we'll go call in the alleys.

SECOND COLONEL: There's a "Southseas Hostel" here in Sappanwood Alley, let's ask the constables.

(*They call out*)

VOICE (*from offstage*): What's your business, gentlemen?

TWO COLONELS: Matters of highest import, and here you are fast asleep! Pay attention:

  IIIa We seek the newly announced Prize Candidate.

  We seek the newly announced Prize Candidate.

VOICE: Where's he from?

TWO COLONELS:

  A southerner.

VOICE: What name?

TWO COLONELS:

  Liu Mengmei, fair complexion, no defects.

VOICE: Who's looking for him?

TWO COLONELS:

  His Imperial Majesty in person,

  His Imperial Majesty in person:

    this "willow" must be found
    or the Almond Park stays closed.
VOICE: No one of that description in any of our places around here,
but there's one of those scruffy southerners staying at Big Sister
Wang's in the tile market.[1]
TWO COLONELS: Aha, off we go then, off we go.
    Ah Heaven, Liu Mengmei!
    Ah Heaven, Liu Mengmei!
    So many twists and turns
    and still no sign of you!

(Exeunt)

BIG SISTER WANG *(a prostitute of the pleasure quarter; enters, and recites
a pastiche of lines from Tang poems)*:
    The oriole left behind—
        doesn't she know it's autumn?[2]
    Day by day more sad to see
        the river's lonesome flow.
    All the way from Ba Peak
        through to Witch's Mount[3]
    still mistaking Hangzhou
        for old Kaifeng.[4]
Big Sister Wang, with a house here open and at your service.
Heavens, not a customer in sight, but here's a whole posse of
officers in a hurry!
TWO COLONELS *(reenter)*: Greetings, Big Sister Wang! Is Prize Candi-
date Liu with you?
BIG SISTER WANG: Who's this Prize Candidate Liu?
TWO COLONELS: One of those southern beggars.
BIG SISTER WANG: Never heard of him.
TWO COLONELS: We have the constables' word for it:
    IIIb "Willow" lulled by smiling blossoms,
        "willow" lulled by smiling blossoms!
BIG SISTER WANG: There was a customer yesterday, up and off before
he could get his trousers back on.

---

1. The old Hangzhou pleasure quarter.
2. Oriole is one of numerous euphemisms for prostitute.
3. See scene 1, note 4.
4. Kaifeng was the capital of the northern Song dynasty, Hangzhou (Lin'an) the
southern Song substitute.

TWO COLONELS:
>A clue, a certain clue!
>Here's the "willow" fooling us,
>hiding among the flowers!

You've got the Prize Ca-handidate then?

BIG SISTER WANG: I've got a prize co-habitant.

SECOND COLONEL: In with you, then, let's do some co-habiting.

*(They enter her house to search. In the process they
maul her about and she runs off)*

TWO COLONELS:
>An amorous Prize Candidate we seek,
>an amorous Prize Candidate we seek!
>Fondly we pursue, whoever's embrace he's in
>trying to lose his sorrows!

Come on!
>Ah Heaven, Liu Mengmei!
>Ah Heaven, Liu Mengmei!
>So many twists and turns
>and still no sign of you!

(Exeunt)

GUO *(enters, leaning on a staff)·*
>IIIc   Here in the capital, close to the sun,
>here in the capital, close to the sun,
>truly a city of majesty:
>broad boulevards on every hand,
>markets at every corner.

But ah, Master Liu,
>no trace of your whereabouts,
>no trace of your whereabouts!
>Now you have taken this fine young wife
>in whose inn does gossip have you hiding?

Nothing for it but to keep on along these broad streets.
>Ah Heaven, Liu Mengmei!

TWO COLONELS *(reenter):*
>Ah Heaven, Liu Mengmei!
>So many twists and turns
>and still no sign of you!

(SECOND COLONEL bumps GUO and sends him sprawling)

GUO (*yells*): You knocked me flying! I'm dead!

SECOND COLONEL (*grabs GUO by the neck*): How come, just as we're calling for Liu Mengmei, you're calling for Liu Mengmei as well? We're taking you to court.

GUO (*kowtows*): Very well, I can see the Apricot Shrine affair has come to light. I know nothing about it.

TWO COLONELS (*laugh*): Then it's obvious you *do* know about it! What's your relationship with him?

GUO: Sirs, I'll tell you:

> IId His family's orchards were in my care,
> his family's orchards were in my care
> and I've come all this way in search of him.

TWO COLONELS (*eagerly*): And you've found him?

GUO:

> Nowhere in the red dust of this world
> can I find a glimpse of my master.

TWO COLONELS: You must know where he is.

GUO: Have pity on me, sirs, I heard tell he reached Nan'an, after that I've no idea.

TWO COLONELS: What a joke! He came here to Hangzhou, took the examinations, and ended up winning the title of Prize Candidate!

GUO (*amazed and delighted*):

> He is named Prize Candidate,
> he is named Prize Candidate!
> He has trampled the vegetable garden[5]
> and is gone to pluck the cassia blooms
> in the Imperial demesne.

Sirs, how can there be any problem finding him if he's been named Prize Candidate?

TWO COLONELS: How indeed!

> Ah Heaven, Liu Mengmei!
> Ah Heaven, Liu Mengmei!
> So many twists and turns
> and still no sign of you!

All right then, old fellow, we'll let you off and you can come along and help us search for him.

---

5. From an old joke about a poor scholar, long condemned to a diet of vegetables, who once ate a dish of mutton. He went to bed and dreamed of the Spirit of the Entrails, who told him, "That sheep is trampling your vegetable garden."

Envoi:

FIRST COLONEL:

> The road to advancement in the world
> a single examination.

SECOND COLONEL:

> The dragon's scales[6]
> lost in storms of dawn.

GUO:

> From the red dust I've gazed my fill
> down path to royal court.

TWO COLONELS, GUO:

> Where is the man
> who dwells now in alien land?

SCENE FIFTY-THREE: *Interrogation under the Rod*

LIU MENGMEI:

> 1   Beaks of malicious sparrows
> landed me in jail:
> what kind of treatment this for one
> who would hit the painted peacock's eye![1]
> For son-in-law-to-be, a cup of thin gruel,
> a palliasse of straw for head that should rest
> on hibiscus-embroidered pillow!

Ah Heaven, when

> one who at the Inn of Betrothals was linked
> by red thread with phoenix partner[2]
> now is trussed as prisoner;
> one who should tryst at Blue Bridge[3]
> is dragged along, a captive;

---

6. Dragon (metamorphosed from fish) symbolizes Prize Candidate.

1. The founder of the Tang dynasty won his bride by accepting her father's challenge to shoot an arrow into the eye of a peacock painted on a screen.

2. The Inn of Betrothals is where an old man links with red thread the feet of those predestined to marry.

3. Blue Bridge was the site of a legendary tryst between mortal man and fairy maiden.

one who should mount the dragon[4]
is made a common convict!

(He recites a Tang pastiche)

Spirit, in dream, south of the river,
   body fettered to lonely inn,
this youth hiding in shame
   covered in disgrace.
That my own wife's father
   should behave like this—
ask a passing stranger,
   what could he tell you?

Here I came, Liu Mengmei, at Miss Du's command, to pay my respects to her father the Commissioner in Huaiyang. Displeased by my appearance as a penurious scholar before his assembled staff, he deliberately declined to recognize me and ordered me back to Hangzhou under escort as a convict. But he is now on his way to his new appointment, and when he sees his daughter's self-portrait he cannot fail to acknowledge me. Until then, what a miserable situation!

JAILER *(enters, accompanied by* TURNKEY, *each with rod in hand):* "Summon Gao Yao, the Prison God, and you'll learn the jailer's might!" So, where is the new prisoner from Huaian prefecture?

(LIU salutes him with folded hands)

How about my introduction fee?
LIU: I have nothing.
JAILER: Entrance money?
LIU: Likewise.
JAILER *(annoyed):* Ha, nothing to offer, yet you have the impudence to salute me! *(He beats him)*
LIU: Don't hit me, just see what you can find in my baggage.
TURNKEY *(searches baggage):* Penniless bastard—one raggedy blanket wrapped around a little painting scroll. *(He unrolls the painting)* It's a bodhisattva Guanyin, I'll give it to Mum to make her offerings to.
LIU: It's all yours, but please leave me the painting.

---

4. "Mounting the dragon" refers both to Liu's examination honors and to his successful marriage.

(*TURNKEY tries to make off with the painting; LIU holds him back*)

MESSENGER (*enters*): "Dragon-riding son-in-law bound hand and foot, sorely wronged in the meeting with His Excellency." Where's the turnkey?

TURNKEY (*bows*): So it's our brother who attends the Minister of State.

MESSENGER (*shows his warrant*): One criminal required for delivery to the office of the Minister of State, to attend with baggage for investigation.

TURNKEY: Here's the prisoner, no baggage.

LIU: The jailers took it all!

MESSENGER: What did they take? To the Minister's office with these dogs of flunkeys too!

JAILER, TURNKEY (*frantically kowtowing*): It's just this scroll and this blanket.

MESSENGER: Give them back to this scholar, you creatures, and let's be on our way at once.

> (*JAILER and TURNKEY assent, and MESSENGER
> starts to lead LIU off*)

Better move a little faster, sir. "He who knows something of Confucian rites won't transgress the laws of Xiao He."[5]

> (*Exeunt. Enter DU BAO with ATTENDANTS*)

DU BAO:

> II   Girdle of jade, crimson robe serpent-patterned,
> I take my station here at center of universe.
> Clear as autumn frost
> I have rested my sword against the Kongtong Mountains
> yet now that I return
> as Chief Minister to the court
> my hair no longer gleams a glossy black.

> (*He recites a Tang pastiche*)

With autumn we spent the last of our strength
   to break the besiegers' lines
to take charge of "Silver Terrace and Crape Myrtle Court"
   in our office of Chief Minister.

---

5. Xiao He instituted the first code of laws at the beginning of the Han period.

But looking back, the sighs that fall
   for sorrows of this floating life
and the constant disputation
   before the east wind's blowing!
Chief Minister Du Bao, appointed to this lofty post by Imperial
favor for my pacification of the Huaiyang rebels. But here comes
some strolling vagabond, just the other day, with a tale of being my
son-in-law. I committed him to detention in the Hangzhou prefectural jail, and today must have him brought in for interrogation.

(*Enter JAILER and TURNKEY, escorting LIU, fettered*)

GATEKEEPER: Prisoner from Hangzhou prefectural jail, enter!
LIU: My respects to you, esteemed father-in-law! (*DU remains seated
and laughs scornfully*) The rites, and music, should come foremost in
men's estimation! (*ATTENDANTS bellow at him. He sighs*)
    III Mere timid student
      though his talents like a rainbow arch overhead
      faces the awful majesty,
      the overbearing pomp
      of the Chief Minister's court.
      How can I bring myself to compromise
      to bow and scrape
      while he makes not a move
      but sits there proud and stiff?
DU: You, penniless bookworm, what sort of a man are you, dragged
here as a criminal yet refusing to kneel before the seat of the Chief
Minister?
LIU: I am the scholar Liu Mengmei from South of the Ridge, and
Your Excellency's son-in-law.
DU: Tchah, my daughter died three years ago. She had known
neither exchange of betrothal gifts of silks and teas, nor any "point-
ing to the belly" of a prenatal match: so where would any son-in-
law of mine come from? Ridiculous! Disgraceful! Guards, take him
away!
LIU: Who'll dare to take me?
DU:
    IV A daughter I had, but partnerless
      and dead in the flower of her youth.
      Your tale is a baseless slander
for how could you claim even the most distant kinship,
      you from South of the Ridge,
      myself from far Sichuan,

too widely separate to breed
even our livestock in heat?
Where did it happen that you attached yourself
like a climbing vine to our house of Du?
A vagabond in search of patronage
babbling of relationship
to deceive the citizenry!

LIU: I am such a son-in-law of yours as has studied day and night, taking the light reflected from snow, to establish his name on the cloudy heights of the examination lists! Would I be so bereft of all resource as to come before Your Excellency with a tale of deception?

DU: Still answering back! Search this man's baggage, it is sure to contain some forged document or seal and we shall take thief and booty together.

TURNKEY (*opens LIU's baggage roll*): One tattered blanket, one Guan-yin scroll.

DU (*examines scroll and starts in surprise*): Ha, here's proof of robbery, this is my daughter's likeness! Have you ever visited Nan'an, and are you acquainted with a certain Sister Stone?

LIU: I am.

DU: And Tutor Chen?

LIU: Yes.

DU: Heaven is all-seeing! It's you who plundered my daughter's tomb! Take him away and beat him!

LIU: Who'll dare to beat me?

DU: Have this thief brought to a speedy confession.

LIU: Who are you calling thief? You speak of "thief and booty together," when what you should be seeking is lovers "in flagrante"!
　　v　You call this portrait "proof . . ."

DU: The portrait was obviously buried in my daughter's grave!

LIU: . . . but you must learn how
from fissure between mossy rocks
a trace came into view . . .

DU: A confession, at once!

LIU:

. . . and my "confession" must be a riddle
of resurrection's bliss
that "warded off evil only to court disaster"!

DU: And did the vault contain also jade fish and golden bowl?

LIU: Indeed, a golden bowl
from which two lovers drank in celebration,
a jade fish

whose twin eyes symbolized
our happy union in the shades!

DU: Anything else?

LIU:

Tinkling jade roller,
clinking golden chain.

DU: This was all the work of that Sister Stone!

LIU:

Ah, Sister Stone in her wisdom
helped the lovers on their way
while His Excellency Du cares only
to shine as a thief taker!

DU: He has openly confessed. Have my clerk bring a sheet of good, sturdy official paper, and indite thereon his confession: "The criminal Liu Mengmei, for opening of coffin and theft of contents, sentence: to be beheaded." When this has been drawn up let it be presented to the convicted party and have him sign below the word "beheaded." Completed document to be placed on file.

CLERK (*enters, bearing charge sheet*): May Your Excellency be pleased to indite the sentence.

(*DU does so; CLERK orders LIU to sign; LIU refuses*)

DU: What a scoundrel, born for the executioner's sword!
　　　VI   Thief born and bred, every inch a villain
　　　　　up to every wicked scheme.
You still refuse to sign?

LIU: Who am I, to sign such a thing?

DU:

A painter, used to brush and paper,
ink and inkstone—
use them now to make confession.

LIU: I have committed no theft, no villainy.

DU:

Your villainy was the fruit
of false, malicious scheming.

LIU: My actions were for your esteemed daughter's sake.

DU:

Such ingenuity, and stubborn with it—
all to deceive and cheat.

LIU: Your daughter lives!

DU: Lives, does she, when you

have scattered her jade-like bones
and stabbed my heart with pain!

LIU: Scattered them where?

DU:

There in the garden pond,
setting her lonely spirit
to grieve in the moon's cold light.

LIU: Who's witness to all this?

DU: I have the report of Tutor Chen.

LIU: The lengths I went to for my lady Heaven witnessed and earth witnessed, but what could Tutor Chen know of all this? For love's sake I

VII   worshipped her portrait, called her name aloud,
awaited in dread our ghostly assignation,
burnt holy incense, broke the grave's strong seal,
revived her heart with magic elixir,
bestowed my warmth upon her quickening flesh,
bathed her cheek to new luster,
infused love's stirrings in her heart,
raised her jade limbs, gently supported her;

for love's sake I

battled with breath of life for her dear fragrance,
rescued her, mortal, from the dark paths of Hell.
With love's own magic
I healed this maiden, brought her to breathe and move—
does it make sense
that now our romance,
all our "moonlit breezes,"
should come to nought?

DU: What kind of rambling tale is this thief telling? He is possessed by demons. You there, bring peach-wood rod to beat him, fresh-flowing river water to spurt over him, and we will exorcise these demons once for all.

TURNKEY (*exits, and returns, bearing peach-wood rod*): "To rid your gate of demons, first plant peach trees in your garden." Peach-wood rod, ready and waiting.

DU: String him high and beat him.

(*ATTENDANTS string LIU high on a frame and mime the motions of beating him. As LIU yells and writhes in pain, ATTENDANTS go through a comic routine of beating and spurting water over the imaginary "demons" that flee from his body*)

TWO COLONELS (*enter, bearing regalia, and followed by* CAMEL GUO, *supporting himself with his staff*):
>What a commotion, early and late—
>
>no one can find the Prize Candidate!

We've spent all this time seeking Liu Mengmei; if today goes by without our finding him we'll just have to beat Camel Guo!

CAMEL GUO: You mean I have to stand in for him? Here, I'll buy you some wine and we'll go on calling for him. (*He shouts*) Prize Candidate Liu Mengmei, where are you?

>(DU *listens intently as they exit, still calling,*
>*then turns to question the* TURNKEY)

TURNKEY: They can't find the Prize Candidate from the recent examinations, and His Majesty has ordered them to search the streets calling his name.

LIU: Brother, tell me the results—who is the new Prize Candidate?

DU (*annoyed*): Inquisitive scoundrel—slap his face!

>(TURNKEY *does so;* LIU *yells in protest*)

TWO COLONELS (*reenter, still accompanied by* GUO): Voices from the Prime Minister's mansion, still no sign of Prize Candidate. Eh? What's all the fuss in the Chief Minister's mansion? (*They listen*)

GUO: That voice from within—sounds like my master! (*They enter the mansion;* GUO *recognizes* LIU, *and bursts into tears*) It's my master they've strung up and beaten!

LIU: Help, save me, all of you!

GUO: Who ordered you beaten, sir?

LIU: This Chief Minister here.

GUO (*beats* DU *with his staff*): Then I'll beat the Chief Minister if it costs me my old life!

DU (*furious*): How dare you behave like this?

TWO COLONELS: We are under Imperial command to seek the Prize Candidate Liu Mengmei.

LIU: Brothers, I am Liu Mengmei.

>(GUO *releases* LIU *from his bonds;*
>DU *tries to stop* GUO *but falls to the floor*)

Camel Guo, how did you get here?

GUO: I've been looking for you all this time, sir, and now here you are, Prize Candidate, I'm overjoyed!

LIU: Can it be? Quickly, hurry out by the Qiantang Gate and report this to Miss Du!

TWO COLONELS: Now that we've found the Prize Candidate we must leave also to report to the Grand Chamberlain. "Before Imperial audience, first we must bother you, sir." (*They exit*)

DU: Now that that pack of scoundrels has left we can proceed with our interrogation of this fellow. You men, string him up again for me.

LIU: Let me say a word in my own defense—don't you believe I am Prize Candidate?

DU: Whosoever may be Prize Candidate, there will be a list of successful entrants as evidènce. What proofs can you show me? Tie him up again, beat him, and there's an end of it.

(*LIU yells again in protest*)

MIAO SHUNBIN (*enters, followed by ATTENDANTS bearing ceremonial headdress and robe*):
  Straw sandals worn through, still no sign—
  here was our quarry all the time!
Stay your hand, sir, here is the list of successful candidates.
    VIII   See now this name, inscribed in first place,
    by the vermilion Imperial brush:
    Liu Mengmei, the very peak and ridgepole.

DU: Must be someone else.

MIAO: My humble self examined and proposed him.

LIU: Tutor Miao! Save me, save your student![6]

MIAO (*laughs*):
    You have strung up and beaten
    a giant of the world of letters
    making too free with your peachwood rod!
Now that the Chief Minister is aware of the situation, make haste, you officers, to invite the Prize Candidate down from his bonds!

(*ATTENDANT releases LIU, who yells "It hurts!"*)

Poor fellow, poor fellow!
    A gentle scholar's pain
    by scholarly gent inflicted,
    sensitive soul in agony
    from the insensitive rod!

LIU: He is my father-in-law!

---

6. The successful examination candidate regarded his examiner in the light of teacher.

MIAO: So, then,

> the fledgling phoenix crushed
> beneath the weight of Mount Tai![7]

ATTENDANT: Scholars of old tied their hair to a beam to keep from nodding off, pricked their thighs with an awl to stay awake, but the Prize Candidate hurts worse than these!

MIAO: Enough of this, clothe him now in his robe of honor.

DU: What robe of honor, strip it off him! (*He tries to do so*)

LIU: Ha, so you would dare

> IX   resist Imperial proclamation,
> rail against His Majesty's hand,
> rip apart the royal gift that cloaks me!
> The visit from a son-in-law should be
> a solemn occasion of "mounting the dragon"
> yet here in bridegroom's finery I call in vain,
> the blooming peach trees of my marriage
> all ruined by your peachwood rod!

(*ATTENDANT adjusts LIU's headdress and sticks a flower in it*)

Now feast your eyes, Your Excellency,

> on headdress decked with flowers
> in token of the weight of royal favor!

DU: This Liu Mengmei must be some other person. And if this is really he, attending the examinations as a mere first-degree scholar, then surely he should have been awaiting publication of the results. What was he doing, examinations over but the lists still unpublished, to go stirring up a fuss in Huaiyang?

LIU: Your Excellency was not to know. Publication of the lists was delayed by the insurrection of Li Quan. Your daughter, learning that you were engaged in action against the rebels, bade me come to you: first, to present myself, second, to bring you the glad word of her return to life, and third, to offer my services as your aide. These good intentions have been sadly betrayed, but I am still your son-in-law!

DU: No son-in-law of mine!

MIAO, ATTENDANTS:

> x   Shame on Your Excellency, judged capable
> of service as Chief Minister

---

7. Mount Tai, in the sense of prop or support, was a metaphor for father-in-law.

yet ignoring this worthy Lü Mengzheng
in the poverty of his disused kiln![8]
Such stubbornness, such wrath
we find among our elders!

(*They laugh*)

Up on Mount Tai
the Father-in-law Peak is toppling!
DU: I regret only that I did not jail this grave robber until his sentence was confirmed!
LIU:

XI Confucius bestowed his daughter's hand
on Gongye Chang, held prisoner though innocent—
but you would place me in bonds of your own accord!
Liu Daozhi was antiquity's worst thief—
but Liu Mengmei stole to win himself a bride!
Your Excellency has powers of life and death
to "regulate yin and yang"—
yet faced with this task, you would have stayed
"speechless before the spring breeze."
I thought to be welcomed in gilded hall
with singing and music of pipes,
to flourish my silken whip
along the capital's boulevards,
to feast like Liu Yi in the Dragon King's Palace—[9]
but like old Fucha you scorned
this suitor for your daughter's hand.[10]
What pride will be mine on the day
when Your Excellency bows before me
ushering the Prize Candidate
to the bridegroom's place of honor!
Ah, then we shall see the fruition of
cuckoo's fading dream
by peony pavilion![11]

---

8. A classic instance of the man of worth in straitened circumstances, Lü Mengzheng has already been alluded to by Tutor Chen in scene 22.

9. Liu Yi, hero of a famous Tang tale, rescued the daughter of the Dragon King and received her hand in marriage.

10. See scene 36, note 1.

11. For the connotations of the cuckoo, see scene 10, note 2.

Your Excellency must excuse me now—your son-in-law is off to attend his banquet!

>　　XII　Be careful lest you
>　　　　sweep from the astronomers' view
>　　　　the star of the God of Letters
>　　　　or melt with the flames of your fury
>　　　　a talented son-in-law pure as ice!

It seems to me the time is close at hand when all will recognize
>　　　　the worth of a bridegroom "at home with
>　　　　　flowers and *willows*"—

if only there could come
>　　　　some understanding from Your Excellency
>　　　　overaddicted to peachwood rod!

(Exit)

DU: A strange, strange affair! A thief—or a demon? Attendant, I
should like a word with Chen, the newly appointed Grand Chamberlain.

ATTENDANT: Very good, Your Excellency. "It's chamberlains look like
demons—the Prize Candidate's quite human!" *(He exits)*

CHAMBERLAIN *(enters; he is of course none other than TUTOR CHEN,
newly dignified)*:

>　　Sleepless in old age, bustling about my duties,
>　　thrice cracks the whip at every morning levee.
>　　Now court emoluments from our Sacred Master
>　　replace the petty fees of village school!

Chen Zuiliang at your service, but Grand Chamberlain now, appointed by His Imperial Majesty in recognition of my services
against the rebels. All this I owe to the gracious patronage of His
Excellency Du Bao, to whom I am even now on my way to express
my gratitude.

ATTENDANT *(reenters and greets CHEN)*: I was just in search of you.
Please wait while I announce you.

(He does so. CHEN greets DU)

DU *(smiles)*: My best congratulations! "Yesterday a tutor, simple and
plain, now behold our Grand Chamberlain!"

CHAMBERLAIN CHEN: "New favors I cannot repay, but old griefs may
be swept away." —These recent days have brought three causes,
sir, for your rejoicing: number one, appointment as Chief Minister;
number two, your daughter once more among the living; number
three, your son-in-law named Prize Candidate.

DU: Fine lessons you must have given the girl, to turn her into a demon like this!

CHEN: Your Excellency should overcome such scruples and accept her.

DU: No, sir, you are mistaken. This is some evil witchcraft. My duty as a leading servant of the throne is to expose and exorcise it.

CHEN: If that is your intention, will you permit me to submit the matter to His Majesty at once and inform you of the Imperial will?

DU: That will be best to do.

Envoi:

DU:

> Night studies at Cangzhou
> and the monsters listening too.

CHEN:

> Is it the breath of demons
> that dims the Star of Letters?

DU:

> What man can determine
> the affairs of this world?

CHEN:

> Hang high the magic mirror
> to banish a hundred sprites.

SCENE FIFTY-FOUR: *Glad News*

SPRING FRAGRANCE:

> 1 Dew strikes chill to timid soul,
> plane tree trembles by painted well
> and like the windlass, round and round
> endless turns love's karma.

Ah me, three years now since my young mistress dreamed of a handsome scholar, took sick and died. The master and mistress grieved over and over for her solitary spirit—never realizing that there she was, alive and well, settled in with her penniless student-lover down by the Qiantang River! Now mother and daughter are reunited: of all the strange and wonderful things in Heaven and here on earth, nothing is impossible! Today my young mistress plans to do some embroidery and has ordered her needlework table prepared. And here she is.

BRIDAL DU *(enters):*

> II Swiftly declines the sun,
> the autumn equinox past,
> swallows twitter their regret
> to leave the friendly rafters.
> Empty river, no sign of him who departed,
> and for me, lodged here in wayside hostel,
> no perfumed carriage in view.
>
> Autumn wind blows cold
> through window's tattered gauze;
> husband away to Yangzhou
> still does not return.
> Tears fall as jade-white fingers
> pluck herbs north of the River;
> my golden needle embroiders still
> flowers from South of the Ridge.

Spring Fragrance, you know that after Master Liu had brought me here he left for the examinations. Before the lists could be published there came word of an insurrection about Yangzhou. I sent Master Liu to hasten day and night in search of news of my father and mother. To our great joy my mother and I met here by chance, but we have still no news of His Excellency. Master Liu must surely arrive at any minute, and I am certain his name has been placed high on the lists. I must cut out a new gown of finest gauze to match his forthcoming splendor!

FRAGRANCE: The table is all prepared for you to cut it out.

BRIDAL *(cuts out the silk gauze):* There's the cutting done, now I must sew. *(She begins to sew)*

FRAGRANCE: Young mistress, forgive my impertinence, but what was it like, you and Master Liu, in your dream and in the shades?

BRIDAL:

> IIIa First a dream in springtime garden,
> then in the shades love grew
> for in dream our shadows
> so briefly joined were parted
> but in the shades love twined us close together.

FRAGRANCE: What was it like when you came back to life?

BRIDAL:

> As one who wakes from dream
> I started, looked back, and stumbled.

FRAGRANCE: But is there anywhere nice in Hades?
BRIDAL:

> The Road to Incarnation
> we traversed in perfumed carriage
> and wrote our love on red leaves[1]
> by the River of Regret
> gazing each night from Demons' Gate
> at clear autumn moon.

FRAGRANCE:

> IIIb   Beauty so bewitching,
> so cruel the pangs of passion!

My lady,

> while your fragrant soul
> fluttered like butterfly in dream[2]
> your poor mother tormented her heart
> with shadow of snake in goblet![3]
> But now let swallow tomb[4]
> be desolate as it may,
> the lovebirds can build a new nest!

But I have questions yet:

> How did you hide from lamp in lover's study?
> Where did you buy the wine to pledge your love?

And when you took your pleasure

> was there no speck of blood in the breaching?

BRIDAL: Silly girl, in our time of bliss in the shades we were to each other as beings in dream, what point is there in such questions? Ha, but here comes my mother in great haste!
MADAM DU (*enters in a flurry*):

> IVa   Such a chitter-chatter on every hand
> and from the sound of it
> something to my daughter's benefit!

My child, there's a hubbub outside, they're saying the new Prize Candidate is Liu Mengmei from South of the Ridge!
BRIDAL: Can it be possible?

---

1. See scene 10, note 4.
2. Allusion to the most celebrated of all dreams, that of the Taoist philosopher Zhuang Zi. Waking from a dream in which he was a butterfly, he could not be sure whether he was not now a butterfly dreaming that it was Zhuang Zi.
3. Allusion to an old story of a man who fell sick of fright on seeing the shadow of a bow, which he took to be a snake, in his wine goblet.
4. Allusion to the story of a courtesan of the Southern Dynasties who succeeded in becoming a virtuous wife and widow. She kept a pet swallow, which after her death flew to her tomb and died there.

SISTER STONE (*enters in haste*):
>   IVb   Pennants flutter with dragon and serpent—
>   what officers
>   are these approaching?

Madam, young mistress, there are messengers here from the court.
I'll go let them in. (*She exits*)

TWO COLONELS (*enter, bearing yellow banners*):
>   v   Tumbledown gateway in humble alley
>   hardly a fitting residence
>   for a Prize Candidate!

But here we are. (*They knock at the door*)

MADAM DU:
>   What a terrifying commotion!
>   Let my spy who it is through the door crack.

(*She opens the door and the* COLONELS *burst through*)

What officers are you?

COLONELS:
>   As meteors we speed,
>   our purpose clear from these our banners:
>   straight from the Chamberlain's office
>   we bear the Imperial edict.

MADAM DU: Daughter, here's an Imperial edict!

BRIDAL:
>   I make bold to inquire:
>   When are the golden tablets to be posted
>   and is the name of Liu Mengmei
>   inscribed there in high place?

COLONELS: He is named Prize Candidate.

BRIDAL: Truly, Prize Candidate?

COLONELS:
>   Yet though Prize Candidate
>   within an ace of perishing!

BRIDAL (*in alarm*): What do you mean?

COLONELS:
>   In Huaiyang he offended
>   the Minister Du Bao
>   and was hauled back to the capital
>   for arraignment as a grave robber.

MADAM DU: Daughter, give thanks to Heaven and earth, your father
is safely returned to the capital! How could he know of such a thing
as your return to life?

BRIDAL: But what happened then?

COLONELS:

> High they strung him for sound thrashing
> with cruel peachwood rod—
> only to have court officers release him
> to tour the streets in victory!

BRIDAL: So all is well!

COLONELS: But the Chief Minister in all the might of his authority has submitted a memorial, protesting the naming of a grave robber as Prize Candidate.

BRIDAL: But can't the Prize Candidate counter this with a memorial of his own?

COLONELS: He has done so. The Chief Minister accuses him of
> viciously plundering a body from the shades

while the Prize Candidate for his part claims that
> with star of God of Letters upon his brow
> he is proof against all demons.

Their stories have
> sadly perplexed His Majesty
> Lord of Myriad Years.

BRIDAL: What is the result?

COLONELS: It so happens that the new Chamberlain, Chen, is an old acquaintance of the Chief Minister, and he has proposed that the Chief Minister, the Prize Candidate, and yourself, young mistress, attend all three in audience to present the case for His Majesty's decision.

MADAM DU: Who then is this Chamberlain Chen?

COLONELS:

> Chen Zuiliang, who claims
> to have served as tutor in Nan'an
> whence by grace of Chief Minister Du
> he is elevated to the charge
> of the Imperial audience chamber.

MADAM DU: Ever more astonishing!

COLONELS: It is on his command that we bear the Imperial edict to you. Your daughter is ordered at the first watch to perform her ablutions, at the second watch to break her fast, at the third watch to robe herself, at the fourth watch to leave the house,
> till at midpoint of fifth watch, at dawn
> tinkling of girdle ornaments
> announces the hour of audience.

BRIDAL: I shall be so frightened, all alone.

COLONELS: No call for alarm
   for daughter of Chief Minister,
   wife of Prize Candidate!
We must take our leave now.
BRIDAL: Let us discuss further before you go.
COLONELS:
   At dawn tomorrow in halls of gold
   we shall await
   some slight token of your appreciation.

(Exeunt)

BRIDAL: So, Mother, my father is appointed to highest office, and
Master Liu heads the list of candidates.
   Banners proclaiming victory
   announce also their safety.
   Let Heaven accept my grateful prostrations,
   let Heaven accept my grateful prostrations!

(She prostrates herself)

VIa From days long gone,
   from days long gone
   root of apricot, leaf of willow
   on lightless path,
   on lightless path
   reunited with my wandering spirit,
   fulfilling garden dream
   then striving on
   to win the highest honors
   and confirm in mortal world
   this match made in the shades.
MADAM DU:
   VIb Though this indeed,
   though this indeed
   was strange and rare adventure
   yet where was cause,
   yet where was cause
   to distress His Majesty?
   Protesting you
   some fearful harpy
   and Liu Mengmei
   the lustful plunderer of your tomb!

Ah child, your father—
> why did he fail
> to summon the Flower Spirit as witness?
Now, daughter, you must
> VII with gown and headdress properly bedecked
> and ritual posturings
> present your peach-bloom cheeks before His Majesty.

BRIDAL: But what am I to say?

MADAM DU:
> Your living presence alone
> is proof to confute all doubt.

BRIDAL:
> Surely the Lord of Myriad Years
> must hear his subject's plea.

CAMEL GUO *(enters):* "To find the giant turtle's hole, first cross the Magpie Bridge."[5] For two days I sought fruitlessly by the Qiantang Gate, before I chanced on officers who told me of the ladies' whereabouts. Now I must collect my wits and enter. *(He greets them)*

MADAM DU: Who are you?

GUO: I'm old Camel Guo of the Prize Candidate's household, here to offer my congratulations.

BRIDAL: That's kind of you. Have you seen the Prize Candidate?

GUO: It was I who went to the Chief Minister's mansion and secured his release, and now he wants you to join him.

Envoi:

MADAM DU:
> Testimony of bygone deeds
> to resolve our dream

BRIDAL:
> now the dawn suddenly reveals
> the gate that leads to Heaven.

GUO:
> Lofty spirits now receive
> just and due reward

BRIDAL:
> brows drawn fine as moth antennae
> for audience at court.

---

5. Allusion to the description of a fantastic landscape in two lines by the Tang poet Du Fu. The "turtle's hole" (river's depths) reminds us that Bridal's lodging is by the Qiantang River; for the bridge formed by magpies, see scene 44, note 3.

SCENE FIFTY-FIVE: *Reunion at Court*

TWO GENERALS OF THE GUARD (*bearing Imperial orb*):
"Sun and moon radiate Heaven's virtue,
hill and stream secure the royal dwelling."
The Lord of Myriad Years gives audience, and we take up our stations here.

CHAMBERLAIN CHEN (*enters*):

> Ia Clouds lift over jeweled palace
> from royal censers haze of smoke ascends
> in universal peace.

(*He prostrates himself in the direction of the Emperor, offstage*)

> As sun throws shadows over steps of gold
> accept, Majesty, your Chamberlain's prostrations.

(*He recites a Tang pastiche*)

> Phoenix pennants wave
>   at first touch of dawn
> now be the royal wisdom
>   conferred on all his subjects.
> A beneficent prince has power
>   to cleanse all impure vapors:
> ask not after mortals
>   but after ghosts and spirits.

Chen Zuiliang at your service, newly appointed Chamberlain in the court of the great Song Empire. Your servant began his career as a learned but lowly scholar in the prefecture of Nan'an. When Liu Mengmei opened the tomb in which the daughter of His Excellency Du Bao lay buried, I hastened at once to Yangzhou to report. Out of consideration for his former employee, His Excellency commissioned me to negotiate the surrender of the rebel Li Quan. My success in this was reported to His Majesty, who graciously rewarded me with appointment as his Chamberlain. Who could foresee that prior to His Excellency's return to the court he would receive a visit from Master Liu? He seized him at once and sent him under escort into custody in Hangzhou. But, strange to relate, Master Liu had already submitted an examination essay that secured him the honor of Prize Candidate. Court officers sought this Prize Candidate—and discovered him strung up for interrogation under the rod in His Excellency's mansion! The officers burst through the gates of the residency, released the Prize Candidate, and bore him away, mounted in triumph. But so much for all this. Next people were saying that Bridal Du, whom formerly I tutored, had returned from the dead and was in the capital. His Excellency the Chief Minister was enraged by the notion that his late daughter had turned into some lustful harpy, and asked me to present his memorial requesting the extermination of demon and grave robber alike. In his submission he accused Liu Mengmei of plundering the tomb, and some malevolent sprite of posing as his late daughter, and he insisted that both be executed. This memorial of His Excellency's was a succinct exposition of the facts of the case. But right on its heels came Liu Mengmei with his own memorial in his own defense. The Imperial edict came down: "We have perused both submissions and find subtle mysteries therein. This woman returned from the dead shall appear in audience to present her case for our Imperial verdict." I began to wonder whether Miss Du might not truly have returned from the dead, and so I had court officers inform her of the edict and summon her to audience at the fifth watch. Truly,

by the Rock of Three Incarnations[1]
   see them pass and repass
before the Dais of Myriad Years
   discriminate true from false.

But here as I am addressing you come the Chief Minister and the Prize Candidate in person.

> (*Enter* DU BAO, *followed by* LIU MENGMEI, *each dressed in court hat and robes, and carrying the long ceremonial tablet for recording Imperial instructions*)

DU BAO:
      1b Disgruntled I don my robes of state,
      bewildered attend in audience
      a most mysterious case.

LIU MENGMEI:
      Riddle hard to solve
      we submit for His Majesty's decision.

My respects to you, father-in-law.

---

1. See scene 1, note 3.

DU: No father-in-law of yours!

LIU: My respects, then, Chief Minister.

DU: No minister to you, either!

LIU (*laughs*): As the old poem says,

> "Apricot bloom and snowflake
>   vied to crown the spring
> and the poet laid down his brush
>   to administer their dispute."[2]

Here come I, Dream-of-Apricot, vying for recognition: it is for you, Chief Minister, to lay down your brush!

DU: Ha, a criminal who can twist a literary allusion!

LIU: What crime have I committed? It is you, Chief Minister, who are the criminal.

DU: I, who have achieved the pacification of the rebel Li Quan, what crime is mine?

LIU: Li Quan, "Li the Whole"? That's something the court was not informed of: you never pacified "Li the Whole," only his better half!

DU: What do you mean, "only his better half"?

LIU (*laughs*): All you did was offer Dame Li a pacifier to trick her into withdrawing her men—that's why I say, only the half, not the whole!

DU (*enraged, makes to tussle with* LIU): Who says this? We'll argue this out in court!

CHEN (*rushes forward*): Who dares create such a commotion before the Imperial gate?

(*They confront each other*)

So, it is Your Excellency! And this is the new Prize Candidate. Please desist!

(*DU releases LIU*)

What has the Prize Candidate done to annoy Your Excellency in this way?

DU: He has called me a criminal—what crime have I committed?

LIU: You ask what crime: three major faults in your treatment of your daughter.

DU: What faults?

---

2. The quatrain, by the Song poet Lu Meipo, concludes that though the snowflake excels in whiteness it must yield on the point of fragrance. The punning relates to "apricot" (Liu's personal name) and "minister" (Du's title).

LIU: Fault number one: as Prefect in Nan'an you permitted your daughter a spring stroll.

DU: True!

LIU: Fault number two: upon your daughter's death you failed to ensure the return of her body to her native place for burial, but built instead a private shrine.

DU: Enough!

LIU: To reject a son-in-law in disdain of his poverty, to string up and beat a Prize Candidate Imperially appointed—does this not make a third major fault?

CHEN (*laughs*): But the Prize Candidate has committed faults of his own in the past. Make peace between you now, for the sake of your humble servant and our past relationship.

LIU: What past relationship dare I claim with the esteemed Grand Chamberlain?

CHEN (*laughs*): I believe you are unaware, sir, that your lady wife once engaged me as her tutor!

LIU: What—a ghost engage a teacher?

CHEN: You are unmindful of past connections, sir.

LIU (*remembers*): Then you, Sir Chamberlain, are none other than Tutor Chen of Nan'an?

CHEN: None other.

LIU: Then, sir, we have a past relationship indeed, and no slight one! What possessed you to spread false reports of me as a robber? If as a tutor you made false report, then I fear for the truth of your submissions as Grand Chamberlain!

CHEN (*laughs*): Today my submissions shall be the truth. I see your lady approaching, it is time for you two gentlemen to make your kowtows in preparation for audience.

VOICE (*from within*): Let the supplicants present themselves.

(*DU and LIU advance together and perform their kowtows*)

DU: Your Majesty's servant Du Bao craves audience.

LIU: Your Majesty's servant Liu Mengmei craves audience.

CHEN: Rise!

(*DU and LIU take their stations to left and right*)

BRIDAL DU (*enters*):
　　Bridal, maiden from the springs below
　　restored to light of sun, enters the court.
　　　II　On all sides, halls of gold,

spreading roofs of emerald glaze,
tiles paired as mandarin ducks;
crack of ceremonial whips
filling the ear.

TWO GENERALS (*shout*): What woman is this, blundering up the steps
to the throne? Seize her!

BRIDAL (*alarmed*):
Ruffians so fierce
screaming at me:

ah, in Yama's palace in Hades were
blue-faced demons, jutting tusks,
yet not so fearful as these!

CHEN: Is it my student Miss Du who approaches?

BRIDAL: This Chamberlain looks very like Tutor Chen; I'll call him:
Tutor Chen! Tutor Chen!

CHEN: Here!

BRIDAL: Blessing on you, Tutor Chen!

CHEN: My pupil, now a ghost—take care lest you affright His
Majesty!

BRIDAL: No more of this! Say not
some third-ranked devil
of a "Blossom Seeker" pretends to highest honors[3]

but rather
the wife of the Prize Candidate
presents herself for audience.

(*Exit* GENERALS)

VOICE: Let the supplicant approach with ceremonial posturings.

(BRIDAL *does so, and cries* "Myriad years to His Majesty!")

Rise!

(*She does so*)

Hear our decree: let her father, Du Bao, and the Prize Candidate,
Liu Mengmei, advance and declare whether this be the true Bridal
Du or an impostor!

LIU (*gazes at* BRIDAL, *and makes a gesture of distress*): Bridal, my wife!

DU (*gazes at* BRIDAL, *and makes a gesture of rage*): Diabolical! The liv-

---

3. "Blossom Seeker" (*tanhua*) was the title given to the candidate who placed third
in the palace examination, behind the Prize Candidate.

ing image—what impudence! (*Turns again to face backstage, kneeling to make his submission*) Your Majesty's servant Du Bao begs reverently to submit: my daughter died three years ago, but this woman is her very likeness. Beyond all doubt this is a false impersonation by some fair-featured harpy or seductive fox-spirit. Hear my plea, my prince:

> III   Years, now, since my daughter perished:
> by laws of yin and yang, of light and dark
> how could she live again?
> One stroke from Your Imperial Majesty
> here on the golden steps to the throne
> and this demon will stand revealed.

LIU (*weeps*): How hard this father's heart!

> (*Kneels in turn to make his submission*)

> The very pattern of stern fatherhood
> with his Five Thunders he would obliterate[4]
> my wife's fair name and history.

DU, LIU (*rising*):

> Not the earthly Yama, Judge Bao himself,[5]
> could crack this mystery
> that only the Imperial will can mediate.

VOICE: Hear our decree: it is our understanding that a human being will cast a shadow, and a demon fear its own reflection in a mirror. In the possession of our court astronomers is the magic mirror of the First Emperor, which reveals internal structure. Let our Chamberlain place Bridal Du before this mirror, and report also whether her form casts a shadow or her feet leave footprints when she walks by the blossoming trees.

CHEN (*assents, and shows* BRIDAL *the mirror*): My pupil, are you truly mortal or ghost?

BRIDAL:

> IV   Mortal or ghost—how to reply?
> Let my image fall now
> on flower-patterned mirror's face.

CHEN: No change in the mirror image, this is indeed a human form. Now we must walk by the blossoming trees to report upon your shadow.

---

4. Five Thunders is a formula used by Taoist priests in exorcism.
5. Bao Zheng, incorruptible and sagacious judge of the Song dynasty, was known as the mortal Yama (King of Hades), and is the hero of many stories and plays. The infernal Judge of scene 23 alludes to him toward the end of his long second aria.

(They walk, and CHEN *observes* BRIDAL's *shadow)*

BRIDAL:

Fresh tribulation:
but here in flower-filled shade
lotus-bud feet in swaying gait
leave as they must
their shallow imprint on the earth.

CHEN *(in response to the Emperor offstage):* Bridal Du leaves foot-prints and casts a shadow, she is indeed of human mold.

VOICE: Hear our decree: Since Bridal Du is of human form, let her now report the circumstances of her death and resurrection.

BRIDAL: Myriad years to Your Majesty! Your servant in the sixteenth year of her blooming painted her own self-portrait, after a dream in which a young scholar appeared amid the willows and flowering apricots. Your servant sickened of longing, died, and was buried beneath an apricot tree in the rear garden. Then came in truth this scholar, surnamed Liu for "Willow," and with the name Mengmei, "Dream-of-Apricots." He found my portrait and gazed on it long-ingly morn and eve. From this cause your servant appeared to him and became his bride. *(She grieves)*

Ai-yo, the desolation!
Here was in truth my death and resurrection
and such the reversal
of yin and yang, of dark and light.

VOICE: Hear our decree: Let the Prize Candidate Liu testify whether these words of Bridal Du be true or false. And how did it come about that he bore in advance the name Mengmei, Dream-of-Apricot?

LIU *(bows and shouts "Myriad years!"):*

v   Your servant from the southern shores
drifted far in search of partner
until in dream before a smiling beauty
he bore a branch of blossoming apricot.
Waking, your servant
set out to attend examination
and rested from a sickness in Nan'an
to him unreal as Nanke's anthill kingdom.[6]

---

6. In a well-known Tang story, the Prefect of Nanke served a king who proved to be an ant, his kingdom an anthill under an old tree stump.

Your servant found temporary lodging in the Apricot Shrine of Nan'an prefecture. There in the rear garden he discovered Bridal Du's self-portrait. Moved by compassion for this mortal soul, he was successful in restoring her to living human form.

DU (*kneels*): This man who dares to lie in Your Majesty's very presence has already debauched my daughter's memory. For your servant's daughter

> was buried a virgin maid
> among the springs of Hades—
> how should she consent to wild liaison
> with this adventurer?

DU, LIU:

> Not the earthly Yama, Judge Bao himself,
> could crack this mystery
> that only the Imperial will can mediate.

VOICE: Hear our decree: We have heard the saying, "One who waits not upon the command of father and mother and the ministrations of the matchmakers will be disdained by parents throughout the land." What is your justification, Bridal Du, for yourself negotiating your own betrothal?

BRIDAL (*weeps*): Myriad years! In return for the grace of Liu Mengmei by which your servant returned to life, she was indeed

> VI betrothed without matchmaker's intercession.

DU: Who was your guarantor?

BRIDAL: My guarantor was

> the baleful funeral star.

DU: And your attendants?

BRIDAL: My attendants were

> female yakshas, sprites of Hell.

DU: Preposterous!

LIU: All was in proper form for union of yin and yang, of dark and light.

DU: Proper form! Fine words from a red-lipped southern barbarian!

LIU: You mock me, Chief Minister, as a betel-chewing barbarian from South of the Ridge—but Liu Mengmei's red lips, white teeth are nature's own.

BRIDAL: No more of this! Father, your daughter stands living here before you and you refuse to acknowledge her, yet Liu Mengmei took me in marriage though three years a ghost!

> Your spite bitter as wolfsbane
> to one returned to world of light

yet you revile the mildness
of betel-red on my husband's lips!
Father, will you not acknowledge me, even in the presence of my
mother? (*She points offstage*) Admit now
my mother, gentle as lily-herb,[7]
to free the throat's obstruction!

MADAM DU (*enters*): Observing that my daughter is still in audience
before His Majesty, I make my way through the palace gates to
plead her case. (*She enters the audience chamber, performs salutations,
and kneels*) Lord of Myriad Years! Zhen, Lady of the First Rank and
wife of Chief Minister Du Bao, presents herself in audience before
Your Majesty.

DU (*reacts in astonishment, as does* CHEN): Where can this lady have
come from? Surely it is my wife! (*He kneels*) Your Majesty's servant
begs to submit: Madam Du died at the hands of the Yangzhou
rebels, your servant has already besought the Imperial grace of
posthumous honors. This is beyond doubt some malicious sprite to
complete the imposture of mother and daughter, daring the light of
day to deceive Heaven itself! (*He rises*)

LIU: This lady I have never seen before.

VOICE: Hear our decree: Since Madam Du died in rebel hands, how
could she be accompanying her daughter here in Hangzhou?

MADAM DU: Myriad years! (*She rises*)
VII On the Yangzhou road
beset by rebels raping and plundering
what course for us
but to seek refuge in the capital?
To Hangzhou we came by night
there to encounter Bridal in the darkness
startling our very souls to flight.
Then mother and daughter, hearts as one
from death released found a new life together.

VOICE: Madam Du's submission places her daughter's return to life
beyond question. But the maid Bridal, three years in the shades,
must have been witness to many mysteries of karma. Those princes

---

7. In this song Bridal alludes to her father's condemnation of her southerner husband as a chewer of betel nut (which is in fact a mild aid to digestion) and puns on
two medicinal herbs, wolfsbane (*fuzi* "attached child"), a harsh drug that she associ-
ates with her father, and a kind of fritillaria, *beimu* "cowrie mother," a mild sedative
that represents her mother.

and ministers of former days who lacked virtue: what punishment was theirs? Let Bridal Du make true submission of these things.

BRIDAL: These matters might be left untold, but there is much to tell.

CHEN: My pupil, "the Master never talked of prodigies, feats of strength, disorders or spirits."[8] In the world of men, the records of every prefecture and county are carefully checked to guard against misrepresentation, but what kind of safeguards can they have *there*?

BRIDAL:

> VIII   In the courts of Hell, each case
> is precisely documented—
> no possibility there of libel or falsehood.
> The panoply of princes there is halved
> and ministers bear chains of jade
> and golden cangues about their necks.[9]

CHEN: The word of a girl pupil, not to be taken as serious proof. But if this is what you say—what treatment was meted out in Hades to the old Grand Tutor Qin Hui?[10]

BRIDAL: Of this I know something. What treatment indeed! No sooner did he step inside the gates than

> thud, thud, black heart pounded with a thousand mallets,
> squish, squish, purple liver ripped in three.

ALL *(startled)*: Ripped in three?

BRIDAL: They said it was one piece for the great Song court, one for the court of Jin, and one for that long-tongued wife of his.

CHEN: And what was the treatment for the lady of the long tongue?

BRIDAL: The punishment for Madam Wang, on her arrival in the shades, was to strip off her phoenix headdress and robe of sunset gauze till she stood stark naked. Then out leaped bull-headed yakshas with fingernails seven inches, eight inches long, who softly raked her throat and

> tore that long tongue from its roots.

CHEN: Why was this?

BRIDAL: Because

> the east-window plot was exposed!

---

8. *Analects of Confucius*, VII, 20 (Waley's translation).

9. The cangue was a kind of portable pillory locked round the neck of a criminal, whose hands were clamped to the bottom of the frame.

10. Minister to the Song court and the most notorious traitor in Chinese history. Numerous stories and plays treat of the "east-window plot" which he and his malicious wife, Madam Wang, devised to entrap the patriotic General Yue Fei.

DU: Devil talk! But let me put this question to you, fiend: In the mortal world there is a punishment prescribed for elopement and abduction, is there such punishment also in the shades?

BRIDAL: Indeed, there is. The seventy strokes upon Liu Mengmei were given on your orders, Father, but won your daughter's ransom in the shades.

> Blows fell from peachwood rod
> on criminal condemned

and honored scholar

> suffered at the hands of minions.

And if there be untruth in this, and your daughter

> guilty of love's sweet crime—

still can you not find it in you to forgive

> so gently nurtured a child?

VOICE: Hear our decree: Having given careful attention to the deposition of Bridal Du, we are no longer inclined to question her rebirth. Now let our eunuchs escort her past the Southern Gate, and let father and child, husband and wife acknowledge each other and all return home to resume their proper relationships.

(ALL shout "Myriad years!" and
move in procession round the stage)

MADAM DU: Felicitations, my lord, on your high advancement.

DU: How could I ever have hoped to find you safe and sound, my dear!

BRIDAL *(weeps):* Oh, my father!

DU *(refuses to look at her):* Here in broad daylight—keep your distance, demon, keep your distance! Tutor Chen, I'm beginning to entertain suspicions about Liu Mengmei, that he is a ghost also.

CHEN *(laughs):* Then he must be the Demon Kick-the-Dipper![11]

MADAM DU *(joyously):* Now that we find our son-in-law to be the new Prize Candidate, our daughter's return to life is doubly joyful! Come, sir, salute your mother-in-law.

LIU *(bows):* I was remiss in welcoming you, Mother-in-Law, on your arrival here. I humbly ask your pardon.

BRIDAL: Congratulations, sir, my best congratulations.

LIU: Who told you my news?

BRIDAL: I heard it from Tutor Chen.

---

11. See scene 22, note 2.

LIU: But I have been the victim of your father's rage.

CHEN: Let the Prize Candidate salute his father-in-law.

LIU: As my father-in-law I salute you, Yama, authentic King of the Ten Courts of Hell!

CHEN: Sir Prize Candidate, let me try to ease matters between you: now that

> IX man and wife have ridden round
> the transsubstantial wheel
> and our lord the Prince
> smiles on the course you have set.
> I fear only that the Chief Minister
> will disclaim his dowry obligation
> so let us now see mother and daughter,
> father and son-in-law
> signed, sealed and delivered.

LIU: Sir Chamberlain, I am a criminal.

CHEN *(laughs):* You should make it easier for me—

> not joke with me!
> We hail your seizure of the cassia bough from Heaven
> yet close-matched to this feat
> was the snatching of a sweet flower from caverns of earth!

BRIDAL *(sighs):* Tutor Chen, if you had not set me to strolling in the rear garden, how should I ever have set eyes on this captor of the cassia bough?

DU: Diabolical! As if there were no suitors of matching rank and status—what is this nonsense about "setting eyes on" Liu Mengmei?

BRIDAL *(laughs):* It's the sight of his

> x black silk scholar's cap
> and court robes draped about him
> gives a spark, spark,
> sparkle to my eye.

Ah my parents, there are people who build high towers decked out with colored silks, yet even in broad daylight can't succeed in attracting a son-in-law of official rank. And here I, your daughter, from ghostly caverns of my dreams have made the conquest of no less than the Prize Candidate—what is this talk now of "family rank and status"?

> Descendant of the great Du Fu
> you are grown so used to browbeating your daughter

> you fail to recognize the eminence
> of a scion of Liu Zongyuan![12]

Father, please acknowledge me as your daughter.

DU: Leave this Liu Mengmei, and I will acknowledge you when you return to my house.

BRIDAL:

> You would have me return to my girlhood home,
> quit my husband's house.
> I'd be an azalea blooming still for you
> but that would not stop the cuckoo's crimson tears.[13]

(She weeps)

Ai-yo, here before

> the father I knew in life,
> the mother who gave me birth
> my dizzy soul loses its hold on sense.

(She faints away)

DU *(startled)*: Bridal, my daughter!

CHEN *(gazes offstage)*: Now what is this old Taoist sister doing here—and Spring Fragrance with her, still among the living? Curious, curious—what was I shown, then, there in the rebel camp?

SISTER STONE, SPRING FRAGRANCE *(enter)*:

> XI   A settlement in court,
> a settlement in court.

(They look about them)

A whole host of high officers! And the Prize Candidate too, standing there pouting by our young mistress!

SISTER STONE:

> Surely they've made
> some crazy judgment in this case
> if they've heeded the babblings
> of that crazy tutor!

CHEN: So it's you, Spring Fragrance, my former pupil! But this old nun is a fraud.

SISTER STONE: Ha, Teacher Chen, fraud is it? When it was you who reported Madam Du dead, and Spring Fragrance dead as well!

---

12. See scene 2, note 5, and scene 3, note 1.
13. See scene 10, note 2.

You buried them in paper coffin
with your own tongue as shovel!

(She turns to LIU)

Greetings, Master Liu.

LIU: Greetings, Aunt Stone. But where have I met this servant girl before?

FRAGRANCE: I was there at the peony pavilion, sir, when you and my young mistress had your dream.

LIU: A living soul in living witness!

SISTER STONE, FRAGRANCE:

Beyond imagining
from spectral return to mortal union,
beyond conceiving
ghostly tricks forsworn for living fullness!

And you, our Master Du Bao,
were you King Yama in person
this would escape your judgment!

(Exeunt)

CHEN: Here within the Imperial palace, where men kneel in reverence and ghosts fall in submission, who dare show disobedience? Now, young mistress, it is for you to urge the Prize Candidate to acknowledge the Chief Minister as his father-in-law and thus bring all to completion.

BRIDAL *(smiling, she coaxes LIU)*: Master Liu, make your prostrations before your father-in-law!

(LIU refuses to budge)

XII How, how, how
can you be so stubborn?

(She tugs at his hands, then tries to press his shoulders down)

Please, please, please
straighten your girdle of jade,
bend your waist
cross jade-white hands in reverence!

LIU: Blows by the hundred from that peach-wood rod!

BRIDAL:

Blows, blows, blows
in penitence like King Wen in the old tale.

(She tugs at DU's sleeve)

Come, come, come
lay aside a father-in-law's
majestic wrath!

(She points to LIU)

This, this, this
is he who burnt paper cash
to invite me as his bride;
his, his, his
was the tea I drank on the Feast of Cold Food.

(She points to CHEN)

You, you, you
in search of office
babbled your tongue dry
with false reports.

(She points to LIU)

Let, let, let
his fault be absolved
in the opening of my coffin!

(She points to DU)

Now, now, now
you have railed enough, my father,
at your diabolical child!

HAN ZICAI *(enters, wearing headdress and girdle of office, and bearing the Imperial proclamation)*: Kneel one and all for the reading of the Imperial decree: "In consequence of the marvels related to us we are pleased to bestow our Imperial blessing on this family reunion. The Chief Minister Du Bao to be advanced to the first rank of the nobility. His lady Madam Zhen to be invested as Dame of Huaiyin Commandery. The Prize Candidate Liu Mengmei to be appointed Scholar of our Imperial Hanlin Academy. His wife Bridal Du to be invested Mistress of Yanghe County. All to be escorted to their place of residence by our Courier Han Zicai." Kowtow, give thanks for the Imperial favor! *(He turns to LIU)* My felicitations to the Prize Candidate!

LIU: Han Zicai, old friend! How came you to this position?

HAN: After we two parted I was entered for examination by the

Prefect of my locality as a descendant of the sage Han Yu. I came
here to the capital and won appointment as Imperial Courier, and
this is how we are able to meet again.

LIU: A marvel to match the rest!

CHEN: So Scholar Han is your old friend!

(ALL *move in procession round the stage*)

ALL:

> XIII Predestined match to astonish belief,
> predestined match to astonish belief,
> dreamer from the shades, from the Yellow Springs below,
> so greatly blessed,
> so greatly blessed,
> her nuptial hall the Imperial court!
> In audience all,
> in audience all,
> joyously rejoined,
> joyously rejoined,
> as edict from world of light
> dispels the darkness of the courts of Hades.

LIU: Henceforth

> XIV together we shall trace
> our peony-pavilion dream.

BRIDAL:

> My bridegroom, sun-warmed "southern branch"
> whereon I, northern bloom, may rest—
> did ever ghost in all the world
> know such a love as mine?

Envoi:

BRIDAL:

> So green the grass on Imperial tomb
>   in time of the Cold Food Feast;
> all other music ceases
>   when deerskin drum beats loud.
> Ah sorrow, when our fragrant souls
>   yearned but failed to meet
> and springtime heart was tortured
>   by peony pavilion.
> Thousandfold regrets
>   for the passing of the blossoms:

travelers leave, travelers come,
  a single cup of wine.
New songs sung to an end—
  joy still unseen,
birdcalls rising
  from the blossoming branch.

Index of Aria Patterns